OXFORD WORLD'S CLASSICS

THIS SIDE OF PARADISE

FRANCIS SCOTT KEY FITZGERALD (1896–1940) was born in St Paul, Minnesota, and named after his second cousin three times removed, the author of 'The Star-Spangled Banner'. He went to Princeton University, but dropped out, eventually joining the Army in 1917. While in the service he began writing a novel, and also met and fell in love with Zelda Sayre, of Montgomery, Alabama, whom he married in the spring of 1920, the year in which he published his first novel, *This Side of Paradise*. The novel, a thinly disguised fictional account of Fitzgerald's Princeton years, made its author an instant literary success, and a celebrity as well. Dividing his time between the East Coast of the United States and France during the 1920s, Fitzgerald wrote short stories in order to earn enough money to sustain himself and his family between novels. His second novel, *The Beautiful and Damned* (1922), was not nearly as critically successful as his first. It was followed by a brief but disastrous excursion into drama, *The Vegetable* (1923), and by his acknowledged masterpiece, *The Great Gatsby* (1925), which marked a departure for Fitzgerald in its poetic style, its narrative complexity, and its highly controlled concise structure. Beset during the late 1920s and early 1930s by his wife's psychiatric difficulties, which required periodic hospitalization, and by his own financial problems, he did not produce another novel until 1934, when *Tender Is the Night* appeared—to mixed reviews and disappointing sales. In 1937 Fitzgerald went to Hollywood to write film scripts; despite working on numerous movies, he received screen credit for only one, but he paid off most of his debts and began a novel about the movie industry. *The Last Tycoon* was nearly half-completed in first draft form when, on 21 December 1940, Fitzgerald died of a heart attack.

JACKSON R. BRYER is Professor Emeritus at the University of Maryland. He has published widely on F. Scott Fitzgerald, including an edition of the love letters of F. Scott and Zelda Fitzgerald, *Dear Scott, Dearest Zelda* (2002), and he has been President of the F. Scott Fitzgerald Society since 1990. His most recent book is *The Selected Letters of Thornton Wilder* (2008).

OXFORD WORLD'S CLASSICS

*For over 100 years Oxford World's Classics have brought
readers closer to the world's great literature. Now with over 700
titles—from the 4,000-year-old myths of Mesopotamia to the
twentieth century's greatest novels—the series makes available
lesser-known as well as celebrated writing.*

*The pocket-sized hardbacks of the early years contained
introductions by Virginia Woolf, T. S. Eliot, Graham Greene,
and other literary figures which enriched the experience of reading.
Today the series is recognized for its fine scholarship and
reliability in texts that span world literature, drama and poetry,
religion, philosophy, and politics. Each edition includes perceptive
commentary and essential background information to meet the
changing needs of readers.*

OXFORD WORLD'S CLASSICS

F. SCOTT FITZGERALD

This Side of Paradise

Edited with an Introduction and Notes by
JACKSON R. BRYER

OXFORD
UNIVERSITY PRESS

OXFORD

UNIVERSITY PRESS

Great Clarendon Street, Oxford OX2 6DP

Oxford University Press is a department of the University of Oxford.
It furthers the University's objective of excellence in research, scholarship,
and education by publishing worldwide in

Oxford New York

Auckland Cape Town Dar es Salaam Hong Kong Karachi
Kuala Lumpur Madrid Melbourne Mexico City Nairobi
New Delhi Shanghai Taipei Toronto

With offices in

Argentina Austria Brazil Chile Czech Republic France Greece
Guatemala Hungary Italy Japan Poland Portugal Singapore
South Korea Switzerland Thailand Turkey Ukraine Vietnam

Oxford is a registered trade mark of Oxford University Press
in the UK and in certain other countries

Published in the United States
by Oxford University Press Inc., New York

Editorial material © Jackson R. Bryer 2009

The moral rights of the author have been asserted
Database right Oxford University Press (maker)

First published as an Oxford World's Classics paperback 2009

British Library Cataloguing in Publication Data

Data available

Library of Congress Cataloging-in-Publication Data

Fitzgerald, F. Scott (Francis Scott), 1896-1940.
This Side of Paradise / F. Scott Fitzgerald;
edited, with an introduction and notes by Jackson R. Bryer.
p. cm.
Includes bibliographical references.
ISBN 978–0–19–954621–3 (pbk.)
1. World War, 1914–1918—Veterans—Fiction. 2. Children of the rich—Fiction.
3. College students—Fiction. 4. Advertising—Fiction. 5. Young men—Fiction.
I. Bryer, Jackson R. II. Title.
PS3511.I9T48 2009
813'.52—dc22
2009029696

Typeset by Cepha Imaging Private Ltd., Bangalore, India
Printed in Great Britain
on acid-free paper by
Clays Ltd., St Ives plc

ISBN 978–0–19–954621–3

5

CONTENTS

INTRODUCTION

SOMETIME in the fall of 1917, in Princeton, New Jersey, awaiting his commission as an Army officer, 21-year-old F. Scott Fitzgerald began work on his first novel.[1] He had completed a lacklustre academic career at Princeton University the previous spring, deciding not to return to finish his degree, instead enlisting in the Army after the United States entered the First World War in April. While he waited for his military assignment, Fitzgerald attended lectures and helped his college roommate John Biggs Jr. edit the school's literary magazine.

Although he had not previously written a novel, Fitzgerald was hardly a novice author. From the age of 13, when he published his first story, 'The Mystery of the Raymond Mortgage', in *The St. Paul Academy Now and Then*, through his high school years at the Newman School in Hackensack, New Jersey, in whose *Newman News* he published fiction, poetry, and journalism, to his years at Princeton, where he contributed fiction, drama, and poetry to the *Nassau Literary Magazine*, humorous verse and articles to *The Princeton Tiger*, news articles and book reviews to *The Daily Princetonian*, and wrote the lyrics for three Triangle Club musicals, he had had an active and successful—albeit non-professional—writing career. He was soon to discover, however, that writing in an extended form for commercial purposes was a much more difficult task.

Fitzgerald had originally planned that his first book-length work would be a volume of poetry, inspired by his literary heroes Rupert Brooke and Algernon Swinburne (he was to quote from their work often in *This Side of Paradise*); but eventually he decided instead on a novel that would mingle verse and prose. Soon after he began writing, he was deployed to Fort Leavenworth, Kansas, for basic training and there he continued to work on his novel under less than ideal conditions. As he recalled three years later:

Every evening, concealing my pad behind Small Problems for Infantry, I wrote paragraph after paragraph on a somewhat edited history of me and

---

[1] James L. W. West III, in *The Making of* This Side of Paradise (Philadelphia, 1983), 5–6, suggests that Fitzgerald began the novel in October while in Princeton. Matthew J. Bruccoli, in *Some Sort of Epic Grandeur: The Life of F. Scott Fitzgerald*, 2nd rev. edn. (Columbia, SC, 2002), 80, contends that he did not begin writing it until he got to training camp at Fort Leavenworth.

my imagination. The outline of twenty-two chapters, four of them in verse, was made, two chapters were completed; and then I was detected and the game was up. I could write no more during study period.

There was a distinct complication. I had only three months to live—in those days all infantry officers thought they had only three months to live—and I had left no mark on the world. But such consuming ambition was not to be thwarted by a mere war. Every Saturday at one o'clock when the week's work was over I hurried to the Officers' Club, and there, in a corner of a roomful of smoke, conversation and rattling newspapers, I wrote a one-hundred-and-twenty-thousand-word novel on the consecutive week-ends of three months. There was no revising; there was no time for it.[2]

In early January 1918, after he had completed eighteen chapters out of a planned twenty-three and titled the book 'The Romantic Egotist', he described it to his college friend Edmund Wilson as 'a prose, modernistic Child Harolde', which

purports to be the picaresque ramble of one Stephen Palms from the San Francisco fire, thru School, Princeton to the end where at twenty one he writes his autobiography at the Princeton aviation school. It shows traces of Tarkington, Chesterton, Chambers Wells, Benson (Robert Hugh), Rupert Brooke and includes Compton McKenzie-like love-affairs and three psychic adventures including an encounter with the devil in a harlots apartment.[3]

By the time Fitzgerald completed his training in Kansas and moved on to Camp Zachary Taylor, near Louisville, Kentucky, in March 1918, he had finished the book and given it to Anglo-Irish writer Shane Leslie, whom he had met in 1912 through Monsignor Sigourney Fay, a teacher at the Newman School who became Fitzgerald's mentor and to whom he ultimately dedicated his first novel, to send to the venerable and prestigious Charles Scribner's Sons. Scribner's was not only Leslie's publisher but also that of such literary lions of the day as Edith Wharton, Henry James, John Galsworthy, and J. M. Barrie. Leslie sent Fitzgerald's manuscript to Scribner's in May, admitting in his covering letter that 'I marvel at it's [*sic*] crudity and its cleverness. It is naive in places, shocking in

---

[2] 'Who's Who and Why', *Saturday Evening Post*, 18 September 1920; repr. in *Afternoon of an Author: A Selection of Uncollected Stories and Essays by F. Scott Fitzgerald* (New York, 1958), 84–5.

[3] Matthew J. Bruccoli (ed.), with the assistance of Judith S. Baughman, *F. Scott Fitzgerald: A Life in Letters* (New York, 1994), 17. Punctuation is Fitzgerald's.

others, painful to the conventional and not without a trace of ironic sublimity especially toward the end,' but he added, 'It interests me as a boy's book and I think gives expression to that real American youth that the sentimentalists and super patriots are so anxious to drape behind the canvas of the Y.M.C.A. tent.' Although its author was 'still alive it has a literary value. Of course when he is killed it will also have a commercial value.'[4]

The prospect of Fitzgerald's imminent demise did not convince Scribner's. As a very conservative firm, it is surprising that they actually seemed to be divided whether or not to accept this manuscript with its candid descriptions of youthful indiscretions. A junior editor, Maxwell Perkins, was apparently in favour of publishing it; but after considerable delay, in August 1918, Scribner's sent the author a remarkably encouraging letter of rejection, inviting him to revise and resubmit. After referencing wartime strictures that increased their costs and limited the number of books they could publish, they suggested two specific areas of revision: 'the story does not seem to us to work up to a conclusion;—neither the hero's career nor his character are shown to be brought to any stage which justifies an ending' and 'not enough significance is given to some of those salient incidents and scenes, such as the affairs with girls. . . . it would be well if the high points were heightened so far as justifiable.'[5] In less than a month, Fitzgerald made revisions and sent the manuscript back to Scribner's, but it was rejected again, this time within a month.

Unlike the first one, this second rejection does not seem to have encouraged Fitzgerald to do further work on the novel and resubmit it; but even if it had, he probably would not have done so as rapidly as he had previously because his life was now undergoing major changes that must have preoccupied him. In July 1918, while he was stationed at Camp Sheridan, outside Montgomery, Alabama, he had met and fallen in love with Zelda Sayre, a popular and flirtatious member of a locally prominent family. Throughout that summer and fall, they engaged in an emotionally charged courtship, conducted primarily in letters after Fitzgerald was transferred to Camp Mills, on Long Island, to await overseas assignment. Much to Fitzgerald's disappointment, Armistice was declared before he could embark.

[4] West, *The Making of* This Side of Paradise, 14.
[5] Matthew J. Bruccoli and Margaret M. Duggan (eds.), with the assistance of Susan Walker, *Correspondence of F. Scott Fitzgerald* (New York, 1980), 31.

In February 1919, he was discharged from the Army and, now engaged to Zelda, he went to New York and began working for an advertising agency by day and writing short stories by night—in an effort to convince his fiancée and her parents that he was a productive and promising candidate for marriage. None of his stories sold, however—he later wrote that he had 'one hundred and twenty-two rejection slips pinned in a frieze about my room'[6]—and, in June, Zelda broke off their engagement.

Determined to redo his novel, sell it, and win back Zelda, Fitzgerald quit his job and retreated to the attic room of his parents' home in St Paul. As in so much of his fiction, including *This Side of Paradise*, in his life also winning the girl was inextricably tied to material success, in this case writing a best-selling book. In two months, he completed an extensive revision of 'The Romantic Egotist', first retitling it 'The Education of a Personage' before finally settling on *This Side of Paradise*, based on a line from a poem by Rupert Brooke, a writer who *had* seen active duty in the war and had died while serving. Because only a few sections of the manuscript of 'The Romantic Egotist' survive, it is not possible to trace exactly how Fitzgerald altered it; it is clear that, in doing so, he did use full sections of it, simply inserting portions of the typescript directly into the new manuscript. He also used a good deal of his previously written fiction and poetry, some published while he was at Princeton and some written and rejected during his six months in New York in early 1919. But he made other significant changes: most importantly, he changed the novel's point of view from first-person to third-person, thus establishing an at-times ironic distance between the narrative voice and the central character's actions where previously there had too often been immature self-absorption. Stephen Palms became Amory Blaine; and he removed direct description of his hero's service in the war, substituting a brief 'Interlude' in which his participation is inferred through letters and poems.

The 'Interlude' material typifies another characteristic of *This Side of Paradise* which, as with his reuse of old material, was probably a result of Fitzgerald's desire to finish his revision quickly for both romantic and financial reasons. The letters from Thayer Darcy in 'Interlude' are heavily based on actual letters Fitzgerald received from Monsignor Fay, and Darcy's 'A Lament for a Lost Son' in the

---

[6] Fitzgerald, 'Who's Who—and Why', in *Afternoon of an Author*, 85.

section is entirely Fay's. In other places in *This Side of Paradise*, he borrowed from a January 1919 letter from Shane Leslie describing Fay's funeral to describe Darcy's funeral, and he also used passages from Zelda's letters. 'The Débutante' and 'Babes in the Woods' sections are lightly revised versions of *Nassau Literary Magazine* pieces; while several other passages in the novel are derived from earlier published poems and stories.[7]

By early September 1919, Fitzgerald had had his revision typed and he resubmitted it to Scribner's. The response this time was rapid: in less than two weeks, Maxwell Perkins wrote to him that 'we are all for publishing your book. . . . Viewing it as the same book that was here before, which in a sense it is, though translated into somewhat different terms and extended further, I think that you have improved it enormously.'[8] As Fitzgerald recalled almost two decades later, 'the postman rang, and that day I quit work [repairing car roofs at the Northern Pacific railroad] and ran along the streets, stopping automobiles to tell friends and acquaintances about it—my novel . . . was accepted for publication . . . I paid off my terrible small debts, bought a suit, and woke up every morning with a world of ineffable toploftiness and promise.'[9] Buoyed by this new-found confidence, he revised some of the stories that had been rejected while he was in New York and others that he had published at Princeton, and now the results were immediate and spectacular. Between November 1919 and June 1920, a dozen Fitzgerald stories appeared in such leading magazines as the *Smart Set*, *Scribner's Magazine*, and the *Saturday Evening Post*; his earnings from his writing leaped from $879 in 1919 to $18,850 in 1920.[10] With Scribner's acceptance in hand, Fitzgerald also convinced Zelda to resume their engagement; they were married in New York on 3 April 1920, eight days after the publication of *This Side of Paradise*.

The haste that characterized Fitzgerald's second reworking of his novel, combined with his lifelong spelling difficulties and with poor

---

[7] For a complete listing of the previously published writings incorporated into *This Side of Paradise*, see F. Scott Fitzgerald, *This Side of Paradise*, ed. James L. W. West III (Cambridge and New York, 1995), p. xxii, n. 13.

[8] John Kuehl and Jackson R. Bryer (eds.), *Dear Scott/Dear Max: The Fitzgerald–Perkins Correspondence* (New York, 1971), 21.

[9] 'Early Success', *American Cavalcade* (Oct. 1937); repr. in Edmund Wilson (ed.), *The Crack-Up* (New York, 1945), 86.

[10] Bruccoli, *Some Sort of Epic Grandeur*, 101–2, 133; *F. Scott Fitzgerald's Ledger: A Facsimile* (Washington, DC, 1972), 51–2.

copy-editing at Scribner's, resulted in a book riddled with embarrassing errors. Names were misspelled, book titles were incorrect, and words were used improperly or ungrammatically. In 1922, Edmund Wilson, who was one of its admirers, called *This Side of Paradise* 'one of the most illiterate books of any merit ever published'.[11] Within a week of publication, both Fitzgerald and Robert Bridges, the respected editor of *Scribner's Magazine*, had submitted lists of errors to the publisher. Eventually, a total of eleven such lists were prepared, the two most public of which appeared in Franklin P. Adams's popular *New York Tribune* column 'The Conning Tower' on 6 and 14 July 1920. Scribner's incorporated thirty-two corrections into its fourth printing of May 1920 and eleven more into its seventh printing in August 1920; but many errors persisted throughout the novel's many reprintings well into the late twentieth century.[12] It was not until James L. W. West III's 1995 edition in the Cambridge Edition of the Works of F. Scott Fitzgerald that a reliable, accurate rendering of the text was made available. The text of this edition is much indebted to West's careful research.

It is difficult today to understand the sensation *This Side of Paradise* caused upon its publication. One way to comprehend it might be to compare it to the impact of such other novels of the twentieth century as *The Grapes of Wrath* in 1939, *The Naked and the Dead* in 1948, *The Catcher in the Rye* in 1951, and *Portnoy's Complaint* in 1969. In each of these instances, literary subjects previously depicted with restraint or not at all were now faced directly and explicitly. So it was with *This Side of Paradise* in 1920. Another way to gauge its impact is, as Henry Dan Piper, author of one of the first critical biographies of Fitzgerald, first suggested, to look at the authors and titles of the best-selling novels of 1920. They included such potboilers by largely forgotten authors as Zane Grey's *The Man of the Forest*, Peter B. Kyne's *Kindred of the Dust*, Harold Bell Wright's *The Re-creation of Brian Kent*, Eleanor H. Porter's *May-Marie*, and Kathleen Norris's *Harriet and the Piper*.[13] Grey and Wright are among the American writers that Amory's poet friend Tom D'Invilliers singles out in his

---

[11] Edmund Wilson, 'The Literary Spotlight—VI. F. Scott Fitzgerald', *The Bookman* (March 1922); repr. as 'F. Scott Fitzgerald before *The Great Gatsby*', in Alfred Kazin (ed.), *F. Scott Fitzgerald: The Man and His Work* (Cleveland, 1951), 78.

[12] See 'Lists of Errors' in Fitzgerald, *This Side of Paradise*, ed. West, 401–7.

[13] Henry Dan Piper, *F. Scott Fitzgerald: A Critical Portrait* (New York, 1965), 42.

'slaughter of American literature' late in *This Side of Paradise* for being unable to write 'one honest novel' (p. 185).

'Honest' is one of the adjectives that recurred frequently in contemporary reviews of *This Side of Paradise*, along with 'original', 'daring', 'clever', 'astonishing', and 'refreshing'. One can almost hear jaded reviewers' relief, surprise, and pleasure as they encountered this new novel by an unknown author. Typically, Robert C. Benchley observed:

In these days when any one can (and does) turn out a book which has been done hundreds of times before and bids fair to be done hundreds of times again, . . . I should be inclined to hail as a genius any twenty-three-year-old author who can think up something new and say it in a new way so that it will be interesting to a great many people.[14]

While there certainly were dissenting opinions—Heywood Broun remained 'unconvinced as to the authenticity of the atmosphere which [Fitzgerald] creates' and the reviewer for the *Providence Sunday Journal* complained that Amory Blaine 'bores us in the book just as he would have bored us in the flesh'—the great majority agreed with H. L. Mencken, who called it '[t]he best American novel that I have seen of late' and 'truly amazing', adding that it was 'original in structure, extremely sophisticated in manner, and adorned with a brilliancy that is as rare in American writing as honesty is in American statecraft'.[15]

Many contemporary reviewers, not surprisingly, felt the need to stress, either implicitly or explicitly, how *This Side of Paradise* revealed new and exciting aspects of adolescent behaviour not previously depicted in American fiction. Although the conservative Catholic journal *America* lamented that 'If the parties to Amory's various love-affairs are faithful portraits of the modern American girl, the country is going to the dogs rapidly,' the reviewer for Dartmouth College's undergraduate newspaper may well have spoken for many of Fitzgerald's younger readers when he asserted that '*This Side of Paradise* fulfills the demands of readers who know undergraduate life at first-hand and who wish to have it described in an entertaining yet always faithful manner.' Speaking from an elder perspective, William Huse predicted that 'beginning-to-be-middle-aged

---

[14] Jackson R. Bryer (ed.), *F. Scott Fitzgerald: The Critical Reception* (New York, 1978), 14.

[15] Ibid. 10, 13, 28.

people will disapprove of its disconcerting frankness' and Burton Rascoe declared tantalizingly that Fitzgerald's novel 'shows definitely that, whatever the teachings of our elders, the Victorian checks, taboos, and reticences are no longer in force among the flappers, the debutantes, and collegians of the present generation'.[16] Several reviewers prominently featured such provocative quotes from the text as 'Amory found it rather fascinating to feel that any popular girl he met before eight he might quite possibly kiss before twelve' (p. 55) and 'None of the Victorian mothers—and most of the mothers were Victorian—had any idea how casually their daughters were accustomed to be kissed' (p. 54). Appearing as it did, in the aftermath of the First World War, at the dawning of the 1920s, and at the beginning of Prohibition, at a time when America was undergoing major social and economic upheavals and the Victorian era was giving way to the Jazz Age, *This Side of Paradise* clearly documents these sweeping changes. When Rosalind Connage says to her mother, '[Y]ou can't run everything now the way you did in the early nineties' (p. 154) or when she tells her hapless suitor Howard Gillespie, 'If Mr. Jones of the nineties bragged he'd kissed a girl, every one knew he was through with her. If Mr. Jones of 1919 brags the same every one knows it's because he can't kiss her any more' (p. 156), she is articulating a new order that readers and reviewers of the day surely recognized but that it took Fitzgerald's novel to certify.

The reviews and the other publicity attendant on the book's publication—Scribner's ads called it 'a novel about flappers for philosophers'—had an immediate and dramatic effect. Within three days of its publication, the first printing of 3,000 copies was sold. Scribner's reprinted it eight more times in 1920; by the end of the year, over 36,000 copies were in print, and by the end of 1921, there had been twelve printings totalling 49,075 copies. No other Fitzgerald book published in his lifetime sold as well. *The Great Gatsby* (1925) only went through two printings and 23,870 copies (copies of the second printing were still in Scribner's warehouse when its author died in 1940); and *Tender Is the Night* (1934) had three printings (15,195 copies) in its year of publication and then was not reprinted again until 1951.[17] Despite these comparative sales figures, *This Side of Paradise* has not fared nearly as well in the

[16] Bryer (ed.), *F. Scott Fitzgerald: The Critical Reception*, 25, 16, 18, 4–5.
[17] Bruccoli, *Some Sort of Epic Grandeur*, 133, 217; Matthew J. Bruccoli, *F. Scott Fitzgerald: A Descriptive Bibliography*, rev. edn. (Pittsburgh, 1987), 65, 67, 92, 94.

decades since its publication as it did in 1920. It has been overlooked by general readers and its reputation even among many Fitzgerald scholars and critics is mixed at best; it has been buried under the steady stream of commentary on *The Great Gatsby* and *Tender Is the Night*. Piper set the tone in 1965: 'For all its commercial success and literary influence, *This Side of Paradise* was not an especially good novel.' Richard D. Lehan a year later dismissed it as 'hopelessly sentimental', noting that 'Fitzgerald seems to have an idea but scarcely a story; there is not enough to hold the reader's attention; . . . and the plot is trite' and Milton Hindus in 1968 contended that, 'in retrospect, it seems that its ideas are threadbare and inadequate'.[18] Up until very recently, there have been few free-standing essays on *This Side of Paradise*; the critical commentary, such as it is, can primarily be found in chapters or brief sections of books that survey Fitzgerald's career and/or life.

Why then reissue *This Side of Paradise* almost ninety years after its original publication in a series that attaches the word 'Classics' to its titles? Simply stated, it is because the reviewers in 1920, notwithstanding the fact that what they regarded then as an 'iconoclastic social document'[19] now seems in many respects quaintly old-fashioned, were more accurate in their assessments of it than more recent commentators who have for the most part casually dismissed it. One respect in which the contemporary reviewers were certainly prescient was in foreseeing a bright future for Fitzgerald. He would 'grow to a maturity that will stamp itself on the palimpsest of American letters', predicted the *Philadelphia North American*; 'Mr. Fitzgerald has something to tell the world', asserted the *Philadelphia Sunday Press*, 'And he will tell it. Better and better, we believe, as time goes on'.[20] And among more recent critics, even those who have harsh words for it see significant foreshadowing of Fitzgerald's later themes and characters in his first novel. Kenneth Eble contends that 'Though it is still not a novel that can stand solely on its own merits'—a debatable assertion—'it offers a good deal to the understanding of Fitzgerald as a writer'; and Milton R. Stern, in what is the fullest and most incisive analysis of *This Side of Paradise* to date,

---

[18] Piper, *F. Scott Fitzgerald*, 42; Richard D. Lehan, *F. Scott Fitzgerald and the Craft of Fiction* (Carbondale, Ill., 1966), 63; Milton Hindus, *F. Scott Fitzgerald: An Introduction and Interpretation* (New York, 1968), 17.

[19] Bruccoli, *Some Sort of Epic Grandeur*, 117.

[20] Bryer, *F. Scott Fitzgerald: The Critical Reception*, 6.

while acknowledging that 'it *is* a silly and adolescent book', also
finds it 'highly important . . . for our understanding of the writings
of Fitzgerald'.[21]

One important and enduring Fitzgerald theme appears very early
in *This Side of Paradise*. Thirteen-year-old Amory Blaine has just
kissed Myra St Claire—'[h]e had never kissed a girl before'—and
we learn:

Sudden revulsion seized Amory, disgust, loathing for the whole incident.
He desired frantically to be away, never to see Myra again, never to kiss
any one; he became conscious of his face and hers, of their clinging hands,
and he wanted to creep out of his body and hide somewhere safe out of
sight, up in the corner of his mind. (p. 18)

Thus begins a linking of women and sex (in *This Side of Paradise*
represented by chaste kisses and vague references to 'petting') with
evil. An apparition representing the Devil appears to Amory at two
points in the narrative and both are associated with what might be
considered illicit behaviour. The first is when Amory and his drunken
friend Sloane are concluding a night of partying at the far-uptown
(that is, unfashionable and lower-class) apartment of Phoebe Column,
one of two showgirls with whom they have spent the evening. As
Axia, Amory's 'friend' for the evening, 'laid her yellow head on his
shoulder' and 'temptation crept over him' (p. 99), he sees the Devil
figure and flees the scene. The second occurs in an Atlantic City hotel
room, where Amory sacrifices his honour to save his friend Alec
Connage and the latter's 'gaudy, vermilion-lipped blonde' consort
(p. 207) Jill, and sees 'over by the window . . . something . . . featureless and indistinguishable, yet strangely familiar' (p. 210).

This same motif recurs elsewhere in the novel. In a section titled
'Petting', Amory, on tour with Princeton's Triangle Club, finds himself in a car with a girl 'outside the Country Club in Louisville' and
asks, 'Why on earth are we here?' 'I don't know. I'm just full of the
devil,' she replies (p. 55). About Rosalind Connage, the great love of
Amory's young life, we read: '*Women she detested. They represented
qualities that she felt and despised in herself—incipient meanness, conceit, cowardice, and petty dishonesty*' (p. 148). And introducing Eleanor
Savage (a surname that was surely carefully chosen), Amory's final
love interest in the novel, the author tells us, 'Eleanor was . . . the last

---

[21] Kenneth Eble, *F. Scott Fitzgerald*, rev. edn. (Boston, 1977), 44; Milton R. Stern,
The Golden Moment: The Novels of F. Scott Fitzgerald (Urbana, Ill., 1970), 36–7.

time that evil crept close to Amory under the mask of beauty' (p. 190). 'The problem of evil', Fitzgerald declares near the end of *This Side of Paradise*, 'had solidified for Amory into the problem of sex' (p. 238). This equation foreshadows virtually all of Fitzgerald's major female characters, most notably, of course, Daisy Buchanan of *The Great Gatsby*, who, with her husband Tom, 'smashed up things and creatures and then retreated back into their money or their vast carelessness . . . and let other people clean up the mess they had made'.[22]

But Fitzgerald's conception of the women in *This Side of Paradise* and elsewhere in his fiction is by no means completely negative. Amory and his creator are fascinated and irresistibly drawn to them as well. As Stern has correctly observed, the author and his male protagonists 'loved them, wanted them, [and] admired them', while simultaneously he 'hated the hard, petty, rapacious selfishness that protects their chrome-bright, pampered, and fashionable desireability'.[23] That both these attitudes are readily apparent in *This Side of Paradise* is particularly important in light of the fact that Fitzgerald's first novel has been so frequently devalued for, as Paul Rosenfeld puts it, 'not sustainedly perceiv[ing] his girls and men for what they are, and tend[ing] to invest them with precisely the glamour with which they in pathetic assurance rather childishly invest themselves'.[24] Consider our first sighting of Isabelle Borgé:

She paused at the top of the staircase. The sensations attributed to divers on spring-boards, leading ladies on opening nights, and lumpy, husky young men on the day of the Big Game, crowded through her. She should have descended to a burst of drums or a discordant blend of themes from 'Thaïs' and 'Carmen.' She had never been so curious about her appearance, she had never been so satisfied with it. She had been sixteen years old for six months. (p. 56)

The reiteration of the same pronoun in four of the five sentences in the paragraph creates an almost poetic effect, and the dead-pan understated satire of the last sentence shows clearly that Fitzgerald is not just skilfully describing Isabelle but is at the same time humorously commenting on her. The paragraph is also enriched by the

---

[22] F. Scott Fitzgerald, *The Great Gatsby*, ed. Matthew J. Bruccoli (Cambridge and New York, 1991), 139.

[23] Stern, *The Golden Moment*, 83.

[24] Paul Rosenfeld, 'F. Scott Fitzgerald', in *Men Seen* (New York, 1925); repr. in Wilson (ed.), *The Crack-Up*, 319.

fact that, in this introduction to Isabelle, Fitzgerald subtly but deliberately also inserts passing references to the two metaphoric motifs
he will use to describe her strategy in romantic situations: an actress
on the stage ('As an actress even in the fullest flush of her own conscious magnetism gets a deep impression of most of the people in the
front row, so Isabelle sized up her antagonist' (p. 59)) and as a competitor in a sporting event ('he knew that he stood for merely the best
game in sight, and that he would have to improve his opportunity
before he lost his advantage' (p. 61)).

The ability to immerse himself fully in the social scene he is
describing, to evoke it accurately, while at the same time being skep-
tical about and even critical of it is one of the major aspects of
Fitzgerald's artistry—and, surely, of such other great social novelists
as Henry James, Edith Wharton, and William Faulkner. His Princeton
classmate John Peale Bishop, the model for Tom D'Invilliers in *This
Side of Paradise*, said that '[h]e had the rare faculty of being able to
experience romantic and ingenuous emotions and half an hour later
regard them with satiric detachment'. 'At his best,' his first bio-
grapher Arthur Mizener observed, 'his mind apprehended things
simultaneously with a participant's vividness of feeling and an
intelligent stranger's acuteness of observation.'[25]

Contrary to what Rosenfeld and other critics of *This Side of Paradise*
claim—James E. Miller, in the first book-length critical study of
Fitzgerald, faults his 'inability to remain detached and unin-
volved'[26]—both Mizener's 'participant' and 'intelligent stranger' are
abundantly evident in Fitzgerald's first novel, often simultaneously
and with great wit; all are present in our introduction to Isabelle—and
in this passage about Amory's mother:

All in all Beatrice O'Hara absorbed the sort of education that will be
quite impossible ever again; a tutelage measured by the number of things
and people one could be contemptuous of and charming about; a culture
rich in all arts and traditions, barren of all ideas, in the last of those
days when the great gardener clipped the inferior roses to produce one
perfect bud. (p. 9)

The characteristics of tone apparent here—genuine feeling, satire,
and wit—are perhaps most apparent in Amory's encounters with the

[25] Arthur Mizener, *The Far Side of Paradise: A Biography of F. Scott Fitzgerald*
(New York, 1959), pp. xix–xx.
[26] James E. Miller, Jr., *F. Scott Fitzgerald: His Art and His Technique* (New York,
1964), 29.

women he successively meets and woos in the novel. Because they were based on the author's own romances—Isabelle was modelled after Ginevra King, the teenaged Chicago socialite who was his first great love, Rosalind after Ginevra and Zelda Sayre, Clara probably after his cousin 'Ceci' Taylor, and Eleanor also to some extent on Zelda and her daring and outrageousness—each has the ring of authentic emotion leavened and sometimes even undercut by humour and ironic self-awareness, as in Amory and Isabelle's first conversation:

'I've got an adjective that just fits you.' This was one of his favorite starts—he seldom had a word in mind, but it was a curiosity provoker, and he could always produce something complimentary if he got in a tight corner.

'Oh—what?' Isabelle's face was a study in enraptured curiosity.

Amory shook his head.

'I don't know you very well yet.'

'Will you tell me—afterward?' she half whispered.

He nodded.

'We'll sit out.'

Isabelle nodded.

'Did any one ever tell you, you have keen eyes?' she said.

Amory attempted to make them look even keener. He fancied, but he was not sure, that her foot had just touched his under the table. But it might possibly have been only the table leg. It was so hard to tell. Still it thrilled him. He wondered quickly if there would be any difficulty in securing the little den up-stairs. (pp. 60–1)

That Amory's first and last meeting with Rosalind Connage are rendered in dramatic form is highly appropriate—and is in itself a satiric comment—in that it signals that Fitzgerald saw their interaction, as Amory's with Isabelle had been to some extent, as that of actors on a stage assuming prescribed roles. But Amory's romance with Rosalind also features another theme that was to be paramount in much of Fitzgerald's later fiction, a theme no doubt suggested to him by the end of his real-life infatuation with Ginevra King and the breaking of his engagement to Zelda Sayre. As was mentioned earlier, Fitzgerald always viewed romance and money as intertwined. This was based on personal experience: he felt that Ginevra had rejected him because of his inferior social standing—the quotation 'poor boys shouldn't think of marrying rich girls' is an entry in his personal Ledger at about the point their romance ended; some have attributed it to Ginevra's father[27]—and because, as he wrote looking back on his broken engagement to Zelda later in his life:

The man with the jingle of money in his pocket who married the girl a year later would always cherish an abiding distrust, an animosity, toward the leisure class—not the conviction of a revolutionist but the smouldering hatred of a peasant. In the years since then I have never been able to stop wondering where my friends' money came from, nor to stop thinking that at one time a sort of *droit de seigneur* might have been exercised to give one of them my girl.[28]

Fitzgerald had been aware of his social status from an early age. Although his maternal grandfather had been quite successful in the wholesale grocery business, leaving an estate of more than a quarter of a million dollars when he died at 43 in 1877, his parents' home was a somewhat shabby building on the edge of St Paul's most fashionable neighbourhood. His childhood playmates were the offspring of the city's wealthiest families; but he was always aware of his position as outside their social sphere. When Rosalind rejects Amory, she is the first in a long line of Fitzgerald's so-called Golden Girl(s)—beautiful, rich, selfish, and destructive women who represent, in Stern's words, 'at once the object of our collective American longing, the dream, and the revelation of the vast, vulgar, shallow, adolescent emptiness and meretriciousness of that dream in its attainment'[29]—who choose men of their own class, despite a genuine attraction to someone outside it. Rosalind selecting Dawson Rider, whom she casually calls 'a background' (p. 166), is Daisy remaining with her unfaithful husband Tom Buchanan despite her romantic nostalgic attraction to Jay Gatsby, or Judy Jones in Fitzgerald's 1922 story 'Winter Dreams' discarding self-made Dexter Green in favour of alcoholic, dissolute socialite Lud Simms. When Rosalind exclaims, 'The very qualities I love you for are the ones that will always make you a failure' (p. 166), she is voicing the very complex truth that Fitzgerald sees at the basis of the triangular relationships present in so many of his stories and novels. In his fictional world, social position even in the person of

---

[27] *F. Scott Fitzgerald's Ledger*, 170.
[28] 'Pasting It Together', *Esquire* (March 1936); repr. in Wilson (ed.), *The Crack-Up*, 77. In the first edition of *The Crack-Up*, the titles of 'Handle With Care' and 'Pasting It Together' were reversed; the essay therein titled 'Handle With Care' should be titled 'Pasting It Together' and the essay titled 'Pasting It Together' should be titled 'Handle With Care'.
[29] Stern, *The Golden Moment*, 67–8.

someone of low or dubious moral standards will always win out over the socially inferior man with pure and genuine romantic feelings. Amory recognizes this at the end of *This Side of Paradise* when he declares, 'I'm sick of a system where the richest man gets the beautiful girl if he wants her, where the artist without an income has to sell his talents to a button manufacturer' (p. 235) and 'It's essentially cleaner to be corrupt and rich than it is to be innocent and poor' (p. 218); and Rosalind speaks for a long line of fictional successors when she tells Amory:

I like sunshine and pretty things and cheerfulness—and I dread responsibility. I don't want to think about pots and kitchens and brooms. I want to worry whether my legs will get slick and brown when I swim in the summer. (p. 168)

Stern is probably correct when he maintains that Fitzgerald's portrait of Clara Page is weaker than that of Amory's other love interests because she has so little in common with Fitzgerald's Golden Girl(s).[30] Because she was not based on any of the author's own romantic attachments, she is less fully realized, and because he depicted her as an angel ('Amory wasn't good enough for Clara, . . . but then no man was' is how she is introduced (p. 119)), his portrait does not contain any of the rich ambivalence present in the portrayals of Isabelle, Rosalind, and Eleanor. Eleanor, on the other hand, also presents yet another facet of Fitzgerald's understanding of the complexities of women. As unpredictable and eccentric as she is ('I'm one of those people who go through the world giving other people thrills, but getting few myself except those I read into men on such nights as these' (p. 195)), on their last night together, she poignantly explains a dilemma to Amory that, while it certainly applied more acutely to girls of her age in 1920, nonetheless has a resonance today and, once more, shows Fitzgerald to have been a keen observer of the subtleties of his social scene:

Look at you; you're stupider than I am, not much, but some, and you can lope about and get bored and then lope somewhere else, and you can play around with girls without being involved in meshes of sentiment, and you can do anything and be justified—and here am I with the brains to do everything, yet tied to the sinking ship of future matrimony. If I were born a hundred years from now, well and good, but now what's in store for me—I have to marry, that goes without saying. Who? I'm too bright for

[30] Ibid. 93–4.

most men, and yet I have to descend to their level and let them patronize my intellect in order to get their attention. Every year that I don't marry I've got less chance for a first-class man. At the best I can have my choice from one or two cities and, of course, I have to marry into a dinner-coat. (p. 202)

If one compares this passage with an excerpt from a letter Zelda wrote to her fiancé in the spring of 1919, it is evident what at least one of the sources for this insight was:

It's funny, but I like being 'pink and helpless'—When I know I seem that way, I feel terribly competent—and superior. I keep thinking, 'Now those men think I'm purely decorative, and they're just fools for not knowing better'—and I love being rather unfathomable. . . . Men love me cause I'm pretty—and they're always afraid of mental wickedness—and men love me cause I'm clever, and they're always afraid of my prettiness—One or two have even loved me cause I'm lovable, and then, of cource, I was acting.[31]

Although Zelda, in contrast to Eleanor's bitter tone, seems to have relished her role in the society of that time, both she and Fitzgerald's fictional character evidence an understanding that young women of the day had to feign intellectual inferiority in order to attract a husband and that the latter pursuit was their only avenue to a successful future.

The awareness of social distinctions found in Fitzgerald's portrayal of male–female relationships is also present in his depiction of Princeton University. Just as with the women characters in the novel, Fitzgerald is able to depict evocatively while at the same time making acute observations and judgements. Thus we get a truly poetic descriptive passage like the following:

The night mist fell. From the moon it rolled, clustered about the spires and towers, and then settled below them, so that the dreaming peaks were still in lofty aspiration toward the sky. Figures that dotted the day like ants now breathed along as shadowy ghosts, in and out of the foreground. The Gothic halls and cloisters were infinitely more mysterious as they loomed suddenly out of the darkness, outlined each by myriad faint squares of yellow light. Indefinitely from somewhere a bell boomed the quarter-hour, and Amory, pausing by the sun-dial, stretched himself out full length on the damp grass. The cool bathed his eyes and showed the

---

[31] Jackson R. Bryer and Cathy W. Barks (eds.), *Dear Scott, Dearest Zelda: The Love Letters of F. Scott and Zelda Fitzgerald* (New York, 2002), 34. Spelling is Zelda's.

flight of time—time that had crept so insidiously through the lazy April afternoons, seemed so intangible in the long spring twilights. Evening after evening the senior singing had drifted over the campus in melancholy beauty, and through the shell of his undergraduate consciousness had broken a deep and reverent devotion to the gray walls and Gothic peaks and all they symbolized as warehouses of dead ages. (pp. 50–1)

We get as well authentic and affectionate first-hand accounts of preparing one of Princeton's famous Triangle Club musicals for its annual Christmas road tour (pp. 52–4), of the selection process for Princeton's clubs (pp. 65–6), of a tumultuous weekend at the Jersey shore with some of his classmates (pp. 66–72), of a spring prom weekend (pp. 78–80), of a remedial mathematics course Amory is forced to take to stay in school (pp. 84–6), of an English lecture class (pp. 130–1), and a hilarious depiction of the football-weekend high jinks Amory's friends Burne Holiday and Fred Sloane perpetrate on 'intercollegiate prom-trotter' Phyllis Styles when she tricks Burne into inviting her to the Princeton–Harvard game (pp. 109–11). But in the midst of all this, we read of McDowell, a 'young sophomore' enrolled in the remedial class, who 'thought it was quite a sporting thing to be tutoring here with all these prominent athletes':

'Those poor birds who haven't a cent to tutor and have to study during the term are the ones I pity,' he announced to Amory one day, with a flaccid camaraderie in the droop of the cigarette from his pale lips. 'I should think it would be such a bore, there's so much else to do in New York during the term. I suppose they don't know what they miss, anyhow.' There was such an air of 'you and I' about Mr. McDowell that Amory very nearly pushed him out of the open window when he said this . . . Next February his mother would wonder why he didn't make a club and increase his allowance . . . simple little nut. . . . (p. 85)

The marvellous phrase 'a flaccid camaraderie in the droop of the cigarette from his pale lips' not only brilliantly presents a vivid picture; but 'flaccid', 'droop', and 'pale' also perfectly capture Fitzgerald's attitude toward McDowell and the author's understanding of the social distinctions present at Princeton. We get further evidence of this understanding in a conversation between Amory and Tom D'Invilliers, when the latter complains, 'I'm sick of adapting myself to the local snobbishness of this corner of the world. I want to go where people aren't barred because of the color of their neckties and the roll of their coats' and Amory replies 'You've just had your eyes

opened to the snobbishness of the world in a rather abrupt manner.
Princeton invariably gives the thoughtful man a social sense' (p. 75).
Amory and Fitzgerald are drawn to Princeton as 'lazy and good-
looking and aristocratic' (p. 27) and 'the pleasantest country club in
America' (p. 36), just as they are attracted to the Golden Girl, but as
with the latter, they also have a clear-eyed view—in this case, of undergraduates from the elite prep schools, 'St. Paul's, Hill, Pomfret, eating
at certain tacitly reserved tables in Commons, dressing in their own
corners of the gymnasium, and drawing unconsciously about them a
barrier of the slightly less important but socially ambitious to protect
them from the friendly, rather puzzled high-school element' (p. 42).

Aside from the salaciousness of *This Side of Paradise*, what most
interested reviewers in 1920 was what Burton Rascoe called its 'peculiarly individual method of presentation'.[32] The novel's mixture of
prose narrative, poems (some rhymed, others in blank verse),
playlets, prose poems, letters, and stream-of-consciousness (sometimes rendered in italics), along with its frequent quotations from
and references to literary works (Fitzgerald himself described it as
'A Romance and a Reading List'[33]) charmed and astonished its
contemporary critics. Fitzgerald 'blazes new paths in story structure', declared John Black; he 'has cast away every thought of form
and coherence to the winds and has written a novel that is nothing
if not unconventional', asserted Edwin Francis Edgett; and the
reviewer for the *New Republic* called it '[t]he collected works of
F. Scott Fitzgerald'.[34] While the loose form of *This Side of Paradise*
may have surprised and seemed innovative to Fitzgerald's contemporaries, Northrop Frye, in his discussion of the 'anatomy' as a narrative
form in *Anatomy of Criticism* (1957), implies that it was actually part
of a venerable literary tradition that includes such classics as Joyce's
Finnegans Wake, Sterne's *Tristram Shandy*, and Burton's *Anatomy
of Melancholy*. Although Frye does not mention Fitzgerald's novel,
his discussion of the anatomy as a form that 'has baffled critics'
and is 'not organized on familiar principles of prose fiction', certainly
indicates that *This Side of Paradise* did not 'blaze a new path'.
When Frye speaks of 'violent dislocations in the customary logic of

---

[32] Bryer, *F. Scott Fitzgerald: The Critical Reception*, 4.
[33] Matthew J. Bruccoli (ed.), *The Notebooks of F. Scott Fitzgerald* (New York, 1978),
158.
[34] Bryer, *F. Scott Fitzgerald: The Critical Reception*, 9, 22.

narrative' that give 'the appearance of carelessness', he is not only describing Fitzgerald's novel but also the reactions of many of its critics who have derided its polyglot structure as results of Fitzgerald's rawness as a novelist and of his haste in revising his manuscript. Frye uses such words and phrases as 'the digressing narrative', 'catalogues', 'the stylizing of characters along "humor" lines', 'dialogues', a 'pervading tone of contemplative irony', 'verse interludes', 'display of erudition', a 'mixture of prose and verse', and 'symposium discussions' to characterize the anatomy.[35] All are surely present in *This Side of Paradise*; many have been mentioned above. One that has not been noted, 'symposium discussions', certainly is an apt description of any one of Amory's numerous 'bull sessions' with his Princeton classmates and of 'The Big Man with Goggles', 'Amory Coins a Phrase', 'Going Faster', and 'The Little Man Gets His' sections at the book's end (pp. 226–37).

It is customary to criticize *This Side of Paradise* for the puerility of its characters and attitudes and for the closeness of its author and his material. To be sure, there is much writing in the novel that makes one wince—'His entity dropped out of her plane' (p. 125) and 'it seemed that he had closed the book of fading harmonies at last and stepped into the sensuous vibrant walks of life' (pp. 160-1) are but two examples of many—but what is more noteworthy is that, at 23 and only two or three years removed from the experiences about which he was writing, Fitzgerald was able to be so relatively objective, so humorously ironic, in depicting them. The callowness of his characters and their dialogue, allowing as we must for the less permissive social customs of the day, is probably quite accurate. Who among us would not be embarrassed by a recording of their first attempts at verbal flirtation? As Mizener has reminded us, 'however immature they are these lovers are not dull characters; on the contrary, they are hauntingly and embarrassingly real. They make us aware of how we would remember ourselves, had we Fitzgerald's gift for remembering the precise feelings which belonged to our experience as we lived it.'[36] Stern identifies 'three basic characters in Fitzgerald's fiction'—'the innocent', 'the moral commentator', and 'the Golden Girl';[37] all three are fully present in his first novel, ready to be further developed as his writing career progressed.

[35] Northrop Frye, *Anatomy of Criticism: Four Essays* (Princeton, 1957), 308–14.

[36] Mizener, *The Far Side of Paradise*, 116.

[37] Stern, *The Golden Moment*, 5–7.

But *This Side of Paradise* should and can stand on its own merits as a significant literary achievement.

Burton Rascoe, one of the earliest reviewers of *This Side of Paradise*, made a very wise observation about it, an observation that seems far more relevant today than many of the curt dismissals of Fitzgerald's first novel that have followed:

Ten years from now, it seems safe to say, Mr. Fitzgerald could not have written this book. He may—I think he will—write better books, but, ten years from now, he could not, probably, give us so sincere a record of the activities, the reactions, the reflections, and the problems of the adolescent and immature. At 35 the episodes herein reported would have taken on a more romantic cast; nostalgia would have empurpled the grayest fact; the skepticism of age would have discounted the relevance of important points; and caution would have killed its charming frankness.[38]

Fitzgerald himself, looking back at *This Side of Paradise* in 1937, remarked, 'A lot of people thought it was a fake, and perhaps it was, and a lot of others thought it was a lie, which it was not.'[39]

[38] Bryer, *F. Scott Fitzgerald: The Critical Reception*, 4.
[39] 'Early Success', in Wilson (ed.), *The Crack-Up*, 88.

NOTE ON THE TEXT

THE text used in this edition is that of the eighth printing of the first edition, dated September 1920. Revisions to the text, which in most cases consisted of correcting spelling errors, were made in the fourth (May 1920) and seventh (August 1920) printings. Despite these corrections, numerous errors remained. What have not been changed for this edition are Fitzgerald's practices of treating as two words such words as *some one*, *worth while*, *per cent*, *under classman*, *every one*, and *any more*, his treating as hyphenated words such words as *to-day*, *quarterback*, *week-ends*, *ski-ing*, and *down-stairs*, and his habit of using such British spellings as *centre*, *sombre*, *spectre*, and *programme*. James L. W. West III provided generous assistance in the emendation of the text. For this edition, the following emendations have been made.

p. 12 Asheville] Ashville
p. 14 Daniell's] Daniel's
p. 16 Arrow-collar]
        arrow-collar
p. 17 chaperone] chaperon
p. 20 Arsène] Arsene
p. 20 Christy] Christie
p. 20 Din] Dhin
p. 20 biases] biasses
p. 20 Rinehart] Rineheart
p. 23 Brooks] Brooks'
p. 27 biases] biasses
p. 28 ingenuous] ingenious
p. 28 Good-bye] Good-by
p. 33 Montmartre]
        Mont Martre
p. 37 confectionery]
        confectionary
p. 39 *Prince*] Prince
p. 39 *Daily Princetonian*]
        Daily Princetonian
p. 43 flamboyant] flambuoyant
p. 43 teetotaling] tetotalling
p. 44 swath] swathe

p. 44 *Lit*] Lit
p. 45 *Princetonian*]
        Princetonian
p. 49 O'Flahertie] O'Flaherty
p. 49 Commons] commons
p. 50 Ballads] Ballades
p. 56 Thaïs] Thais
p. 57 clenched] clinched
p. 61 distinctly] distinctively
p. 64 cosy] cosey
p. 65 upperclassmen]
        upper classmen
p. 65 edges] edge
p. 68 *Princetonian*]
        Princetonian
p. 69 dumbfounded]
        dumfounded
p. 71 *Illustrated London News*]
        Illustrated London
        News
p. 71 *Lukannon*] *Lukanon*
p. 74 Good-bye] Good-by
p. 78 upperclassmen]
        upper classmen

SELECT BIBLIOGRAPHY

Selected Fiction by F. Scott Fitzgerald

This Side of Paradise (New York, 1920); ed. James L. W. West III (Cambridge and New York, 1995).

The Beautiful and Damned (New York, 1922); ed. James L. W. West III (Cambridge and New York, 2008).

The Great Gatsby (New York, 1925); ed. Matthew J. Bruccoli (Cambridge and New York, 1991).

Tender is the Night (New York, 1934); rev. edn. (New York, 1951).

The Last Tycoon (New York, 1941); *The Love of the Last Tycoon*, ed. Matthew J. Bruccoli (Cambridge and New York, 1993).

The Bodley Head Scott Fitzgerald, 6 vols. (London, 1958–63).

The Apprentice Fiction of F. Scott Fitzgerald: 1909–1917, ed. John Kuehl (New Brunswick, NJ, 1965).

The Price Was High: The Last Uncollected Stories of F. Scott Fitzgerald, ed. Matthew J. Bruccoli (New York, 1979).

The Short Stories of F. Scott Fitzgerald: A New Collection, ed. Matthew J. Bruccoli (New York, 1989).

Letters

The Letters of F. Scott Fitzgerald, ed. Andrew Turnbull (New York, 1963).

Dear Scott/Dear Max: The Fitzgerald–Perkins Correspondence, ed. John Kuehl and Jackson R. Bryer (New York, 1971).

As Ever, Scott Fitz——: Letters Between F. Scott Fitzgerald and His Literary Agent, Harold Ober, 1919–1940, ed. Matthew J. Bruccoli, with the assistance of Jennifer McCabe Atkinson (Philadelphia, 1972).

Correspondence of F. Scott Fitzgerald, ed. Matthew J. Bruccoli and Margaret M. Duggan, with the assistance of Susan Walker (New York, 1980).

F. Scott Fitzgerald: A Life in Letters, ed. Matthew J. Bruccoli, with the assistance of Judith S. Baughman (New York, 1994).

Dear Scott, Dearest Zelda: The Love Letters of F. Scott and Zelda Fitzgerald, ed. Jackson R. Bryer and Cathy W. Barks (New York, 2002).

Bibliography

Bruccoli, Matthew J., 'A Collation of F. Scott Fitzgerald's *This Side of Paradise*', *Studies in Bibliography*, 9 (1957), 263–5.

—— 'Fitzgerald's Marked Copy of *This Side of Paradise*', *Fitzgerald/Hemingway Annual*, 3 (1971), 64–9.

Bruccoli, Matthew J., *F. Scott Fitzgerald: A Descriptive Bibliography*, rev. edn. (Pittsburgh, 1987).

—— (ed.), *This Side of Paradise: The Manuscripts and Typescripts*, 2 vols. (New York and London, 1990).

Bryer, Jackson R., 'The Critical Reputation of F. Scott Fitzgerald', in Ruth Prigozy (ed.), *The Cambridge Companion to F. Scott Fitzgerald* (Cambridge, 2002), 208–34.

—— *The Critical Reputation of F. Scott Fitzgerald: A Bibliographical Study* (Hamden, Conn., 1967).

—— *The Critical Reputation of F. Scott Fitzgerald: A Bibliographical Study. Supplement One Through 1981* (Hamden, Conn., 1984).

—— 'F. Scott Fitzgerald', in Jackson R. Bryer (ed.), *Sixteen Modern American Authors: A Survey of Research and Criticism* (Durham, NC, 1974), 277–321.

—— 'F. Scott Fitzgerald', in Jackson R. Bryer (ed.), *Sixteen Modern American Authors*, vol. ii, *A Survey of Research and Criticism Since 1972* (Durham, NC, 1990), 301–59.

Good, Dorothy Ballweg, '"A Romance and a Reading List": The Literary References in *This Side of Paradise*', *Fitzgerald/Hemingway Annual*, 8 (1976), 35–64.

Haywood, Lynn, 'Historical Notes for *This Side of Paradise*', *Resources for American Literary Study*, 10 (Autumn 1980), 191–208.

Stanley, Linda C., *The Foreign Critical Reputation of F. Scott Fitzgerald: An Analysis and Annotated Bibliography* (Westport, Conn., 1980).

—— *The Foreign Critical Reputation of F. Scott Fitzgerald, 1980–2000: An Analysis and Annotated Bibliography* (Westport, Conn., 2004).

Tate, Mary Jo, *F. Scott Fitzgerald A to Z: The Essential Reference to His Life and Work* (New York, 1998).

West, James L. W., III, 'The Correction Lists for F. Scott Fitzgerald's *This Side of Paradise*', *Studies in Bibliography*, 26 (1973), 254–64.

Biography

Bruccoli, Matthew J., *Some Sort of Epic Grandeur: The Life of F. Scott Fitzgerald*, 2nd rev. edn. (Columbia, SC, 2002).

Donaldson, Scott, *Fool for Love: F. Scott Fitzgerald* (New York, 1983).

Le Vot, André, *F. Scott Fitzgerald: A Biography*, tr. William Byron (Garden City, NY, 1983).

Mellow, James R., *Invented Lives: F. Scott & Zelda Fitzgerald* (Boston, 1984).

Mizener, Arthur, *The Far Side of Paradise: A Biography of F. Scott Fitzgerald*, rev. edn. (New York, 1959).

Piper, Henry Dan, *F. Scott Fitzgerald: A Critical Portrait* (New York, 1965).

Turnbull, Andrew, *Scott Fitzgerald* (New York, 1962).

Criticism

Collections

Assadi, Jamal, and Freedman, William (eds.), *A Distant Drummer: Foreign Perspectives on F. Scott Fitzgerald* (New York, 2007).

Bruccoli, Matthew J., and Baughman, Judith S. (eds.), *Conversations with F. Scott Fitzgerald* (Jackson, Miss., 2004).

—— and Bryer, Jackson R. (eds.), *F. Scott Fitzgerald in His Own Time: A Miscellany* (Kent, OH, 1971).

—— Smith, Scottie Fitzgerald, and Kerr, Joan P. (eds.), *The Romantic Egoists: A Pictorial Autobiography from the Scrapbooks and Albums of Scott and Zelda Fitzgerald* (New York, 1974).

Bryer, Jackson R. (ed.), *F. Scott Fitzgerald: The Critical Reception* (New York, 1978).

—— Margolies, Alan, and Prigozy, Ruth (eds.), *F. Scott Fitzgerald: New Perspectives* (Athens, Ga., 2000).

—— Prigozy, Ruth, and Stern, Milton R. (eds.), *F. Scott Fitzgerald in the Twenty-First Century* (Tuscaloosa, Ala., and London, 2003).

Claridge, Henry (ed.), *F. Scott Fitzgerald: Critical Assessments*, 4 vols. (Robertsbridge, 1991).

Curnutt, Kirk (ed.), *A Historical Guide to F. Scott Fitzgerald* (New York and Cambridge, 2004).

Kazin, Alfred (ed.), *F. Scott Fitzgerald: The Man and His Work* (Cleveland, 1951).

Kennedy, J. Gerald, and Bryer, Jackson R. (eds.), *French Connections: Hemingway and Fitzgerald Abroad* (New York, 1998).

Lee, A. Robert (ed.), *Scott Fitzgerald: The Promises of Life* (London and New York, 1989).

Mizener, Arthur (ed.), *F. Scott Fitzgerald: A Collection of Critical Essays* (Englewood Cliffs, NJ, 1968).

Noble, Donald R. (ed.), *Zelda & Scott/Scott & Zelda: New Writings on Their Works, Lives and Times* (Albany, NY, 2005).

Prigozy, Ruth (ed.), *The Cambridge Companion to F. Scott Fitzgerald* (Cambridge and New York, 2002).

Wilson, Edmund (ed.), *The Crack-Up* (New York, 1945).

Books and Essays

Allen, Joan M., *Candles and Carnival Lights: The Catholic Sensibility of F. Scott Fitzgerald* (New York, 1978).

Burhans, Clinton S., Jr., 'Structure and Theme in *This Side of Paradise*', *Journal of English and Germanic Philology*, 68 (October 1969), 605–24.

Chambers, John B., *The Novels of F. Scott Fitzgerald* (New York, 1989).

Cross, K. G. W., *F. Scott Fitzgerald* (Edinburgh and New York, 1964).

Curnutt, Kirk, *The Cambridge Introduction to F. Scott Fitzgerald* (Cambridge and New York, 2007).

—— 'Youth Culture and the Spectacle of Waste: *This Side of Paradise* and *The Beautiful and Damned*', in Jackson R. Bryer, Ruth Prigozy, and Milton R. Stern (eds.), *F. Scott Fitzgerald in the Twenty-First Century* (Tuscaloosa, Ala., and London, 2003), 79–103.

Eble, Kenneth, *F. Scott Fitzgerald*, rev. edn. (Boston, 1977).

Fryer, Sarah Beebe, *Fitzgerald's New Women: Harbingers of Change* (Ann Arbor, 1988).

Gallo, Rose Adrienne, *F. Scott Fitzgerald* (New York, 1978).

Gillin, Edward, 'Princeton, Pragmatism, and Fitzgerald's Sentimental Journey', in Jackson R. Bryer, Ruth Prigozy, and Milton R. Stern (eds.), *F. Scott Fitzgerald in the Twenty-First Century* (Tuscaloosa, Ala., and London, 2003), 38–53.

Goldhurst, William, *F. Scott Fitzgerald and His Contemporaries* (Cleveland, 1963).

Graham, T. Austin, 'Fitzgerald's "Riotous Mystery": *This Side of Paradise* as Musical Theater', *F. Scott Fitzgerald Review*, 6 (2007–8), 21–53.

Gross, Barry, '*This Side of Paradise*: The Dominating Intention', *Studies in the Novel*, 1 (Spring 1969), 51–9.

Hebel, Udo J., '"Platitudes and Prejudices and Sentimentalisms": F. Scott Fitzgerald's *This Side of Paradise* and Sentimental Popular Culture', in Winifried Herget (ed.), *Sentimentality in Modern Literature and Popular Culture* (Tübingen, 1991), 139–53.

Hendriksen, Jack, This Side of Paradise *as a Bildungsroman* (New York, 1993).

Hindus, Milton, *F. Scott Fitzgerald: An Introduction and Interpretation* (New York, 1968).

Hoffman, Madelyn, '*This Side of Paradise*: A Study of Pathological Narcissism', *Literature and Psychology*, 28 3–4 (1978), 178–85.

Hook, Andrew, 'Cases for Reconsideration: Fitzgerald's *This Side of Paradise* and *The Beautiful and Damned*', in A. Robert Lee (ed.), *Scott Fitzgerald: The Promises of Life* (London and New York, 1989), 17–36.

—— *F. Scott Fitzgerald* (London and New York, 1992).

James, Pearl, 'History and Masculinity in F. Scott Fitzgerald's *This Side of Paradise*', *Modern Fiction Studies*, 51 (Spring 2005), 1–33.

Kahn, Sy, '*This Side of Paradise*: The Pageantry of Disillusion', *Midwest Quarterly*, 7 (Winter 1966), 177–94.

Lehan, Richard D., *F. Scott Fitzgerald and the Craft of Fiction* (Carbondale, Ill., 1966).

Liebling, A. J. 'Books: Amory, We're Beautiful', *New Yorker*, 27 (19, May 1951), 129–36.

Long, Richard Emmet, *The Achieving of* The Great Gatsby: *F. Scott Fitzgerald, 1920–1925* (Lewisburg, Penn., 1979).

McDonald, Jarom Lyle, *Sports, Narrative, and Nation in the Fiction of F. Scott Fitzgerald* (New York and London, 2007).

Marquand, John P., 'Looking Backwards. Fitzgerald: "This Side of Paradise"', *Saturday Review of Literature*, 22 (Aug. 6, 1949), 30–1.

Miller, James E., Jr., *F. Scott Fitzgerald: His Art and His Technique* (New York, 1964).

Monk, Craig, 'The Political F. Scott Fitzgerald: Liberal Illusion and Disillusion in *This Side of Paradise* and *The Beautiful and Damned*', *American Studies International*, 33 (October 1995), 60–70.

Moore, Benita A., *Escape into a Labyrinth: F. Scott Fitzgerald, Catholic Sensibility, and the American Way* (New York and London, 1988).

Perosa, Sergio, *The Art of F. Scott Fitzgerald*, tr. Charles Matz and Sergio Perosa (Ann Arbor, 1965).

Raubicheck, Walter, 'The Catholic Romanticism of *This Side of Paradise*', in Jackson R. Bryer, Ruth Prigozy, and Milton R. Stern (eds.), *F. Scott Fitzgerald in the Twenty-First Century* (Tuscaloosa, Ala., and London, 2003), 54–65.

Roulston, Robert, '*This Side of Paradise*: The Ghost of Rupert Brooke', *Fitzgerald/Hemingway Annual*, 7 (1975), 117–30.

——and Roulston, Helen H., *The Winding Road to West Egg: The Artistic Development of F. Scott Fitzgerald* (Lewisburg, Penn., 1995).

Schiff, Jonathan, *Ashes to Ashes: Mourning and Social Difference in F. Scott Fitzgerald's Fiction* (Cranbury, NJ, 2001).

Seiters, Dan, *Image Patterns in the Novels of F. Scott Fitzgerald* (Ann Arbor, 1986).

Sklar, Robert, *F. Scott Fitzgerald: The Last Laocoön* (New York, 1967).

Smith, Susan Harris, 'Some Biographical Aspects of *This Side of Paradise*', *Fitzgerald/Hemingway Annual*, 2 (1970), 96–101.

Stavola, Thomas J., *Scott Fitzgerald: Crisis in an American Identity* (New York, 1979).

Stern, Milton R., *The Golden Moment: The Novels of F. Scott Fitzgerald* (Urbana, Ill., 1970).

Tanner, Stephen L., 'The Devil and F. Scott Fitzgerald', in Jackson R. Bryer, Ruth Prigozy, and Milton R. Stern (eds.), *F. Scott Fitzgerald in the Twenty-First Century* (Tuscaloosa, Ala., and London, 2003), 66–78.

Tuttleton, James W., 'The Presence of Poe in *This Side of Paradise*', *English Language Notes*, 3 (June 1966), 384–9.

Ullrich, David W., 'Reconstructing Fitzgerald's "Twice-Told Tales": Intertextuality in *This Side of Paradise* and *Tender Is the Night*', *F. Scott Fitzgerald Review*, 3 (2004), 43–71.

Van Arsdale, Nancy P., 'Princeton as Modernist's Hermeneutics: Rereading *This Side of Paradise*', in Jackson R. Bryer, Alan Margolies, and Ruth Prigozy (eds.), *F. Scott Fitzgerald: New Perspectives* (Athens, Ga., 2000), 39–50.

Way, Brian, *F. Scott Fitzgerald and the Art of Social Fiction* (London, 1980).

West, James L. W., III, *The Making of* This Side of Paradise (Philadelphia, 1983).

—— 'The Question of Vocation in *This Side of Paradise* and *The Beautiful and Damned*', in Ruth Prigozy (ed.), *The Cambridge Companion to F. Scott Fitzgerald* (Cambridge and New York, 2002), 48–56.

Zhang, Aiping, *Enchanted Places: The Use of Setting in F. Scott Fitzgerald's Fiction* (Westport, Conn., 1997).

Further Reading in Oxford World's Classics

Fitzgerald, F. Scott, *The Beautiful and Damned*, ed. Alan Margolies.

—— *The Great Gatsby*, ed. Ruth Prigozy.

A CHRONOLOGY OF
F. SCOTT FITZGERALD

1896   Francis Scott Key Fitzgerald born on 24 September, first surviving child (two others having died) of Edward Fitzgerald and Mollie McQuillan, in St Paul, Minnesota.

1898   Family moves to Buffalo, New York, where Edward Fitzgerald takes a job as a salesman for Proctor & Gamble.

1901   Family moves to Syracuse, New York, in January; in May, Fitzgerald's only sibling, his sister Annabel, is born.

1903   Family moves back to Buffalo.

1908–10 After Edward Fitzgerald loses his job, the family returns to St Paul in July; Fitzgerald enrols at St Paul Academy in September. His first publication, the story 'The Mystery of the Raymond Mortgage', appears in the *St Paul Academy Now and Then* in October.

1910–11 He publishes three other stories in the *Now and Then*.

1911–12 Fitzgerald writes and produces his first play, *The Girl from Lazy J*, in St Paul in August; subsequently, in the summers of 1912, 1913, and 1914, he writes and produces three more plays. In September 1911, he enrols at the Newman School in Hackensack, New Jersey; while at Newman, he publishes three stories in the *Newman School News* and graduates in the spring of 1913.

1913   In September Fitzgerald enters Princeton University as a member of the Class of 1917, where he meets Edmund Wilson and John Peale Bishop, and almost immediately becomes involved with the principal literary and dramatic groups on campus. Between 1914 and 1918 Fitzgerald's poetry, fiction, parodies, and plays appear in the *Nassau Literary Magazine* and the *Princeton Tiger*, and he writes the book and lyrics for one Triangle Club show and the lyrics for two others.

1914   While home for Christmas Fitzgerald meets and falls in love with Ginevra King, a 16-year-old beauty from a wealthy Lake Forest, Illinois, family, with whom he corresponds frequently and whom he sees occasionally until she terminates their relationship in August 1916.

1915 In December, Fitzgerald drops out of Princeton, with illness as his official excuse but with poor grades due to over-concentration on extracurricular activities as the true reason.

1916 Fitzgerald returns to Princeton in September as a member of the Class of 1918.

1917 On 26 October Fitzgerald enlists as a second lieutenant in the army infantry; on 20 November he reports to Fort Leavenworth, Kansas, for training. While there he begins work on a novel entitled 'The Romantic Egotist'.

1918 Fitzgerald is transferred to Camp Taylor in Louisville, Kentucky, in March; while on leave at Princeton he completes a first draft of 'The Romantic Egotist' and submits it to Charles Scribner's Sons. In April Fitzgerald is sent to Camp Gordon in Georgia and in June he is transferred to Camp Sheridan, outside Montgomery, Alabama. In July, at a dance at a country club in Montgomery, he meets Zelda Sayre, daughter of Anthony Sayre, an Associate Justice of the Supreme Court of Alabama. In August Scribner's rejects 'The Romantic Egotist', which Fitzgerald revises and resubmits, only to have the revised version rejected in October. In November, Fitzgerald goes to Camp Mills on Long Island, New York, to await assignment overseas, but the war ends before he can embark.

1919 Fitzgerald is discharged from the army in February; engaged to marry Zelda, he goes to New York and works for the Barron Collier advertising agency. He visits Zelda in Montgomery during the spring and, in June, she breaks off their engagement because of his uncertain future. He quits the ad agency job in the summer and returns to St Paul, where he lives with his parents while he rewrites his novel. On 16 September Maxwell Perkins of Scribner's accepts his novel, now titled *This Side of Paradise*, and his magazine stories, all of which had been rejected previously, now begin to be accepted.

1920 Between January and March the *Smart Set* publishes three Fitzgerald stories and a play, and the *Saturday Evening Post* publishes two stories. In January he is re-engaged to Zelda. On 26 March *This Side of Paradise* is published, and on 3 April Fitzgerald marries Zelda Sayre in the rectory of St Patrick's Cathedral in New York City. From May until September they live in a rented house in Westport, Connecticut. In September *Flappers and Philosophers*, his first short story collection, is published; and in October the Fitzgeralds move to New York City.

1921 From May until July the Fitzgeralds visit England, France, and Italy. In August they move back to the St Paul area; and on 26 October their daughter Frances Scott (Scottie) is born.

1922   In March Fitzgerald's second novel, *The Beautiful and Damned*, is published; and in September his second collection of short stories, *Tales of the Jazz Age*, appears. In October the Fitzgeralds move to a rented house in Great Neck, Long Island, New York.

1923   Fitzgerald's play *The Vegetable* is published in April; it fails as a stage vehicle at a tryout in Atlantic City, New Jersey, in November.

1924   In April the Fitzgeralds sail for France, settling in St Raphael on the Riviera. During the summer, Zelda briefly becomes romantically involved with Édouard Jozan, a French aviator. In the early winter, the Fitzgeralds go to Italy, where Fitzgerald revises his new novel.

1925   *The Great Gatsby* is published on 10 April; late that month the Fitzgeralds rent an apartment in Paris, where, in April, Fitzgerald meets Ernest Hemingway at the Dingo bar.

1926   *All the Sad Young Men*, a collection of short stories, is published in February; in March the Fitzgeralds return to the Riviera, where they remain until December, when they sail back to America.

1927   In January Fitzgerald goes to Hollywood to work on a screenplay (which is never produced) for United Artists; while there he meets and has a flirtation with a young starlet, Lois Moran. In March the Fitzgeralds move to Ellerslie, a large rented home near Wilmington, Delaware, and Zelda starts to take ballet lessons.

1928   The Fitzgeralds return to Europe in April and settle in Paris, where Zelda continues her ballet lessons. In September they return to Ellerslie.

1929   In March the Fitzgeralds go back to Europe, visiting Italy and the Riviera before taking an apartment in Paris in October.

1930   After a trip to North Africa in February the Fitzgeralds return to Paris where, in late April, Zelda suffers her first nervous breakdown and enters Malmaison clinic outside the city. A month later she is moved to Valmont clinic in Switzerland and then, in June, to Prangins clinic, also in Switzerland. During the summer and autumn Fitzgerald lives in Switzerland.

1931   Fitzgerald's father dies in late January and Fitzgerald returns to America briefly for the funeral. When Zelda is released from Prangins in September the Fitzgeralds rent a house in Montgomery, Alabama. Late in the year Fitzgerald makes his second visit to Hollywood, this time to work on a script for Metro-Goldwyn-Mayer.

1932   In February, Zelda suffers another breakdown and is sent to the Phipps Psychiatric Clinic in Baltimore, Maryland, and Fitzgerald, in May, rents La Paix, a house just outside the city. In June Zelda is discharged from Phipps and joins him. In October Zelda's novel, *Save Me the Waltz*, which she completed while at Phipps, is published.

1933–4   In December 1933 Fitzgerald moves to Baltimore; and in January, Zelda suffers her third breakdown and enters Sheppard-Pratt Hospital outside Baltimore. In March she is sent to Craig House in Beacon, New York, but is returned to Sheppard-Pratt in May. On 15 April *Tender Is the Night*, Fitzgerald's fourth novel, is published.

1935–6   Fitzgerald spends most of the year 1935 in North Carolina, first at the Oak Hall Hotel in Tryon, then the summer at the Grove Park Inn in Asheville, and finally at the Skyland Hotel in Hendersonville in November (where he begins 'The Crack-Up' essays). In March 1935 *Taps at Reveille*, his fourth collection of short stories, is published; and in September 1935 he rents an apartment in downtown Baltimore. Zelda enters Highland Hospital in Asheville in April 1936, and Fitzgerald returns to the Grove Park Inn in July, remaining there until December.

1937   Fitzgerald spends the first six months of the year at the Oak Park Hotel in Tryon; in July, deeply in debt, he goes to Hollywood under a six-month contract with Metro-Goldwyn-Mayer at $1,000 per week. On 14 July he meets columnist Sheilah Graham at a party and, soon after, initiates a romantic relationship with her which ends only at his death. Beginning in the late summer, Fitzgerald writes the script for *Three Comrades*, the only sound film for which he received screen credit. In December his contract with M-G-M is renewed for a year at $1,250 per week.

1938–9   In September 1938 Scottie Fitzgerald enrols at Vassar College in Poughkeepsie, New York. In December Fitzgerald's M-G-M contract is terminated; he works briefly on the script of *Gone With the Wind* in early 1939, and in February goes to Dartmouth College in New Hampshire with Budd Schulberg to work on the movie *Winter Carnival* but is fired from the project for drinking. Thereafter, he takes free-lance screenwriting jobs at Paramount, Universal, Columbia, Goldwyn, and Twentieth Century-Fox studios. In October 1939 he begins work on a novel about Hollywood.

1940   In April Zelda is discharged from Highland Hospital and goes to Montgomery, Alabama, to live with her mother. On 21 December Fitzgerald dies of a heart attack at Sheilah Graham's apartment in Hollywood.

1947–8   Zelda returns to Highland Hospital in November 1947 and dies in a fire there on 10 March 1948.

THIS SIDE OF PARADISE

. . . Well this side of Paradise! . . .
There's little comfort in the wise.

—*Rupert Brooke.**

Experience is the name so many people
give to their mistakes.

—*Oscar Wilde.**

CONTENTS

BOOK ONE: THE ROMANTIC EGOTIST

[Interlude: May, 1917–February, 1919.]

BOOK TWO: THE EDUCATION OF A PERSONAGE

BOOK ONE

THE ROMANTIC EGOTIST

CHAPTER I

AMORY, SON OF BEATRICE

AMORY BLAINE inherited from his mother every trait, except the stray inexpressible few, that made him worth while. His father, an ineffectual, inarticulate man with a taste for Byron and a habit of drowsing over the *Encyclopædia Britannica*, grew wealthy at thirty through the death of two elder brothers, successful Chicago brokers, and in the first flush of feeling that the world was his, went to Bar Harbor* and met Beatrice O'Hara. In consequence, Stephen Blaine handed down to posterity his height of just under six feet and his tendency to waver at crucial moments, these two abstractions appearing in his son Amory. For many years he hovered in the background of his family's life, an unassertive figure with a face half-obliterated by lifeless, silky hair, continually occupied in "taking care" of his wife, continually harassed by the idea that he didn't and couldn't understand her.

But Beatrice Blaine! There was a woman! Early pictures taken on her father's estate at Lake Geneva, Wisconsin, or in Rome at the Sacred Heart Convent—an educational extravagance that in her youth was only for the daughters of the exceptionally wealthy—showed the exquisite delicacy of her features, the consummate art and simplicity of her clothes. A brilliant education she had—her youth passed in renaissance glory, she was versed in the latest gossip of the Older Roman Families; known by name as a fabulously wealthy American girl to Cardinal Vitori and Queen Margherita* and more subtle celebrities that one must have had some culture even to have heard of. She learned in England to prefer whiskey and soda to wine, and her small talk was broadened in two senses during a winter in Vienna. All in all Beatrice O'Hara absorbed the sort of education that will be quite impossible ever again; a tutelage measured by the number of things and people one could be contemptuous of and charming about; a culture rich in all arts and traditions, barren of all ideas, in the last of those days when the great gardener clipped the inferior roses to produce one perfect bud.

In her less important moments she returned to America, met Stephen Blaine and married him—this almost entirely because she was a little bit weary, a little bit sad. Her only child was carried through a tiresome season and brought into the world on a spring day in ninety-six.

When Amory was five he was already a delightful companion for her. He was an auburn-haired boy, with great, handsome eyes which he would grow up to in time, a facile imaginative mind and a taste for fancy dress. From his fourth to his tenth year he *did* the country with his mother in her father's private car, from Coronado,* where his mother became so bored that she had a nervous breakdown in a fashionable hotel, down to Mexico City, where she took a mild, almost epidemic consumption. This trouble pleased her, and later she made use of it as an intrinsic part of her atmosphere—especially after several astounding bracers.

So, while more or less fortunate little rich boys were defying governesses on the beach at Newport,* or being spanked or tutored or read to from "Do and Dare," or "Frank on the Lower Mississippi,"* Amory was biting acquiescent bell-boys in the Waldorf,* outgrowing a natural repugnance to chamber music and symphonies, and deriving a highly specialized education from his mother.

"Amory."

"Yes, Beatrice." (Such a quaint name for his mother; she encouraged it.)

"Dear, don't *think* of getting out of bed yet. I've always suspected that early rising in early life makes one nervous. Clothilde is having your breakfast brought up."

"All right."

"I am feeling very old to-day, Amory," she would sigh, her face a rare cameo of pathos, her voice exquisitely modulated, her hands as facile as Bernhardt's.* "My nerves are on edge—on edge. We must leave this terrifying place to-morrow and go searching for sunshine."

Amory's penetrating green eyes would look out through tangled hair at his mother. Even at this age he had no illusions about her.

"Amory."

"Oh, *yes*."

"I want you to take a red-hot bath—as hot as you can bear it, and just relax your nerves. You can read in the tub if you wish."

She fed him sections of the "Fêtes Galantes"* before he was ten; at eleven he could talk glibly, if rather reminiscently, of Brahms and Mozart and Beethoven. One afternoon, when left alone in the hotel at Hot Springs,* he sampled his mother's apricot cordial, and as the taste pleased him, he became quite tipsy. This was fun for a while, but he essayed a cigarette in his exaltation, and succumbed to a vulgar, plebeian reaction. Though this incident horrified Beatrice, it also secretly amused her and became part of what in a later generation would have been termed her "line."

"This son of mine," he heard her tell a room full of awe-struck, admiring women one day, "is entirely sophisticated and quite charming—but delicate—we're all delicate; *here*, you know." Her hand was radiantly outlined against her beautiful bosom; then sinking her voice to a whisper, she told them of the apricot cordial. They rejoiced, for she was a brave raconteuse, but many were the keys turned in sideboard locks that night against the possible defection of little Bobby or Barbara. . . .

These domestic pilgrimages were invariably in state; two maids, the private car, or Mr. Blaine when available, and very often a physician. When Amory had the whooping-cough four disgusted specialists glared at each other hunched around his bed; when he took scarlet fever the number of attendants, including physicians and nurses, totalled fourteen. However, blood being thicker than broth, he was pulled through.

The Blaines were attached to no city. They were the Blaines of Lake Geneva; they had quite enough relatives to serve in place of friends, and an enviable standing from Pasadena to Cape Cod.* But Beatrice grew more and more prone to like only new acquaintances, as there were certain stories, such as the history of her constitution and its many amendments, memories of her years abroad, that it was necessary for her to repeat at regular intervals. Like Freudian dreams, they must be thrown off, else they would sweep in and lay siege to her nerves. But Beatrice was critical about American women, especially the floating population of ex-Westerners.

"They have accents, my dear," she told Amory, "not Southern accents or Boston accents, not an accent attached to any locality, just an accent"—she became dreamy. "They pick up old, moth-eaten London accents that are down on their luck and have to be used by some one. They talk as an English butler might after several years in a Chicago grand-opera company." She became almost incoherent—"Suppose—time in every Western woman's life—she feels her husband is prosperous enough for her to have—accent—they try to impress *me*, my dear——"

Though she thought of her body as a mass of frailties, she considered her soul quite as ill, and therefore important in her life. She had once been a Catholic, but discovering that priests were infinitely more attentive when she was in process of losing or regaining faith in Mother Church, she maintained an enchantingly wavering attitude. Often she deplored the bourgeois quality of the American Catholic clergy, and was quite sure that had she lived in the shadow of the great Continental cathedrals her soul would still be a thin flame on the mighty altar of Rome. Still, next to doctors, priests were her favorite sport.

"Ah, Bishop Wiston," she would declare, "I do not *want* to talk of myself. I can imagine the stream of hysterical women fluttering at your doors, beseeching you to be sim*pati*co"—then after an interlude filled by the clergyman—"but my mood—is—oddly dissimilar."

Only to bishops and above did she divulge her clerical romance. When she had first returned to her country there had been a pagan, Swinburnian young man in Asheville,* for whose passionate kisses and unsentimental conversations she had taken a decided penchant—they had discussed the matter pro and con with an intellectual romancing quite devoid of soppiness. Eventually she had decided to marry for background, and the young pagan from Asheville had gone through a spiritual crisis, joined the Catholic Church, and was now—Monsignor Darcy.

"Indeed, Mrs. Blaine, he is still delightful company—quite the cardinal's right-hand man."

"Amory will go to him one day, I know," breathed the beautiful lady, "and Monsignor Darcy will understand him as he understood me."

Amory became thirteen, rather tall and slender, and more than ever on to his Celtic mother. He had tutored occasionally—the idea being that he was to "keep up," at each place "taking up the work where he left off," yet as no tutor ever found the place he left off, his mind was still in very good shape. What a few more years of this life would have made of him is problematical. However, four hours out from land, Italy bound, with Beatrice, his appendix burst, probably from too many meals in bed, and after a series of frantic telegrams to Europe and America, to the amazement of the passengers the great ship slowly wheeled around and returned to New York to deposit Amory at the pier. You will admit that if it was not life it was magnificent.

After the operation Beatrice had a nervous breakdown that bore a suspicious resemblance to delirium tremens, and Amory was left in Minneapolis, destined to spend the ensuing two years with his aunt and uncle. There the crude, vulgar air of Western civilization first catches him—in his underwear, so to speak.

A Kiss For Amory

His lip curled when he read it.

> *"I am going to have a bobbing party,"* it said, *"on Thursday, December the seventeenth, at five o'clock, and I would like it very much if you could come.*
>
> *Yours truly,*
>
> R.S.V.P. *Myra St. Claire."*

He had been two months in Minneapolis, and his chief struggle had been the concealing from "the other guys at school" how particularly superior he felt himself to be, yet this conviction was built upon shifting sands. He had shown off one day in French class (he was in senior French class) to the utter confusion of Mr. Reardon, whose accent Amory damned contemptuously, and to the delight of the class. Mr. Reardon, who had spent several weeks in Paris ten years before, took his revenge on the verbs, whenever he had his book open. But another time Amory showed off in history class, with quite disastrous results, for the boys there were his own age, and they shrilled innuendoes at each other all the following week:

"Aw—I b'lieve, doncherknow, the Umuricun revolution was *lawgely* an affair of the middul *clawses*," or

"Washington came of very good blood—aw, quite good—I b'lieve."

Amory ingeniously tried to retrieve himself by blundering on purpose. Two years before he had commenced a history of the United States which, though it only got as far as the Colonial Wars, had been pronounced by his mother completely enchanting.

His chief disadvantage lay in athletics, but as soon as he discovered that it was the touchstone of power and popularity at school, he began to make furious, persistent efforts to excel in the winter sports, and with his ankles aching and bending in spite of his efforts, he skated valiantly around the Lorelie rink every afternoon, wondering how soon he would be able to carry a hockey-stick without getting it inexplicably tangled in his skates.

The invitation to Miss Myra St. Claire's bobbing party spent the morning in his coat pocket, where it had an intense physical affair with a dusty piece of peanut brittle. During the afternoon he brought it to light with a sigh, and after some consideration and a preliminary draft in the back of Collar and Daniell's "First-Year Latin," composed an answer:

My dear Miss St. Claire:
  Your truly charming envitation for the evening of next Thursday evening was truly delightful to recieve this morning. I will be charm and inchanted indeed to present my compliments on next Thursday evening.
                    Faithfully,
                              Amory Blaine.

On Thursday, therefore, he walked pensively along the slippery, shovel-scraped sidewalks, and came in sight of Myra's house, on the half-hour after five, a lateness which he fancied his mother would have favored. He waited on the door-step with his eyes nonchalantly half-closed, and planned his entrance with precision. He would cross the floor, not too hastily, to Mrs. St. Claire, and say with exactly the correct modulation:

"My *dear* Mrs. St. Claire, I'm *frightfully* sorry to be late, but my maid"—he paused there and realized he would be quoting—"but my uncle and I had to see a fella— Yes, I've met your enchanting daughter at dancing-school."

Then he would shake hands, using that slight, half-foreign bow, with all the starchy little females, and nod to the fellas who would be standing 'round, paralyzed into rigid groups for mutual protection.

A butler (one of the three in Minneapolis) swung open the door. Amory stepped inside and divested himself of cap and coat. He was mildly surprised not to hear the shrill squawk of conversation from the next room, and he decided it must be quite formal. He approved of that—as he approved of the butler.

"Miss Myra," he said.

To his surprise the butler grinned horribly.

"Oh, yeah," he declared, "she's here." He was unaware that his failure to be cockney was ruining his standing. Amory considered him coldly.

"But," continued the butler, his voice rising unnecessarily, "she's the only one what *is* here. The party's gone."

Amory gasped in sudden horror.

"What?"

"She's been waitin' for Amory Blaine. That's you, ain't it? Her mother says that if you showed up by five-thirty you two was to go after 'em in the Packard."

Amory's despair was crystallized by the appearance of Myra herself, bundled to the ears in a polo coat, her face plainly sulky, her voice pleasant only with difficulty.

"'Lo, Amory."

"'Lo, Myra." He had described the state of his vitality.

"Well—you *got* here, *any*ways."

"Well—I'll tell you. I guess you don't know about the auto accident," he romanced.

Myra's eyes opened wide.

"Who was it to?"

"Well," he continued desperately, "uncle 'n aunt 'n I."

"Was any one *killed?*"

Amory paused and then nodded.

"Your uncle?"—alarm.

"Oh, no—just a horse—a sorta gray horse."

At this point the Erse butler snickered.

"Probably killed the engine," he suggested. Amory would have put him on the rack without a scruple.

"We'll go now," said Myra coolly. "You see, Amory, the bobs were ordered for five and everybody was here, so we couldn't wait——"

"Well, I couldn't help it, could I?"

"So mama said for me to wait till ha'past five. We'll catch the bob before it gets to the Minnehaha Club, Amory."

Amory's shredded poise dropped from him. He pictured the happy party jingling along snowy streets, the appearance of the limousine, the horrible public descent of him and Myra before sixty reproachful eyes, his apology—a real one this time. He sighed aloud.

"What?" inquired Myra.

"Nothing. I was just yawning. Are we going to *surely* catch up with 'em before they get there?" He was encouraging a faint hope that they might slip into the Minnehaha Club and meet the others there, be found in blasé seclusion before the fire and quite regain his lost attitude.

"Oh, sure Mike, we'll catch 'em all right—let's hurry."

He became conscious of his stomach. As they stepped into the machine he hurriedly slapped the paint of diplomacy over a rather box-like plan he had conceived. It was based upon some "trade-lasts"* gleaned at dancing-school, to the effect that he was "awful good-looking and *English*, sort of."

"Myra," he said, lowering his voice and choosing his words carefully, "I beg a thousand pardons. Can you ever forgive me?"

She regarded him gravely, his intent green eyes, his mouth, that to her thirteen-year-old, Arrow-collar* taste was the quintessence of romance. Yes, Myra could forgive him very easily.

"Why—yes—sure."

He looked at her again, and then dropped his eyes. He had lashes.

"I'm awful," he said sadly. "I'm diff'runt. I don't know why I make faux pas. 'Cause I don't care, I s'pose." Then, recklessly: "I been smoking too much. I've got t'bacca heart."

Myra pictured an all-night tobacco debauch, with Amory pale and reeling from the effect of nicotined lungs. She gave a little gasp.

"Oh, *Amory*, don't smoke. You'll stunt your *growth!*"

"I don't care," he persisted gloomily. "I gotta. I got the habit. I've done a lot of things that if my fambly knew"—he hesitated, giving her imagination time to picture dark horrors—"I went to the burlesque show last week."

Myra was quite overcome. He turned the green eyes on her again.

"You're the only girl in town I like much," he exclaimed in a rush of sentiment. "You're simpatico."

Myra was not sure that she was, but it sounded stylish though vaguely improper.

Thick dusk had descended outside, and as the limousine made a sudden turn she was jolted against him; their hands touched.

"You shouldn't smoke, Amory," she whispered. "Don't you know that?"

He shook his head.

"Nobody cares."

Myra hesitated.

"*I* care."

Something stirred within Amory.

"Oh, yes, you do! You got a crush on Froggy Parker. I guess everybody knows that."

"No, I haven't," very slowly.

A silence, while Amory thrilled. There was something fascinating about Myra, shut away here cosily from the dim, chill air. Myra, a little bundle of clothes, with strands of yellow hair curling out from under her skating cap.

"Because I've got a crush, too——" He paused, for he heard in the distance the sound of young laughter, and, peering through the frosted glass along the lamp-lit street, he made out the dark outline of the bobbing party. He must act quickly. He reached over with a violent, jerky effort, and clutched Myra's hand—her thumb, to be exact.

"Tell him to go to the Minnehaha straight," he whispered. "I wanta talk to you—I *got* to talk to you."

Myra made out the party ahead, had an instant vision of her mother, and then—alas for convention—glanced into the eyes beside.

"Turn down this side street, Richard, and drive straight to the Minnehaha Club!" she cried through the speaking tube. Amory sank back against the cushions with a sigh of relief.

"I can kiss her," he thought. "I'll bet I can. I'll *bet* I can!"

Overhead the sky was half crystalline, half misty, and the night around was chill and vibrant with rich tension. From the Country Club steps the roads stretched away, dark creases on the white blanket; huge heaps of snow lining the sides like the tracks of giant moles. They lingered for a moment on the steps, and watched the white holiday moon.

"Pale moons like that one"—Amory made a vague gesture—"make people mysterieuse. You look like a young witch with her cap off and her hair sorta mussed"—her hands clutched at her hair—"Oh, leave it, it looks *good*."

They drifted up the stairs and Myra led the way into the little den of his dreams, where a cosy fire was burning before a big sink-down couch. A few years later this was to be a great stage for Amory, a cradle for many an emotional crisis. Now they talked for a moment about bobbing parties.

"There's always a bunch of shy fellas," he commented, "sitting at the tail of the bob, sorta lurkin' an' whisperin' an' pushin' each other off. Then there's always some crazy cross-eyed girl"—he gave a terrifying imitation—"she's always talkin' *hard*, sorta, to the chaperone."

"You're such a funny boy," puzzled Myra.

"How d'y' mean?" Amory gave immediate attention, on his own ground at last.

"Oh—always talking about crazy things. Why don't you come skiing with Marylyn and I to-morrow?"

"I don't like girls in the daytime," he said shortly, and then, thinking this a bit abrupt, he added: "But I like you." He cleared his throat. "I like you first and second and third."

Myra's eyes became dreamy. What a story this would make to tell Marylyn! Here on the couch with this *wonderful*-looking boy—the little fire—the sense that they were alone in the great building——

Myra capitulated. The atmosphere was too appropriate.

"I like you the first twenty-five," she confessed, her voice trembling, "and Froggy Parker twenty-sixth."

Froggy had fallen twenty-five places in one hour. As yet he had not even noticed it.

But Amory, being on the spot, leaned over quickly and kissed Myra's cheek. He had never kissed a girl before, and he tasted his lips curiously, as if he had munched some new fruit. Then their lips brushed like young wild flowers in the wind.

"We're awful," rejoiced Myra gently. She slipped her hand into his, her head drooped against his shoulder. Sudden revulsion seized Amory, disgust, loathing for the whole incident. He desired frantically to be away, never to see Myra again, never to kiss any one; he became conscious of his face and hers, of their clinging hands, and he wanted to creep out of his body and hide somewhere safe out of sight, up in the corner of his mind.

"Kiss me again." Her voice came out of a great void.

"I don't want to," he heard himself saying. There was another pause.

"I don't want to!" he repeated passionately.

Myra sprang up, her cheeks pink with bruised vanity, the great bow on the back of her head trembling sympathetically.

"I hate you!" she cried. "Don't you ever dare to speak to me again!"

"What?" stammered Amory.

"I'll tell mama you kissed me! I will too! I will too! I'll tell mama, and she won't let me play with you!"

Amory rose and stared at her helplessly, as though she were a new animal of whose presence on the earth he had not heretofore been aware.

The door opened suddenly, and Myra's mother appeared on the threshold, fumbling with her lorgnette.

"Well," she began, adjusting it benignantly, "the man at the desk told me you two children were up here—How do you do, Amory."

Amory watched Myra and waited for the crash—but none came. The pout faded, the high pink subsided, and Myra's voice was placid as a summer lake when she answered her mother.

"Oh, we started so late, mama, that I thought we might as well——"

He heard from below the shrieks of laughter, and smelled the vapid odor of hot chocolate and tea-cakes as he silently followed mother and daughter down-stairs. The sound of the graphophone* mingled with the voices of many girls humming the air, and a faint glow was born and spread over him:

> *"Casey-Jones—mounted to the cab-un*
> *Casey-Jones—'th his orders in his hand.*
> *Casey-Jones—mounted to the cab-un*
> *Took his farewell journey to the prom-ised land."*

Snapshots of the Young Egotist

Amory spent nearly two years in Minneapolis. The first winter he wore moccasins that were born yellow, but after many applications of oil and dirt assumed their mature color, a dirty, greenish brown; he wore a gray plaid mackinaw coat, and a red toboggan cap. His dog, Count Del Monte, ate the red cap, so his uncle gave him a gray one that pulled down over his face. The trouble with this one was that you breathed into it and your breath froze; one day the darn thing froze his cheek. He rubbed snow on his cheek, but it turned bluish-black just the same.

The Count Del Monte ate a box of bluing once, but it didn't hurt him. Later, however, he lost his mind and ran madly up the street, bumping into fences, rolling in gutters, and pursuing his eccentric course out of Amory's life. Amory cried on his bed.

"Poor little Count," he cried. "Oh, *poor* little *Count!*"

After several months he suspected Count of a fine piece of emotional acting.

Amory and Frog Parker considered that the greatest line in literature occurred in Act III of "Arsène Lupin."*

They sat in the first row at the Wednesday and Saturday matinées. The line was:

"If one can't be a great artist or a great soldier, the next best thing is to be a great criminal."

Amory fell in love again, and wrote a poem. This was it:

> "Marylyn and Sallee,
> Those are the girls for me.
> Marylyn stands above
> Sallee in that sweet, deep love."

He was interested in whether McGovern of Minnesota* would make the first or second All-American, how to do the card-pass, how to do the coin-pass, chameleon ties, how babies were born, and whether Three-fingered Brown was really a better pitcher than Christy Mathewson.*

Among other things he read: "For the Honor of the School," "Little Women" (twice), "The Common Law," "Sapho," "Dangerous Dan McGrew," "The Broad Highway" (three times), "The Fall of the House of Usher," "Three Weeks," "Mary Ware, the Little Colonel's Chum," "Gunga Din,"* *The Police Gazette*, and *Jim-Jam Jems.**

He had all the Henty biases in history, and was particularly fond of the cheerful murder stories of Mary Roberts Rinehart.*

School ruined his French and gave him a distaste for standard authors. His masters considered him idle, unreliable and superficially clever.

He collected locks of hair from many girls. He wore the rings of several. Finally he could borrow no more rings, owing to his nervous habit of chewing them out of shape. This, it seemed, usually aroused the jealous suspicions of the next borrower.

All through the summer months Amory and Frog Parker went each week to the Stock Company. Afterward they would stroll home in the balmy air of August night, dreaming along Hennepin and Nicollet Avenues, through the gay crowd. Amory wondered how people could fail to notice that he was a boy marked for glory, and when faces of the throng turned toward him and ambiguous eyes stared into his, he assumed the most romantic of expressions and walked on the air cushions that lie on the asphalts of fourteen.

Always, after he was in bed, there were voices—indefinite, fading, enchanting—just outside his window, and before he fell asleep he would dream one of his favorite waking dreams, the one about becoming a great half-back, or the one about the Japanese invasion, when he was rewarded by being made the youngest general in the world. It was always the becoming he dreamed of, never the being. This, too, was quite characteristic of Amory.

Code of the Young Egotist

Before he was summoned back to Lake Geneva, he had appeared, shy but inwardly glowing, in his first long trousers, set off by a purple accordion tie and a "Belmont" collar with the edges unassailably meeting, purple socks, and handkerchief with a purple border peeping from his breast pocket. But more than that, he had formulated his first philosophy, a code to live by, which, as near as it can be named, was a sort of aristocratic egotism.

He had realized that his best interests were bound up with those of a certain variant, changing person, whose label, in order that his past might always be identified with him, was Amory Blaine. Amory marked himself a fortunate youth, capable of infinite expansion for good or evil. He did not consider himself a "strong char'c'ter," but relied on his facility (learn things sorta quick) and his superior mentality (read a lotta deep books). He was proud of the fact that he could never become a mechanical or scientific genius. From no other heights was he debarred.

Physically.—Amory thought that he was exceedingly handsome. He was. He fancied himself an athlete of possibilities and a supple dancer.

Socially.—Here his condition was, perhaps, most dangerous. He granted himself personality, charm, magnetism, poise, the power

of dominating all contemporary males, the gift of fascinating all
women.

Mentally.—Complete, unquestioned superiority.

Now a confession will have to be made. Amory had rather a
Puritan conscience. Not that he yielded to it—later in life he almost
completely slew it—but at fifteen it made him consider himself a
great deal worse than other boys . . . unscrupulousness . . . the desire
to influence people in almost every way, even for evil . . . a certain
coldness and lack of affection, amounting sometimes to cruelty . . . a
shifting sense of honor . . . an unholy selfishness . . . a puzzled, furtive interest in everything concerning sex.

There was, also, a curious strain of weakness running crosswise
through his make-up . . . a harsh phrase from the lips of an older
boy (older boys usually detested him) was liable to sweep him off his
poise into surly sensitiveness, or timid stupidity . . . he was a slave
to his own moods and he felt that though he was capable of reckless-
ness and audacity, he possessed neither courage, perseverance, nor
self-respect.

Vanity, tempered with self-suspicion if not self-knowledge, a
sense of people as automatons to his will, a desire to "pass" as many
boys as possible and get to a vague top of the world . . . with this
background did Amory drift into adolescence.

Preparatory to the Great Adventure

The train slowed up with midsummer languor at Lake Geneva, and
Amory caught sight of his mother waiting in her electric on the grav-
elled station drive. It was an ancient electric, one of the early types,
and painted gray. The sight of her sitting there, slenderly erect, and
of her face, where beauty and dignity combined, melting to a dreamy
recollected smile, filled him with a sudden great pride of her. As they
kissed coolly and he stepped into the electric, he felt a quick fear lest
he had lost the requisite charm to measure up to her.

"Dear boy—you're *so* tall . . . look behind and see if there's anything coming . . ."

She looked left and right, she slipped cautiously into a speed of
two miles an hour, beseeching Amory to act as sentinel; and at one
busy crossing she made him get out and run ahead to signal her
forward like a traffic policeman. Beatrice was what might be termed
a careful driver.

"You *are* tall—but you're still very handsome—you've skipped the awkward age, or is that sixteen; perhaps it's fourteen or fifteen; I can never remember; but you've skipped it."

"Don't embarrass me," murmured Amory.

"But, my dear boy, what odd clothes! They look as if they were a *set*—don't they? Is your underwear purple, too?"

Amory grunted impolitely

"You must go to Brooks* and get some really nice suits. Oh, we'll have a talk to-night or perhaps to-morrow night. I want to tell you about your heart—you've probably been neglecting your heart—and you don't *know*."

Amory thought how superficial was the recent overlay of his own generation. Aside from a minute shyness, he felt that the old cynical kinship with his mother had not been one bit broken. Yet for the first few days he wandered about the gardens and along the shore in a state of superloneliness, finding a lethargic content in smoking "Bull"* at the garage with one of the chauffeurs.

The sixty acres of the estate were dotted with old and new summer houses and many fountains and white benches that came suddenly into sight from foliage-hung hiding-places; there was a great and constantly increasing family of white cats that prowled the many flower-beds and were silhouetted suddenly at night against the darkening trees. It was on one of the shadowy paths that Beatrice at last captured Amory, after Mr. Blaine had, as usual, retired for the evening to his private library. After reproving him for avoiding her, she took him for a long tête-à-tête in the moonlight. He could not reconcile himself to her beauty, that was mother to his own, the exquisite neck and shoulders, the grace of a fortunate woman of thirty.

"Amory, dear," she crooned softly, "I had such a strange, weird time after I left you."

"Did you, Beatrice?"

"When I had my last breakdown"—she spoke of it as a sturdy, gallant feat.

"The doctors told me"—her voice sang on a confidential note—"that if any man alive had done the consistent drinking that I have, he would have been physically *shattered*, my dear, and in his *grave*—long in his grave."

Amory winced, and wondered how this would have sounded to Froggy Parker.

"Yes," continued Beatrice tragically, "I had dreams—wonderful visions." She pressed the palms of her hands into her eyes. "I saw bronze rivers lapping marble shores, and great birds that soared through the air, parti-colored birds with iridescent plumage. I heard strange music and the flare of barbaric trumpets—what?"

Amory had snickered.

"What, Amory?"

"I said go on, Beatrice."

"That was all—it merely recurred and recurred—gardens that flaunted coloring against which this would be quite dull, moons that whirled and swayed, paler than winter moons, more golden than harvest moons——"

"Are you quite well now, Beatrice?"

"Quite well—as well as I will ever be. I am not understood, Amory. I know that can't express it to you, Amory, but—I am not understood."

Amory was quite moved. He put his arm around his mother, rubbing his head gently against her shoulder.

"Poor Beatrice—poor Beatrice."

"Tell me about *you*, Amory. Did you have two *horrible* years?"

Amory considered lying, and then decided against it.

"No, Beatrice. I enjoyed them. I adapted myself to the bourgeoisie. I became conventional." He surprised himself by saying that, and he pictured how Froggy would have gaped.

"Beatrice," he said suddenly, "I want to go away to school. Everybody in Minneapolis is going to go away to school."

Beatrice showed some alarm.

"But you're only fifteen."

"Yes, but everybody goes away to school at fifteen, and I *want* to, Beatrice."

On Beatrice's suggestion the subject was dropped for the rest of the walk, but a week later she delighted him by saying:

"Amory, I have decided to let you have your way. If you still want to, you can go to school."

"Yes?"

"To St. Regis's in Connecticut."

Amory felt a quick excitement.

"It's being arranged," continued Beatrice. "It's better that you should go away. I'd have preferred you to have gone to Eton, and

then to Christ Church, Oxford, but it seems impracticable now—and
for the present we'll let the university question take care of itself."

"What are you going to do, Beatrice?"

"Heaven knows. It seems my fate to fret away my years in this
country. Not for a second do I regret being American—indeed,
I think that a regret typical of very vulgar people, and I feel sure we
are the great coming nation—yet"—and she sighed—"I feel my life
should have drowsed away close to an older, mellower civilization,
a land of greens and autumnal browns——"

Amory did not answer, so his mother continued:

"My regret is that you haven't been abroad, but still, as you are
a man, it's better that you should grow up here under the snarling
eagle—is that the right term?"

Amory agreed that it was. She would not have appreciated the
Japanese invasion.

"When do I go to school?"

"Next month. You'll have to start East a little early to take your
examinations. After that you'll have a free week, so I want you to go
up the Hudson and pay a visit."

"To who?"

"To Monsignor Darcy, Amory. He wants to see you. He went to
Harrow and then to Yale—became a Catholic. I want him to talk to
you—I feel he can be such a help——" She stroked his auburn hair
gently. "Dear Amory, dear Amory——"

"Dear Beatrice——"

So early in September Amory, provided with "six suits summer
underwear, six suits winter underwear, one sweater or T shirt, one
jersey, one overcoat, winter, etc.," set out for New England, the land
of schools.

There were Andover and Exeter with their memories of New
England dead—large, college-like democracies; St. Mark's, Groton,
St. Regis'—recruited from Boston and the Knickerbocker families of
New York; St. Paul's, with its great rinks; Pomfret and St. George's,
prosperous and well-dressed; Taft and Hotchkiss, which prepared
the wealth of the Middle West for social success at Yale; Pawling,
Westminster, Choate, Kent, and a hundred others; all milling out
their well-set-up, conventional, impressive type, year after year; their
mental stimulus the college entrance exams; their vague purpose

set forth in a hundred circulars as "To impart a Thorough Mental, Moral, and Physical Training as a Christian Gentleman, to fit the boy *for meeting the problems of his day and generation*, and to give a solid foundation in the Arts and Sciences."

At St. Regis' Amory stayed three days and took his exams with a scoffing confidence, then doubling back to New York to pay his tutelary visit. The metropolis, barely glimpsed, made little impression on him, except for the sense of cleanliness he drew from the tall white buildings seen from a Hudson River steamboat in the early morning. Indeed, his mind was so crowded with dreams of athletic prowess at school that he considered this visit only as a rather tiresome prelude to the great adventure. This, however, it did not prove to be.

Monsignor Darcy's house was an ancient, rambling structure set on a hill overlooking the river, and there lived its owner, between his trips to all parts of the Roman-Catholic world, rather like an exiled Stuart king waiting to be called to the rule of his land. Monsignor was forty-four then, and bustling—a trifle too stout for symmetry, with hair the color of spun gold, and a brilliant, enveloping personality. When he came into a room clad in his full purple regalia from thatch to toe, he resembled a Turner sunset,* and attracted both admiration and attention. He had written two novels: one of them violently anti-Catholic, just before his conversion, and five years later another, in which he had attempted to turn all his clever jibes against Catholics into even cleverer innuendoes against Episcopalians. He was intensely ritualistic, startlingly dramatic, loved the idea of God enough to be a celibate, and rather liked his neighbor.

Children adored him because he was like a child; youth revelled in his company because he was still a youth, and couldn't be shocked. In the proper land and century he might have been a Richelieu—at present he was a very moral, very religious (if not particularly pious) clergyman, making a great mystery about pulling rusty wires, and appreciating life to the fullest, if not entirely enjoying it.

He and Amory took to each other at first sight—the jovial, impressive prelate who could dazzle an embassy ball, and the green-eyed, intent youth, in his first long trousers, accepted in their own minds a relation of father and son within a half-hour's conversation.

"My dear boy, I've been waiting to see you for years. Take a big chair and we'll have a chat."

"I've just come from school—St. Regis's, you know."

"So your mother says—a remarkable woman; have a cigarette—I'm sure you smoke. Well, if you're like me, you loathe all science and mathematics——"

Amory nodded vehemently.

"Hate 'em all. Like English and history."

"Of course. You'll hate school for a while, too, but I'm glad you're going to St. Regis's."

"Why?"

"Because it's a gentleman's school, and democracy won't hit you so early. You'll find plenty of that in college."

"I want to go to Princeton," said Amory. "I don't know why, but I think of all Harvard men as sissies, like I used to be, and all Yale men as wearing big blue sweaters and smoking pipes."

Monsignor chuckled.

"I'm one, you know."

"Oh, you're different—I think of Princeton as being lazy and good-looking and aristocratic—you know, like a spring day. Harvard seems sort of indoors——"

"And Yale is November, crisp and energetic," finished Monsignor.

"That's it."

They slipped briskly into an intimacy from which they never recovered.

"I was for Bonnie Prince Charlie," announced Amory.

"Of course you were—and for Hannibal——"*

"Yes, and for the Southern Confederacy." He was rather sceptical about being an Irish patriot—he suspected that being Irish was being somewhat common—but Monsignor assured him that Ireland was a romantic lost cause and Irish people quite charming, and that it should, by all means, be one of his principal biases.

After a crowded hour which included several more cigarettes, and during which Monsignor learned, to his surprise but not to his horror, that Amory had not been brought up a Catholic, he announced that he had another guest. This turned out to be the Honorable Thornton Hancock, of Boston, ex-minister to The Hague, author of an erudite history of the Middle Ages and the last of a distinguished, patriotic, and brilliant family.

"He comes here for a rest," said Monsignor confidentially, treating Amory as a contemporary. "I act as an escape from the weariness of agnosticism, and I think I'm the only man who knows how his staid old mind is really at sea and longs for a sturdy spar like the Church to cling to."

Their first luncheon was one of the memorable events of Amory's early life. He was quite radiant and gave off a peculiar brightness and charm. Monsignor called out the best that he had thought by question and suggestion, and Amory talked with an ingenuous brilliance of a thousand impulses and desires and repulsions and faiths and fears. He and Monsignor held the floor, and the older man, with his less receptive, less accepting, yet certainly not colder mentality, seemed content to listen and bask in the mellow sunshine that played between these two. Monsignor gave the effect of sunlight to many people; Amory gave it in his youth and, to some extent, when he was very much older, but never again was it quite so mutually spontaneous.

"He's a radiant boy," thought Thornton Hancock, who had seen the splendor of two continents and talked with Parnell and Gladstone and Bismarck*—and afterward he added to Monsignor: "But his education ought not to be intrusted to a school or college."

But for the next four years the best of Amory's intellect was concentrated on matters of popularity, the intricacies of a university social system and American Society as represented by Biltmore Teas and Hot Springs golf-links.*

. . . In all, a wonderful week, that saw Amory's mind turned inside out, a hundred of his theories confirmed, and his joy of life crystallized to a thousand ambitions. Not that the conversation was scholastic—heaven forbid! Amory had only the vaguest idea as to what Bernard Shaw was—but Monsignor made quite as much out of "The Beloved Vagabond" and "Sir Nigel,"* taking good care that Amory never once felt out of his depth.

But the trumpets were sounding for Amory's preliminary skirmish with his own generation.

"You're not sorry to go, of course. With people like us our home is where we are not," said Monsignor.

"I *am* sorry——"

"No, you're not. No one person in the world is necessary to you or to me."

"Well——"

"Good-bye."

The Egotist Down

Amory's two years at St. Regis', though in turn painful and triumphant, had as little real significance in his own life as the American "prep" school, crushed as it is under the heel of the universities, has to American life in general. We have no Eton to create the self-consciousness of a governing class; we have, instead, clean, flaccid and innocuous preparatory schools.

He went all wrong at the start, was generally considered both conceited and arrogant, and universally detested. He played football intensely, alternating a reckless brilliancy with a tendency to keep himself as safe from hazard as decency would permit. In a wild panic he backed out of a fight with a boy his own size, to a chorus of scorn, and a week later, in desperation, picked a battle with another boy very much bigger, from which he emerged badly beaten, but rather proud of himself.

He was resentful against all those in authority over him, and this, combined with a lazy indifference toward his work, exasperated every master in school. He grew discouraged and imagined himself a pariah; took to sulking in corners and reading after lights. With a dread of being alone he attached a few friends, but since they were not among the élite of the school, he used them simply as mirrors of himself, audiences before which he might do that posing absolutely essential to him. He was unbearably lonely, desperately unhappy.

There were some few grains of comfort. Whenever Amory was submerged, his vanity was the last part to go below the surface, so he could still enjoy a comfortable glow when "Wookey-wookey," the deaf old housekeeper, told him that he was the best-looking boy she had ever seen. It had pleased him to be the lightest and youngest man on the first football squad; it pleased him when Doctor Dougall told him at the end of a heated conference that he could, if he wished, get the best marks in school. But Doctor Dougall was wrong. It was temperamentally impossible for Amory to get the best marks in school.

Miserable, confined to bounds, unpopular with both faculty and students—that was Amory's first term. But at Christmas he had returned to Minneapolis, tight-lipped and strangely jubilant.

"Oh, I was sort of fresh at first," he told Frog Parker patronizingly, "but I got along fine—lightest man on the squad. You ought to go away to school, Froggy. It's great stuff."

Incident of the Well-Meaning Professor

On the last night of his first term, Mr. Margotson, the senior master, sent word to study hall that Amory was to come to his room at nine. Amory suspected that advice was forthcoming, but he determined to be courteous, because this Mr. Margotson had been kindly disposed toward him.

His summoner received him gravely, and motioned him to a chair. He hemmed several times and looked consciously kind, as a man will when he knows he's on delicate ground.

"Amory," he began. "I've sent for you on a personal matter."

"Yes, sir."

"I've noticed you this year and I—I like you. I think you have in you the makings of a—a very good man."

"Yes, sir," Amory managed to articulate. He hated having people talk as if he were an admitted failure.

"But I've noticed," continued the older man blindly, "that you're not very popular with the boys."

"No, sir." Amory licked his lips.

"Ah—I thought you might not understand exactly what it was they—ah—objected to. I'm going to tell you, because I believe—ah—that when a boy knows his difficulties he's better able to cope with them—to conform to what others expect of him." He a-hemmed again with delicate reticence, and continued: "They seem to think that you're—ah—rather too fresh——"

Amory could stand no more. He rose from his chair, scarcely controlling his voice when he spoke.

"I know—oh, *don't* you s'pose I know." His voice rose. "I know what they think; do you s'pose you have to *tell* me!" He paused. "I'm—I've got to go back now—hope I'm not rude——"

He left the room hurriedly. In the cool air outside, as he walked to his house, he exulted in his refusal to be helped.

"That *damn* old fool!" he cried wildly. "As if I didn't *know!*"

He decided, however, that this was a good excuse not to go back to study hall that night, so, comfortably couched up in his room, he munched nabiscos and finished "The White Company."*

Incident of the Wonderful Girl

There was a bright star in February. New York burst upon him on Washington's Birthday with the brilliance of a long-anticipated event.

His glimpse of it as a vivid whiteness against a deep-blue sky had left a picture of splendor that rivalled the dream cities in the Arabian Nights; but this time he saw it by electric light, and romance gleamed from the chariot-race sign on Broadway* and from the women's eyes at the Astor, where he and young Paskert from St. Regis' had dinner. When they walked down the aisle of the theatre, greeted by the nervous twanging and discord of untuned violins and the sensuous, heavy fragrance of paint and powder, he moved in a sphere of epicurean delight. Everything enchanted him. The play was "The Little Millionaire,"* with George M. Cohan, and there was one stunning young brunette who made him sit with brimming eyes in the ecstasy of watching her dance.

> *"Oh—you—wonderful girl,*
> *What a wonderful girl you are—"*

sang the tenor, and Amory agreed silently, but passionately.

> *"All—your—wonderful words*
> *Thrill me through——"*

The violins swelled and quavered on the last notes, the girl sank to a crumpled butterfly on the stage, a great burst of clapping filled the house. Oh, to fall in love like that, to the languorous magic melody of such a tune!

The last scene was laid on a roof-garden, and the 'cellos sighed to the musical moon, while light adventure and facile froth-like comedy flitted back and forth in the calcium. Amory was on fire to be an habitué of roof-gardens, to meet a girl who should look like that—better, that very girl; whose hair would be drenched with golden moonlight, while at his elbow sparkling wine was poured by an unintelligible waiter. When the curtain fell for the last time he gave such a long sigh that the people in front of him twisted around and stared and said loud enough for him to hear:

"What a *remarkable*-looking boy!"

This took his mind off the play, and he wondered if he really did seem handsome to the population of New York.

Paskert and he walked in silence toward their hotel. The former was the first to speak. His uncertain fifteen-year-old voice broke in in a melancholy strain on Amory's musings:

"I'd marry that girl to-night."

There was no need to ask what girl he referred to.

"I'd be proud to take her home and introduce her to my people," continued Paskert.

Amory was distinctly impressed. He wished he had said it instead of Paskert. It sounded so mature.

"I wonder about actresses; are they all pretty bad?"

"No, *sir*, not by a darn sight," said the worldly youth with emphasis, "and I know that girl's as good as gold. I can tell."

They wandered on, mixing in the Broadway crowd, dreaming on the music that eddied out of the cafés. New faces flashed on and off like myriad lights, pale or rouged faces, tired, yet sustained by a weary excitement. Amory watched them in fascination. He was planning his life. He was going to live in New York, and be known at every restaurant and café, wearing a dress-suit from early evening to early morning, sleeping away the dull hours of the forenoon.

"Yes, *sir*, I'd marry that girl to-night!"

Heroic in General Tone

October of his second and last year at St. Regis' was a high point in Amory's memory. The game with Groton was played from three of a snappy, exhilarating afternoon far into the crisp autumnal twilight, and Amory at quarter-back, exhorting in wild despair, making impossible tackles, calling signals in a voice that had diminished to a hoarse, furious whisper, yet found time to revel in the blood-stained bandage around his head, and the straining, glorious heroism of plunging, crashing bodies and aching limbs. For those minutes courage flowed like wine out of the November dusk, and he was the eternal hero, one with the sea-rover on the prow of a Norse galley, one with Roland and Horatius, Sir Nigel and Ted Coy,* scraped and stripped into trim and then flung by his own will into the breach, beating back the tide, hearing from afar the thunder of cheers . . . finally bruised and weary, but still elusive, circling an end, twisting, changing pace, straight-arming . . . falling behind the Groton goal with two men on his legs, in the only touchdown of the game.

The Philosophy of the Slicker

From the scoffing superiority of sixth-form year and success Amory looked back with cynical wonder on his status of the year before. He was changed as completely as Amory Blaine could ever be changed.

Amory plus Beatrice plus two years in Minneapolis—these had been his ingredients when he entered St. Regis'. But the Minneapolis years were not a thick enough overlay to conceal the "Amory plus Beatrice" from the ferreting eyes of a boarding-school, so St. Regis' had very painfully drilled Beatrice out of him, and begun to lay down new and more conventional planking on the fundamental Amory. But both St. Regis' and Amory were unconscious of the fact that this fundamental Amory had not in himself changed. Those qualities for which he had suffered, his moodiness, his tendency to pose, his laziness, and his love of playing the fool, were now taken as a matter of course, recognized eccentricities in a star quarter-back, a clever actor, and the editor of the *St. Regis Tattler*; it puzzled him to see impressionable small boys imitating the very vanities that had not long ago been contemptible weaknesses.

After the football season he slumped into dreamy content. The night of the pre-holiday dance he slipped away and went early to bed for the pleasure of hearing the violin music cross the grass and come surging in at his window. Many nights he lay there dreaming awake of secret cafés in Montmartre, where ivory women delved in romantic mysteries with diplomats and soldiers of fortune, while orchestras played Hungarian waltzes and the air was thick and exotic with intrigue and moonlight and adventure. In the spring he read "L'Allegro," by request, and was inspired to lyrical outpourings on the subject of Arcady and the pipes of Pan. He moved his bed so that the sun would wake him at dawn that he might dress and go out to the archaic swing that hung from an apple-tree near the sixth-form house. Seating himself in this he would pump higher and higher until he got the effect of swinging into the wide air, into a fairy-land of piping satyrs and nymphs with the faces of fair-haired girls he passed in the streets of Eastchester. As the swing reached its highest point, Arcady really lay just over the brow of a certain hill, where the brown road dwindled out of sight in a golden dot.

He read voluminously all spring, the beginning of his eighteenth year: "The Gentleman from Indiana," "The New Arabian Nights," "The Morals of Marcus Ordeyne," "The Man Who Was Thursday,"* which he liked without understanding; "Stover at Yale,"* that became somewhat of a text-book; "Dombey and Son," because he thought he really should read better stuff; Robert Chambers, David Graham Phillips, and E. Phillips Oppenheim* complete, and a scattering of

Tennyson and Kipling. Of all his class work only "L'Allegro" and some quality of rigid clarity in solid geometry stirred his languid interest.

As June drew near, he felt the need of conversation to formulate his own ideas, and, to his surprise, found a co-philosopher in Rahill, the president of the sixth form. In many a talk, on the highroad or lying belly-down along the edge of the baseball diamond, or late at night with their cigarettes glowing in the dark, they threshed out the questions of school, and there was developed the term "slicker."

"Got tobacco?" whispered Rahill one night, putting his head inside the door five minutes after lights.

"Sure."

"I'm coming in."

"Take a couple of pillows and lie in the window-seat, why don't you."

Amory sat up in bed and lit a cigarette while Rahill settled for a conversation. Rahill's favorite subject was the respective futures of the sixth form, and Amory never tired of outlining them for his benefit.

"Ted Converse? 'At's easy. He'll fail his exams, tutor all summer at Harstrum's,* get into Sheff* with about four conditions, and flunk out in the middle of the freshman year. Then he'll go back West and raise hell for a year or so; finally his father will make him go into the paint business. He'll marry and have four sons, all bone heads. He'll always think St. Regis's spoiled him, so he'll send his sons to day school in Portland. He'll die of locomotor ataxia* when he's forty-one, and his wife will give a baptizing stand or whatever you call it to the Presbyterian Church, with his name on it——"

"Hold up, Amory. That's too darned gloomy. How about yourself?"

"I'm in a superior class. You are, too. We're philosophers."

"I'm not."

"Sure you are. You've got a darn good head on you." But Amory knew that nothing in the abstract, no theory or generality, ever moved Rahill until he stubbed his toe upon the concrete minutiæ of it.

"Haven't," insisted Rahill. "I let people impose on me here and don't get anything out of it. I'm the prey of my friends, damn it—do their lessons, get 'em out of trouble, pay 'em stupid summer visits, and always entertain their kid sisters; keep my temper when they get selfish and *then* they think they pay me back by voting for me and telling me I'm the 'big man' of St. Regis's. I want to get where everybody does their own work and I can tell people where to go. I'm tired of being nice to every poor fish in school."

"You're not a slicker," said Amory suddenly.

"A what?"

"A slicker."

"What the devil's that?"

"Well, it's something that—that—there's a lot of them. You're not one, and neither am I, though I am more than you are."

"Who is one? What makes you one?"

Amory considered.

"Why—why, I suppose that the *sign* of it is when a fellow slicks his hair back with water."

"Like Carstairs?"

"Yes—sure. He's a slicker."

They spent two evenings getting an exact definition. The slicker was good-looking or *clean*-looking; he had brains, social brains, that is, and he used all means on the broad path of honesty to get ahead, be popular, admired, and never in trouble. He dressed well, was particularly neat in appearance, and derived his name from the fact that his hair was inevitably worn short, soaked in water or tonic, parted in the middle, and slicked back as the current of fashion dictated. The slickers of that year had adopted tortoise-shell spectacles as badges of their slickerhood, and this made them so easy to recognize that Amory and Rahill never missed one. The slicker seemed distributed through school, always a little wiser and shrewder than his contemporaries, managing some team or other, and keeping his cleverness carefully concealed.

Amory found the slicker a most valuable classification until his junior year in college, when the outline became so blurred and indeterminate that it had to be subdivided many times, and became only a quality. Amory's secret ideal had all the slicker qualifications, but, in addition, courage and tremendous brains and talents—also Amory conceded him a bizarre streak that was quite irreconcilable to the slicker proper.

This was a first real break from the hypocrisy of school tradition. The slicker was a definite element of success, differing intrinsically from the prep school "big man."

"THE SLICKER"	"THE BIG MAN"
1. Clever sense of social values.	1. Inclined to stupidity and unconscious of social values.
2. Dresses well. Pretends that dress is superficial—but knows that it isn't.	2. Thinks dress is superficial, and is inclined to be careless about it.
3. Goes into such activities as he can shine in.	3. Goes out for everything from a sense of duty.
4. Gets to college and is, in a worldly way, successful.	4. Gets to college and has a problematical future. Feels lost without his circle, and always says that school days were happiest, after all. Goes back to school and makes speeches about what St. Regis's boys are doing.
5. Hair slicked.	5. Hair not slicked.

Amory had decided definitely on Princeton, even though he would be the only boy entering that year from St. Regis'. Yale had a romance and glamour from the tales of Minneapolis, and St. Regis' men who had been "tapped for Skull and Bones,"* but Princeton drew him most, with its atmosphere of bright colors and its alluring reputation as the pleasantest country club in America. Dwarfed by the menacing college exams, Amory's school days drifted into the past. Years afterward, when he went back to St. Regis', he seemed to have forgotten the successes of sixth-form year, and to be able to picture himself only as the unadjustable boy who had hurried down corridors, jeered at by his rabid contemporaries mad with common sense.

CHAPTER II
SPIRES AND GARGOYLES

At first Amory noticed only the wealth of sunshine creeping across the long, green swards, dancing on the leaded window-panes, and swimming around the tops of spires and towers and battlemented walls. Gradually he realized that he was really walking up University Place, self-conscious about his suitcase, developing a new tendency to glare straight ahead when he passed any one. Several times he could have sworn that men turned to look at him critically. He wondered vaguely if there was something the matter with his clothes, and wished he had shaved that morning on the train. He felt unnecessarily stiff and awkward among these white-flannelled, bareheaded youths, who must be juniors and seniors, judging from the savoir faire with which they strolled.

He found that 12 University Place was a large, dilapidated mansion, at present apparently uninhabited, though he knew it housed usually a dozen freshmen. After a hurried skirmish with his landlady he sallied out on a tour of exploration, but he had gone scarcely a block when he became horribly conscious that he must be the only man in town who was wearing a hat. He returned hurriedly to 12 University, left his derby, and, emerging bareheaded, loitered down Nassau Street, stopping to investigate a display of athletic photographs in a store window, including a large one of Allenby, the football captain, and next attracted by the sign "Jigger Shop" over a confectionery window. This sounded familiar, so he sauntered in and took a seat on a high stool.

"Chocolate sundae," he told a colored person.

"Double chocolate jiggah? Anything else?"

"Why—yes."

"Bacon bun?"

"Why—yes."

He munched four of these, finding them of pleasing savor, and then consumed another double-chocolate jigger before ease descended upon him. After a cursory inspection of the pillow-cases, leather pennants, and Gibson Girls* that lined the walls, he left, and continued along Nassau Street with his hands in his pockets.

Gradually he was learning to distinguish between upper classmen and entering men, even though the freshman cap* would not appear until the following Monday. Those who were too obviously, too nervously at home were freshmen, for as each train brought a new contingent it was immediately absorbed into the hatless, white-shod, book-laden throng, whose function seemed to be to drift endlessly up and down the street, emitting great clouds of smoke from brand-new pipes. By afternoon Amory realized that now the newest arrivals were taking him for an upper classman, and he tried conscientiously to look both pleasantly blasé and casually critical, which was as near as he could analyze the prevalent facial expression.

At five o'clock he felt the need of hearing his own voice, so he retreated to his house to see if any one else had arrived. Having climbed the rickety stairs he scrutinized his room resignedly, concluding that it was hopeless to attempt any more inspired decoration than class banners and tiger pictures.* There was a tap at the door.

"Come in!"

A slim face with gray eyes and a humorous smile appeared in the doorway.

"Got a hammer?"

"No—sorry. Maybe Mrs. Twelve, or whatever she goes by, has one."

The stranger advanced into the room.

"You an inmate of this asylum?"

Amory nodded.

"Awful barn for the rent we pay."

Amory had to agree that it was.

"I thought of the campus," he said, "but they say there's so few freshmen that they're lost. Have to sit around and study for something to do."

The gray-eyed man decided to introduce himself.

"My name's Holiday."

"Blaine's my name."

They shook hands with the fashionable low swoop. Amory grinned.

"Where'd you prep?"

"Andover—where did you?"

"St Regis's."

"Oh, did you? I had a cousin there."

They discussed the cousin thoroughly, and then Holiday announced that he was to meet his brother for dinner at six.

"Come along and have a bite with us."

"All right."

At the Kenilworth Amory met Burne Holiday—he of the gray eyes was Kerry—and during a limpid meal of thin soup and anæmic vegetables they stared at the other freshmen, who sat either in small groups looking very ill at ease, or in large groups seeming very much at home.

"I hear Commons is pretty bad," said Amory.

"That's the rumor. But you've got to eat there—or pay anyways."

"Crime!"

"Imposition!"

"Oh, at Princeton you've got to swallow everything the first year. It's like a damned prep school."

Amory agreed.

"Lot of pep, though," he insisted. "I wouldn't have gone to Yale for a million."

"Me either."

"You going out for anything?" inquired Amory of the elder brother.

"Not me—Burne here is going out for the *Prince*—the *Daily Princetonian*, you know."

"Yes, I know."

"You going out for anything?"

"Why—yes. I'm going to take a whack at freshman football."

"Play at St. Regis's?"

"Some," admitted Amory depreciatingly, "but I'm getting so damned thin."

"You're not thin."

"Well, I used to be stocky last fall."

"Oh!"

After supper they attended the movies, where Amory was fascinated by the glib comments of a man in front of him, as well as by the wild yelling and shouting.

"*Yoho!*"

"Oh, honey-*baby*—you're so big and strong, but oh, so *gentle!*"

"Clinch!"

"Oh, *Clinch!*"

"Kiss her, kiss, 'at lady, *quick!*"

"Oh-h-h——!"

A group began whistling "By the Sea,"* and the audience took it up noisily. This was followed by an indistinguishable song that included much stamping and then by an endless, incoherent dirge.

> "Oh-h-h-h-h
> She works in a Jam Factoree
> And—that-may-be-all-right
> But you can't-fool-me
> For I know—DAMN—WELL
> That she DON'T-make-jam-all-night!
> Oh-h-h-h!"

As they pushed out, giving and receiving curious impersonal glances, Amory decided that he liked the movies, wanted to enjoy them as the row of upper classmen in front had enjoyed them, with their arms along the backs of the seats, their comments Gaelic and caustic, their attitude a mixture of critical wit and tolerant amusement.

"Want a sundae—I mean a jigger?" asked Kerry.

"Sure."

They suppered heavily and then, still sauntering, eased back to 12.

"Wonderful night."

"It's a whiz."

"You men going to unpack?"

"Guess so. Come on, Burne."

Amory decided to sit for a while on the front steps, so he bade them good night.

The great tapestries of trees had darkened to ghosts back at the last edge of twilight. The early moon had drenched the arches with pale blue, and, weaving over the night, in and out of the gossamer rifts of moon, swept a song, a song with more than a hint of sadness, infinitely transient, infinitely regretful.

He remembered that an alumnus of the nineties had told him of one of Booth Tarkington's amusements: standing in mid-campus in the small hours and singing tenor songs to the stars, arousing mingled emotions in the couched undergraduates according to the sentiment of their moods.

Now, far down the shadowy line of University Place a white-clad phalanx broke the gloom, and marching figures, white-shirted,

white-trousered, swung rhythmically up the street, with linked arms
and heads thrown back:

> *"Going back—going back,*
> *Going—back—to—Nas-sau—Hall,*
> *Going back—going back—*
> *To the—Best—Old—Place—of—All.*
> *Going back—going back,*
> *From all—this—earth-ly—ball,*
> *We'll—clear—the—track—as—we—go—back—*
> *Going—back—to—Nas-sau—Hall!"*

Amory closed his eyes as the ghostly procession drew near. The
song soared so high that all dropped out except the tenors, who bore
the melody triumphantly past the danger-point and relinquished it
to the fantastic chorus. Then Amory opened his eyes, half afraid that
sight would spoil the rich illusion of harmony.

He sighed eagerly. There at the head of the white platoon marched
Allenby, the football captain, slim and defiant, as if aware that this
year the hopes of the college rested on him, that his hundred-
and-sixty pounds were expected to dodge to victory through the
heavy blue and crimson lines.*

Fascinated, Amory watched each rank of linked arms as it came
abreast, the faces indistinct above the polo shirts, the voices blent in a
pæan of triumph—and then the procession passed through shadowy
Campbell Arch, and the voices grew fainter as it wound eastward
over the campus.

The minutes passed and Amory sat there very quietly. He regretted the rule that would forbid freshmen to be outdoors after curfew,
for he wanted to ramble through the shadowy scented lanes, where
Witherspoon brooded like a dark mother over Whig and Clio, her
Attic children, where the black Gothic snake of Little curled down
to Cuyler and Patton, these in turn flinging the mystery out over the
placid slope rolling to the lake.

Princeton of the daytime filtered slowly into his consciousness—
West and Reunion, redolent of the sixties, Seventy-nine Hall, brick-
red and arrogant, Upper and Lower Pyne, aristocratic Elizabethan
ladies not quite content to live among shopkeepers, and, topping
all, climbing with clear blue aspiration, the great dreaming spires of
Holder and Cleveland towers.

From the first he loved Princeton—its lazy beauty, its half-grasped significance, the wild moonlight revel of the rushes, the handsome, prosperous big-game crowds, and under it all the air of struggle that pervaded his class. From the day when, wild-eyed and exhausted, the jerseyed freshmen sat in the gymnasium and elected some one from Hill School class president, a Lawrenceville celebrity vice-president, a hockey star from St. Paul's secretary, up until the end of sophomore year it never ceased, that breathless social system, that worship, seldom named, never really admitted, of the bogey "Big Man."

First it was schools, and Amory, alone from St. Regis', watched the crowds form and widen and form again; St. Paul's, Hill, Pomfret, eating at certain tacitly reserved tables in Commons, dressing in their own corners of the gymnasium, and drawing unconsciously about them a barrier of the slightly less important but socially ambitious to protect them from the friendly, rather puzzled high-school element. From the moment he realized this Amory resented social barriers as artificial distinctions made by the strong to bolster up their weak retainers and keep out the almost strong.

Having decided to be one of the gods of the class, he reported for freshman football practice, but in the second week, playing quarter-back, already paragraphed in corners of the *Princetonian*, he wrenched his knee seriously enough to put him out for the rest of the season. This forced him to retire and consider the situation.

"12 Univee" housed a dozen miscellaneous question-marks. There were three or four inconspicuous and quite startled boys from Lawrenceville, two amateur wild men from a New York private school (Kerry Holiday christened them the "plebeian drunks"), a Jewish youth, also from New York, and, as compensation for Amory, the two Holidays, to whom he took an instant fancy.

The Holidays were rumored twins, but really the dark-haired one, Kerry, was a year older than his blond brother, Burne. Kerry was tall, with humorous gray eyes, and a sudden, attractive smile; he became at once the mentor of the house, reaper of ears that grew too high, censor of conceit, vendor of rare, satirical humor. Amory spread the table of their future friendship with all his ideas of what college should and did mean. Kerry, not inclined as yet to take things seriously, chided him gently for being curious at this inopportune time about the intricacies of the social system, but liked him and was both interested and amused.

Burne, fair-haired, silent, and intent, appeared in the house only as a busy apparition, gliding in quietly at night and off again in the early morning to get up his work in the library—he was out for the *Princetonian*, competing furiously against forty others for the coveted first place. In December he came down with diphtheria, and some one else won the competition, but, returning to college in February, he dauntlessly went after the prize again. Necessarily, Amory's acquaintance with him was in the way of three-minute chats, walking to and from lectures, so he failed to penetrate Burne's one absorbing interest and find what lay beneath it.

Amory was far from contented. He missed the place he had won at St. Regis', the being known and admired, yet Princeton stimulated him, and there were many things ahead calculated to arouse the Machiavelli latent in him, could he but insert a wedge. The upper-class clubs, concerning which he had pumped a reluctant graduate during the previous summer, excited his curiosity: Ivy, detached and breathlessly aristocratic; Cottage, an impressive mélange of brilliant adventurers and well-dressed philanderers; Tiger Inn, broad-shouldered and athletic, vitalized by an honest elaboration of prep-school standards; Cap and Gown, anti-alcoholic faintly religious and politically powerful; flamboyant Colonial; literary Quadrangle; and the dozen others, varying in age and position.

Anything which brought an under classman into too glaring a light was labelled with the damning brand of "running it out." The movies thrived on caustic comments, but the men who made them were generally running it out; talking of clubs was running it out; standing for anything very strongly, as, for instance, drinking parties or teetotaling, was running it out; in short, being personally conspicuous was not tolerated, and the influential man was the non-committal man, until at club elections in sophomore year every one should be sewed up in some bag for the rest of his college career.

Amory found that writing for the *Nassau Literary Magazine* would get him nothing, but that being on the board of the *Daily Princetonian* would get any one a good deal. His vague desire to do immortal acting with the English Dramatic Association faded out when he found that the most ingenious brains and talents were concentrated upon the Triangle Club, a musical comedy organization that every year took a great Christmas trip. In the meanwhile, feeling strangely alone and restless in Commons, with new desires and ambitions stirring in his mind, he let the first term go by between an envy of the embryo successes and a puzzled fretting with Kerry as to why they were not accepted immediately among the élite of the class.

Many afternoons they lounged in the windows of 12 Univee and watched the class pass to and from Commons, noting satellites already attaching themselves to the more prominent, watching the lonely grind with his hurried step and downcast eye, envying the happy security of the big school groups.

"We're the damned middle class, that's what!" he complained to Kerry one day as he lay stretched out on the sofa, consuming a family of Fatimas* with contemplative precision.

"Well, why not? We came to Princeton so we could feel that way toward the small colleges—have it on 'em, more self-confidence, dress better, cut a swath——"

"Oh, it isn't that I mind the glittering caste system," admitted Amory. "I like having a bunch of hot cats on top, but gosh, Kerry, I've got to be one of them."

"But just now, Amory, you're only a sweaty bourgeois."

Amory lay for a moment without speaking.

"I won't be—long," he said finally. "But I hate to get anywhere by working for it. I'll show the marks, don't you know."

"Honorable scars." Kerry craned his neck suddenly at the street. "There's Langueduc, if you want to see what he looks like—and Humbird just behind."

Amory rose dynamically and sought the windows.

"Oh," he said, scrutinizing these worthies, "Humbird looks like a knockout, but this Langueduc—he's the rugged type, isn't he? I distrust that sort. All diamonds look big in the rough."

"Well," said Kerry, as the excitement subsided, "you're a literary genius. It's up to you."

"I wonder"—Amory paused—"if I could be. I honestly think so sometimes. That sounds like the devil, and I wouldn't say it to anybody except you."

"Well—go ahead. Let your hair grow and write poems like this guy D'Invilliers in the *Lit*."

Amory reached lazily at a pile of magazines on the table.

"Read his latest effort?"

"Never miss 'em. They're rare."

Amory glanced through the issue.

"Hello!" he said in surprise, "he's a freshman, isn't he?"

"Yeah."

"Listen to this! My God!

> *"'A serving lady speaks:*
> *Black velvet trails its folds over the day,*
> *White tapers, prisoned in their silver frames,*
> *Wave their thin flames like shadows in the wind,*
> *Pia, Pompia, come—come away—'*

"Now, what the devil does that mean?"

"It's a pantry scene."

> *"'Her toes are stiffened like a stork's in flight;*
> *She's laid upon her bed, on the white sheets,*
> *Her hands pressed on her smooth bust like a saint,*
> *Bella Cunizza, come into the light!'*

"My gosh, Kerry, what in hell is it all about? I swear I don't get him at all, and I'm a literary bird myself."

"It's pretty tricky," said Kerry, "only you've got to think of hearses and stale milk when you read it. That isn't as pash as some of them."

Amory tossed the magazine on the table.

"Well," he sighed, "I sure am up in the air. I know I'm not a regular fellow, yet I loathe anybody else that isn't. I can't decide whether to cultivate my mind and be a great dramatist, or to thumb my nose at the Golden Treasury* and be a Princeton slicker."

"Why decide?" suggested Kerry. "Better drift, like me. I'm going to sail into prominence on Burne's coat-tails."

"I can't drift—I want to be interested. I want to pull strings, even for somebody else, or be *Princetonian* chairman or Triangle president. I want to be admired, Kerry."

"You're thinking too much about yourself."

Amory sat up at this.

"No. I'm thinking about you, too. We've got to get out and mix around the class right now, when it's fun to be a snob. I'd like to bring a sardine to the prom in June, for instance, but I wouldn't do it unless I could be damn debonaire about it—introduce her to all the prize parlor-snakes, and the football captain, and all that simple stuff."

"Amory," said Kerry impatiently, "you're just going around in a circle. If you want to be prominent, get out and try for something;

if you don't, just take it easy." He yawned. "Come on, let's let the smoke drift off. We'll go down and watch football practice."

Amory gradually accepted this point of view, decided that next fall would inaugurate his career, and relinquished himself to watching Kerry extract joy from 12 Univee.

They filled the Jewish youth's bed with lemon pie; they put out the gas all over the house every night by blowing into the jet in Amory's room, to the bewilderment of Mrs. Twelve and the local plumber; they set up the effects of the plebeian drunks—pictures, books, and furniture—in the bathroom, to the confusion of the pair, who hazily discovered the transposition on their return from a Trenton spree; they were disappointed beyond measure when the plebeian drunks decided to take it as a joke; they played red-dog and twenty-one and jackpot from dinner to dawn, and on the occasion of one man's birthday persuaded him to buy sufficient champagne for a hilarious celebration. The donor of the party having remained sober, Kerry and Amory accidently dropped him down two flights of stairs and called, shame-faced and penitent, at the infirmary all the following week.

"Say, who are all these women?" demanded Kerry one day, protesting at the size of Amory's mail. "I've been looking at the postmarks lately—Farmington and Dobbs and Westover and Dana Hall*—what's the idea?"

Amory grinned.

"All from the Twin Cities."* He named them off. "There's Marylyn De Witt—she's pretty, got a car of her own and that's damn convenient; there's Sally Weatherby—she's getting too fat; there's Myra St. Claire, she's an old flame, easy to kiss if you like it——"

"What line do you throw 'em?" demanded Kerry. "I've tried everything, and the mad wags aren't even afraid of me."

"You're the 'nice boy' type," suggested Amory.

"That's just it. Mother always feels the girl is safe if she's with me. Honestly, it's annoying. If I start to hold somebody's hand, they laugh at me, and *let* me, just as if it wasn't part of them. As soon as I get hold of a hand they sort of disconnect it from the rest of them."

"Sulk," suggested Amory. "Tell 'em you're wild and have 'em reform you—go home furious—come back in half an hour—startle 'em."

Kerry shook his head.

"No chance. I wrote a St. Timothy* girl a really loving letter last year. In one place I got rattled and said: 'My God, how I love you!' She took a nail scissors, clipped out the 'My God' and showed the rest of the letter all over school. Doesn't work at all. I'm just 'good old Kerry' and all that rot."

Amory smiled and tried to picture himself as "good old Amory." He failed completely.

February dripped snow and rain, the cyclonic freshman mid-years passed, and life in 12 Univee continued interesting if not purposeful. Once a day Amory indulged in a club sandwich, cornflakes, and Julienne potatoes at "Joe's," accompanied usually by Kerry or Alec Connage. The latter was a quiet, rather aloof slicker from Hotchkiss, who lived next door and shared the same enforced singleness as Amory, due to the fact that his entire class had gone to Yale. "Joe's" was unæsthetic and faintly unsanitary, but a limitless charge account could be opened there, a convenience that Amory appreciated. His father had been experimenting with mining stocks and, in consequence, his allowance, while liberal, was not at all what he had expected.

"Joe's" had the additional advantage of seclusion from curious upper-class eyes, so at four each afternoon Amory, accompanied by friend or book, went up to experiment with his digestion. One day in March, finding that all the tables were occupied, he slipped into a chair opposite a freshman who bent intently over a book at the last table. They nodded briefly. For twenty minutes Amory sat consuming bacon buns and reading "Mrs. Warren's Profession"* (he had discovered Shaw quite by accident while browsing in the library during mid-years); the other freshman, also intent on his volume, meanwhile did away with a trio of chocolate malted milks.

By and by Amory's eyes wandered curiously to his fellow-luncher's book. He spelled out the name and title upside down—"Marpessa," by Stephen Phillips.* This meant nothing to him, his metrical education having been confined to such Sunday classics as "Come into the Garden, Maude,"* and what morsels of Shakespeare and Milton had been recently forced upon him.

Moved to address his vis-à-vis, he simulated interest in his book for a moment, and then exclaimed aloud as if involuntarily:

"Ha! Great stuff!"

The other freshman looked up and Amory registered artificial embarrassment.

"Are you referring to your bacon buns?" His cracked, kindly voice went well with the large spectacles and the impression of a voluminous keenness that he gave.

"No," Amory answered. "I was referring to Bernard Shaw." He turned the book around in explanation.

"I've never read any Shaw. I've always meant to." The boy paused and then continued: "Did you ever read Stephen Phillips, or do you like poetry?"

"Yes, indeed," Amory affirmed eagerly. "I've never read much of Phillips, though." (He had never heard of any Phillips except the late David Graham.)

"It's pretty fair, I think. Of course he's a Victorian." They sallied into a discussion of poetry, in the course of which they introduced themselves, and Amory's companion proved to be none other than "that awful highbrow, Thomas Parke D'Invilliers," who signed the passionate love-poems in the *Lit*. He was, perhaps, nineteen, with stooped shoulders, pale blue eyes, and, as Amory could tell from his general appearance, without much conception of social competition and such phenomena of absorbing interest. Still, he liked books, and it seemed forever since Amory had met any one who did; if only that St. Paul's crowd at the next table would not mistake *him* for a bird, too, he would enjoy the encounter tremendously. They didn't seem to be noticing, so he let himself go, discussed books by the dozens—books he had read, read about, books he had never heard of, rattling off lists of titles with the facility of a Brentano's clerk. D'Invilliers was partially taken in and wholly delighted. In a good-natured way he had almost decided that Princeton was one part deadly Philistines and one part deadly grinds, and to find a person who could mention Keats without stammering, yet evidently washed his hands, was rather a treat.

"Ever read any Oscar Wilde?" he asked.

"No. Who wrote it?"

"It's a man—don't you know?"

"Oh, surely." A faint chord was struck in Amory's memory. "Wasn't the comic opera, 'Patience,'* written about him?"

"Yes, that's the fella. I've just finished a book of his, 'The Picture of Dorian Gray,'* and I certainly wish you'd read it. You'd like it. You can borrow it if you want to."

"Why, I'd like it a lot—thanks."

"Don't you want to come up to the room? I've got a few other books."

Amory hesitated, glanced at the St. Paul's group—one of them was the magnificent, exquisite Humbird—and he considered how determinate the addition of this friend would be. He never got to the stage of making them and getting rid of them—he was not hard enough for that—so he measured Thomas Parke D'Invilliers' undoubted attractions and value against the menace of cold eyes behind tortoise-rimmed spectacles that he fancied glared from the next table.

"Yes, I'll go."

So he found "Dorian Gray" and the "Mystic and Somber Dolores" and the "Belle Dame sans Merci";* for a month was keen on naught else. The world became pale and interesting, and he tried hard to look at Princeton through the satiated eyes of Oscar Wilde and Swinburne—or "Fingal O'Flahertie"* and "Algernon Charles," as he called them in précieuse jest. He read enormously every night—Shaw, Chesterton, Barrie, Pinero, Yeats, Synge, Ernest Dowson, Arthur Symons, Keats, Sudermann, Robert Hugh Benson,* the Savoy Operas*—just a heterogeneous mixture, for he suddenly discovered that he had read nothing for years.

Tom D'Invilliers became at first an occasion rather than a friend. Amory saw him about once a week, and together they gilded the ceiling of Tom's room and decorated the walls with imitation tapestry, bought at an auction, tall candlesticks and figured curtains. Amory liked him for being clever and literary without effeminacy or affectation. In fact, Amory did most of the strutting and tried painfully to make every remark an epigram, than which, if one is content with ostensible epigrams, there are many feats harder. 12 Univee was amused. Kerry read "Dorian Gray" and simulated Lord Henry, following Amory about, addressing him as "Dorian" and pretending to encourage in him wicked fancies and attenuated tendencies to ennui. When he carried it into Commons, to the amazement of the others at table, Amory became furiously embarrassed, and after that made epigrams only before D'Invilliers or a convenient mirror.

One day Tom and Amory tried reciting their own and Lord Dunsany's poems* to the music of Kerry's graphophone.

"Chant!" cried Tom. "Don't recite! *Chant!*"

Amory, who was performing, looked annoyed, and claimed that he needed a record with less piano in it. Kerry thereupon rolled on the floor in stifled laughter.

"Put on 'Hearts and Flowers'!"* he howled. "Oh, my Lord, I'm going to cast a kitten."

"Shut off the damn graphophone," Amory cried, rather red in the face. "I'm not giving an exhibition."

In the meanwhile Amory delicately kept trying to awaken a sense of the social system in D'Invilliers, for he knew that this poet was really more conventional than he, and needed merely watered hair, a smaller range of conversation, and a darker brown hat to become quite regular. But the liturgy of Livingstone collars and dark ties fell on heedless ears; in fact D'Invilliers faintly resented his efforts; so Amory confined himself to calls once a week, and brought him occasionally to 12 Univee. This caused mild titters among the other freshmen, who called them "Doctor Johnson and Boswell."

Alec Connage, another frequent visitor, liked him in a vague way, but was afraid of him as a highbrow. Kerry, who saw through his poetic patter to the solid, almost respectable depths within, was immensely amused and would have him recite poetry by the hour, while he lay with closed eyes on Amory's sofa and listened:

> *"Asleep or waking is it? for her neck*
> *Kissed over close, wears yet a purple speck*
> *Wherein the pained blood falters and goes out;*
> *Soft and stung softly—fairer for a fleck . . ."**

"That's good," Kerry would say softly. "It pleases the elder Holiday. That's a great poet, I guess." Tom, delighted at an audience, would ramble through the "Poems and Ballads" until Kerry and Amory knew them almost as well as he.

Amory took to writing poetry on spring afternoons, in the gardens of the big estates near Princeton, while swans made effective atmosphere in the artificial pools, and slow clouds sailed harmoniously above the willows. May came too soon, and suddenly unable to bear walls, he wandered the campus at all hours through starlight and rain.

A Damp Symbolic Interlude

The night mist fell. From the moon it rolled, clustered about the spires and towers, and then settled below them, so that the dreaming peaks were still in lofty aspiration toward the sky. Figures that dotted the day like ants now brushed along as shadowy ghosts, in and out of the foreground. The Gothic halls and cloisters were infinitely more mysterious as they loomed suddenly out of the darkness, out-lined each by myriad faint squares of yellow light. Indefinitely from somewhere a bell boomed the quarter-hour, and Amory, pausing by the sun-dial, stretched himself out full length on the damp grass. The cool bathed his eyes and slowed the flight of time—time that had crept so insidiously through the lazy April afternoons, seemed so intangible in the long spring twilights. Evening after evening the senior singing had drifted over the campus in melancholy beauty, and through the shell of his undergraduate consciousness had broken a deep and reverent devotion to the gray walls and Gothic peaks and all they symbolized as warehouses of dead ages.

The tower that in view of his window sprang upward, grew into a spire, yearning higher until its uppermost tip was half invisible against the morning skies, gave him the first sense of the transiency and unimportance of the campus figures except as holders of the apostolic succession. He liked knowing that Gothic architecture, with its upward trend, was peculiarly appropriate to universities, and the idea became personal to him. The silent stretches of green, the quiet halls with an occasional late-burning scholastic light held his imagination in a strong grasp, and the chastity of the spire became a symbol of this perception.

"Damn it all," he whispered aloud, wetting his hands in the damp and running them through his hair. "Next year I work!" Yet he knew that where now the spirit of spires and towers made him dreamily acquiescent, it would then overawe him. Where now he realized only his own inconsequence, effort would make him aware of his own impotency and insufficiency.

The college dreamed on—awake. He felt a nervous excitement that might have been the very throb of its slow heart. It was a stream where he was to throw a stone whose faint ripple would be vanishing almost as it left his hand. As yet he had given nothing, he had taken nothing.

A belated freshman, his oilskin slicker rasping loudly, slushed along the soft path. A voice from somewhere called the inevitable formula, "Stick out your head!" below an unseen window. A hundred little sounds of the current drifting on under the fog pressed in finally on his consciousness.

"Oh, *God!*" he cried suddenly, and started at the sound of his voice in the stillness. The rain dripped on. A minute longer he lay without moving, his hands clinched. Then he sprang to his feet and gave his clothes a tentative pat.

"I'm very damn wet!" he said aloud to the sundial.

Historical

The war began in the summer following his freshman year. Beyond a sporting interest in the German dash for Paris the whole affair failed either to thrill or interest him. With the attitude he might have held toward an amusing melodrama he hoped it would be long and bloody. If it had not continued he would have felt like an irate ticket-holder at a prize-fight where the principals refused to mix it up.

That was his total reaction.

"Ha-Ha Hortense!"

"All right, po*nies!*"

"Shake it up!"

"Hey, ponies—how about easing up on that crap game and shaking a mean hip?"

"Hey, *ponies!*"

The coach fumed helplessly, the Triangle Club president, glowering with anxiety, varied between furious bursts of authority and fits of temperamental lassitude, when he sat spiritless and wondered how the devil the show was ever going on tour by Christmas.

"All right. We'll take the pirate song."

The ponies took last drags at their cigarettes and slumped into place; the leading lady rushed into the foreground, setting his hands and feet in an atmospheric mince; and as the coach clapped and stamped and tumped and da-da'd, they hashed out a dance.

A great, seething ant-hill was the Triangle Club. It gave a musical comedy every year, travelling with cast, chorus, orchestra, and scenery all through Christmas vacation. The play and music were the work of undergraduates, and the club itself was the most influential of institutions, over three hundred men competing for it every year.

Amory, after an easy victory in the first sophomore *Princetonian* competition, stepped into a vacancy of the cast as *Boiling Oil, a Pirate Lieutenant*. Every night for the last week they had rehearsed "Ha-Ha Hortense!" in the Casino, from two in the afternoon until eight in the morning, sustained by dark and powerful coffee, and sleeping in lectures through the interim. A rare scene, the Casino. A big, barnlike auditorium, dotted with boys as girls, boys as pirates, boys as babies; the scenery in course of being violently set up; the spotlight man rehearsing by throwing weird shafts into angry eyes; over all the constant tuning of the orchestra or the cheerful tumpty-tump of a Triangle tune. The boy who writes the lyrics stands in the corner, biting a pencil, with twenty minutes to think of an encore; the business manager argues with the secretary as to how much money can be spent on "those damn milkmaid costumes"; the old graduate, president in ninety-eight, perches on a box and thinks how much simpler it was in his day.

How a Triangle show ever got off was a mystery, but it was a riotous mystery, anyway, whether or not one did enough service to wear a little gold Triangle on his watch-chain. "Ha-Ha Hortense!" was written over six times and had the names of nine collaborators on the programme. All Triangle shows started by being "something different—not just a regular musical comedy," but when the several authors, the president, the coach and the faculty committee finished with it, there remained just the old reliable Triangle show with the old reliable jokes and the star comedian who got expelled or sick or something just before the trip, and the dark-whiskered man in the pony-ballet, who "absolutely won't shave twice a day, dog-gone it!"

There was one brilliant place in "Ha-Ha Hortense!" It is a Princeton tradition that whenever a Yale man who is a member of the widely advertised "Skull and Bones" hears the sacred name mentioned, he must leave the room. It is also a tradition that the members are invariably successful in later life, amassing fortunes or votes or coupons or whatever they choose to amass. Therefore, at each performance of "Ha-Ha Hortense!" half-a-dozen seats were kept from sale and occupied by six of the worst-looking vagabonds that could be hired from the streets, further touched up by the Triangle make-up man. At the moment in the show where *Firebrand, the Pirate Chief*, pointed at his black flag and said, "I am a Yale graduate—note my Skull and Bones !"—at this very moment the six vagabonds were instructed to rise *conspicuously* and leave the theatre with looks of deep melancholy and an injured dignity. It was claimed though never proved that on one occasion the hired Elis* were swelled by one of the real thing.

They played through vacation to the fashionable of eight cities. Amory liked Louisville and Memphis best: these knew how to meet strangers, furnished extraordinary punch, and flaunted an astonishing array of feminine beauty. Chicago he approved for a certain verve that transcended its loud accent—however, it was a Yale town, and as the Yale Glee Club was expected in a week the Triangle received only divided homage. In Baltimore, Princeton was at home, and every one fell in love. There was a proper consumption of strong waters all along the line; one man invariably went on the stage highly stimulated, claiming that his particular interpretation of the part required it. There were three private cars; however, no one slept except in the third car, which was called the "animal car," and where were herded the spectacled wind-jammers of the orchestra. Everything was so hurried that there was no time to be bored, but when they arrived in Philadelphia, with vacation nearly over, there was rest in getting out of the heavy atmosphere of flowers and grease-paint, and the ponies took off their corsets with abdominal pains and sighs of relief.

When the disbanding came, Amory set out post-haste for Minneapolis, for Sally Weatherby's cousin, Isabelle Borgé, was coming to spend the winter in Minneapolis while her parents went abroad. He remembered Isabelle only as a little girl with whom he had played sometimes when he first went to Minneapolis. She had gone to Baltimore to live—but since then she had developed a past.

Amory was in full stride, confident, nervous, and jubilant. Scurrying back to Minneapolis to see a girl he had known as a child seemed the interesting and romantic thing to do, so without compunction he wired his mother not to expect him . . . sat in the train, and thought about himself for thirty-six hours.

"Petting"

On the Triangle trip Amory had come into constant contact with that great current American phenomenon, the "petting party."

None of the Victorian mothers—and most of the mothers were Victorian—had any idea how casually their daughters were accustomed to be kissed. "*Servant*-girls are that way," says Mrs. Huston-Carmelite to her popular daughter. "They are kissed first and proposed to afterward."

But the Popular Daughter becomes engaged every six months between sixteen and twenty-two, when she arranges a match with young Hambell, of Cambell & Hambell, who fatuously considers himself her first love, and between engagements the P. D. (she is selected by the cut-in system at dances, which favors the survival of the fittest) has other sentimental last kisses in the moonlight, or the firelight, or the outer darkness.

Amory saw girls doing things that even in his memory would have been impossible: eating three-o'clock, after-dance suppers in impossible cafés, talking of every side of life with an air half of earnestness, half of mockery, yet with a furtive excitement that Amory considered stood for a real moral let-down. But he never realized how widespread it was until he saw the cities between New York and Chicago as one vast juvenile intrigue.

Afternoon at the Plaza, with winter twilight hovering outside and faint drums down-stairs . . . they strut and fret in the lobby, taking another cocktail, scrupulously attired and waiting. Then the swinging doors revolve and three bundles of fur mince in. The theatre comes afterward; then a table at the Midnight Frolic*—of course, mother will be along there, but she will serve only to make things more secretive and brilliant as she sits in solitary state at the deserted table and thinks such entertainments as this are not half so bad as they are painted, only rather wearying. But the P. D. is in love again . . . it was odd, wasn't it?—that though there was so much room left in the taxi the P. D. and the boy from Williams* were somehow crowded out and had to go in a separate car. Odd! Didn't you notice how flushed the P. D. was when she arrived just seven minutes late? But the P. D. "gets away with it."

The "belle" had become the "flirt," the "flirt" had become the "baby vamp." The "belle" had five or six callers every afternoon. If the P. D., by some strange accident, has two, it is made pretty uncomfortable for the one who hasn't a date with her. The "belle" was surrounded by a dozen men in the intermissions between dances. Try to find the P. D. between dances, just *try* to find her.

The same girl . . . deep in an atmosphere of jungle music and the questioning of moral codes. Amory found it rather fascinating to feel that any popular girl he met before eight he might quite possibly kiss before twelve.

"Why on earth are we here?" he asked the girl with the green combs one night as they sat in some one's limousine, outside the Country Club in Louisville.

"I don't know. I'm just full of the devil."

"Let's be frank—we'll never see each other again. I wanted to come out here with you because I thought you were the best-looking girl in sight. You really don't care whether you ever see me again, do you?"

"No—but is this your line for every girl? What have I done to deserve it?"

"And you didn't feel tired dancing or want a cigarette or any of the things you said? You just wanted to be——"

"Oh, let's go in," she interrupted, "if you want to *analyze*. Let's not *talk* about it."

When the hand-knit, sleeveless jerseys were stylish, Amory, in a burst of inspiration, named them "petting shirts." The name travelled from coast to coast on the lips of parlor-snakes and P. D.'s.

Descriptive

Amory was now eighteen years old, just under six feet tall and exceptionally, but not conventionally, handsome. He had rather a young face, the ingenuousness of which was marred by the penetrating green eyes, fringed with long dark eyelashes. He lacked somehow that intense animal magnetism that so often accompanies beauty in men or women; his personality seemed rather a mental thing, and it was not in his power to turn it on and off like a water-faucet. But people never forgot his face.

Isabelle

She paused at the top of the staircase. The sensations attributed to divers on spring-boards, leading ladies on opening nights, and lumpy, husky young men on the day of the Big Game, crowded through her. She should have descended to a burst of drums or a discordant blend of themes from "Thaïs" and "Carmen."* She had never been so curious about her appearance, she had never been so satisfied with it. She had been sixteen years old for six months.

"Isabelle!" called her cousin Sally from the doorway of the dressing-room.

"I'm ready." She caught a slight lump of nervousness in her throat.

"I had to send back to the house for another pair of slippers. It'll be just a minute."

Isabelle started toward the dressing-room for a last peek in the mirror, but something decided her to stand there and gaze down the broad stairs of the Minnehaha Club. They curved tantalizingly, and she could catch just a glimpse of two pairs of masculine feet in the hall below. Pump-shod in uniform black, they gave no hint of identity, but she wondered eagerly if one pair were attached to Amory Blaine. This young man, not as yet encountered, had nevertheless taken up a considerable part of her day—the first day of her arrival. Coming up in the machine from the station, Sally had volunteered, amid a rain of question, comment, revelation, and exaggeration:

"You remember Amory Blaine, of *course*. Well, he's simply mad to see you again. He's stayed over a day from college, and he's coming to-night. He's heard so much about you—says he remembers your eyes."

This had pleased Isabelle. It put them on equal terms, although she was quite capable of staging her own romances, with or without advance advertising. But following her happy tremble of anticipation, came a sinking sensation that made her ask:

"How do you mean he's heard about me? What sort of things?"

Sally smiled. She felt rather in the capacity of a showman with her more exotic cousin.

"He knows you're—you're considered beautiful and all that"— she paused—"and I guess he knows you've been kissed."

At this Isabelle's little fist had clenched suddenly under the fur robe. She was accustomed to be thus followed by her desperate past, and it never failed to rouse in her the same feeling of resentment; yet—in a strange town it was an advantageous reputation. She was a "Speed," was she? Well—let them find out.

Out of the window Isabelle watched the snow glide by in the frosty morning. It was ever so much colder here than in Baltimore; she had not remembered; the glass of the side door was iced, the windows were shirred with snow in the corners. Her mind played still with one subject. Did *he* dress like that boy there, who walked calmly down a bustling business street, in moccasins and winter-carnival costume? How very *Western!* Of course he wasn't that way: he went to Princeton, was a sophomore or something. Really she had no distinct idea of him. An ancient snap-shot she had preserved in an old kodak book had impressed her by the big eyes (which he had probably grown up to by now). However, in the last month, when her winter visit to Sally had been decided on, he had assumed the proportions of a worthy adversary. Children, most astute of match-makers, plot their campaigns quickly, and Sally had played a clever correspondence sonata to Isabelle's excitable temperament. Isabelle had been for some time capable of very strong, if very transient emotions. . . .

They drew up at a spreading, white-stone building, set back from the snowy street. Mrs. Weatherby greeted her warmly and her various younger cousins were produced from the corners where they skulked politely. Isabelle met them tactfully. At her best she allied all with whom she came in contact—except older girls and some women. All the impressions she made were conscious. The half-dozen girls she renewed acquaintance with that morning were all rather impressed and as much by her direct personality as by her reputation. Amory Blaine was an open subject. Evidently a bit light of love, neither popular nor unpopular—every girl there seemed to have had an affair with him at some time or other, but no one volunteered any really useful information. He was going to fall for her. . . . Sally had published that information to her young set and they were retailing it back to Sally as fast as they set eyes on Isabelle. Isabelle resolved secretly that she would, if necessary, *force* herself to like him—she owed it to Sally. Suppose she were terribly disappointed. Sally had painted him in such glowing colors—he was good-looking, "sort of distinguished, when he wants to be," had a line, and was properly inconstant. In fact, he summed up all the romance that her age and environment led her to desire. She wondered if those were his dancing-shoes that fox-trotted tentatively around the soft rug below.

All impressions and, in fact, all ideas were extremely kaleidoscopic to Isabelle. She had that curious mixture of the social and the artistic temperaments found often in two classes, society women and actresses. Her education or, rather, her sophistication, had been absorbed from the boys who had dangled on her favor; her tact was instinctive, and her capacity for love-affairs was limited only by the number of the susceptible within telephone distance. Flirt smiled from her large black-brown eyes and shone through her intense physical magnetism.

So she waited at the head of the stairs that evening while slippers were fetched. Just as she was growing impatient, Sally came out of the dressing-room, beaming with her accustomed good nature and high spirits, and together they descended to the floor below, while the shifting search-light of Isabelle's mind flashed on two ideas: she was glad she had high color to-night, and she wondered if he danced well.

Down-stairs, in the club's great room, she was surrounded for a moment by the girls she had met in the afternoon, then she heard Sally's voice repeating a cycle of names, and found herself bowing to a sextet of black and white, terribly stiff, vaguely familiar figures. The name Blaine figured somewhere, but at first she could not place him. A very confused, very juvenile moment of awkward backings and bumpings followed, and every one found himself talking to the person he least desired to. Isabelle manœuvred herself and Froggy Parker, freshman at Harvard, with whom she had once played hop-scotch, to a seat on the stairs. A humorous reference to the past was all she needed. The things Isabelle could do socially with one idea were remarkable. First, she repeated it rapturously in an enthusiastic contralto with a soupçon of Southern accent; then she held it off at a distance and smiled at it—her wonderful smile; then she delivered it in variations and played a sort of mental catch with it, all this in the nominal form of dialogue. Froggy was fascinated and quite unconscious that this was being done, not for him, but for the green eyes that glistened under the shining carefully watered hair, a little to her left, for Isabelle had discovered Amory. As an actress even in the fullest flush of her own conscious magnetism gets a deep impression of most of the people in the front row, so Isabelle sized up her antagonist. First, he had auburn hair, and from her feeling of disappointment she knew that she had expected him to be dark and of garter-advertisement slenderness. . . . For the rest, a faint flush and a straight, romantic profile; the effect set off by a close-fitting dress suit and a silk ruffled shirt of the kind that women still delight to see men wear, but men were just beginning to get tired of.

During this inspection Amory was quietly watching.

"Don't *you* think so?" she said suddenly, turning to him, innocent-eyed.

There was a stir, and Sally led the way over to their table. Amory struggled to Isabelle's side, and whispered:

"You're my dinner partner, you know. We're all coached for each other."

Isabelle gasped—this was rather right in line. But really she felt as if a good speech had been taken from the star and given to a minor character. . . . She mustn't lose the leadership a bit. The dinner-table glittered with laughter at the confusion of getting places, and then curious eyes were turned on her, sitting near the head. She was enjoying this immensely, and Froggy Parker was so engrossed with the added sparkle of her rising color that he forgot to pull out Sally's chair, and fell into a dim confusion. Amory was on the other side, full of confidence and vanity, gazing at her in open admiration. He began directly, and so did Froggy:

"I've heard a lot about you since you wore braids——"

"Wasn't it funny this afternoon——"

Both stopped. Isabelle turned to Amory shyly. Her face was always enough answer for any one, but she decided to speak.

"How—from whom?"

"From everybody—for all the years since you've been away." She blushed appropriately. On her right Froggy was *hors de combat* already, although he hadn't quite realized it.

"I'll tell you what I remembered about you all these years," Amory continued. She leaned slightly toward him and looked modestly at the celery before her. Froggy sighed—he knew Amory, and the situations that Amory seemed born to handle. He turned to Sally and asked her if she was going away to school next year. Amory opened with grape-shot.

"I've got an adjective that just fits you." This was one of his favorite starts—he seldom had a word in mind, but it was a curiosity provoker, and he could always produce something complimentary if he got in a tight corner.

"Oh—what?" Isabelle's face was a study in enraptured curiosity.

Amory shook his head.

"I don't know you very well yet."

"Will you tell me—afterward?" she half whispered.

He nodded.

"We'll sit out."

Isabelle nodded.

"Did any one ever tell you, you have keen eyes?" she said.

Amory attempted to make them look even keener. He fancied, but he was not sure, that her foot had just touched his under the table. But it might possibly have been only the table leg. It was so hard to tell. Still it thrilled him. He wondered quickly if there would be any difficulty in securing the little den up-stairs.

Babes in the Woods

Isabelle and Amory were distinctly not innocent, nor were they particularly brazen. Moreover, amateur standing had very little value in the game they were playing, a game that would presumably be her principal study for years to come. She had begun as he had, with good looks and an excitable temperament, and the rest was the result of accessible popular novels and dressing-room conversation culled from a slightly older set. Isabelle had walked with an artificial gait at nine and a half, and when her eyes, wide and starry, proclaimed the ingenue most, Amory was proportionately less deceived. He waited for the mask to drop off, but at the same time he did not question her right to wear it. She, on her part, was not impressed by his studied air of blasé sophistication. She had lived in a larger city and had slightly an advantage in range. But she accepted his pose—it was one of the dozen little conventions of this kind of affair. He was aware that he was getting this particular favor now because she had been coached; he knew that he stood for merely the best game in sight, and that he would have to improve his opportunity before he lost his advantage. So they proceeded with an infinite guile that would have horrified her parents.

After the dinner the dance began . . . smoothly. Smoothly?—boys cut in on Isabelle every few feet and then squabbled in the corners with: "You might let me get more than an inch!" and "She didn't like it either—she told me so next time I cut in." It was true—she told every one so, and gave every hand a parting pressure that said: "You know that your dances are *making* my evening."

But time passed, two hours of it, and the less subtle beaux had better learned to focus their pseudo-passionate glances elsewhere, for eleven o'clock found Isabelle and Amory sitting on the couch in the little den off the reading-room up-stairs. She was conscious that they were a handsome pair, and seemed to belong distinctly in this seclusion, while lesser lights fluttered and chattered down-stairs.

Boys who passed the door looked in enviously—girls who passed only laughed and frowned and grew wise within themselves.

They had now reached a very definite stage. They had traded accounts of their progress since they had met last, and she had listened to much she had heard before. He was a sophomore, was on the

Princetonian board, hoped to be chairman in senior year. He learned that some of the boys she went with in Baltimore were "terrible speeds" and came to dances in states of artificial stimulation; most of them were twenty or so, and drove alluring red Stutzes.* A good half seemed to have already flunked out of various schools and colleges, but some of them bore athletic names that made him look at her admiringly. As a matter of fact, Isabelle's closer acquaintance with the universities was just commencing. She had bowing acquaintance with a lot of young men who thought she was a "pretty kid—worth keeping an eye on." But Isabelle strung the names into a fabrication of gayety that would have dazzled a Viennese nobleman. Such is the power of young contralto voices on sink-down sofas.

He asked her if she thought he was conceited. She said there was a difference between conceit and self-confidence. She adored self-confidence in men.

"Is Froggy a good friend of yours?" she asked.

"Rather—why?"

"He's a bum dancer."

Amory laughed.

"He dances as if the girl were on his back instead of in his arms."

She appreciated this.

"You're awfully good at sizing people up."

Amory denied this painfully. However, he sized up several people for her. Then they talked about hands.

"You've got awfully nice hands," she said. "They look as if you played the piano. Do you?"

I have said they had reached a very definite stage—nay, more, a very critical stage. Amory had stayed over a day to see her, and his train left at twelve-eighteen that night. His trunk and suitcase awaited him at the station; his watch was beginning to hang heavy in his pocket.

"Isabelle," he said suddenly, "I want to tell you something." They had been talking lightly about "that funny look in her eyes," and Isabelle knew from the change in his manner what was coming—indeed, she had been wondering how soon it would come. Amory reached above their heads and turned out the electric light, so that they were in the dark, except for the red glow that fell through the door from the reading-room lamps. Then he began:

"I don't know whether or not you know what you—what I'm going to say. Lordy, Isabelle—this *sounds* like a line, but it isn't."

"I know," said Isabelle softly.

"Maybe we'll never meet again like this—I have darned hard luck sometimes." He was leaning away from her on the other arm of the lounge, but she could see his eyes plainly in the dark.

"You'll meet me again—silly." There was just the slightest emphasis on the last word—so that it became almost a term of endearment. He continued a bit huskily:

"I've fallen for a lot of people—girls—and I guess you have, too—boys, I mean, but, honestly, you—" he broke off suddenly and leaned forward, chin on his hands: "Oh, what's the use—you'll go your way and I suppose I'll go mine."

Silence for a moment. Isabelle was quite stirred; she wound her handkerchief into a tight ball, and by the faint light that streamed over her, dropped it deliberately on the floor. Their hands touched for an instant, but neither spoke. Silences were becoming more frequent and more delicious. Outside another stray couple had come up and were experimenting on the piano in the next room. After the usual preliminary of "chopsticks," one of them started "Babes in the Woods"* and a light tenor carried the words into the den:

> *"Give me your hand—*
> *I'll understand*
> *We're off to slumberland."*

Isabelle hummed it softly and trembled as she felt Amory's hand close over hers.

"Isabelle," he whispered. "You know I'm mad about you. You *do* give a darn about me."

"Yes."

"How much do you care—do you like any one better?"

"No." He could scarcely hear her, although he bent so near that he felt her breath against his cheek.

"Isabelle, I'm going back to college for six long months, and why shouldn't we—if I could only just have one thing to remember you by——"

"Close the door. . . ." Her voice had just stirred so that he half wondered whether she had spoken at all. As he swung the door softly shut, the music seemed quivering just outside.

> *"Moonlight is bright,*
> *Kiss me good night."*

What a wonderful song, she thought—everything was wonderful to-night, most of all this romantic scene in the den, with their hands clinging and the inevitable looming charmingly close. The future vista of her life seemed an unending succession of scenes like this: under moonlight and pale starlight, and in the backs of warm limousines and in low, cosy roadsters stopped under sheltering trees—only the boy might change, and this one was *so* nice. He took her hand softly. With a sudden movement he turned it and, holding it to his lips, kissed the palm.

"Isabelle!" His whisper blended in the music, and they seemed to float nearer together. Her breath came faster. "Can't I kiss you, Isabelle—Isabelle?" Lips half parted, she turned her head to him in the dark. Suddenly the ring of voices, the sound of running footsteps surged toward them. Quick as a flash Amory reached up and turned on the light, and when the door opened and three boys, the wrathy and dance-craving Froggy among them, rushed in, he was turning over the magazines on the table, while she sat without moving, serene and unembarrassed, and even greeted them with a welcoming smile. But her heart was beating wildly, and she felt somehow as if she had been deprived.

It was evidently over. There was a clamor for a dance, there was a glance that passed between them—on his side despair, on hers regret, and then the evening went on, with the reassured beaux and the eternal cutting in.

At quarter to twelve Amory shook hands with her gravely, in the midst of a small crowd assembled to wish him good-speed. For an instant he lost his poise, and she felt a bit rattled when a satirical voice from a concealed wit cried:

"Take her outside, Amory!" As he took her hand he pressed it a little, and she returned the pressure as she had done to twenty hands that evening—that was all.

At two o'clock back at the Weatherbys' Sally asked her if she and Amory had had a "time" in the den. Isabelle turned to her quietly. In her eyes was the light of the idealist, the inviolate dreamer of Joan-like dreams.

"No," she answered. "I don't do that sort of thing any more; he asked me to, but I said no."

As she crept in bed she wondered what he'd say in his special delivery to-morrow. He had such a good-looking mouth—would she ever——?

"Fourteen angels were watching o'er them," sang Sally sleepily from the next room.

"Damn!" muttered Isabelle, punching the pillow into a luxurious lump and exploring the cold sheets cautiously. "Damn!"

Carnival

Amory, by way of the *Princetonian*, had arrived. The minor snobs, finely balanced thermometers of success, warmed to him as the club elections grew nigh, and he and Tom were visited by groups of upperclassmen who arrived awkwardly, balanced on the edges of the furniture and talked of all subjects except the one of absorbing interest. Amory was amused at the intent eyes upon him, and, in case the visitors represented some club in which he was not interested, took great pleasure in shocking them with unorthodox remarks.

"Oh, let me see——" he said one night to a flabbergasted delegation, "what club do you represent?"

With visitors from Ivy and Cottage and Tiger Inn he played the "nice, unspoilt, ingenuous boy" very much at ease and quite unaware of the object of the call.

When the fatal morning arrived, early in March, and the campus became a document in hysteria, he slid smoothly into Cottage with Alec Connage and watched his suddenly neurotic class with much wonder.

There were fickle groups that jumped from club to club; there were friends of two or three days who announced tearfully and wildly that they must join the same club, nothing should separate them; there were snarling disclosures of long-hidden grudges as the Suddenly Prominent remembered snubs of freshman year. Unknown men were elevated into importance when they received certain coveted bids; others who were considered "all set" found that they had made unexpected enemies, felt themselves stranded and deserted, talked wildly of leaving college.

In his own crowd Amory saw men kept out for wearing green hats, for being "a damn tailor's dummy," for having "too much pull in heaven," for getting drunk one night "not like a gentleman, by God," or for unfathomable secret reasons known to no one but the wielders of the black balls.*

This orgy of sociability culminated in a gigantic party at the Nassau Inn, where punch was dispensed from immense bowls, and the whole down-stairs became a delirious, circulating, shouting pattern of faces and voices.

"Hi, Dibby—'gratulations!"

"Goo' boy, Tom, you got a good bunch in Cap."

"Say, Kerry——"

"Oh, Kerry—I hear you went Tiger with all the weight-lifters!"

"Well, I didn't go Cottage—the parlor-snakes' delight."

"They say Overton fainted when he got his Ivy bid—Did he sign up the first day?—oh, *no*. Tore over to Murray-Dodge on a bicycle—afraid it was a mistake."

"How'd you get into Cap—you old roué?"

"'Gratulations!"

"'Gratulations yourself. Hear you got a good crowd."

When the bar closed, the party broke up into groups and streamed, singing, over the snow-clad campus, in a weird delusion that snobbishness and strain were over at last, and that they could do what they pleased for the next two years.

Long afterward Amory thought of sophomore spring as the happiest time of his life. His ideas were in tune with life as he found it; he wanted no more than to drift and dream and enjoy a dozen new-found friendships through the April afternoons.

Alec Connage came into his room one morning and woke him up into the sunshine and peculiar glory of Campbell Hall shining in the window.

"Wake up, Original Sin, and scrape yourself together. Be in front of Renwick's in half an hour. Somebody's got a car." He took the bureau cover and carefully deposited it, with its load of small articles, upon the bed.

"Where'd you get the car?" demanded Amory cynically.

"Sacred trust, but don't be a critical goopher or you can't go!"

"I think I'll sleep," Amory said calmly, resettling himself and reaching beside the bed for a cigarette.

"Sleep!"

"Why not? I've got a class at eleven-thirty."

"You damned gloom! Of course, if you don't want to go to the coast——"

With a bound Amory was out of bed, scattering the bureau cover's burden on the floor. The coast . . . he hadn't seen it for years, since he and his mother were on their pilgrimage.

"Who's going?" he demanded as he wriggled into his B. V. D.'s.

"Oh, Dick Humbird and Kerry Holiday and Jesse Ferrenby and—oh about five or six. Speed it up, kid!"

In ten minutes Amory was devouring cornflakes in Renwick's, and at nine-thirty they bowled happily out of town, headed for the sands of Deal Beach.

"You see," said Kerry, "the car belongs down there. In fact, it was stolen from Asbury Park* by persons unknown, who deserted it in Princeton and left for the West. Heartless Humbird here got permission from the city council to deliver it."

"Anybody got any money?" suggested Ferrenby, turning around from the front seat.

There was an emphatic negative chorus.

"That makes it interesting."

"Money—what's money? We can sell the car."

"Charge him salvage or something."

"How're we going to get food?" asked Amory.

"Honestly," answered Kerry, eying him reprovingly, "do you doubt Kerry's ability for three short days? Some people have lived on nothing for years at a time. Read the Boy Scout Monthly."

"Three days," Amory mused, "and I've got classes."

"One of the days is the Sabbath."

"Just the same, I can only cut six more classes, with over a month and a half to go."

"Throw him out!"

"It's a long walk back."

"Amory, you're running it out, if I may coin a new phrase."

"Hadn't you better get some dope on yourself, Amory?"

Amory subsided resignedly and drooped into a contemplation of the scenery. Swinburne seemed to fit in somehow.

> *"Oh, winter's rains and ruins are over,*
> *And all the seasons of snows and sins;*
> *The days dividing lover and lover,*
> *The light that loses, the night that wins;*
> *And time remembered is grief forgotten,*

And frosts are slain and flowers begotten,
And in green underwood and cover,
   Blossom by blossom the spring begins.

   *"The full streams feed on flower of——"**

   "What's the matter, Amory? Amory's thinking about poetry, about the pretty birds and flowers. I can see it in his eye."

   "No, I'm not," he lied. "I'm thinking about the *Princetonian*. I ought to make up to-night; but I can telephone back, I suppose."

   "Oh," said Kerry respectfully, "these important men——"

   Amory flushed and it seemed to him that Ferrenby, a defeated competitor, winced a little. Of course, Kerry was only kidding, but he really mustn't mention the *Princetonian*.

   It was a halcyon day, and as they neared the shore and the salt breezes scurried by, he began to picture the ocean and long, level stretches of sand and red roofs over blue sea. Then they hurried through the little town and it all flashed upon his consciousness to a mighty pæan of emotion. . . .

   "Oh, good Lord! *Look* at it!" he cried.

   "What?"

   "Let me out, quick—I haven't seen it for eight years! Oh, gentlefolk, stop the car!"

   "What an odd child!" remarked Alec.

   "I do believe he's a bit eccentric."

   The car was obligingly drawn up at a curb, and Amory ran for the boardwalk. First, he realized that the sea was blue and that there was an enormous quantity of it, and that it roared and roared—really all the banalities about the ocean that one could realize, but if any one had told him then that these things were banalities, he would have gaped in wonder.

   "Now we'll get lunch," ordered Kerry, wandering up with the crowd. "Come on, Amory, tear yourself away and get practical."

   "We'll try the best hotel first," he went on, "and thence and so forth."

   They strolled along the boardwalk to the most imposing hostelry in sight, and, entering the dining-room, scattered about a table.

   "Eight Bronxes," commanded Alec, "and a club sandwich and Juliennes. The food for one. Hand the rest around."

Amory ate little, having seized a chair where he could watch the sea and feel the rock of it. When luncheon was over they sat and smoked quietly.

"What's the bill?"

Some one scanned it.

"Eight twenty-five."

"Rotten overcharge. We'll give them two dollars and one for the waiter. Kerry, collect the small change."

The waiter approached, and Kerry gravely handed him a dollar, tossed two dollars on the check, and turned away. They sauntered leisurely toward the door, pursued in a moment by the suspicious Ganymede.*

"Some mistake, sir."

Kerry took the bill and examined it critically.

"No mistake!" he said, shaking his head gravely, and, tearing it into four pieces he handed the scraps to the waiter, who was so dumbfounded that he stood motionless and expressionless while they walked out.

"Won't he send after us?"

"No," said Kerry; "for a minute he'll think we're the proprietor's sons or something; then he'll look at the check again and call the manager, and in the meantime——"

They left the car at Asbury and street-car'd to Allenhurst, where they investigated the crowded pavilions for beauty. At four there were refreshments in a lunch-room, and this time they paid an even smaller per cent on the total cost; something about the appearance and savoir-faire of the crowd made the thing go, and they were not pursued.

"You see, Amory, we're Marxian Socialists," explained Kerry. "We don't believe in property and we're putting it to the great test."

"Night will descend," Amory suggested.

"Watch, and put your trust in Holiday."

They became jovial about five-thirty and, linking arms, strolled up and down the boardwalk in a row, chanting a monotonous ditty about the sad sea waves. Then Kerry saw a face in the crowd that attracted him and, rushing off, reappeared in a moment with one of the homeliest girls Amory had ever set eyes on. Her pale mouth extended from ear to ear, her teeth projected in a solid wedge, and she had little, squinty eyes that peeped ingratiatingly over the side sweep of her nose. Kerry presented them formally.

"Name of Kaluka, Hawaiian queen! Let me present Messrs. Connage, Sloane, Humbird, Ferrenby, and Blaine."

The girl bobbed courtesies all around. Poor creature; Amory supposed she had never before been noticed in her life—possibly she was half-witted. While she accompanied them (Kerry had invited her to supper) she said nothing which could discountenance such a belief.

"She prefers her native dishes," said Alec gravely to the waiter, "but any coarse food will do."

All through supper he addressed her in the most respectful language, while Kerry made idiotic love to her on the other side, and she giggled and grinned. Amory was content to sit and watch the by-play, thinking what a light touch Kerry had, and how he could transform the barest incident into a thing of curve and contour. They all seemed to have the spirit of it more or less, and it was a relaxation to be with them. Amory usually liked men individually, yet feared them in crowds unless the crowd was around *him*. He wondered how much each one contributed to the party, for there was somewhat of a spiritual tax levied. Alec and Kerry were the life of it, but not quite the centre. Somehow the quiet Humbird, and Sloane, with his impatient superciliousness, were the centre.

Dick Humbird had, ever since freshman year, seemed to Amory a perfect type of aristocrat. He was slender but well-built—black curly hair, straight features, and rather a dark skin. Everything he said sounded intangibly appropriate. He possessed infinite courage, an averagely good mind, and a sense of honor with a clear charm and noblesse oblige that varied it from righteousness. He could dissipate without going to pieces, and even his most bohemian adventures never seemed "running it out." People dressed like him, tried to talk as he did. . . . Amory decided that he probably held the world back, but he wouldn't have changed him. . . .

He differed from the healthy type that was essentially middle-class—he never seemed to perspire. Some people couldn't be familiar with a chauffeur without having it returned; Humbird could have lunched at Sherry's with a colored man, yet people would have somehow known that it was all right. He was not a snob, though he knew only half his class. His friends ranged from the highest to the lowest, but it was impossible to "cultivate" him. Servants worshipped him, and treated him like a god. He seemed the eternal example of what the upper class tries to be.

"He's like those pictures in the *Illustrated London News* of the English officers who have been killed," Amory had said to Alec.

"Well," Alec had answered, "if you want to know the shocking truth, his father was a grocery clerk who made a fortune in Tacoma real estate and came to New York ten years ago."

Amory had felt a curious sinking sensation.

This present type of party was made possible by the surging together of the class after club elections—as if to make a last desperate attempt to know itself, to keep together, to fight off the tightening spirit of the clubs. It was a let-down from the conventional heights they had all walked so rigidly.

After supper they saw Kaluka to the boardwalk, and then strolled back along the beach to Asbury. The evening sea was a new sensation, for all its color and mellow age was gone, and it seemed the bleak waste that made the Norse sagas sad; Amory thought of Kipling's

*"Beaches of Lukannon before the sealers came."**

It was still a music, though, infinitely sorrowful.

Ten o'clock found them penniless. They had supped greatly on their last eleven cents and, singing, strolled up through the casinos and lighted arches on the boardwalk, stopping to listen approvingly to all band concerts. In one place Kerry took up a collection for the French War Orphans which netted a dollar and twenty cents, and with this they bought some brandy in case they caught cold in the night. They finished the day in a moving-picture show and went into solemn systematic roars of laughter at an ancient comedy, to the startled annoyance of the rest of the audience. Their entrance was distinctly strategic, for each man as he entered pointed reproachfully at the one just behind him. Sloane, bringing up the rear, disclaimed all knowledge and responsibility as soon as the others were scattered inside; then as the irate ticket-taker rushed in he followed nonchalantly.

They reassembled later by the Casino and made arrangements for the night. Kerry wormed permission from the watchman to sleep on the platform and, having collected a huge pile of rugs from the booths to serve as mattresses and blankets, they talked until midnight, and then fell into a dreamless sleep, though Amory tried hard to stay awake and watch that marvellous moon settle on the sea.

So they progressed for two happy days, up and down the shore by
street-car or machine, or by shoe-leather on the crowded boardwalk;
sometimes eating with the wealthy, more frequently dining frugally
at the expense of an unsuspecting restaurateur. They had their photos
taken, eight poses, in a quick-development store. Kerry insisted on
grouping them as a "varsity" football team, and then as a tough gang
from the East Side, with their coats inside out, and himself sitting in
the middle on a cardboard moon. The photographer probably has them
yet—at least, they never called for them. The weather was perfect, and
again they slept outside, and again Amory fell unwillingly asleep.

Sunday broke stolid and respectable, and even the sea seemed to
mumble and complain, so they returned to Princeton via the Fords
of transient farmers, and broke up with colds in their heads, but
otherwise none the worse for wandering.

Even more than in the year before, Amory neglected his work,
not deliberately but lazily and through a multitude of other interests.
Co-ordinate geometry and the melancholy hexameters of Corneille
and Racine* held forth small allurements, and even psychology,
which he had eagerly awaited, proved to be a dull subject full of
muscular reactions and biological phrases rather than the study
of personality and influence. That was a noon class, and it always
sent him dozing. Having found that "subjective and objective, sir,"
answered most of the questions, he used the phrase on all occasions,
and it became the class joke when, on a query being levelled at him,
he was nudged awake by Ferrenby or Sloane to gasp it out.

Mostly there were parties—to Orange or the Shore, more rarely
to New York and Philadelphia, though one night they marshalled
fourteen waitresses out of Childs' and took them to ride down
Fifth Avenue on top of an auto bus. They all cut more classes
than were allowed, which meant an additional course the following year, but spring was too rare to let anything interfere with their
colorful ramblings. In May Amory was elected to the Sophomore
Prom Committee, and when after a long evening's discussion
with Alec they made out a tentative list of class probabilities for the
senior council, they placed themselves among the surest. The senior
council was composed presumably of the eighteen most representative seniors, and in view of Alec's football managership and Amory's
chance of nosing out Burne Holiday as *Princetonian* chairman,
they seemed fairly justified in this presumption. Oddly enough, they

both placed D'Invilliers as among the possibilities, a guess that a year before the class would have gaped at.

All through the spring Amory had kept up an intermittent correspondence with Isabelle Borgé, punctuated by violent squabbles and chiefly enlivened by his attempts to find new words for love. He discovered Isabelle to be discreetly and aggravatingly unsentimental in letters, but he hoped against hope that she would prove not too exotic a bloom to fit the large spaces of spring as she had fitted the den in the Minnehaha Club. During May he wrote thirty-page documents almost nightly, and sent them to her in bulky envelopes exteriorly labelled "Part I" and "Part II."

"Oh, Alec, I believe I'm tired of college," he said sadly, as they walked the dusk together.

"I think I am, too, in a way."

"All I'd like would be a little home in the country, some warm country, and a wife, and just enough to do to keep from rotting."

"Me, too."

"I'd like to quit."

"What does your girl say?"

"Oh!" Amory gasped in horror. "She wouldn't *think* of marrying . . . that is, not now. I mean the future, you know."

"My girl would. I'm engaged."

"Are you really?"

"Yes. Don't say a word to anybody, please, but I am. I may not come back next year."

"But you're only twenty! Give up college?"

"Why, Amory, you were saying a minute ago——"

"Yes," Amory interrupted, "but I was just wishing. I wouldn't think of leaving college. It's just that I feel so sad these wonderful nights. I sort of feel they're never coming again, and I'm not really getting all I could out of them. I wish my girl lived here. But marry—not a chance. Especially as father says the money isn't forthcoming as it used to be."

"What a waste these nights are!" agreed Alec.

But Amory sighed and made use of the nights. He had a snapshot of Isabelle, enshrined in an old watch, and at eight almost every night he would turn off all the lights except the desk lamp and, sitting by the open windows with the picture before him, write her rapturous letters.

. . . Oh, it's so hard to write you what I really *feel* when I think about you so much; you've gotten to mean to me a *dream* that I can't put on paper any more. Your last letter came and it was wonderful! I read it over about six times, especially the *last* part, but I do wish, sometimes, you'd be more *frank* and tell me what you really do think of me, yet your last letter was too good to be true, and I can hardly wait until June! Be sure and be able to come to the prom. It'll be fine, I think, and I want to bring *you* just at the end of a wonderful year. I often think over what you said on that night and wonder how much you meant. If it were any one but you—but you see I *thought* you were fickle the first time I saw you and you are so popular and everything that I can't imagine your really liking me *best*.

Oh, Isabelle, dear—it's a wonderful night. Somebody is playing "Love Moon" on a mandolin far across the campus, and the music seems to bring you into the window. Now he's playing "Good-bye, Boys, I'm Through,"* and how well it suits me. For I *am* through with everything. I have decided never to take a cocktail again, and I know I'll never again fall in love—I couldn't—you've been too much a part of my days and nights to ever let me think of another girl. I meet them all the time and they don't interest me. I'm not pretending to be blasé, because it's not that. It's just that I'm in love. Oh, *dearest* Isabelle (somehow I can't call you just Isabelle, and I'm afraid I'll come out with the "dearest" before your family this June), you've *got* to come to the prom, and then I'll come up to your house for a day and everything'll be perfect. . . .

And so on in an eternal monotone that seemed to both of them infinitely charming, infinitely new.

June came and the days grew so hot and lazy that they could not worry even about exams, but spent dreamy evenings on the court of Cottage, talking of long subjects until the sweep of country toward Stony Brook became a blue haze and the lilacs were white around tennis-courts, and words gave way to silent cigarettes. . . . Then down deserted Prospect and along McCosh with song everywhere around them, up to the hot joviality of Nassau Street.

Tom D'Invilliers and Amory walked late in those days. A gambling fever swept through the sophomore class and they bent over the bones till three o'clock many a sultry night. After one session they came out of Sloane's room to find the dew fallen and the stars old in the sky.

"Let's borrow bicycles and take a ride," Amory suggested.

"All right. I'm not a bit tired and this is almost the last night of the year, really, because the prom stuff starts Monday."

They found two unlocked bicycles in Holder Court and rode out about half-past three along the Lawrenceville Road.

"What are you going to do this summer, Amory?"

"Don't ask me—same old things, I suppose. A month or two in Lake Geneva—I'm counting on you to be there in July, you know—then there'll be Minneapolis, and that means hundreds of summer hops, parlor-snaking, getting bored—But oh, Tom," he added suddenly, "hasn't this year been slick!"

"No," declared Tom emphatically, a new Tom, clothed by Brooks, shod by Franks,* "I've won this game, but I feel as if I never want to play another. You're all right—you're a rubber ball, and somehow it suits you, but I'm sick of adapting myself to the local snobbishness of this corner of the world. I want to go where people aren't barred because of the color of their neckties and the roll of their coats."

"You can't, Tom," argued Amory, as they rolled along through the scattering night; "wherever you go now you'll always unconsciously apply these standards of 'having it' or 'lacking it.' For better or worse we've stamped you; you're a Princeton type!"

"Well, then," complained Tom, his cracked voice rising plaintively, "why do I have to come back at all? I've learned all that Princeton has to offer. Two years more of mere pedantry and lying around a club aren't going to help. They're just going to disorganize me, conventionalize me completely. Even now I'm so spineless that I wonder how I get away with it."

"Oh, but you're missing the real point, Tom," Amory interrupted. "You've just had your eyes opened to the snobbishness of the world in a rather abrupt manner. Princeton invariably gives the thoughtful man a social sense."

"You consider you taught me that, don't you?" he asked quizzically, eying Amory in the half dark.

Amory laughed quietly.

"Didn't I?"

"Sometimes," he said slowly, "I think you're my bad angel. I might have been a pretty fair poet."

"Come on, that's rather hard. You chose to come to an Eastern college. Either your eyes were opened to the mean scrambling quality of people, or you'd have gone through blind, and you'd hate to have done that—been like Marty Kaye."

"Yes," he agreed, "you're right. I wouldn't have liked it. Still, it's hard to be made a cynic at twenty."

"I was born one," Amory murmured. "I'm a cynical idealist." He paused and wondered if that meant anything.

They reached the sleeping school of Lawrenceville, and turned to ride back.

"It's good, this ride, isn't it?" Tom said presently.

"Yes; it's a good finish, it's knock-out; everything's good to-night. Oh, for a hot, languorous summer and Isabelle!"

"Oh, you and your Isabelle! I'll bet she's a simple one . . . let's say some poetry."

So Amory declaimed "The Ode to a Nightingale" to the bushes they passed.

"I'll never be a poet," said Amory as he finished. "I'm not enough of a sensualist really; there are only a few obvious things that I notice as primarily beautiful: women, spring evenings, music at night, the sea; I don't catch the subtle things like 'silver-snarling trumpets.'* I may turn out an intellectual, but I'll never write anything but mediocre poetry."

They rode into Princeton as the sun was making colored maps of the sky behind the graduate school, and hurried to the refreshment of a shower that would have to serve in place of sleep. By noon the bright-costumed alumni crowded the streets with their bands and choruses, and in the tents there was great reunion under the orange-and-black banners that curled and strained in the wind. Amory looked long at one house which bore the legend "Sixty-nine." There a few gray-haired men sat and talked quietly while the classes swept by in panorama of life.

Under the Arc-Light

Then tragedy's emerald eyes glared suddenly at Amory over the edge of June. On the night after his ride to Lawrenceville a crowd sallied to New York in quest of adventure, and started back to Princeton about twelve o'clock in two machines. It had been a gay party and different stages of sobriety were represented. Amory was in the car behind; they had taken the wrong road and lost the way, and so were hurrying to catch up.

It was a clear night and the exhilaration of the road went to Amory's head. He had the ghost of two stanzas of a poem forming in his mind. . . .

So the gray car crept nightward in the dark and there was no life stirred as it went by. . . . As the still ocean paths before the shark in starred and glittering waterways, beauty-high, the moon-swathed trees divided, pair on pair, while flapping nightbirds cried across the air. . . .

A moment by an inn of lamps and shades, a yellow inn under a yellow moon—then silence, where crescendo laughter fades . . . the car swung out again to the winds of June, mellowed the shadows where the distance grew, then crushed the yellow shadows into blue. . . .

They jolted to a stop, and Amory peered up, startled. A woman was standing beside the road, talking to Alec at the wheel. Afterward he remembered the harpy effect that her old kimono gave her, and the cracked hollowness of her voice as she spoke:

"You Princeton boys?"

"Yes."

"Well, there's one of you killed here, and two others about dead."

"*My God!*"

"Look!" She pointed and they gazed in horror. Under the full light of a roadside arc-light lay a form, face downward in a widening circle of blood.

They sprang from the car. Amory thought of the back of that head—that hair—that hair . . . and then they turned the form over.

"It's Dick—Dick Humbird!"

"Oh, Christ!"

"Feel his heart!"

Then the insistent voice of the old crone in a sort of croaking triumph:

"He's quite dead, all right. The car turned over. Two of the men that weren't hurt just carried the others in, but this one's no use."

Amory rushed into the house and the rest followed with a limp mass that they laid on the sofa in the shoddy little front parlor. Sloane, with his shoulder punctured, was on another lounge. He was half delirious, and kept calling something about a chemistry lecture at 8:10.

"I don't know what happened," said Ferrenby in a strained voice. "Dick was driving and he wouldn't give up the wheel; we told him he'd been drinking too much—then there was this damn curve—oh, my *God!* . . ." He threw himself face downward on the floor and broke into dry sobs.

The doctor had arrived, and Amory went over to the couch, where some one handed him a sheet to put over the body. With a sudden hardness, he raised one of the hands and let it fall back inertly. The brow was cold but the face not expressionless. He looked at the shoe-laces—Dick had tied them that morning. *He* had tied them—and now he was this heavy white mass. All that remained of the charm and personality of the Dick Humbird he had known—oh, it was all so horrible and unaristocratic and close to the earth. All tragedy has that strain of the grotesque and squalid—so useless, futile . . . the way animals die. . . . Amory was reminded of a cat that had lain horribly mangled in some alley of his childhood.

"Some one go to Princeton with Ferrenby."

Amory stepped outside the door and shivered slightly at the late night wind—a wind that stirred a broken fender on the mass of bent metal to a plaintive, tinny sound.

Crescendo!

Next day, by a merciful chance, passed in a whirl. When Amory was by himself his thoughts zigzagged inevitably to the picture of that red mouth yawning incongruously in the white face, but with a determined effort he piled present excitement upon the memory of it and shut it coldly away from his mind.

Isabelle and her mother drove into town at four, and they rode up smiling Prospect Avenue, through the gay crowd, to have tea at Cottage. The clubs had their annual dinners that night, so at seven he loaned her to a freshman and arranged to meet her in the gymnasium at eleven, when the upperclassmen were admitted to the freshman dance. She was all he had expected, and he was happy and eager to make that night the centre of every dream. At nine the upper classes stood in front of the clubs as the freshman torchlight parade rioted past, and Amory wondered if the dress-suited groups against the dark, stately backgrounds and under the flare of the torches made the night as brilliant to the staring, cheering freshmen as it had been to him the year before.

The next day was another whirl. They lunched in a gay party of six in a private dining-room at the club, while Isabelle and Amory looked at each other tenderly over the fried chicken and knew that their love was to be eternal. They danced away the prom until five, and the stags cut in on Isabelle with joyous abandon, which grew more and more enthusiastic as the hour grew late, and their wines, stored in overcoat pockets in the coat room, made old weariness wait until another day. The stag line is a most homogeneous mass of men. It fairly sways with a single soul. A dark-haired beauty dances by and there is a half-gasping sound as the ripple surges forward and some one sleeker than the rest darts out and cuts in. Then when the six-foot girl (brought by Kaye in your class, and to whom he has been trying to introduce you all evening) gallops by, the line surges back and the groups face about and become intent on far corners of the hall, for Kaye, anxious and perspiring, appears elbowing through the crowd in search of familiar faces.

"I say, old man, I've got an awfully nice——"

"Sorry, Kaye, but I'm set for this one. I've got to cut in on a fella."

"Well, the next one?"

"What—ah—er—I swear I've got to go cut in—look me up when she's got a dance free."

It delighted Amory when Isabelle suggested that they leave for a while and drive around in her car. For a delicious hour that passed too soon they glided the silent roads about Princeton and talked from the surface of their hearts in shy excitement. Amory felt strangely ingenuous and made no attempt to kiss her.

Next day they rode up through the Jersey country, had luncheon in New York, and in the afternoon went to see a problem play at which Isabelle wept all through the second act, rather to Amory's embarrassment—though it filled him with tenderness to watch her. He was tempted to lean over and kiss away her tears, and she slipped her hand into his under cover of darkness to be pressed softly.

Then at six they arrived at the Borgés' summer place on Long Island, and Amory rushed up-stairs to change into a dinner coat. As he put in his studs he realized that he was enjoying life as he would probably never enjoy it again. Everything was hallowed by the haze of his own youth. He had arrived, abreast of the best in his generation at Princeton. He was in love and his love was returned. Turning on all the lights, he looked at himself in the mirror, trying to find in his own face the qualities that made him see clearer than the great crowd of people, that made him decide firmly, and able to influence and follow his own will. There was little in his life now that he would have changed. . . . Oxford might have been a bigger field.

Silently he admired himself. How conveniently well he looked, and how well a dinner coat became him. He stepped into the hall and then waited at the top of the stairs, for he heard footsteps coming. It was Isabelle, and from the top of her shining hair to her little golden slippers she had never seemed so beautiful.

"Isabelle!" he cried, half involuntarily, and held out his arms. As in the story-books, she ran into them, and on that half-minute, as their lips first touched, rested the high point of vanity, the crest of his young egotism.

CHAPTER III

THE EGOTIST CONSIDERS

"Ouch! Let me go!"

He dropped his arms to his sides.

"What's the matter?"

"Your shirt stud—it hurt me—look!" She was looking down at her neck, where a little blue spot about the size of a pea marred its pallor.

"Oh, Isabelle," he reproached himself, "I'm a goopher. Really, I'm sorry—I shouldn't have held you so close."

She looked up impatiently.

"Oh, Amory, of course you couldn't help it, and it didn't hurt much; but what *are* we going to do about it?"

"*Do* about it?" he asked. "Oh—that spot; it'll disappear in a second."

"It isn't," she said, after a moment of concentrated gazing, "it's still there—and it looks like Old Nick—oh, Amory, what'll we do! It's *just* the height of your shoulder."

"Massage it," he suggested, repressing the faintest inclination to laugh.

She rubbed it delicately with the tips of her fingers, and then a tear gathered in the corner of her eye, and slid down her cheek.

"Oh, Amory," she said despairingly, lifting up a most pathetic face, "I'll just make my whole neck *flame* if I rub it. What'll I do?"

A quotation sailed into his head and he couldn't resist repeating it aloud.

"All the perfumes of Arabia will not whiten this little hand."*

She looked up and the sparkle of the tear in her eye was like ice.

"You're not very sympathetic."

Amory mistook her meaning.

"Isabelle, darling, I think it'll——"

"Don't touch me!" she cried. "Haven't I enough on my mind and you stand there and *laugh!*"

Then he slipped again.

"Well, it *is* funny, Isabelle, and we were talking the other day about a sense of humor being——"

She was looking at him with something that was not a smile, rather the faint, mirthless echo of a smile, in the corners of her mouth.

"Oh, shut up!" she cried suddenly, and fled down the hallway toward her room. Amory stood there, covered with remorseful confusion.

"Damn!"

When Isabelle reappeared she had thrown a light wrap about her shoulders, and they descended the stairs in a silence that endured through dinner.

"Isabelle," he began rather testily, as they arranged themselves in the car, bound for a dance at the Greenwich Country Club,* "you're angry, and I'll be, too, in a minute. Let's kiss and make up."

Isabelle considered glumly.

"I hate to be laughed at," she said finally.

"I won't laugh any more. I'm not laughing now, am I?"

"You did."

"Oh, don't be so darned feminine."

Her lips curled slightly.

"I'll be anything I want."

Amory kept his temper with difficulty. He became aware that he had not an ounce of real affection for Isabelle, but her coldness piqued him. He wanted to kiss her, kiss her a lot, because then he knew he could leave in the morning and not care. On the contrary, if he didn't kiss her, it would worry him. . . . It would interfere vaguely with his idea of himself as a conqueror. It wasn't dignified to come off second best, *pleading*, with a doughty warrior like Isabelle.

Perhaps she suspected this. At any rate, Amory watched the night that should have been the consummation of romance glide by with great moths overhead and the heavy fragrance of roadside gardens, but without those broken words, those little sighs. . . .

Afterward they supped on ginger ale and devil's food in the pantry, and Amory announced a decision.

"I'm leaving early in the morning."

"Why?"

"Why not?" he countered.

"There's no need."

"However, I'm going."

"Well, if you insist on being ridiculous——"

"Oh, don't put it that way," he objected.

"—just because I won't let you kiss me. Do you think——"

"Now, Isabelle," he interrupted, "you know it's not that—even suppose it is. We've reached the stage where we either ought to kiss—or—or—nothing. It isn't as if you were refusing on moral grounds."

She hesitated.

"I really don't know what to think about you," she began, in a feeble, perverse attempt at conciliation. "You're so funny."

"How?"

"Well, I thought you had a lot of self-confidence and all that; remember you told me the other day that you could do anything you wanted, or get anything you wanted?"

Amory flushed. He *had* told her a lot of things.

"Yes."

"Well, you didn't seem to feel so self-confident to-night. Maybe you're just plain conceited."

"No, I'm not," he hesitated. "At Princeton——"

"Oh, you and Princeton! You'd think that was the world, the way you talk! Perhaps you *can* write better than anybody else on your old *Princetonian;* maybe the freshmen *do* think you're important——"

"You don't understand——"

"Yes, I do," she interrupted. "I *do*, because you're always talking about yourself and I used to like it; now I don't."

"Have I to-night?"

"That's just the point," insisted Isabelle. "You got all upset to-night. You just sat and watched my eyes. Besides, I have to think all the time I'm talking to you—you're so critical."

"I make you think, do I?" Amory repeated with a touch of vanity.

"You're a nervous strain"—this emphatically—"and when you analyze every little emotion and instinct I just don't have 'em."

"I know." Amory admitted her point and shook his head helplessly.

"Let's go." She stood up.

He rose abstractedly and they walked to the foot of the stairs.

"What train can I get?"

"There's one about 9:11 if you really must go."

"Yes, I've got to go, really. Good night."

"Good night."

They were at the head of the stairs, and as Amory turned into his room he thought he caught just the faintest cloud of discontent in her face. He lay awake in the darkness and wondered how much he cared—how much of his sudden unhappiness was hurt vanity—whether he was, after all, temperamentally unfitted for romance.

When he awoke, it was with a glad flood of consciousness. The early wind stirred the chintz curtains at the windows and he was idly puzzled not to be in his room at Princeton with his school football picture over the bureau and the Triangle Club on the wall opposite. Then the grandfather's clock in the hall outside struck eight, and the memory of the night before came to him. He was out of bed, dressing, like the wind; he must get out of the house before he saw Isabelle. What had seemed a melancholy happening, now seemed a tiresome anticlimax. He was dressed at half past, so he sat down by the window; felt that the sinews of his heart were twisted somewhat more than he had thought. What an ironic mockery the morning seemed!—bright and sunny, and full of the smell of the garden; hearing Mrs. Borgé's voice in the sun-parlor below, he wondered where was Isabelle.

There was a knock at the door.

"The car will be around at ten minutes of nine, sir."

He returned to his contemplation of the outdoors, and began repeating over and over, mechanically, a verse from Browning, which he had once quoted to Isabelle in a letter:

> *"Each life unfulfilled, you see,*
> *It hangs still, patchy and scrappy;*
> *We have not sighed deep, laughed free,*
> *Starved, feasted, despaired—been happy."**

But his life would not be unfulfilled. He took a sombre satisfaction in thinking that perhaps all along she had been nothing except what he had read into her; that this was her high point, that no one else would ever make her think. Yet that was what she had objected to in him; and Amory was suddenly tired of thinking, thinking!

"Damn her!" he said bitterly, "she's spoiled my year!"

The Superman Grows Careless

On a dusty day in September Amory arrived in Princeton and joined the sweltering crowd of conditioned men* who thronged the streets. It seemed a stupid way to commence his upper-class years, to spend four hours a morning in the stuffy room of a tutoring school, imbibing the infinite boredom of conic sections. Mr. Rooney, pander to the dull, conducted the class and smoked innumerable Pall Malls as he drew diagrams and worked equations from six in the morning until midnight.

"Now, Langueduc, if I used that formula, where would my *A* point be?"

Langueduc lazily shifts his six-foot-three of football material and tries to concentrate.

"Oh—ah—I'm damned if I know, Mr. Rooney."

"Oh, why of course, of course you can't *use* that formula. *That's* what I wanted you to say."

"Why, sure, of course."

"Do you see why?"

"You bet—I suppose so."

"If you don't see, tell me. I'm here to show you."

"Well, Mr. Rooney, if you don't mind, I wish you'd go over that again."

"Gladly. Now here's '*A*' . . ."

The room was a study in stupidity—two huge stands for paper, Mr. Rooney in his shirt-sleeves in front of them, and slouched around on chairs, a dozen men: Fred Sloane, the pitcher, who absolutely *had* to get eligible; "Slim" Langueduc, who would beat Yale this fall, if only he could master a poor fifty per cent; McDowell, gay young sophomore, who thought it was quite a sporting thing to be tutoring here with all these prominent athletes.

"Those poor birds who haven't a cent to tutor, and have to study during the term are the ones I pity," he announced to Amory one day, with a flaccid camaraderie in the droop of the cigarette from his pale lips. "I should think it would be such a bore, there's so much else to do in New York during the term. I suppose they don't know what they miss, anyhow." There was such an air of "you and I" about Mr. McDowell that Amory very nearly pushed him out of the open window when he said this. . . . Next February his mother would wonder why he didn't make a club and increase his allowance . . . simple little nut. . . .

Through the smoke and the air of solemn, dense earnestness that filled the room would come the inevitable helpless cry:

"I don't get it! Repeat that, Mr. Rooney!" Most of them were so stupid or careless that they wouldn't admit when they didn't understand,

and Amory was of the latter. He found it impossible to study conic sections; something in their calm and tantalizing respectability breathing defiantly through Mr. Rooney's fetid parlors distorted their equations into insoluble anagrams. He made a last night's effort with the proverbial wet towel, and then blissfully took the exam, wondering unhappily why all the color and ambition of the spring before had faded out. Somehow, with the defection of Isabelle the idea of undergraduate success had loosed its grasp on his imagination, and he contemplated a possible failure to pass off his condition with equanimity, even though it would arbitrarily mean his removal from the *Princetonian* board and the slaughter of his chances for the Senior Council.

There was always his luck.

He yawned, scribbled his honor pledge on the cover, and sauntered from the room.

"If you don't pass it," said the newly arrived Alec as they sat on the window-seat of Amory's room and mused upon a scheme of wall decoration, "you're the world's worst goopher. Your stock will go down like an elevator at the club and on the campus."

"Oh, hell, I know it. Why rub it in?"

"'Cause you deserve it. Anybody that'd risk what you were in line for *ought* to be ineligible for *Princetonian* chairman."

"Oh, drop the subject," Amory protested. "Watch and wait and shut up. I don't want every one at the club asking me about it, as if I were a prize potato being fattened for a vegetable show."

One evening a week later Amory stopped below his own window on the way to Renwick's, and, seeing a light, called up:

"Oh, Tom, any mail?"

Alec's head appeared against the yellow square of light.

"Yes, your result's here."

His heart clamored violently.

"What is it, blue or pink?"

"Don't know. Better come up."

He walked into the room and straight over to the table, and then suddenly noticed that there were other people in the room.

"'Lo, Kerry." He was most polite. "Ah, men of Princeton." They seemed to be mostly friends, so he picked up the envelope marked "Registrar's Office," and weighed it nervously.

"We have here quite a slip of paper."

"Open it, Amory."

"Just to be dramatic, I'll let you know that if it's blue, my name is withdrawn from the editorial board of the *Prince*, and my short career is over."

He paused, and then saw for the first time Ferrenby's eyes, wearing a hungry look and watching him eagerly. Amory returned the gaze pointedly.

"Watch my face, gentlemen, for the primitive emotions."

He tore it open and held the slip up to the light.

"Well?"

"Pink or blue?"

"Say what it is."

"We're all ears, Amory."

"Smile or swear—or something."

There was a pause . . . a small crowd of seconds swept by . . . then he looked again and another crowd went on into time.

"Blue as the sky, gentlemen. . . ."

Aftermath

What Amory did that year from early September to late in the spring was so purposeless and inconsecutive that it seems scarcely worth recording. He was, of course, immediately sorry for what he had lost. His philosophy of success had tumbled down upon him, and he looked for the reasons.

"Your own laziness," said Alec later.

"No—something deeper than that. I've begun to feel that I was meant to lose this chance."

"They're rather off you at the club, you know; every man that doesn't come through makes our crowd just so much weaker."

"I hate that point of view."

"Of course, with a little effort you could still stage a comeback."

"No—I'm through—as far as ever being a power in college is concerned."

"But, Amory, honestly, what makes me the angriest isn't the fact that you won't be chairman of the *Prince* and on the Senior Council, but just that you didn't get down and pass that exam."

"Not me," said Amory slowly; "I'm mad at the concrete thing. My own idleness was quite in accord with my system, but the luck broke."

"Your system broke, you mean."

"Maybe."

"Well, what are you going to do? Get a better one quick, or just bum around for two more years as a has-been?"

"I don't know yet . . ."

"Oh, Amory, buck up!"

"Maybe."

Amory's point of view, though dangerous, was not far from the true one. If his reactions to his environment could be tabulated, the chart would have appeared like this, beginning with his earliest years:

1. The fundamental Amory.

2. Amory plus Beatrice.

3. Amory plus Beatrice plus Minneapolis.

Then St. Regis' had pulled him to pieces and started him over again:

4. Amory plus St. Regis'.

5. Amory plus St. Regis' plus Princeton.

That had been his nearest approach to success through conformity. The fundamental Amory, idle, imaginative, rebellious, had been nearly snowed under. He had conformed, he had succeeded, but as his imagination was neither satisfied nor grasped by his own success, he had listlessly, half-accidentally chucked the whole thing and become again:

6. The fundamental Amory.

Financial

His father died quietly and inconspicuously at Thanksgiving. The incongruity of death with either the beauties of Lake Geneva or with his mother's dignified, reticent attitude diverted him, and he looked at the funeral with an amused tolerance. He decided that burial was after all preferable to cremation, and he smiled at his old boyhood choice, slow oxidation in the top of a tree. The day after the ceremony he was amusing himself in the great library by sinking back on a couch in graceful mortuary attitudes, trying to determine whether he would, when his day came, be found with his arms crossed piously over his chest (Monsignor Darcy had once advocated this posture as being the most distinguished), or with his hands clasped behind his head, a more pagan and Byronic attitude.

What interested him much more than the final departure of his father from things mundane was a tri-cornered conversation between Beatrice, Mr. Barton, of Barton and Krogman, their lawyers, and himself, that took place several days after the funeral. For the first time he came into actual cognizance of the family finances, and realized what a tidy fortune had once been under his father's management. He took a ledger labelled "1906" and ran through it rather carefully. The total expenditure that year had come to something over one hundred and ten thousand dollars. Forty thousand of this had been Beatrice's own income, and there had been no attempt to account for it: it was all under the heading, "Drafts, checks, and letters of credit forwarded to Beatrice Blaine." The dispersal of the rest was rather minutely itemized: the taxes and improvements on the Lake Geneva estate had come to almost nine thousand dollars; the general up-keep, including Beatrice's electric and a French car, bought that year, was over thirty-five thousand dollars. The rest was fully taken care of, and there were invariably items which failed to balance on the right side of the ledger.

In the volume for 1912 Amory was shocked to discover the decrease in the number of bond holdings and the great drop in the income. In the case of Beatrice's money this was not so pronounced, but it was obvious that his father had devoted the previous year to several unfortunate gambles in oil. Very little of the oil had been burned, but Stephen Blaine had been rather badly singed. The next year and the next and the next showed similar decreases, and Beatrice had for the first time begun using her own money for keeping up the house. Yet her doctor's bill for 1913 had been over nine thousand dollars.

About the exact state of things Mr. Barton was quite vague and confused. There had been recent investments, the outcome of which was for the present problematical, and he had an idea there were further speculations and exchanges concerning which he had not been consulted.

It was not for several months that Beatrice wrote Amory the full situation. The entire residue of the Blaine and O'Hara fortunes consisted of the place at Lake Geneva and approximately a half million dollars, invested now in fairly conservative six-per-cent holdings. In fact, Beatrice wrote that she was putting the money into railroad and street-car bonds as fast as she could conveniently transfer it.

"I am quite sure," she wrote to Amory, "that if there is one thing we can be positive of, it is that people will not stay in one place. This Ford person has certainly made the most of that idea. So I am instructing Mr. Barton to specialize on such things as Northern Pacific and these Rapid Transit Companies, as they call the street-cars. I shall never forgive myself for not buying Bethlehem Steel. I've heard the most *fascinating* stories. You must go into finance, Amory. I'm sure you would revel in it. You start as a messenger or a teller, I believe, and from that you go up—almost indefinitely. I'm sure if I were a man I'd love the handling of money; it has become quite a senile passion with me. Before I get any farther I want to discuss something. A Mrs. Bispam, an overcordial little lady whom I met at a tea the other day, told me that her son, he is at Yale, wrote her that all the boys there wore their summer underwear *all during the winter*, and also went about with their heads wet and in low shoes on the *coldest days*. Now, Amory, I don't know whether that is a fad at Princeton too, but I don't want you to be so foolish. It not only inclines a young man to *pneumonia* and *infantile paralysis*, but to all forms of lung trouble, to which you are particularly *inclined*. You cannot experiment with your health. I have found that out. I will not make myself ridiculous as some mothers no doubt do, by insisting that you wear overshoes, though I remember one Christmas you wore them around *constantly* without a single buckle latched, making such a curious swishing sound, and you refused to buckle them because it was not the thing to do. The very *next* Christmas you would not wear even *rubbers*, though I begged you. You are nearly twenty years old now, dear, and I can't be with you constantly to find whether you are doing the sensible thing.

"This has been a very *practical* letter. I warned you in my last that the lack of money to do the things one wants to makes one quite prosy and domestic, but there is still plenty for everything if we are not too extravagant. Take care of yourself, my dear boy, and do try to write at least *once* a week, because I imagine all sorts of horrible things if I don't hear from you.

Affectionately,   MOTHER."

First Appearance of the Term "Personage"

Monsignor Darcy invited Amory up to the Stuart palace on the Hudson for a week at Christmas, and they had enormous conversations around the open fire. Monsignor was growing a trifle stouter and his personality had expanded even with that, and Amory felt both rest and security in sinking into a squat, cushioned chair and joining him in the middle-aged sanity of a cigar.

"I've felt like leaving college, Monsignor."

"Why?"

"All my career's gone up in smoke; you think it's petty and all that, but——"

"Not at all petty. I think it's most important. I want to hear the whole thing. Everything you've been doing since I saw you last."

Amory talked; he went thoroughly into the destruction of his egotistic highways, and in a half-hour the listless quality had left his voice.

"What would you do if you left college?" asked Monsignor.

"Don't know. I'd like to travel, but of course this tiresome war prevents that. Anyways, mother would hate not having me graduate. I'm just at sea. Kerry Holiday wants me to go over with him and join the Lafayette Escadrille."*

"You know you wouldn't like to go."

"Sometimes I would—to-night I'd go in a second."

"Well, you'd have to be very much more tired of life than I think you are. I know you."

"I'm afraid you do," agreed Amory reluctantly. "It just seemed an easy way out of everything—when I think of another useless, draggy year."

"Yes, I know; but to tell you the truth, I'm not worried about you; you seem to me to be progressing perfectly naturally."

"No," Amory objected. "I've lost half my personality in a year."

"Not a bit of it!" scoffed Monsignor. "You've lost a great amount of vanity and that's all."

"Lordy! I feel, anyway, as if I'd gone through another fifth form at St. Regis's."

"No." Monsignor shook his head. "That was a misfortune; this has been a good thing. Whatever worth while comes to you, won't be through the channels you were searching last year."

"What could be more unprofitable than my present lack of pep?"

"Perhaps in itself . . . but you're developing. This has given you time to think and you're casting off a lot of your old luggage about success and the superman and all. People like us can't adopt whole theories, as you did. If we can do the next thing, and have an hour a day to think in, we can accomplish marvels, but as far as any high-handed scheme of blind dominance is concerned—we'd just make asses of ourselves."

"But, Monsignor, I can't do the next thing."

"Amory, between you and me, I have only just learned to do it myself. I can do the one hundred things beyond the next thing, but I stub my toe on that, just as you stubbed your toe on mathematics this fall."

"Why do we have to do the next thing? It never seems the sort of thing I should do."

"We have to do it because we're not personalities, but personages."

"That's a good line—what do you mean?"

"A personality is what you thought you were, what this Kerry and Sloane you tell me of evidently are. Personality is a physical matter almost entirely; it lowers the people it acts on—I've seen it vanish in a long sickness. But while a personality is active, it overrides 'the next thing.' Now a personage, on the other hand, gathers. He is never thought of apart from what he's done. He's a bar on which a thousand things have been hung—glittering things sometimes, as ours are; but he uses those things with a cold mentality back of them."

"And several of my most glittering possessions had fallen off when I needed them." Amory continued the metaphor eagerly.

"Yes, that's it; when you feel that your garnered prestige and talents and all that are hung out, you need never bother about anybody; you can cope with them without difficulty."

"But, on the other hand, if I haven't my possessions, I'm helpless!"

"Absolutely."

"That's certainly an idea."

"Now you've a clean start—a start Kerry or Sloane can constitutionally never have. You brushed three or four ornaments down, and, in a fit of pique, knocked off the rest of them. The thing now is to collect some new ones, and the farther you look ahead in the collecting the better. But remember, do the next thing!"

"How clear you can make things!"

So they talked, often about themselves, sometimes of philosophy and religion, and life as respectively a game or a mystery. The priest seemed to guess Amory's thoughts before they were clear in his own head, so closely related were their minds in form and groove.

"Why do I make lists?" Amory asked him one night. "Lists of all sorts of things?"

"Because you're a mediævalist," Monsignor answered. "We both are. It's the passion for classifying and finding a type."

"It's a desire to get something definite."

"It's the nucleus of scholastic philosophy."

"I was beginning to think I was growing eccentric till I came up here. It was a pose, I guess."

"Don't worry about that; for you not posing may be the biggest pose of all. Pose——"

"Yes?"

"But do the next thing."

After Amory returned to college he received several letters from Monsignor which gave him more egotistic food for consumption.

I am afraid that I gave you too much assurance of your inevitable safety, and you must remember that I did that through faith in your springs of effort; not in the silly conviction that you will arrive without struggle. Some nuances of character you will have to take for granted in yourself, though you must be careful in confessing them to others. You are unsentimental, almost incapable of affection, astute without being cunning and vain without being proud.

Don't let yourself feel worthless; often through life you will really be at your worst when you seem to think best of yourself; and don't worry about losing your "personality," as you persist in calling it; at fifteen you had the radiance of early morning, at twenty you will begin to have the melancholy brilliance of the moon, and when you are my age you will give out, as I do, the genial golden warmth of 4 P. M.

If you write me letters, please let them be natural ones. Your last, that dissertation on architecture, was perfectly awful—so "highbrow" that I picture you living in an intellectual and emotional vacuum; and beware of trying to classify people too definitely into types; you will find that all through their youth they will persist annoyingly in jumping from class to class, and by pasting a supercilious label on every one you meet you are merely packing a Jack-in-the-box that will spring up and leer at you when you begin to come into really antagonistic contact with the world. An idealization of some such a man as Leonardo da Vinci would be a more valuable beacon to you at present.

You are bound to go up and down, just as I did in my youth, but do keep your clarity of mind, and if fools or sages dare to criticise don't blame yourself too much.

You say that convention is all that really keeps you straight in this "woman proposition"; but it's more than that, Amory; it's the fear that what you begin you can't stop; you would run amuck, and I know whereof I speak; it's that half-miraculous sixth sense by which you detect evil, it's the half-realized fear of God in your heart.

Whatever your metier proves to be—religion, architecture, literature—I'm sure you would be much safer anchored to the Church, but I won't risk my influence by arguing with you even though I am secretly sure that the "black chasm of Romanism" yawns beneath you. Do write me soon.

With affectionate regards,

THAYER DARCY.

Even Amory's reading paled during this period; he delved further into the misty side streets of literature: Huysmans, Walter Pater, Theophile Gautier, and the racier sections of Rabelais, Boccaccio, Petronius, and Suetonius. One week, through general curiosity, he inspected the private libraries of his classmates and found Sloane's as typical as any: sets of Kipling, O. Henry, John Fox, Jr.,* and Richard Harding Davis; "What Every Middle-Aged Woman Ought to Know," "The Spell of the Yukon";* a "gift" copy of James Whitcomb Riley, an assortment of battered, annotated school-books, and, finally, to his surprise, one of his own late discoveries, the collected poems of Rupert Brooke.

Together with Tom D'Invilliers, he sought among the lights of Princeton for some one who might found the Great American Poetic Tradition.

The undergraduate body itself was rather more interesting that year than had been the entirely Philistine Princeton of two years before. Things had livened surprisingly, though at the sacrifice of much of the spontaneous charm of freshman year. In the old Princeton they would never have discovered Tanaduke Wylie. Tanaduke was a sophomore, with tremendous ears and a way of saying, "The earth swirls down through the ominous moons of pre-considered generations!" that made them vaguely wonder why it did not sound quite clear, but never question that it was the utterance of a supersoul. At least so Tom and Amory took him. They told him in all earnestness that he had a mind like Shelley's, and featured his ultrafree free verse and prose poetry in the *Nassau Literary Magazine*. But Tanaduke's genius absorbed the many colors of the age, and he took to the Bohemian life, to their great disappointment. He talked of Greenwich Village now instead of "noon-swirled moons," and met winter muses, unacademic, and cloistered by Forty-second Street and Broadway, instead of the Shelleyan dream-children with whom he had regaled their expectant appreciation. So they surrendered

Tanaduke to the futurists, deciding that he and his flaming ties would do better there. Tom gave him the final advice that he should stop writing for two years and read the complete works of Alexander Pope four times, but on Amory's suggestion that Pope for Tanaduke was like foot-ease for stomach trouble, they withdrew in laughter, and called it a coin's toss whether this genius was too big or too petty for them.

Amory rather scornfully avoided the popular professors who dispensed easy epigrams and thimblefuls of Chartreuse to groups of admirers every night. He was disappointed, too, at the air of general uncertainty on every subject that seemed linked with the pedantic temperament; his opinions took shape in a miniature satire called "In a Lecture-Room," which he persuaded Tom to print in the *Nassau Lit*.

> "Good-morning, Fool . . .
> 	Three times a week
> You hold us helpless while you speak,
> Teasing our thirsty souls with the
> Sleek 'yeas' of your philosophy . . .
> Well, here we are, your hundred sheep,
> Tune up, play on, pour forth . . . we sleep . . .
> You are a student, so they say;
> You hammered out the other day
> A syllabus, from what we know
> Of some forgotten folio;
> You'd sniffled through an era's must,
> Filling your nostrils up with dust,
> And then, arising from your knees,
> Published, in one gigantic sneeze . . .
> But here's a neighbor on my right,
> An *Eager Ass*, considered bright;
> Asker of questions. . . . How he'll stand,
> With earnest air and fidgy hand,
> After this hour, telling you
> He sat all night and burrowed through
> Your book. . . . Oh, you'll be coy and he
> Will simulate precosity,
> And pedants both, you'll smile and smirk,
> And leer, and hasten back to work. . . .
>
> 'Twas this day week, sir, you returned
> A theme of mine, from which I learned

(Through various comment on the side
Which you had scrawled) that I defied
The *highest rules of criticism*
For *cheap* and *careless* witticism. . . .
   'Are you quite sure that this could be?'
And
   'Shaw is no authority!'
But *Eager Ass*, with what he's sent,
Plays havoc with your best per cent.

Still—still I meet you here and there . . .
When Shakespeare's played you hold a chair,
And some defunct, moth-eaten star
Enchants the mental prig you are . . .
A radical comes down and shocks
The *atheistic orthodox?*—
You're representing *Common Sense*,
Mouth open, in the audience.
And, sometimes, even chapel lures
That conscious tolerance of yours,
That broad and beaming view of truth
(Including *Kant* and *General Booth**. . .)
And so from shock to shock you live,
A hollow, pale affirmative . . .

The hour's up . . . and roused from rest
One hundred children of the blest
Cheat you a word or two with feet
That down the noisy aisle-ways beat . . .
Forget on *narrow-minded earth*
The Mighty Yawn that gave you birth."

In April, Kerry Holiday left college and sailed for France to enroll in the Lafayette Escadrille. Amory's envy and admiration of this step was drowned in an experience of his own to which he never succeeded in giving an appropriate value, but which, nevertheless, haunted him for three years afterward.

The Devil

Healy's they left at twelve and taxied to Bistolary's. There were Axia Marlowe and Phœbe Column, from the Summer Garden show, Fred Sloane and Amory. The evening was so very young that they felt ridiculous with surplus energy, and burst into the café like Dionysian revellers.

"Table for four in the middle of the floor," yelled Phœbe. "Hurry, old dear, tell 'em we're here!"

"Tell 'em to play 'Admiration'!" shouted Sloane. "You two order; Phœbe and I are going to shake a wicked calf," and they sailed off in the muddled crowd. Axia and Amory, acquaintances of an hour, jostled behind a waiter to a table at a point of vantage; there they took seats and watched.

"There's Findle Margotson, from New Haven!" she cried above the uproar. "'Lo, Findle! Whoo-ee!"

"Oh, Axia!" he shouted in salutation. "C'mon over to our table."

"No!" Amory whispered.

"Can't do it, Findle; I'm with somebody else! Call me up to-morrow about one o'clock!"

Findle, a nondescript man-about-Bisty's, answered incoherently and turned back to the brilliant blonde whom he was endeavoring to steer around the room.

"There's a natural damn fool," commented Amory.

"Oh, he's all right. Here's the old jitney waiter.* If you ask me, I want a double Daiquiri."

"Make it four."

The crowd whirled and changed and shifted. They were mostly from the colleges, with a scattering of the male refuse of Broadway, and women of two types, the higher of which was the chorus girl. On the whole it was a typical crowd, and their party as typical as any. About three-fourths of the whole business was for effect and therefore harmless, ended at the door of the café, soon enough for the five-o'clock train back to Yale or Princeton; about one-fourth continued on into the dimmer hours and gathered strange dust from strange places. Their party was scheduled to be one of the harmless kind. Fred Sloane and Phœbe Column were old friends; Axia and Amory new ones. But strange things are prepared even in the dead of night, and the unusual, which lurks least in the café, home of the prosaic and inevitable, was preparing to spoil for him the waning romance of Broadway. The way it took was so inexpressibly terrible, so unbelievable, that afterward he never thought of it as experience; but it was a scene from a misty tragedy, played far behind the veil, and that it meant something definite he knew.

About one o'clock they moved to Maxim's, and two found them in Devinière's. Sloane had been drinking consecutively and was in a state of unsteady exhilaration, but Amory was quite tiresomely sober; they had run across none of those ancient, corrupt buyers of champagne who usually assisted their New York parties.

They were just through dancing and were making their way back to their chairs when Amory became aware that some one at a nearby table was looking at him. He turned and glanced casually . . . a middle-aged man dressed in a brown sack suit, it was, sitting a little apart at a table by himself and watching their party intently. At Amory's glance he smiled faintly. Amory turned to Fred, who was just sitting down.

"Who's that pale fool watching us?" he complained indignantly.

"Where?" cried Sloane. "We'll have him thrown out!" He rose to his feet and swayed back and forth, clinging to his chair. "Where is he?"

Axia and Phœbe suddenly leaned and whispered to each other across the table, and before Amory realized it they found themselves on their way to the door.

"Where now?"

"Up to the flat," suggested Phœbe. "We've got brandy and fizz—and everything's slow down here to-night."

Amory considered quickly. He hadn't been drinking, and decided that if he took no more, it would be reasonably discreet for him to trot along in the party. In fact, it would be, perhaps, the thing to do in order to keep an eye on Sloane, who was not in a state to do his own thinking. So he took Axia's arm and, piling intimately into a taxicab, they drove out over the hundreds and drew up at a tall, white-stone apartment-house. . . . Never would he forget that street. . . . It was a broad street, lined on both sides with just such tall, white-stone buildings, dotted with dark windows; they stretched along as far as the eye could see, flooded with a bright moonlight that gave them a calcium pallor. He imagined each one to have an elevator and a colored hall-boy and a key-rack; each one to be eight stories high and full of three and four room suites. He was rather glad to walk into the cheeriness of Phœbe's living-room and sink onto a sofa, while the girls went rummaging for food.

"Phœbe's great stuff," confided Sloane, sotto voce.

"I'm only going to stay half an hour," Amory said sternly. He wondered if it sounded priggish.

"Hell y' say," protested Sloane. "We're here now—don't le's rush."

"I don't like this place," Amory said sulkily, "and I don't want any food."

Phœbe reappeared with sandwiches, brandy bottle, siphon, and four glasses.

"Amory, pour 'em out," she said, "and we'll drink to Fred Sloane, who has a rare, distinguished edge."

"Yes," said Axia, coming in, "and Amory. I like Amory." She sat down beside him and laid her yellow head on his shoulder.

"I'll pour," said Sloane; "you use siphon, Phœbe."

They filled the tray with glasses.

"Ready, here she goes!"

Amory hesitated, glass in hand.

There was a minute while temptation crept over him like a warm wind, and his imagination turned to fire, and he took the glass from Phœbe's hand. That was all; for at the second that his decision came, he looked up and saw, ten yards from him, the man who had been in the café, and with his jump of astonishment the glass fell from his uplifted hand. There the man half sat, half leaned against a pile of pillows on the corner divan. His face was cast in the same yellow wax as in the café, neither the dull, pasty color of a dead man—rather a sort of virile pallor—nor unhealthy, you'd have called it; but like a strong man who'd worked in a mine or done night shifts in a damp climate. Amory looked him over carefully and later he could have drawn him after a fashion, down to the merest details. His mouth was the kind that is called frank, and he had steady gray eyes that moved slowly from one to the other of their group, with just the shade of a questioning expression. Amory noticed his hands; they weren't fine at all, but they had versatility and a tenuous strength . . . they were nervous hands that sat lightly along the cushions and moved constantly with little jerky openings and closings. Then, suddenly, Amory perceived the feet, and with a rush of blood to the head he realized he was afraid. The feet were all wrong . . . with a sort of wrongness that he felt rather than knew. . . . It was like weakness in a good woman, or blood on satin; one of those terrible incongruities that shake little things in the back of the brain. He wore no shoes, but, instead, a sort of half moccasin, pointed, though, like the shoes they wore in the fourteenth century, and with the little ends curling up.

They were a darkish brown and his toes seemed to fill them to the end. . . . They were unutterably terrible. . . .

He must have said something, or looked something, for Axia's voice came out of the void with a strange goodness.

"Well, look at Amory! Poor old Amory's sick—old head going 'round?"

"Look at that man!" cried Amory, pointing toward the corner divan.

"You mean that purple zebra!" shrieked Axia facetiously. "Ooo-ee! Amory's got a purple zebra watching him!"

Sloane laughed vacantly.

"Ole zebra gotcha, Amory?"

There was a silence. . . . The man regarded Amory quizzically. . . . Then the human voices fell faintly on his ear:

"Thought you weren't drinking," remarked Axia sardonically, but her voice was good to hear; the whole divan that held the man was alive; alive like heat waves over asphalt, like wriggling worms. . . .

"Come back! Come back!" Axia's arm fell on his. "Amory, dear, you aren't going, Amory!" He was half-way to the door.

"Come on, Amory, stick 'th us!"

"Sick, are you?"

"Sit down a second!"

"Take some water."

"Take a little brandy. . . ."

The elevator was close, and the colored boy was half asleep, paled to a livid bronze . . . Axia's beseeching voice floated down the shaft. Those feet . . . those feet . . .

As they settled to the lower floor the feet came into view in the sickly electric light of the paved hall.

In the Alley

Down the long street came the moon, and Amory turned his back on it and walked. Ten, fifteen steps away sounded the footsteps. They were like a slow dripping, with just the slightest insistence in their fall. Amory's shadow lay, perhaps, ten feet ahead of him, and soft shoes was presumably that far behind. With the instinct of a child Amory edged in under the blue darkness of the white buildings, cleaving the moonlight for haggard seconds, once bursting into a slow run with clumsy stumblings. After that he stopped suddenly; he must keep hold, he thought. His lips were dry and he licked them.

If he met any one good—were there any good people left in the world or did they all live in white apartment-houses now? Was every one followed in the moonlight? But if he met some one good who'd know what he meant and hear this damned scuffle . . . then the scuffling grew suddenly nearer, and a black cloud settled over the moon. When again the pale sheen skimmed the cornices, it was almost beside him, and Amory thought he heard a quiet breathing. Suddenly he realized that the footsteps were not behind, had never been behind, they were ahead and he was not eluding but following . . . following. He began to run, blindly, his heart knocking heavily, his hands clinched. Far ahead a black dot showed itself, resolved slowly into a human shape. But Amory was beyond that now; he turned off the street and darted into an alley, narrow and dark and smelling of old rottenness. He twisted down a long, sinuous blackness, where the moonlight was shut away except for tiny glints and patches . . . then suddenly sank panting into a corner by a fence, exhausted. The steps ahead stopped, and he could hear them shift slightly with a continuous motion, like waves around a dock.

He put his face in his hands and covered eyes and ears as well as he could. During all this time it never occurred to him that he was delirious or drunk. He had a sense of reality such as material things could never give him. His intellectual content seemed to submit passively to it, and it fitted like a glove everything that had ever preceded it in his life. It did not muddle him. It was like a problem whose answer he knew on paper, yet whose solution he was unable to grasp. He was far beyond horror. He had sunk through the thin surface of that, now moved in a region where the feet and the fear of white walls were real, living things, things he must accept. Only far inside his soul a little fire leaped and cried that something was pulling him down, trying to get him inside a door and slam it behind him. After that door was slammed there would be only footfalls and white buildings in the moonlight, and perhaps he would be one of the footfalls.

During the five or ten minutes he waited in the shadow of the fence, there was somehow this fire . . . that was as near as he could name it afterward. He remembered calling aloud:

"I want some one stupid. Oh, send some one stupid!" This to the black fence opposite him, in whose shadows the footsteps shuffled . . . shuffled.

He supposed "stupid" and "good" had become somehow intermingled through previous association. When he called thus it was not an act of will at all—will had turned him away from the moving figure in the street; it was almost instinct that called, just the pile on pile of inherent tradition or some wild prayer from way over the night. Then something clanged like a low gong struck at a distance, and before his eyes a face flashed over the two feet, a face pale and distorted with a sort of infinite evil that twisted it like flame in the wind; *but he knew, for the half instant that the gong tanged and hummed, that it was the face of Dick Humbird.*

Minutes later he sprang to his feet, realizing dimly that there was no more sound, and that he was alone in the graying alley. It was cold, and he started on a steady run for the light that showed the street at the other end.

At the Window

It was late morning when he woke and found the telephone beside his bed in the hotel tolling frantically, and remembered that he had left word to be called at eleven. Sloane was snoring heavily, his clothes in a pile by his bed. They dressed and ate breakfast in silence, and then sauntered out to get some air. Amory's mind was working slowly, trying to assimilate what had happened and separate from the chaotic imagery that stacked his memory the bare shreds of truth. If the morning had been cold and gray he could have grasped the reins of the past in an instant, but it was one of those days that New York gets sometimes in May, when the air on Fifth Avenue is a soft, light wine. How much or how little Sloane remembered Amory did not care to know; he apparently had none of the nervous tension that was gripping Amory and forcing his mind back and forth like a shrieking saw.

Then Broadway broke upon them, and with the babel of noise and the painted faces a sudden sickness rushed over Amory.

"For God's sake, let's go back! Let's get off of this—this place!"

Sloane looked at him in amazement.

"What do you mean?"

"This street, it's ghastly! Come on! let's get back to the Avenue!"

"Do you mean to say," said Sloane stolidly, "that 'cause you had some sort of indigestion that made you act like a maniac last night, you're never coming on Broadway again?"

Simultaneously Amory classed him with the crowd, and he seemed no longer Sloane of the debonair humor and the happy personality, but only one of the evil faces that whirled along the turbid stream.

"Man!" he shouted so loud that the people on the corner turned and followed them with their eyes, "it's filthy, and if you can't see it, you're filthy, too!"

"I can't help it," said Sloane doggedly. "What's the matter with you? Old remorse getting you? You'd be in a fine state if you'd gone through with our little party."

"I'm going, Fred," said Amory slowly. His knees were shaking under him, and he knew that if he stayed another minute on this street he would keel over where he stood. "I'll be at the Vanderbilt for lunch." And he strode rapidly off and turned over to Fifth Avenue. Back at the hotel he felt better, but as he walked into the barber-shop, intending to get a head massage, the smell of the powders and tonics brought back Axia's sidelong, suggestive smile, and he left hurriedly. In the doorway of his room a sudden blackness flowed around him like a divided river.

When he came to himself he knew that several hours had passed. He pitched onto the bed and rolled over on his face with a deadly fear that he was going mad. He wanted people, people, some one sane and stupid and good. He lay for he knew not how long without moving. He could feel the little hot veins on his forehead standing out, and his terror had hardened on him like plaster. He felt he was passing up again through the thin crust of horror, and now only could he distinguish the shadowy twilight he was leaving. He must have fallen asleep again, for when he next recollected himself he had paid the hotel bill and was stepping into a taxi at the door. It was raining torrents.

On the train for Princeton he saw no one he knew, only a crowd of fagged-looking Philadelphians. The presence of a painted woman across the aisle filled him with a fresh burst of sickness and he changed to another car, tried to concentrate on an article in a popular magazine. He found himself reading the same paragraphs over and over, so he abandoned this attempt and leaning over wearily pressed his hot forehead against the damp window-pane. The car, a smoker, was hot and stuffy with most of the smells of the state's alien population; he opened a window and shivered against the cloud of fog that drifted in over him. The two hours' ride was like days, and he nearly cried aloud with joy when the towers of Princeton loomed up beside him and the yellow squares of light filtered through the blue rain.

Tom was standing in the centre of the room, pensively relighting a cigar-stub. Amory fancied he looked rather relieved on seeing him.

"Had a hell of a dream about you last night," came in the cracked voice through the cigar smoke. "I had an idea you were in some trouble."

"Don't tell me about it!" Amory almost shrieked. "Don't say a word; I'm tired and pepped out."

Tom looked at him queerly and then sank into a chair and opened his Italian note-book. Amory threw his coat and hat on the floor, loosened his collar, and took a Wells novel at random from the shelf. "Wells is sane," he thought, "and if he won't do I'll read Rupert Brooke."

Half an hour passed. Outside the wind came up, and Amory started as the wet branches moved and clawed with their finger-nails at the window-pane. Tom was deep in his work, and inside the room only the occasional scratch of a match or the rustle of leather as they shifted in their chairs broke the stillness. Then like a zigzag of lightning came the change. Amory sat bolt upright, frozen cold in his chair. Tom was looking at him with his mouth drooping, eyes fixed.

"God help us!" Amory cried.

"Oh, my heavens!" shouted Tom, "look behind!" Quick as a flash Amory whirled around. He saw nothing but the dark window-pane.

"It's gone now," came Tom's voice after a second in a still terror. "Something was looking at you."

Trembling violently, Amory dropped into his chair again.

"I've got to tell you," he said. "I've had one hell of an experience. I think I've—I've seen the devil or—something like him. What face did you just see?—or no," he added quickly, "don't tell me!"

And he gave Tom the story. It was midnight when he finished, and after that, with all lights burning, two sleepy, shivering boys read to each other from "The New Machiavelli,"* until dawn came up out of Witherspoon Hall, and the *Princetonian* fell against the door, and the May birds hailed the sun on last night's rain.

CHAPTER IV

NARCISSUS OFF DUTY

DURING Princeton's transition period, that is, during Amory's last two years there, while he saw it change and broaden and live up to its Gothic beauty by better means than night parades, certain individuals arrived who stirred it to its plethoric depths. Some of them had been freshmen, and wild freshmen, with Amory; some were in the class below; and it was in the beginning of his last year and around small tables at the Nassau Inn that they began questioning aloud the institutions that Amory and countless others before him had questioned so long in secret. First, and partly by accident, they struck on certain books, a definite type of biographical novel that Amory christened "quest" books. In the "quest" book the hero set off in life armed with the best weapons and avowedly intending to use them as such weapons are usually used, to push their possessors ahead as selfishly and blindly as possible, but the heroes of the "quest" books discovered that there might be a more magnificent use for them. "None Other Gods," "Sinister Street," and "The Research Magnificent"* were examples of such books; it was the latter of these three that gripped Burne Holiday and made him wonder in the beginning of senior year how much it was worth while being a diplomatic autocrat around his club on Prospect Avenue and basking in the high lights of class office. It was distinctly through the channels of aristocracy that Burne found his way. Amory, through Kerry, had had a vague drifting acquaintance with him, but not until January of senior year did their friendship commence.

"Heard the latest?" said Tom, coming in late one drizzly evening with that triumphant air he always wore after a successful conversational bout.

"No. Somebody flunked out? Or another ship sunk?"

"Worse than that. About one-third of the junior class are going to resign from their clubs."

"What!"

"Actual fact!"

"Why!"

"Spirit of reform and all that. Burne Holiday is behind it. The club presidents are holding a meeting to-night to see if they can find a joint means of combating it."

"Well, what's the idea of the thing?"

"Oh, clubs injurious to Princeton democracy; cost a lot; draw social lines, take time; the regular line you get sometimes from disappointed sophomores. Woodrow* thought they should be abolished and all that."

"But this is the real thing?"

"Absolutely. I think it'll go through."

"For Pete's sake, tell me more about it."

"Well," began Tom, "it seems that the idea developed simultaneously in several heads. I was talking to Burne a while ago, and he claims that it's a logical result if an intelligent person thinks long enough about the social system. They had a 'discussion crowd' and the point of abolishing the clubs was brought up by some one—everybody there leaped at it—it had been in each one's mind, more or less, and it just needed a spark to bring it out."

"Fine! I swear I think it'll be most entertaining. How do they feel up at Cap and Gown?"

"Wild, of course. Every one's been sitting and arguing and swearing and getting mad and getting sentimental and getting brutal. It's the same at all the clubs; I've been the rounds. They get one of the radicals in the corner and fire questions at him."

"How do the radicals stand up?"

"Oh, moderately well. Burne's a damn good talker, and so obviously sincere that you can't get anywhere with him. It's so evident that resigning from his club means so much more to him than preventing it does to us that I felt futile when I argued; finally took a position that was brilliantly neutral. In fact, I believe Burne thought for a while that he'd converted me."

"And you say almost a third of the junior class are going to resign?"

"Call it a fourth and be safe."

"Lord—who'd have thought it possible!"

There was a brisk knock at the door, and Burne himself came in.

"Hello, Amory—hello, Tom."

Amory rose.

"'Evening, Burne. Don't mind if I seem to rush; I'm going to Renwick's."

Burne turned to him quickly.

"You probably know what I want to talk to Tom about, and it isn't a bit private. I wish you'd stay."

"I'd be glad to." Amory sat down again, and as Burne perched on a table and launched into argument with Tom, he looked at this revolutionary more carefully than he ever had before. Broad-browed and strong-chinned, with a fineness in the honest gray eyes that were like Kerry's, Burne was a man who gave an immediate impression of bigness and security—stubborn, that was evident, but his stubbornness wore no stolidity, and when he had talked for five minutes Amory knew that this keen enthusiasm had in it no quality of dilettantism.

The intense power Amory felt later in Burne Holiday differed from the admiration he had had for Humbird. This time it began as purely a mental interest. With other men of whom he had thought as primarily first-class, he had been attracted first by their personalities, and in Burne he missed that immediate magnetism to which he usually swore allegiance. But that night Amory was struck by Burne's intense earnestness, a quality he was accustomed to associate only with the dread stupidity, and by the great enthusiasm that struck dead chords in his heart. Burne stood vaguely for a land Amory hoped he was drifting toward—and it was almost time that land was in sight. Tom and Amory and Alec had reached an impasse; never did they seem to have new experiences in common, for Tom and Alec had been as blindly busy with their committees and boards as Amory had been blindly idling, and the things they had for dissection—college, contemporary personality and the like—they had hashed and rehashed for many a frugal conversational meal.

That night they discussed the clubs until twelve, and, in the main, they agreed with Burne. To the room-mates it did not seem such a vital subject as it had in the two years before, but the logic of Burne's objections to the social system dovetailed so completely with everything they had thought, that they questioned rather than argued, and envied the sanity that enabled this man to stand out so against all traditions.

Then Amory branched off and found that Burne was deep in other things as well. Economics had interested him and he was turning socialist. Pacifism played in the back of his mind, and he read the *Masses** and Lyof Tolstoi faithfully.

"How about religion?" Amory asked him.

"Don't know. I'm in a muddle about a lot of things—I've just discovered that I've a mind, and I'm starting to read."

"Read what?"

"Everything. I have to pick and choose, of course, but mostly things to make me think. I'm reading the four gospels now, and the 'Varieties of Religious Experience.'"*

"What chiefly started you?"

"Wells, I guess, and Tolstoi, and a man named Edward Carpenter.* I've been reading for over a year now—on a few lines, on what I consider the essential lines."

"Poetry?"

"Well, frankly, not what you call poetry, or for your reasons—you two write, of course, and look at things differently. Whitman is the man that attracts me."

"Whitman?"

"Yes; he's a definite ethical force."

"Well, I'm ashamed to say that I'm a blank on the subject of Whitman. How about you, Tom?"

Tom nodded sheepishly.

"Well," continued Burne, "you may strike a few poems that are tiresome, but I mean the mass of his work. He's tremendous—like Tolstoi. They both look things in the face, and, somehow, different as they are, stand for somewhat the same things."

"You have me stumped, Burne," Amory admitted. "I've read 'Anna Karénina' and the 'Kreutzer Sonata'* of course, but Tolstoi is mostly in the original Russian as far as I'm concerned."

"He's the greatest man in hundreds of years," cried Burne enthusiastically. "Did you ever see a picture of that shaggy old head of his?"

They talked until three, from biology to organized religion, and when Amory crept shivering into bed it was with his mind aglow with ideas and a sense of shock that some one else had discovered the path he might have followed. Burne Holiday was so evidently developing—and Amory had considered that he was doing the same. He had fallen into a deep cynicism over what had crossed his path, plotted the imperfectability of man and read Shaw and Chesterton enough to keep his mind from the edges of decadence—now suddenly all his mental processes of the last year and a half seemed stale and futile—a petty consummation of himself . . . and like a sombre background lay that incident of the spring before, that filled half his nights with a dreary terror and made him unable to pray. He was not even a Catholic, yet that was the only ghost of a code that he had, the gaudy, ritualistic, paradoxical Catholicism whose prophet was Chesterton, whose claqueurs were such reformed rakes of literature as Huysmans and Bourget,* whose American sponsor was Ralph Adams Cram,* with his adulation of thirteenth-century cathedrals—a Catholicism which Amory found convenient and ready-made, without priest or sacraments or sacrifice.

He could not sleep, so he turned on his reading-lamp and, taking down the "Kreutzer Sonata," searched it carefully for the germs of Burne's enthusiasm. Being Burne was suddenly so much realler than being clever. Yet he sighed . . . here were other possible clay feet.

He thought back through two years, of Burne as a hurried, nervous freshman, quite submerged in his brother's personality. Then he remembered an incident of sophomore year, in which Burne had been suspected of the leading rôle.

Dean Hollister had been heard by a large group arguing with a taxi-driver, who had driven him from the junction. In the course of the altercation the dean remarked that he "might as well buy the taxicab." He paid and walked off, but next morning he entered his private office to find the taxicab itself in the space usually occupied by his desk, bearing a sign which read "Property of Dean Hollister. Bought and Paid for." . . . It took two expert mechanics half a day to disassemble it into its minutest parts and remove it, which only goes to prove the rare energy of sophomore humor under efficient leadership.

Then again, that very fall, Burne had caused a sensation. A certain Phyllis Styles, an intercollegiate prom-trotter, had failed to get her yearly invitation to the Harvard-Princeton game.

Jesse Ferrenby had brought her to a smaller game a few weeks before, and had pressed Burne into service—to the ruination of the latter's misogyny.

"Are you coming to the Harvard game?" Burne had asked indiscreetly, merely to make conversation.

"If you ask me," cried Phyllis quickly.

"Of course I do," said Burne feebly. He was unversed in the arts of Phyllis, and was sure that this was merely a vapid form of kidding. Before an hour had passed he knew that he was indeed involved.

Phyllis had pinned him down and served him up, informed him the train she was arriving by, and depressed him thoroughly. Aside from loathing Phyllis, he had particularly wanted to stag that game and entertain some Harvard friends.

"She'll see," he informed a delegation who arrived in his room to josh him. "This will be the last game she ever persuades any young innocent to take her to!"

"But, Burne—why did you *invite* her if you didn't want her?"

"Burne, you *know* you're secretly mad about her—that's the *real* trouble."

"What can *you* do, Burne? What can *you* do against Phyllis?"

But Burne only shook his head and muttered threats which consisted largely of the phrase: "She'll see, she'll see!"

The blithesome Phyllis bore her twenty-five summers gayly from the train, but on the platform a ghastly sight met her eyes. There were Burne and Fred Sloane arrayed to the last dot like the lurid figures on college posters. They had bought flaring suits with huge peg-top trousers and gigantic padded shoulders. On their heads were rakish college hats, pinned up in front and sporting bright orange-and-black bands, while from their celluloid collars blossomed flaming orange ties. They wore black arm-bands with orange "P's," and carried canes flying Princeton pennants, the effect completed by socks and peeping handkerchiefs in the same color motifs. On a clanking chain they led a large, angry tom-cat, painted to represent a tiger.

A good half of the station crowd was already staring at them, torn between horrified pity and riotous mirth, and as Phyllis, with her svelte jaw dropping, approached, the pair bent over and emitted a college cheer in loud, far-carrying voices, thoughtfully adding the name "Phyllis" to the end. She was vociferously greeted and escorted enthusiastically across the campus, followed by half a hundred village urchins—to the stifled laughter of hundreds of alumni and visitors, half of whom had no idea that this was a practical joke, but thought that Burne and Fred were two varsity sports showing their girl a collegiate time.

Phyllis's feelings as she was paraded by the Harvard and Princeton stands, where sat dozens of her former devotees, can be imagined. She tried to walk a little ahead, she tried to walk a little behind—but they stayed close, that there should be no doubt whom she was with, talking in loud voices of their friends on the football team, until she could almost hear her acquaintances whispering:

"Phyllis Styles must be *awfully hard up* to have to come with *those two*."

That had been Burne, dynamically humorous, fundamentally serious. From that root had blossomed the energy that he was now trying to orient with progress. . . .

So the weeks passed and March came and the clay feet that Amory looked for failed to appear. About a hundred juniors and seniors resigned from their clubs in a final fury of righteousness, and the clubs in helplessness turned upon Burne their finest weapon: ridicule. Every one who knew him liked him—but what he stood for (and he began to stand for more all the time) came under the lash of many tongues, until a frailer man than he would have been snowed under.

"Don't you mind losing prestige?" asked Amory one night. They had taken to exchanging calls several times a week.

"Of course I don't. What's prestige, at best?"

"Some people say that you're just a rather original politician."

He roared with laughter.

"That's what Fred Sloane told me to-day. I suppose I have it coming."

One afternoon they dipped into a subject that had interested Amory for a long time—the matter of the bearing of physical attributes on a man's make-up. Burne had gone into the biology of this, and then:

"Of course health counts—a healthy man has twice the chance of being good," he said.

"I don't agree with you—I don't believe in 'muscular Christianity.'"

"I do—I believe Christ had great physical vigor."

"Oh, no," Amory protested. "He worked too hard for that. I imagine that when he died he was a broken-down man—and the great saints haven't been strong."

"Half of them have."

"Well, even granting that, I don't think health has anything to do with goodness; of course, it's valuable to a great saint to be able to stand enormous strains, but this fad of popular preachers rising on their toes in simulated virility, bellowing that calisthenics will save the world—no, Burne, I can't go that."

"Well, let's waive it—we won't get anywhere, and besides I haven't quite made up my mind about it myself. Now, here's something I *do* know—personal appearance has a lot to do with it."

"Coloring?" Amory asked eagerly.

"Yes."

"That's what Tom and I figured," Amory agreed. "We took the year-books for the last ten years and looked at the pictures of the senior council. I know you don't think much of that august body, but it does represent success here in a general way. Well, I suppose only about thirty-five per cent of every class here are blonds, are really light—yet *two-thirds* of every senior council are light. We looked at pictures of ten years of them, mind you; that means that out of every *fifteen* light-haired men in the senior class *one* is on the senior council, and of the dark-haired men it's only one in *fifty*."

"It's true," Burne agreed. "The light-haired man *is* a higher type, generally speaking. I worked the thing out with the Presidents of the United States once, and found that way over half of them were light-haired—yet think of the preponderant number of brunets in the race."

"People unconsciously admit it," said Amory. "You'll notice a blond person is *expected* to talk. If a blonde girl doesn't talk we call her a 'doll'; if a light-haired man is silent he's considered stupid. Yet the world is full of 'dark silent men' and 'languorous brunettes' who haven't a brain in their heads, but somehow are never accused of the dearth."

"And the large mouth and broad chin and rather big nose undoubtedly make the superior face."

"I'm not so sure." Amory was all for classical features.

"Oh, yes—I'll show you," and Burne pulled out of his desk a photographic collection of heavily bearded, shaggy celebrities—Tolstoi, Whitman, Carpenter, and others.

"Aren't they wonderful?"

Amory tried politely to appreciate them, and gave up laughingly.

"Burne, I think they're the ugliest-looking crowd I ever came across. They look like an old men's home."

"Oh, Amory, look at that forehead on Emerson; look at Tolstoi's eyes." His tone was reproachful.

Amory shook his head.

"No! Call them remarkable-looking or anything you want—but ugly they certainly are."

Unabashed, Burne ran his hand lovingly across the spacious fore-heads, and piling up the pictures put them back in his desk.

Walking at night was one of his favorite pursuits, and one night he persuaded Amory to accompany him.

"I hate the dark," Amory objected. "I didn't use to—except when I was particularly imaginative, but now, I really do—I'm a regular fool about it."

"That's useless, you know."

"Quite possibly."

"We'll go east," Burne suggested, "and down that string of roads through the woods."

"Doesn't sound very appealing to me," admitted Amory reluctantly, "but let's go."

They set off at a good gait, and for an hour swung along in a brisk argument until the lights of Princeton were luminous white blots behind them.

"Any person with any imagination is bound to be afraid," said Burne earnestly. "And this very walking at night is one of the things I was afraid about. I'm going to tell you why I can walk anywhere now and not be afraid."

"Go on," Amory urged eagerly. They were striding toward the woods, Burne's nervous, enthusiastic voice warming to his subject.

"I used to come out here alone at night, oh, three months ago, and I always stopped at that cross-road we just passed. There were the woods looming up ahead, just as they do now, there were dogs howl-ing and the shadows and no human sound. Of course, I peopled the woods with everything ghastly, just like you do; don't you?"

"I do," Amory admitted.

"Well, I began analyzing it—my imagination persisted in stick-ing horrors into the dark—so I stuck my imagination into the dark instead, and let it look out at me—I let it play stray dog or escaped convict or ghost, and then saw myself coming along the road. That made it all right—as it always makes everything all right to project yourself completely into another's place. I knew that if I were the dog or the convict or the ghost I wouldn't be a menace to Burne Holiday any more than he was a menace to me. Then I thought of my watch. I'd better go back and leave it and then essay the woods. No; I decided, it's better on the whole that I should lose a watch than that I should turn back—and I did go into them—not only followed the road through them, but walked into them until I wasn't frightened any more—did it until one night I sat down and dozed off in there; then I knew I was through being afraid of the dark."

"Lordy," Amory breathed. "I couldn't have done that. I'd have come out half-way, and the first time an automobile passed and made the dark thicker when its lamps disappeared, I'd have come in."

"Well," Burne said suddenly, after a few moments' silence, "we're half-way through, let's turn back."

On the return he launched into a discussion of will.

"It's the whole thing," he asserted. "It's the one dividing line between good and evil. I've never met a man who led a rotten life and didn't have a weak will."

"How about great criminals?"

"They're usually insane. If not, they're weak. There is no such thing as a strong, sane criminal."

"Burne, I disagree with you altogether; how about the superman?"

"Well?"

"He's evil, I think, yet he's strong and sane."

"I've never met him. I'll bet, though, that he's stupid or insane."

"I've met him over and over and he's neither. That's why I think you're wrong."

"I'm sure I'm not—and so I don't believe in imprisonment except for the insane."

On this point Amory could not agree. It seemed to him that life and history were rife with the strong criminal, keen, but often self-deluding; in politics and business one found him and among the old statesmen and kings and generals; but Burne never agreed and their courses began to split on that point.

Burne was drawing farther and farther away from the world about him. He resigned the vice-presidency of the senior class and took to reading and walking as almost his only pursuits. He voluntarily attended graduate lectures in philosophy and biology, and sat in all of them with a rather pathetically intent look in his eyes, as if waiting for something the lecturer would never quite come to. Sometimes Amory would see him squirm in his seat; and his face would light up; he was on fire to debate a point.

He grew more abstracted on the street and was even accused of becoming a snob, but Amory knew it was nothing of the sort, and once when Burne passed him four feet off, absolutely unseeingly, his mind a thousand miles away, Amory almost choked with the romantic joy of watching him. Burne seemed to be climbing heights where others would be forever unable to get a foothold.

"I tell you," Amory declared to Tom, "he's the first contemporary I've ever met whom I'll admit is my superior in mental capacity."

"It's a bad time to admit it—people are beginning to think he's odd."

"He's way over their heads—you know you think so yourself when you talk to him—Good Lord, Tom, you *used* to stand out against 'people.' Success has completely conventionalized you."

Tom grew rather annoyed.

"What's he trying to do—be excessively holy?"

"No! not like anybody you've ever seen. Never enters the Philadelphian Society.* He has no faith in that rot. He doesn't believe that public swimming-pools and a kind word in time will right the wrongs of the world; moreover, he takes a drink whenever he feels like it."

"He certainly is getting in wrong."

"Have you talked to him lately?"

"No."

"Then you haven't any conception of him."

The argument ended nowhere, but Amory noticed more than ever how the sentiment toward Burne had changed on the campus.

"It's odd," Amory said to Tom one night when they had grown more amicable on the subject, "that the people who violently disapprove of Burne's radicalism are distinctly the Pharisee class—I mean they're the best-educated men in college—the editors of the papers, like yourself and Ferrenby, the younger professors. . . . The illiterate athletes like Langueduc think he's getting eccentric, but they just say, 'Good old Burne has got some queer ideas in his head,' and pass on—the Pharisee class—Gee! they ridicule him unmercifully."

The next morning he met Burne hurrying along McCosh walk after a recitation.

"Whither bound, Tsar?"

"Over to the *Prince* office to see Ferrenby," he waved a copy of the morning's *Princetonian* at Amory. "He wrote this editorial."

"Going to flay him alive?"

"No—but he's got me all balled up. Either I've misjudged him or he's suddenly become the world's worst radical."

Burne hurried on, and it was several days before Amory heard an account of the ensuing conversation. Burne had come into the editor's sanctum displaying the paper cheerfully.

"Hello, Jesse."

"Hello there, Savonarola."*

"I just read your editorial."

"Good boy—didn't know you stooped that low."

"Jesse, you startled me."

"How so?"

"Aren't you afraid the faculty'll get after you if you pull this irreligious stuff?"

"What?"

"Like this morning."

"What the devil—that editorial was on the coaching system."

"Yes, but that quotation——"

Jesse sat up.

"What quotation?"

"You know: 'He who is not with me is against me.'"*

"Well—what about it?"

Jesse was puzzled but not alarmed.

"Well, you say here—let me see." Burne opened the paper and read: "'*He who is not with me is against me*, as that gentleman said who was notoriously capable of only coarse distinctions and puerile generalities.'"

"What of it?" Ferrenby began to look alarmed. "Oliver Cromwell said it, didn't he? or was it Washington, or one of the saints? Good Lord, I've forgotten."

Burne roared with laughter.

"Oh, Jesse, oh, good, kind Jesse."

"Who said it, for Pete's sake?"

"Well," said Burne, recovering his voice, "St. Matthew attributes it to Christ."

"My God!" cried Jesse, and collapsed backward into the waste-basket.

Amory Writes a Poem

The weeks tore by. Amory wandered occasionally to New York on the chance of finding a new shining green auto-bus, that its stick-of-candy glamour might penetrate his disposition. One day he ventured into a stock-company revival of a play whose name was faintly familiar. The curtain rose—he watched casually as a girl entered. A few phrases rang in his ear and touched a faint chord of memory. Where—? When—?

Then he seemed to hear a voice whispering beside him, a very soft, vibrant voice: "Oh, I'm such a poor little fool; *do* tell me when I do wrong."

The solution came in a flash and he had a quick, glad memory of Isabelle.

He found a blank space on his programme, and began to scribble rapidly:

> "Here in the figured dark I watch once more,
>   There, with the curtain, roll the years away;
>   Two years of years—there was an idle day
> Of ours, when happy endings didn't bore
> Our unfermented souls; I could adore
>   Your eager face beside me, wide-eyed, gay,
>   Smiling a repertoire while the poor play
> Reached me as a faint ripple reaches shore.
>
> Yawning and wondering an evening through,
>   I watch alone . . . and chatterings, of course,
>   Spoil the one scene which, somehow, *did* have charms;
> You wept a bit, and I grew sad for you
>   Right here! Where Mr. X defends divorce
>   And What's-Her-Name falls fainting in his arms."

Still Calm

"Ghosts are such dumb things," said Alec, "they're slow-witted. I can always outguess a ghost."

"How?" asked Tom.

"Well, it depends where. Take a bedroom, for example. If you use *any* discretion a ghost can never get you in a bedroom."

"Go on, s'pose you think there's maybe a ghost in your bedroom—what measures do you take on getting home at night?" demanded Amory, interested.

"Take a stick," answered Alec, with ponderous reverence, "one about the length of a broom-handle. Now, the first thing to do is to get the room *cleared*—to do this you rush with your eyes closed into your study and turn on the lights—next, approaching the closet,

carefully run the stick in the door three or four times. Then, if nothing happens, you can look in. *Always, always* run the stick in viciously
first—*never* look first!"

"Of course, that's the ancient Celtic school," said Tom gravely.

"Yes—but they usually pray first. Anyway, you use this method
to clear the closets and also for behind all doors——"

"And the bed," Amory suggested.

"Oh, Amory, no!" cried Alec in horror. "That isn't the way—the
bed requires different tactics—let the bed alone, as you value your
reason—if there is a ghost in the room and that's only about a third
of the time, it is *almost always* under the bed."

"Well—" Amory began.

Alec waved him into silence.

"Of *course* you never look. You stand in the middle of the floor
and before he knows what you're going to do make a sudden leap for
the bed—never walk near the bed; to a ghost your ankle is your most
vulnerable part—once in bed, you're safe; he may lie around under
the bed all night, but you're safe as daylight. If you still have doubts
pull the blanket over your head."

"All that's very interesting, Alec."

"Isn't it?" Alec beamed proudly. "All my own, too—the Sir Oliver
Lodge* of the new world."

Amory was enjoying college immensely again. The sense of going
forward in a direct, determined line had come back; youth was stirring and shaking out a few new feathers. He had even stored enough
surplus energy to sally into a new pose.

"What's the idea of all this 'distracted' stuff, Amory?" asked Alec
one day, and then as Amory pretended to be cramped over his book
in a daze: "Oh, don't try to act Burne, the mystic, to me."

Amory looked up innocently.

"What?"

"What?" mimicked Alec. "Are you trying to read yourself into a
rhapsody with—let's see the book."

He snatched it; regarded it derisively.

"Well?" said Amory a little stiffly.

"'The Life of St. Teresa,'" read Alec aloud. "Oh, my gosh!"

"Say, Alec."

"What?"

"Does it bother you?"

"Does what bother me?"

"My acting dazed and all that?"

"Why, no—of course it doesn't *bother* me."

"Well, then, don't spoil it. If I enjoy going around telling people guilelessly that I think I'm a genius, let me do it."

"You're getting a reputation for being eccentric," said Alec, laughing, "if that's what you mean."

Amory finally prevailed, and Alec agreed to accept his face value in the presence of others if he was allowed rest periods when they were alone; so Amory "ran it out" at a great rate, bringing the most eccentric characters to dinner, wild-eyed grad students, preceptors* with strange theories of God and government, to the cynical amazement of the supercilious Cottage Club.

As February became slashed by sun and moved cheerfully into March, Amory went several times to spend week-ends with Monsignor; once he took Burne, with great success, for he took equal pride and delight in displaying them to each other. Monsignor took him several times to see Thornton Hancock, and once or twice to the house of a Mrs. Lawrence, a type of Rome-haunting American whom Amory liked immediately.

Then one day came a letter from Monsignor, which appended an interesting P. S.:

"Do you know," it ran, "that your third cousin, Clara Page, widowed six months and very poor, is living in Philadelphia? I don't think you've ever met her, but I wish, as a favor to me, you'd go to see her. To my mind, she's rather a remarkable woman, and just about your age."

Amory sighed and decided to go, as a favor. . . .

Clara

She was immemorial. . . . Amory wasn't good enough for Clara, Clara of ripply golden hair, but then no man was. Her goodness was above the prosy morals of the husband-seeker, apart from the dull literature of female virtue.

Sorrow lay lightly around her, and when Amory found her in Philadelphia he thought her steely blue eyes held only happiness; a latent strength, a realism, was brought to its fullest development by the facts that she was compelled to face. She was alone in the world, with two small children, little money, and, worst of all, a host of friends.

He saw her that winter in Philadelphia entertaining a houseful of men for an evening, when he knew she had not a servant in the house except the little colored girl guarding the babies overhead. He saw one of the greatest libertines in that city, a man who was habitually drunk and notorious at home and abroad, sitting opposite her for an evening, discussing *girls' boarding-schools* with a sort of innocent excitement. What a twist Clara had to her mind! She could make fascinating and almost brilliant conversation out of the thinnest air that ever floated through a drawing-room.

The idea that the girl was poverty-stricken had appealed to Amory's sense of situation. He arrived in Philadelphia expecting to be told that 921 Ark Street was in a miserable lane of hovels. He was even disappointed when it proved to be nothing of the sort. It was an old house that had been in her husband's family for years. An elderly aunt, who objected to having it sold, had put ten years' taxes with a lawyer and pranced off to Honolulu, leaving Clara to struggle with the heating-problem as best she could. So no wild-haired woman with a hungry baby at her breast and a sad Amelia-like* look greeted him. Instead, Amory would have thought from his reception that she had not a care in the world.

A calm virility and a dreamy humor, marked contrasts to her level-headedness—into these moods she slipped sometimes as a refuge. She could do the most prosy things (though she was wise enough never to stultify herself with such "household arts" as *knitting* and *embroidery*), yet immediately afterward pick up a book and let her imagination rove as a formless cloud with the wind. Deepest of all in her personality was the golden radiance that she diffused around her. As an open fire in a dark room throws romance and pathos into the quiet faces at its edge, so she cast her lights and shadows around the rooms that held her, until she made of her prosy old uncle a man of quaint and meditative charm, metamorphosed the stray telegraph boy into a Puck-like creature of delightful originality. At first this quality of hers somehow irritated Amory. He considered his own uniqueness sufficient, and it rather embarrassed him when she tried to read new interests into him for the benefit of what other adorers were present. He felt as if a polite but insistent stage-manager were attempting to make him give a new interpretation of a part he had conned for years.

But Clara talking, Clara telling a slender tale of a hat-pin and an inebriated man and herself. . . . People tried afterward to repeat her anecdotes but for the life of them they could make them sound like nothing whatever. They gave her a sort of innocent attention and the best smiles many of them had smiled for long; there were few tears in Clara, but people smiled misty-eyed at her.

Very occasionally Amory stayed for little half-hours after the rest of the court had gone, and they would have bread and jam and tea late in the afternoon or "maple-sugar lunches," as she called them, at night.

"You *are* remarkable, aren't you!" Amory was becoming trite from where he perched in the centre of the dining-room table one six o'clock.

"Not a bit," she answered. She was searching out napkins in the sideboard. "I'm really most humdrum and commonplace. One of those people who have no interest in anything but their children."

"Tell that to somebody else," scoffed Amory. "You know you're perfectly effulgent." He asked her the one thing that he knew might embarrass her. It was the remark that the first bore made to Adam.

"Tell me about yourself." And she gave the answer that Adam must have given.

"There's nothing to tell."

But eventually Adam probably told the bore all the things he thought about at night, when the locusts sang in the sandy grass, and he must have remarked patronizingly how *different* he was from Eve, forgetting how different she was from him . . . at any rate, Clara told Amory much about herself that evening. She had had a harried life from sixteen on, and her education had stopped sharply with her leisure. Browsing in her library, Amory found a tattered gray book out of which fell a yellow sheet that he impudently opened. It was a poem that she had written at school about a gray convent wall on a gray day, and a girl with her cloak blown by the wind sitting atop of it and think-ing about the many-colored world. As a rule such sentiment bored him, but this was done with so much simplicity and atmosphere, that it brought a picture of Clara to his mind, of Clara on such a cool, gray day with her keen blue eyes staring out, trying to see her tragedies come marching over the gardens outside. He envied that poem. How he would have loved to have come along and seen her on the wall and talked nonsense or romance to her, perched above him in the air. He began to be frightfully jealous of everything about Clara: of her past, of her babies, of the men and women who flocked to drink deep of her cool kindness and rest their tired minds as at an absorbing play.

"*Nobody* seems to bore you," he objected.

"About half the world do," she admitted, "but I think that's a pretty good average, don't you?" and she turned to find something in Browning that bore on the subject. She was the only person he ever met who could look up passages and quotations to show him in the middle of the conversation, and yet not be irritating to distraction. She did it constantly, with such a serious enthusiasm that he grew fond of watching her golden hair bent over a book, brow wrinkled ever so little at hunting her sentence.

Through early March he took to going to Philadelphia for week-ends. Almost always there was some one else there and she seemed not anxious to see him alone, for many occasions presented themselves when a word from her would have given him another delicious half-hour of adoration. But he fell gradually in love and began to speculate wildly on marriage. Though this design flowed through his brain even to his lips, still he knew afterward that the desire had not been deeply rooted. Once he dreamt that it had come true and woke up in a cold panic, for in his dream she had been a silly, flaxen Clara, with the gold gone out of her hair and platitudes falling insipidly from her changeling tongue. But she was the first fine woman he ever knew and one of the few good people who ever interested him. She made her goodness such an asset. Amory had decided that most good people either dragged theirs after them as a liability, or else distorted it to artificial geniality, and of course there were the ever-present prig and Pharisee—(but Amory never included *them* as being among the saved).

St. Cecilia

"*Over her gray and velvet dress,*
    Under her molten, beaten hair,
Color of rose in mock distress
    Flushes and fades and makes her fair;
Fills the air from her to him
    With light and languor and little sighs,
Just so subtly he scarcely knows . . .
    Laughing lightning, color of rose."

"Do you like me?"

"Of course I do," said Clara seriously.

"Why?"

"Well, we have some qualities in common. Things that are spontaneous in each of us—or were originally."

"You're implying that I haven't used myself very well?"

Clara hesitated.

"Well, I can't judge. A man, of course, has to go through a lot more, and I've been sheltered."

"Oh, don't stall, please, Clara," Amory interrupted; "but do talk about me a little, won't you?"

"Surely, I'd adore to." She didn't smile.

"That's sweet of you. First answer some questions. Am I painfully conceited?"

"Well—no, you have tremendous vanity, but it'll amuse the people who notice its preponderance."

"I see."

"You're really humble at heart. You sink to the third hell of depression when you think you've been slighted. In fact, you haven't much self-respect."

"Centre of target twice, Clara. How do you do it? You never let me say a word."

"Of course not—I can never judge a man while he's talking. But I'm not through; the reason you have so little real self-confidence, even though you gravely announce to the occasional philistine that you think you're a genius, is that you've attributed all sorts of atrocious faults to yourself and are trying to live up to them. For instance, you're always saying that you are a slave to high-balls."

"But I am, potentially."

"And you say you're a weak character, that you've no will."

"Not a bit of will—I'm a slave to my emotions, to my likes, to my hatred of boredom, to most of my desires——"

"You are not!" She brought one little fist down onto the other. "You're a slave, a bound helpless slave to one thing in the world, your imagination."

"You certainly interest me. If this isn't boring you, go on."

"I notice that when you want to stay over an extra day from college you go about it in a sure way. You never decide at first while the merits of going or staying are fairly clear in your mind. You let your imagination shinny on the side of your desires for a few hours, and then you decide. Naturally your imagination, after a little freedom, thinks up a million reasons why you should stay, so your decision when it comes isn't true. It's biased."

"Yes," objected Amory, "but isn't it lack of will-power to let my imagination shinny on the wrong side?"

"My dear boy, there's your big mistake. This has nothing to do with will-power; that's a crazy, useless word, anyway; you lack judgment—the judgment to decide at once when you know your imagination will play you false, given half a chance."

"Well, I'll be darned!" exclaimed Amory in surprise, "that's the last thing I expected."

Clara didn't gloat. She changed the subject immediately. But she had started him thinking and he believed she was partly right. He felt like a factory-owner who after accusing a clerk of dishonesty finds that his own son, in the office, is changing the books once a week. His poor, mistreated will that he had been holding up to the scorn of himself and his friends, stood before him innocent, and his judgment walked off to prison with the unconfinable imp, imagination, dancing in mocking glee beside him. Clara's was the only advice he ever asked without dictating the answer himself—except, perhaps, in his talks with Monsignor Darcy.

How he loved to do any sort of thing with Clara! Shopping with her was a rare, epicurean dream. In every store where she had ever traded she was whispered about as the beautiful Mrs. Page.

"I'll bet she won't stay single long."

"Well, don't scream it out. She ain't lookin' for no advice."

"*Ain't* she beautiful!"

 (*Enter a floor-walker—silence till he moves forward, smirking.*)

"Society person, ain't she?"

"Yeah, but poor now, I guess; so they say."

"Gee! girls, *ain't* she some kid!"

And Clara beamed on all alike. Amory believed that tradespeople gave her discounts, sometimes to her knowledge and sometimes without it. He knew she dressed very well, had always the best of everything in the house, and was inevitably waited upon by the head floor-walker at the very least.

Sometimes they would go to church together on Sunday and he would walk beside her and revel in her cheeks moist from the soft water in the new air. She was very devout, always had been, and God knows what heights she attained and what strength she drew down to herself when she knelt and bent her golden hair into the stained-glass light.

"St. Cecilia," he cried aloud one day, quite involuntarily, and the people turned and peered, and the priest paused in his sermon and Clara and Amory turned to fiery red.

That was the last Sunday they had, for he spoiled it all that night. He couldn't help it.

They were walking through the March twilight where it was as warm as June, and the joy of youth filled his soul so that he felt he must speak.

"I think," he said and his voice trembled, "that if I lost faith in you I'd lose faith in God."

She looked at him with such a startled face that he asked her the matter.

"Nothing," she said slowly, "only this: five men have said that to me before, and it frightens me."

"Oh, Clara, is that your fate!"

She did not answer.

"I suppose love to you is——" he began.

She turned like a flash.

"I have never been in love."

They walked along, and he realized slowly how much she had told him . . . never in love. . . . She seemed suddenly a daughter of light alone. His entity dropped out of her plane and he longed only to touch her dress with almost the realization that Joseph must have had of Mary's eternal significance. But quite mechanically he heard himself saying:

"And I love you—any latent greatness that I've got is . . . oh, I can't talk, but Clara, if I come back in two years in a position to marry you——"

She shook her head.

"No," she said; "I'd never marry again. I've got my two children and I want myself for them. I like you—I like all clever men, you more than any—but you know me well enough to know that I'd never marry a clever man——" She broke off suddenly.

"Amory."

"What?"

"You're not in love with me. You never wanted to marry me, did you?"

"It was the twilight," he said wonderingly. "I didn't feel as though I were speaking aloud. But I love you—or adore you—or worship you——'

"There you go—running through your catalogue of emotions in five seconds."

He smiled unwillingly.

"Don't make me out such a light-weight, Clara; you *are* depressing sometimes."

"You're not a light-weight, of all things," she said intently, taking his arm and opening wide her eyes—he could see their kindliness in the fading dusk. "A light-weight is an eternal nay."

"There's so much spring in the air—there's so much lazy sweetness in your heart."

She dropped his arm.

"You're all fine now, and I feel glorious. Give me a cigarette. You've never seen me smoke, have you? Well, I do, about once a month."

And then that wonderful girl and Amory raced to the corner like two mad children gone wild with pale-blue twilight.

"I'm going to the country for to-morrow," she announced, as she stood panting, safe beyond the flare of the corner lamp-post. "These days are too magnificent to miss, though perhaps I feel them more in the city."

"Oh, Clara!" Amory said; "what a devil you could have been if the Lord had just bent your soul a little the other way!"

"Maybe," she answered; "but I think not. I'm never really wild and never have been. That little outburst was pure spring."

"And you are, too," said he.

They were walking along now.

"No—you're wrong again, how can a person of your own self-reputed brains be so constantly wrong about me? I'm the opposite of everything spring ever stood for. It's unfortunate, if I happen to look like what pleased some soppy old Greek sculptor, but I assure you that if it weren't for my face I'd be a quiet nun in the convent without"—then she broke into a run and her raised voice floated back to him as he followed—"my precious babies, which I must go back and see."

She was the only girl he ever knew with whom he could understand how another man might be preferred. Often Amory met wives whom he had known as débutantes, and looking intently at them imagined that he found something in their faces which said:

"Oh, if I could only have gotten *you!*" Oh, the enormous conceit of the man!

But that night seemed a night of stars and singing and Clara's bright soul still gleamed on the ways they had trod.

"*Golden, golden is the air*—" he chanted to the little pools of water. . . . "*Golden is the air, golden notes from golden mandolins, golden frets of golden violins, fair, oh, wearily fair. . . . Skeins from braided basket, mortals may not hold; oh, what young extravagant God, who would know or ask it? . . . who could give such gold . . .*"

Amory is Resentful

Slowly and inevitably, yet with a sudden surge at the last, while Amory talked and dreamed, war rolled swiftly up the beach and washed the sands where Princeton played. Every night the gymnasium echoed as platoon after platoon swept over the floor and shuffled out the basket-ball markings. When Amory went to Washington the next week-end he caught some of the spirit of crisis which changed to repulsion in the Pullman car coming back, for the berths across from him were occupied by stinking aliens—Greeks, he guessed, or Russians. He thought how much easier patriotism had been to a homogeneous race, how much easier it would have been to fight as the Colonies fought, or as the Confederacy fought. And he did no sleeping that night, but listened to the aliens guffaw and snore while they filled the car with the heavy scent of latest America.

In Princeton every one bantered in public and told themselves privately that their deaths at least would be heroic. The literary students read Rupert Brooke passionately; the lounge-lizards worried over whether the government would permit the English-cut uniform for officers; a few of the hopelessly lazy wrote to the obscure branches of the War Department, seeking an easy commission and a soft berth.

Then, after a week, Amory saw Burne and knew at once that argument would be futile—Burne had come out as a pacifist. The socialist magazines, a great smattering of Tolstoi, and his own intense longing for a cause that would bring out whatever strength lay in him, had finally decided him to preach peace as a subjective ideal.

"When the German army entered Belgium," he began, "if the inhabitants had gone peaceably about their business, the German army would have been disorganized in——"

"I know," Amory interrupted, "I've heard it all. But I'm not going to talk propaganda with you. There's a chance that you're right—but even so we're hundreds of years before the time when non-resistance can touch us as a reality."

"But, Amory, listen——"

"Burne, we'd just argue——"

"Very well."

"Just one thing—I don't ask you to think of your family or friends, because I know they don't count a picayune with you beside your sense of duty—but, Burne, how do you know that the magazines you read and the societies you join and these idealists you meet aren't just plain *German?*"

"Some of them are, of course."

"How do you know they aren't *all* pro-German—just a lot of weak ones—with German-Jewish names."

"That's the chance, of course," he said slowly. "How much or how little I'm taking this stand because of propaganda I've heard, I don't know; naturally I think that it's my most innermost conviction—it seems a path spread before me just now."

Amory's heart sank.

"But think of the cheapness of it—no one's really going to martyr you for being a pacifist—it's just going to throw you in with the worst——"

"I doubt it," he interrupted.

"Well, it all smells of Bohemian New York to me."

"I know what you mean, and that's why I'm not sure I'll agitate."

"You're one man, Burne—going to talk to people who won't listen—with all God's given you."

"That's what Stephen* must have thought many years ago. But he preached his sermon and they killed him. He probably thought as he was dying what a waste it all was. But you see, I've always felt that Stephen's death was the thing that occurred to Paul on the road to Damascus, and sent him to preach the word of Christ all over the world."

"Go on."

"That's all—this is my particular duty. Even if right now I'm just a pawn—just sacrificed. God! Amory—you don't think *I* like the Germans!"

"Well, I can't say anything else—I get to the end of all the logic about non-resistance, and there, like an excluded middle, stands the huge spectre of man as he is and always will be. And this spectre stands right beside the one logical necessity of Tolstoi's, and the other logical necessity of Nietzsche's—" Amory broke off suddenly. "When are you going?"

"I'm going next week."

"I'll see you, of course."

As he walked away it seemed to Amory that the look in his face bore a great resemblance to that in Kerry's when he had said good-bye under Blair Arch two years before. Amory wondered unhappily why he could never go into anything with the primal honesty of those two.

"Burne's a fanatic," he said to Tom, "and he's dead wrong and, I'm inclined to think, just an unconscious pawn in the hands of anarchistic publishers and German-paid rag wavers—but he haunts me—just leaving everything worth while——"

Burne left in a quietly dramatic manner a week later. He sold all his possessions and came down to the room to say good-bye, with a battered old bicycle, on which he intended to ride to his home in Pennsylvania.

"Peter the Hermit* bidding farewell to Cardinal Richelieu," suggested Alec, who was lounging in the window-seat as Burne and Amory shook hands.

But Amory was not in a mood for that, and as he saw Burne's long legs propel his ridiculous bicycle out of sight beyond Alexander Hall, he knew he was going to have a bad week. Not that he doubted the war—Germany stood for everything repugnant to him; for materialism and the direction of tremendous licentious force; it was just that Burne's face stayed in his memory and he was sick of the hysteria he was beginning to hear.

"What on earth is the use of suddenly running down Goethe," he declared to Alec and Tom. "Why write books to prove he started the war—or that that stupid, overestimated Schiller is a demon in disguise?"

"Have you ever read anything of theirs?" asked Tom shrewdly.

"No," Amory admitted.

"Neither have I," he said laughing.

"People will shout," said Alec quietly, "but Goethe's on his same old shelf in the library—to bore any one that wants to read him!"

Amory subsided, and the subject dropped.

"What are you going to do, Amory?"

"Infantry or aviation, I can't make up my mind—I hate mechanics, but then of course aviation's the thing for me——"

"I feel as Amory does," said Tom. "Infantry or aviation—aviation sounds like the romantic side of the war, of course—like cavalry used to be, you know; but like Amory I don't know a horse-power from a piston-rod."

Somehow Amory's dissatisfaction with his lack of enthusiasm culminated in an attempt to put the blame for the whole war on the ancestors of his generation . . . all the people who cheered for Germany in 1870.* . . . All the materialists rampant, all the idolizers of German science and efficiency. So he sat one day in an English lecture and heard "Locksley Hall" quoted and fell into a brown study with contempt for Tennyson and all he stood for—for he took him as a representative of the Victorians.

> *"Victorians, Victorians, who never learned to weep*
>   *Who sowed the bitter harvest that your children go to reap——"*

scribbled Amory in his note-book. The lecturer was saying something about Tennyson's solidity and fifty heads were bent to take notes. Amory turned over to a fresh page and began scrawling again.

> *"They shuddered when they found what Mr. Darwin was about,*
>   *They shuddered when the waltz came in and Newman hurried out——"*

But the waltz came in much earlier; he crossed that out.

"And entitled 'A Song in Time of Order'," came the professor's voice, droning far away. "Time of Order"—Good Lord! Everything crammed in the box and the Victorians sitting on the lid smiling serenely. . . . With Browning in his Italian villa crying bravely: "All's for the best." Amory scribbled again.

> *"You knelt up in the temple and he bent to hear you pray,*
>   *You thanked him for your 'glorious gains'—reproached him for 'Cathay.'"*

Why could he never get more than a couplet at a time? Now he needed something to rhyme with:

"You would keep Him straight with science, tho He had gone wrong before . . ."

Well, anyway. . . .

"You met your children in your home—'I've fixed it up!' you cried,
Took your fifty years of Europe, and then virtuously—died."

"That was to a great extent Tennyson's idea," came the lecturer's voice. "Swinburne's 'Song in Time of Order' might well have been Tennyson's title. He idealized order against chaos, against waste."

At last Amory had it. He turned over another page and scrawled vigorously for the twenty minutes that were left of the hour. Then he walked up to the desk and deposited a page torn out of his note-book.

"Here's a poem to the Victorians, sir," he said coldly.

The professor picked it up curiously while Amory backed rapidly through the door.

Here is what he had written:

> *"Songs in the time of order*
> *You left for us to sing,*
> *Proofs with excluded middles,*
> *Answers to life in rhyme,*
> *Keys of the prison warder*
> *And ancient bells to ring,*
> *Time was the end of riddles,*
> *We were the end of time . . .*
>
> *Here were domestic oceans*
> *And a sky that we might reach,*
> *Guns and a guarded border,*
> *Gantlets—but not to fling,*
> *Thousands of old emotions*
> *And a platitude for each,*
> *Songs in the time of order—*
> *And tongues, that we might sing."*

The End of Many Things

Early April slipped by in a haze—a haze of long evenings on the club veranda with the graphophone playing "Poor Butterfly"* inside . . . for "Poor Butterfly" had been the song of that last year. The war seemed scarcely to touch them and it might have been one of the senior springs of the past, except for the drilling every other afternoon, yet Amory realized poignantly that this was the last spring under the old régime.

"This is the great protest against the superman," said Amory.

"I suppose so," Alec agreed.

"He's absolutely irreconcilable with any Utopia. As long as he occurs, there's trouble and all the latent evil that makes a crowd list and sway when he talks."

"And of course all that he is is a gifted man without a moral sense."

"That's all. I think the worst thing to contemplate is this—it's all happened before, how soon will it happen again? Fifty years after Waterloo Napoleon was as much a hero to English school children as Wellington. How do we know our grandchildren won't idolize Von Hindenburg* the same way?"

"What brings it about?"

"Time, damn it, and the historian. If we could only learn to look on evil *as* evil, whether it's clothed in filth or monotony or magnificence."

"God! Haven't we raked the universe over the coals for four years?"

Then the night came that was to be the last. Tom and Amory, bound in the morning for different training-camps, paced the shadowy walks as usual and seemed still to see around them the faces of the men they knew.

"The grass is full of ghosts to-night."

"The whole campus is alive with them."

They paused by Little and watched the moon rise, to make silver of the slate roof of Dodd and blue the rustling trees.

"You know," whispered Tom, "what we feel now is the sense of all the gorgeous youth that has rioted through here in two hundred years."

A last burst of singing flooded up from Blair Arch—broken voices for some long parting.

"And what we leave here is more than this class; it's the whole heritage of youth. We're just one generation—we're breaking all the links that seemed to bind us here to top-booted and high-stocked generations. We've walked arm and arm with Burr and Light-Horse Harry Lee* through half these deep-blue nights."

"That's what they are," Tom tangented off, "deep blue—a bit of color would spoil them, make them exotic. Spires, against a sky that's a promise of dawn, and blue light on the slate roofs—it hurts . . . rather——"

"Good-bye, Aaron Burr," Amory called toward deserted Nassau Hall, "you and I knew strange corners of life."

His voice echoed in the stillness.

"The torches are out," whispered Tom. "Ah, Messalina,* the long shadows are building minarets on the stadium——"

For an instant the voices of freshman year surged around them and then they looked at each other with faint tears in their eyes.

"Damn!"

"Damn!"

The last light fades and drifts across the land—the low, long land, the sunny land of spires; the ghosts of evening tune again their lyres and wander singing in a plaintive band down the long corridors of trees; pale fires echo the night from tower top to tower: Oh, sleep that dreams, and dream that never tires, press from the petals of the lotus flower something of this to keep, the essence of an hour.

No more to wait the twilight of the moon in this sequestered vale of star and spire, for one eternal morning of desire passes to time and earthy afternoon. Here, Heraclitus, did you find in fire and shifting things the prophecy you hurled down the dead years; this midnight my desire will see, shadowed among the embers, furled in flame, the splendor and the sadness of the world.*

INTERLUDE

MAY, 1917–FEBRUARY, 1919

A letter dated January, 1918, written by Monsignor Darcy to Amory, who is a second lieutenant in the 171st Infantry, Port of Embarkation, Camp Mills, Long Island.

MY DEAR BOY:—

All you need tell me of yourself is that you still are; for the rest I merely search back in a restive memory, a thermometer that records only fevers, and match you with what I was at your age. But men will chatter and you and I will still shout our futilities to each other across the stage until the last silly curtain falls *plump!* upon our bobbing heads. But you are starting the spluttering magic-lantern show of life with much the same array of slides as I had, so I need to write you if only to shriek the colossal stupidity of *people*. . . .

This is the end of one thing: for better or worse you will never again be quite the Amory Blaine that I knew, never again will we meet as we have met, because your generation is growing hard, much harder than mine ever grew, nourished as they were on the stuff of the nineties.

Amory, lately I reread Æschylus and there in the divine irony of the "Agamemnon" I find the only answer to this bitter age—all the world tumbled about our ears, and the closest parallel ages back in that hopeless resignation. There are times when I think of the men out there as Roman legionaries, miles from their corrupt city, stemming back the hordes . . . hordes a little more menacing, after all, than the corrupt city . . . another blind blow at the race, furies that we passed with ovations years ago, over whose corpses we bleated triumphantly all through the Victorian era. . . .

And afterward an out-and-out materialistic world—and the Catholic Church. I wonder where you'll fit in. Of one thing I'm sure—Celtic you'll live and Celtic you'll die; so if you don't use heaven as a continual referendum for your ideas you'll find earth a continual recall to your ambitions.

Amory, I've discovered suddenly that I'm an old man. Like all old men, I've had dreams sometimes and I'm going to tell you of them. I've enjoyed imagining that you were my son, that perhaps when I was young I went into a state of coma and begat you, and when I came to, had no recollection of it . . . it's the paternal instinct, Amory—celibacy goes deeper than the flesh. . . .

Sometimes I think that the explanation of our deep resemblance is some common ancestor, and I find that the only blood that the Darcys and the O'Haras have in common is that of the O'Donahues . . . Stephen was his name, I think. . . .

When the lightning strikes one of us it strikes both: you had hardly arrived at the port of embarkation when I got my papers to start for Rome, and I am waiting every moment to be told where to take ship. Even before you get this letter I shall be on the ocean; then will come your turn. You went to war as a gentleman should, just as you went to school and college, because it was the thing to do. It's better to leave the blustering and tremulo-heroism to the middle classes; they do it so much better.

Do you remember that week-end last March when you brought Burne Holiday from Princeton to see me? What a magnificent boy he is! It gave me a frightful shock afterward when you wrote that he thought me splendid; how could he be so deceived? Splendid is the one thing that neither you nor I are. We are many other things—we're extraordinary, we're clever, we could be said, I suppose, to be brilliant. We can attract people, we can make atmosphere, we can almost lose our Celtic souls in Celtic subtleties, we can almost always have our own way; but splendid—rather not!

I am going to Rome with a wonderful dossier and letters of introduction that cover every capital in Europe, and there will be "no small stir" when I get there. How I wish you were with me! This sounds like a rather cynical paragraph, not at all the sort of thing that a middle-aged clergyman should write to a youth about to depart for the war; the only excuse is that the middle-aged clergyman is talking to himself. There are deep things in us and you know what they are as well as I do. We have great faith, though yours at present is uncrystallized; we have a terrible honesty that all our sophistry cannot destroy and, above all, a childlike simplicity that keeps us from ever being really malicious.

I have written a keen for you which follows. I am sorry your cheeks are not up to the description I have written of them, but you *will* smoke and read all night——

At any rate here it is:

A Lament for a Foster Son, and He going to the War Against the King of Foreign.

"Ochone
He is gone from me the son of my mind
    And he in his golden youth like Angus Oge
Angus of the bright birds
    And his mind strong and subtle like the mind of Cuchulin on
        Muirtheme.

Awirra sthrue
His brow is as white as the milk of the cows of Maeve
    And his cheeks like the cherries of the tree
And it bending down to Mary and she feeding the Son of God.

Aveelia Vrone
His hair is like the golden collar of the Kings at Tara
    And his eyes like the four gray seas of Erin.
And they swept with the mists of rain.

Mavrone go Gudyo
He to be in the joyful and red battle
    Amongst the chieftains and they doing great deeds of valor
His life to go from him
    It is the chords of my own soul would be loosed.

A Vich Deelish
My heart is in the heart of my son
    And my life is in his life surely
A man can be twice young
    In the life of his sons only.

Jia du Vaha Alanav
May the Son of God be above him and beneath him, before him and
    behind him
    May the King of the elements cast a mist over the eyes of the King
        of Foreign,
May the Queen of the Graces lead him by the hand the way he can go
        through the midst of his enemies and they not seeing him
    May Patrick of the Gael and Collumb of the Churches and the five
        thousand Saints of Erin be better than a shield to him
And he go into the fight.
    Och Ochone."

Amory—Amory—I feel, somehow, that this is all; one or both of us is
not going to last out this war. . . . I've been trying to tell you how much this
reincarnation of myself in you has meant in the last few years . . . curiously
alike we are . . . curiously unlike.
    Good-bye, dear boy, and God be with you.

THAYER DARCY.

Embarking at Night

Amory moved forward on the deck until he found a stool under an
electric light. He searched in his pocket for note-book and pencil and
then began to write, slowly, laboriously:

> *"We leave to-night . . .*
>   *Silent, we filled the still, deserted street,*
>   *A column of dim gray,*
>   *And ghosts rose startled at the muffled beat*
>   *Along the moonless way;*

> *The shadowy shipyards echoed to the feet*
> *That turned from night and day.*
>
> *And so we linger on the windless decks,*
>   *See on the spectre shore*
> *Shades of a thousand days, poor gray-ribbed wrecks . . .*
>   *Oh, shall we then deplore*
> *Those futile years!*
>   *See how the sea is white!*
> *The clouds have broken and the heavens burn*
>   *To hollow highways, paved with gravelled light*
> *The churning of the waves about the stern*
>   *Rises to one voluminous nocturne,*
>   *. . . We leave to-night."*

*A letter from Amory, headed "Brest, March 11th, 1919," to Lieutenant
T. P. D'Invilliers, Camp Gordon. Ga.*

DEAR BAUDELAIRE:—

We meet in Manhattan on the 30th of this very mo.; we then proceed
to take a very sporty apartment, you and I and Alec, who is at me elbow
as I write. I don't know what I'm going to do but I have a vague dream of
going into politics. Why is it that the pick of the young Englishmen from
Oxford and Cambridge go into politics and in the U. S. A. we leave it to
the muckers?—raised in the ward, educated in the assembly and sent to
Congress, fat-paunched bundles of corruption, devoid of "both ideas and
ideals" as the debaters used to say. Even forty years ago we had good men
in politics, but *we*, we are brought up to pile up a million and "show what
we are made of." Sometimes I wish I'd been an Englishman; American life
is so damned dumb and stupid and healthy.

Since poor Beatrice died I'll probably have a little money, but very
darn little. I can forgive mother almost everything except the fact that in a
sudden burst of religiosity toward the end, she left half of what remained to
be spent in stained-glass windows and seminary endowments. Mr. Barton,
my lawyer, writes me that my thousands are mostly in street railways and
that the said Street R.R.s are losing money because of the five-cent fares.
Imagine a salary list that gives $350 a month to a man that can't read and
write!—yet I believe in it, even though I've seen what was once a sizable
fortune melt away between speculation, extravagance, the democratic
administration, and the income tax—modern, that's me all over, Mabel.

At any rate we'll have really knock-out rooms—you can get a job on some
fashion magazine, and Alec can go into the Zinc Company or whatever it
is that his people own—he's looking over my shoulder and he says it's a

brass company, but I don't think it matters much, do you? There's probably as much corruption in zinc-made money as brass-made money. As for the well-known Amory, he would write immortal literature if he were sure enough about anything to risk telling any one else about it. There is no more dangerous gift to posterity than a few cleverly turned platitudes.

Tom, why don't you become a Catholic? Of course to be a good one you'd have to give up those violent intrigues you used to tell me about, but you'd write better poetry if you were linked up to tall golden candlesticks and long, even chants, and even if the American priests are rather burgeois, as Beatrice used to say, still you need only go to the sporty churches, and I'll introduce you to Monsignor Darcy who really is a wonder.

Kerry's death was a blow, so was Jesse's to a certain extent. And I have a great curiosity to know what queer corner of the world has swallowed Burne. Do you suppose he's in prison under some false name? I confess that the war instead of making me orthodox, which is the correct reaction, has made me a passionate agnostic. The Catholic Church has had its wings clipped so often lately that its part was timidly negligible, and they haven't any good writers any more. I'm sick of Chesterton.

I've only discovered one soldier who passed through the much-advertised spiritual crisis, like this fellow, Donald Hankey;* and the one I knew was already studying for the ministry, so he was ripe for it. I honestly think that's all pretty much rot, though it seemed to give sentimental comfort to those at home; and may make fathers and mothers appreciate their children. This crisis-inspired religion is rather valueless and fleeting at best. I think four men have discovered Paris to one that discovered God.

But *us*—you and me and Alec—oh, we'll get a Jap butler and dress for dinner and have wine on the table and lead a contemplative, emotionless life until we decide to use machine-guns with the property owners—or throw bombs with the Bolshevik. God! Tom, I hope something happens. I'm restless as the devil and have a horror of getting fat or falling in love and growing domestic.

The place at Lake Geneva is now for rent but when I land I'm going West to see Mr. Barton and get some details. Write me care of the Blackstone, Chicago.

> S'ever, dear Boswell,
>
> SAMUEL JOHNSON.

BOOK TWO

THE EDUCATION OF A PERSONAGE

CHAPTER I

THE DÉBUTANTE

The time is February. The place is a large, dainty bedroom in the Connage house on Sixty-eighth Street, New York. A girl's room: pink walls and curtains and a pink bedspread on a cream-colored bed. Pink and cream are the motifs of the room, but the only article of furniture in full view is a luxurious dressing-table with a glass top and a three-sided mirror. On the walls there is an expensive print of "Cherry Ripe," a few polite dogs by Landseer, and the "King of the Black Isles," by Maxfield Parrish.*

Great disorder consisting of the following items: (1) seven or eight empty cardboard boxes, with tissue-paper tongues hanging panting from their mouths; (2) an assortment of street dresses mingled with their sisters of the evening, all upon the table, all evidently new; (3) a roll of tulle, which has lost its dignity and wound itself tortuously around everything in sight, and (4) upon the two small chairs, a collection of lingerie that beggars description. One would enjoy seeing the bill called forth by the finery displayed and one is possessed by a desire to see the princess for whose benefit—   Look! There's some one! Disappointment! This is only a maid hunting for something—she lifts a heap from a chair—   Not there; another heap, the dressing-table, the chiffonier drawers. She brings to light several beautiful chemises and an amazing pajama but this does not satisfy her—she goes out.

An indistinguishable mumble from the next room.

Now, we are getting warm. This is Alec's mother, Mrs. Connage, ample, dignified, rouged to the dowager point and quite worn out. Her lips move significantly as she looks for IT. Her search is less thorough than the maid's but there is a touch of fury in it, that quite makes up for its sketchiness. She stumbles on the tulle and her "damn" is quite audible. She retires, empty-handed.

More chatter outside and a girl's voice, a very spoiled voice, says: "Of all the stupid people——"

After a pause a third seeker enters, not she of the spoiled voice, but a younger edition. This is Cecelia Connage, sixteen, pretty, shrewd, and constitutionally good-humored. She is dressed for the evening in a gown the obvious simplicity of which probably bores her. She goes to the nearest pile, selects a small pink garment and holds it up appraisingly.

CECELIA. Pink?

ROSALIND. (*Outside*) Yes!

CECELIA. *Very* snappy?

ROSALIND. Yes!

CECELIA. I've got it!

(*She sees herself in the mirror of the dressing-table and commences to shimmy enthusiastically.*)

ROSALIND. (*Outside*) What are you doing—trying it on?

(CECELIA *ceases and goes out carrying the garment at the right shoulder.*

From the other door, enters ALEC CONNAGE. *He looks around quickly and in a huge voice shouts:* Mama! *There is a chorus of protest from next door and encouraged he starts toward it, but is repelled by another chorus.*)

ALEC. So *that's* where you all are! Amory Blaine is here.

CECELIA. (*Quickly*) Take him down-stairs.

ALEC. Oh, he *is* down-stairs.

MRS. CONNAGE. Well, you can show him where his room is. Tell him I'm sorry that I can't meet him now.

ALEC. He's heard a lot about you all. I wish you'd hurry. Father's telling him all about the war and he's restless. He's sort of temperamental.

(*This last suffices to draw* CECELIA *into the room.*)

CECELIA. (*Seating herself high upon lingerie*) How do you mean—temperamental? You used to say that about him in letters.

ALEC. Oh, he writes stuff.

CECELIA. Does he play the piano?

ALEC. Don't think so.

CECELIA. (*Speculatively*) Drink?

ALEC. Yes—nothing queer about him.

CECELIA. Money?

ALEC. Good Lord—ask him, he used to have a lot, and he's got some income now.

(MRS. CONNAGE *appears.*)

MRS. CONNAGE. Alec, of course we're glad to have any friend of yours——

ALEC. You certainly ought to meet Amory.

MRS. CONNAGE. Of course, I want to. But I think it's so childish of you to leave a perfectly good home to go and live with two other boys in some impossible apartment. I hope it isn't in order that you can all drink as much as you want. (*She pauses.*) He'll be a little neglected to-night. This is Rosalind's week, you see. When a girl comes out, she needs *all* the attention.

ROSALIND. (*Outside*) Well, then, prove it by coming here and hooking me.

(MRS. CONNAGE *goes.*)

ALEC. Rosalind hasn't changed a bit.

CECELIA. (*In a lower tone*) She's awfully spoiled.

ALEC. She'll meet her match to-night.

CECELIA. Who—Mr. Amory Blaine?

(ALEC *nods.*)

CECELIA. Well, Rosalind has still to meet the man she can't outdistance. Honestly, Alec, she treats men terribly. She abuses them and cuts them and breaks dates with them and yawns in their faces—and they come back for more.

ALEC. They love it.

CECELIA. They hate it. She's a—she's a sort of vampire, I think—and she can make girls do what she wants usually—only she hates girls.

ALEC. Personality runs in our family.

CECELIA. (*Resignedly*) I guess it ran out before it got to me.

ALEC. Does Rosalind behave herself?

CECELIA. Not particularly well. Oh, she's average—smokes sometimes, drinks punch, frequently kissed—Oh, yes—common knowledge—one of the effects of the war, you know.

(*Emerges* MRS. CONNAGE.)

MRS. CONNAGE. Rosalind's almost finished so I can go down and meet your friend.

(ALEC *and his mother go out.*)

ROSALIND. (*Outside*) Oh, mother——

CECELIA. Mother's gone down.

(*And now* ROSALIND *enters.* ROSALIND *is—utterly* ROSALIND. *She is one of those girls who need never make the slightest effort to have men fall in love with them. Two types of men seldom do: dull men are usually afraid of her cleverness and intellectual men are usually afraid of her beauty. All others are hers by natural prerogative.*

If ROSALIND *could be spoiled the process would have been complete by this time, and as a matter of fact, her disposition is not all it should be; she wants what she wants when she wants it and she is prone to make every one around her pretty miserable when she doesn't get it—but in the true sense she is not spoiled. Her fresh enthusiasm, her will to grow and learn, her endless faith in the inexhaustibility of romance, her courage and fundamental honesty—these things are not spoiled.*

There are long periods when she cordially loathes her whole family. She is quite unprincipled; her philosophy is carpe diem for herself and laissez faire for others. She loves shocking stories: she has that coarse streak that usually goes with natures that are both fine and big. She wants people to like her, but if they do not it never worries her or changes her.

She is by no means a model character.

The education of all beautiful women is the knowledge of men. ROSALIND *had been disappointed in man after man as individuals, but she had great faith in man as a sex. Women she detested. They represented qualities that she felt and despised in herself—incipient meanness, conceit, cowardice, and petty dishonesty. She once told a roomful of her mother's friends that the only excuse for women was the necessity for a disturbing element among men. She danced exceptionally well, drew cleverly but hastily, and had a startling facility with words, which she used only in love-letters.*

But all criticism of ROSALIND *ends in her beauty. There was that shade of glorious yellow hair, the desire to imitate which supports the dye industry. There was the eternal kissable mouth, small, slightly sensual, and utterly disturbing. There were gray eyes and an unimpeachable skin with two spots of vanishing color. She was slender and athletic, without underdevelopment, and it was a delight to watch her move about a room, walk along a street, swing a golf club, or turn a "cart-wheel."*

A last qualification—her vivid, instant personality escaped that conscious, theatrical quality that AMORY *had found in* ISABELLE. MONSIGNOR DARCY *would have been quite up a tree whether to call her a personality or a personage. She was perhaps the delicious, inexpressible, once-in-a-century blend.*

On the night of her début she is, for all her strange, stray wisdom, quite like a happy little girl. Her mother's maid has just done her hair, but she has decided impatiently that she can do a better job herself. She is too nervous just now to stay in one place. To that

we owe her presence in this littered room. She is going to speak.
ISABELLE'S *alto tones had been like a violin, but if you could hear*
ROSALIND, *you would say her voice was musical as a waterfall.*)

ROSALIND. Honestly, there are only two costumes in the world
that I really enjoy being in— (*Combing her hair at the dressing-
table.*) One's a hoop skirt with pantaloons; the other's a one-piece
bathing-suit. I'm quite charming in both of them.

CECELIA. Glad you're coming out?

ROSALIND. Yes; aren't you?

CECELIA. (*Cynically*) You're glad so you can get married and live
on Long Island with the *fast younger married set*. You want life to be
a chain of flirtation with a man for every link.

ROSALIND. *Want* it to be one! You mean I've *found* it one.

CECELIA. Ha!

ROSALIND. Cecelia, darling, you don't know what a trial it is to
be—like me. I've got to keep my face like steel in the street to keep
men from winking at me. If I laugh hard from a front row in the
theatre, the comedian plays to me for the rest of the evening. If I
drop my voice, my eyes, my handkerchief at a dance, my partner calls
me up on the 'phone every day for a week.

CECELIA. It must be an awful strain.

ROSALIND. The unfortunate part is that the only men who interest me at all are the totally ineligible ones. Now—if I were poor I'd
go on the stage.

CECELIA. Yes, you might as well get paid for the amount of acting
you do.

ROSALIND. Sometimes when I've felt particularly radiant I've
thought, why should this be wasted on one man?

CECELIA. Often when you're particularly sulky, I've wondered why
it should all be wasted on just one family. (*Getting up.*) I think I'll go
down and meet Mr. Amory Blaine. I like temperamental men.

ROSALIND. There aren't any. Men don't know how to be really
angry or really happy—and the ones that do, go to pieces.

CECELIA. Well, I'm glad I don't have all your worries. I'm
engaged.

ROSALIND. (*With a scornful smile*) Engaged? Why, you little
lunatic! If mother heard you talking like that she'd send you off to
boarding-school, where you belong.

CECELIA. You won't tell her, though, because I know things I could tell—and you're too selfish!

ROSALIND. (*A little annoyed*) Run along, little girl! Who are you engaged to, the iceman? the man that keeps the candy-store?

CECELIA. Cheap wit—good-bye, darling, I'll see you later.

ROSALIND. Oh, be *sure* and do that—you're *such* a help.

(*Exit* CECELIA. ROSALIND *finishes her hair and rises, humming. She goes up to the mirror and starts to dance in front of it on the soft carpet. She watches not her feet, but her eyes—never casually but always intently, even when she smiles. The door suddenly opens and then slams behind* AMORY, *very cool and handsome as usual. He melts into instant confusion.*)

HE. Oh, I'm sorry. I thought——

SHE. (*Smiling radiantly*) Oh, you're Amory Blaine, aren't you?

HE. (*Regarding her closely*) And you're Rosalind?

SHE. I'm going to call you Amory—oh, come in—it's all right—mother'll be right in—(*under her breath*) unfortunately.

HE. (*Gazing around*) This is sort of a new wrinkle for me.

SHE. This is No Man's Land.

HE. This is where you—you—(*pause*)

SHE. Yes—all those things. (*She crosses to the bureau.*) See, here's my rouge—eye pencils.

HE. I didn't know you were that way.

SHE. What did you expect?

HE. I thought you'd be sort of—sort of—sexless, you know, swim and play golf.

SHE. Oh, I do—but not in business hours.

HE. Business?

SHE. Six to two—strictly.

HE. I'd like to have some stock in the corporation.

SHE. Oh, it's not a corporation—it's just "Rosalind, Unlimited." Fifty-one shares, name, good-will, and everything goes at $25,000 a year.

HE. (*Disapprovingly*) Sort of a chilly proposition.

SHE. Well, Amory, you don't mind—do you?* When I meet a man that doesn't bore me to death after two weeks, perhaps it'll be different.

HE. Odd, you have the same point of view on men that I have on women.

SHE. I'm not really feminine, you know—in my mind.

HE. (*Interested*) Go on.

SHE. No, you—you go on—you've made me talk about myself. That's against the rules.

HE. Rules?

SHE. My own rules—but you— Oh, Amory, I hear you're brilliant. The family expects *so* much of you.

HE. How encouraging!

SHE. Alec said you'd taught him to think. Did you? I didn't believe any one could.

HE. No. I'm really quite dull.

(*He evidently doesn't intend this to be taken seriously.*)

SHE. Liar.

HE. I'm—I'm religious—I'm literary. I've—I've even written poems.

SHE. Vers libre—splendid! (*She declaims.*)

> "The trees are green,
>   The birds are singing in the trees,
>   The girl sips her poison
>   The bird flies away the girl dies."

HE. (*Laughing*) No, not that kind.

SHE. (*Suddenly*) I like you.

HE. Don't.

SHE. Modest too——

HE. I'm afraid of you. I'm always afraid of a girl—until I've kissed her.

SHE. (*Emphatically*) My dear boy, the war is over.

HE. So I'll always be afraid of you.

SHE. (*Rather sadly*) I suppose you will.

(*A slight hesitation on both their parts.*)

HE. (*After due consideration*) Listen. This is a frightful thing to ask.

SHE. (*Knowing what's coming*) After five minutes.

IIE. But will you—kiss me? Or are you afraid?

SHE. I'm never afraid—but your reasons are so poor.

HE. Rosalind, I really *want* to kiss you.

SHE. So do I.

(*They kiss—definitely and thoroughly.*)

HE. (*After a breathless second*) Well, is your curiosity satisfied?

SHE. Is yours?

HE. No, it's only aroused.

(*He looks it.*)

SHE. (*Dreamily*) I've kissed dozens of men. I suppose I'll kiss dozens more.

HE. (*Abstractedly*) Yes, I suppose you could—like that.

SHE. Most people like the way I kiss.

HE. (*Remembering himself*) Good Lord, yes. Kiss me once more, Rosalind.

SHE. No—my curiosity is generally satisfied at one.

HE (*Discouraged*) Is that a rule?

SHE. I make rules to fit the cases.

HE. You and I are somewhat alike—except that I'm years older in experience.

SHE. How old are you?

HE. Almost twenty-three. You?

SHE. Nineteen—just.

HE. I suppose you're the product of a fashionable school.

SHE. No—I'm fairly raw material. I was expelled from Spence*—I've forgotten why.

HE. What's your general trend?

SHE. Oh, I'm bright, quite selfish, emotional when aroused, fond of admiration——

HE. (*Suddenly*) I don't want to fall in love with you——

SHE. (*Raising her eyebrows*) Nobody asked you to.

HE. (*Continuing coldly*) But I probably will. I love your mouth.

SHE. Hush! Please don't fall in love with my mouth—hair, eyes, shoulders, slippers—but *not* my mouth. Everybody falls in love with my mouth.

HE. It's quite beautiful.

SHE. It's too small.

HE. No it isn't—let's see.

(*He kisses her again with the same thoroughness.*)

SHE. (*Rather moved*) Say something sweet.

HE. (*Frightened*) Lord help me.

SHE. (*Drawing away*) Well, don't—if it's so hard.

HE. Shall we pretend? So soon?

SHE. We haven't the same standards of time as other people.

HE. Already it's—other people.

SHE. Let's pretend.

HE. No—I can't—it's sentiment.

SHE. You're not sentimental?

HE. No, I'm romantic—a sentimental person thinks things will last—a romantic person hopes against hope that they won't. Sentiment is emotional.

SHE. And you're not? (*With her eyes half-closed.*) You probably flatter yourself that that's a superior attitude.

HE. Well—Rosalind, Rosalind, don't argue—kiss me again.

SHE. (*Quite chilly now*) No—I have no desire to kiss you.

HE. (*Openly taken aback*) You wanted to kiss me a minute ago.

SHE. This is now.

HE. I'd better go.

SHE. I suppose so.

(*He goes toward the door.*)

SHE. Oh!

(*He turns.*)

SHE. (*Laughing*) Score—Home Team: One hundred—Opponents: Zero.

(*He starts back.*)

SHE. (*Quickly*) Rain—no game.

(*He goes out.*)

(*She goes quietly to the chiffonier, takes out a cigarette-case and hides it in the side drawer of a desk. Her mother enters, note-book in hand.*)

MRS. CONNAGE. Good—I've been wanting to speak to you alone before we go down-stairs.

ROSALIND. Heavens! you frighten me!

MRS. CONNAGE. Rosalind, you've been a very expensive proposition.

ROSALIND. (*Resignedly*) Yes.

MRS. CONNAGE. And you know your father hasn't what he once had.

ROSALIND. (*Making a wry face*) Oh, please don't talk about money.

MRS. CONNAGE. You can't do anything without it. This is our last year in this house—and unless things change Cecelia won't have the advantages you've had.

ROSALIND. (*Impatiently*) Well—what is it?

MRS. CONNAGE. So I ask you to please mind me in several things I've put down in my note-book. The first one is: don't disappear with young men. There may be a time when it's valuable, but at present I want you on the dance-floor where I can find you. There are certain men I want to have you meet and I don't like finding you in some corner of the conservatory exchanging silliness with any one—or listening to it.

ROSALIND. (*Sarcastically*) Yes, listening to it *is* better.

MRS. CONNAGE. And don't waste a lot of time with the college set—little boys nineteen and twenty years old. I don't mind a prom or a football game, but staying away from advantageous parties to eat in little cafés down-town with Tom, Dick, and Harry——

ROSALIND. (*Offering her code, which is, in its way, quite as high as her mother's*) Mother, it's done—you can't run everything now the way you did in the early nineties.

MRS. CONNAGE. (*Paying no attention*) There are several bachelor friends of your father's that I want you to meet to-night—youngish men.

ROSALIND. (*Nodding wisely*) About forty-five?

MRS. CONNAGE. (*Sharply*) Why not?

ROSALIND. Oh, *quite* all right—they know life and are so adorably tired looking (*shakes her head*)—but they *will* dance.

MRS. CONNAGE. I haven't met Mr. Blaine—but I don't think you'll care for him. He doesn't sound like a money-maker.

ROSALIND. Mother, I never *think* about money.

MRS. CONNAGE. You never keep it long enough to think about it.

ROSALIND. (*Sighs*) Yes, I suppose some day I'll marry a ton of it—out of sheer boredom.

MRS. CONNAGE. (*Referring to note-book*) I had a wire from Hartford. Dawson Ryder is coming up. Now there's a young man I like, and he's floating in money. It seems to me that since you seem tired of Howard Gillespie you might give Mr. Ryder some encouragement. This is the third time he's been up in a month.

ROSALIND. How did you know I was tired of Howard Gillespie?

MRS. CONNAGE. The poor boy looks so miserable every time he comes.

ROSALIND. That was one of those romantic, pre-battle affairs. They're all wrong.

MRS. CONNAGE. (*Her say said*) At any rate, make us proud of you to-night.

ROSALIND. Don't you think I'm beautiful?

MRS. CONNAGE. You know you are.

(*From down-stairs is heard the moan of a violin being tuned, the roll of a drum.* MRS. CONNAGE *turns quickly to her daughter.*)

MRS. CONNAGE. Come!

ROSALIND. One minute!

(*Her mother leaves.* ROSALIND *goes to the glass where she gazes at herself with great satisfaction. She kisses her hand and touches her mirrored mouth with it. Then she turns out the lights and leaves the room. Silence for a moment. A few chords from the piano, the discreet patter of faint drums, the rustle of new silk, all blend on the staircase outside and drift in through the partly opened door. Bundled figures pass in the lighted hall. The laughter heard below becomes doubled and multiplied. Then some one comes in, closes the door, and switches on the lights. It is* CECELIA. *She goes to the chiffonier, looks in the drawers, hesitates—then to the desk whence she takes the cigarette-case and extracts one. She lights it and then, puffing and blowing, walks toward the mirror.*)

CECELIA. (*In tremendously sophisticated accents*) Oh, yes, coming out is *such* a farce nowadays, you know. One really plays around so much before one is seventeen, that it's positively anticlimax. (*Shaking hands with a visionary middle-aged nobleman.*) Yes, your grace—I b'lieve I've heard my sister speak of you. Have a puff—they're very good. They're—they're Coronas.* You don't smoke? What a pity! The king doesn't allow it, I suppose. Yes, I'll dance.

(*So she dances around the room to a tune from down-stairs, her arms outstretched to an imaginary partner, the cigarette waving in her hand.*)

Several Hours Later

The corner of a den down-stairs, filled by a very comfortable leather lounge. A small light is on each side above, and in the middle, over the couch hangs a painting of a very old, very dignified gentleman, period 1860. Outside the music is heard in a fox-trot.

ROSALIND *is seated on the lounge and on her left is* HOWARD GILLESPIE, *a vapid youth of about twenty-four. He is obviously very unhappy, and she is quite bored.*

GILLESPIE. (*Feebly*) What do you mean I've changed. I feel the same toward you.

ROSALIND. But you don't look the same to me.

GILLESPIE. Three weeks ago you used to say that you liked me because I was so blasé, so indifferent—I still am.

ROSALIND. But not about me. I used to like you because you had brown eyes and thin legs.

GILLESPIE. (*Helplessly*) They're still thin and brown. You're a vampire, that's all.

ROSALIND. The only thing I know about vamping is what's on the piano score. What confuses men is that I'm perfectly natural. I used to think you were never jealous. Now you follow me with your eyes wherever I go.

GILLESPIE. I love you.

ROSALIND. (*Coldly*) I know it.

GILLESPIE. And you haven't kissed me for two weeks. I had an idea that after a girl was kissed she was—was—won.

ROSALIND. Those days are over. I have to be won all over again every time you see me.

GILLESPIE. Are you serious?

ROSALIND. About as usual. There used to be two kinds of kisses: First when girls were kissed and deserted; second, when they were engaged. Now there's a third kind, where the man is kissed and deserted. If Mr. Jones of the nineties bragged he'd kissed a girl, every one knew he was through with her. If Mr. Jones of 1919 brags the same every one knows it's because he can't kiss her any more. Given a decent start any girl can beat a man nowadays.

GILLESPIE. Then why do you play with men?

ROSALIND. (*Leaning forward confidentially*) For that first moment, when he's interested. There is a moment—Oh, just before the first kiss, a whispered word—something that makes it worth while.

GILLESPIE. And then?

ROSALIND. Then after that you make him talk about himself. Pretty soon he thinks of nothing but being alone with you—he sulks, he won't fight, he doesn't want to play— Victory!

(*Enter* DAWSON RYDER, *twenty-six, handsome, wealthy, faithful to his own, a bore perhaps, but steady and sure of success.*)

RYDER. I believe this is my dance, Rosalind.

ROSALIND. Well, Dawson, so you recognize me. Now I know I haven't got too much paint on. Mr. Ryder, this is Mr. Gillespie.

(*They shake hands and* GILLESPIE *leaves, tremendously downcast.*)

RYDER. Your party is certainly a success.

ROSALIND. Is it— I haven't seen it lately. I'm weary— Do you mind sitting out a minute?

RYDER. Mind—I'm delighted. You know I loathe this "rushing" idea. See a girl yesterday, to-day, to-morrow.

ROSALIND. Dawson!

RYDER. What?

ROSALIND. I wonder if you know you love me.

RYDER. (*Startled*) What— Oh—you know you're remarkable!

ROSALIND. Because you know I'm an awful proposition. Any one who marries me will have his hands full. I'm mean—mighty mean.

RYDER. Oh, I wouldn't say that.

ROSALIND. Oh, yes, I am—especially to the people nearest to me. (*She rises.*) Come, let's go. I've changed my mind and I want to dance. Mother is probably having a fit.

(*Exeunt. Enter* ALEC *and* CECELIA.)

CECELIA. Just my luck to get my own brother for an intermission.

ALEC. (*Gloomily*) I'll go if you want me to.

CECELIA. Good heavens, no—with whom would I begin the next dance? (*Sighs.*) There's no color in a dance since the French officers went back.*

ALEC. (*Thoughtfully*) I don't want Amory to fall in love with Rosalind.

CECELIA. Why, I had an idea that that was just what you did want.

ALEC. I did, but since seeing these girls—I don't know. I'm awfully attached to Amory. He's sensitive and I don't want him to break his heart over somebody who doesn't care about him.

CECELIA. He's very good looking.

ALEC. (*Still thoughtfully*) She won't marry him, but a girl doesn't have to marry a man to break his heart.

CECELIA. What does it? I wish I knew the secret.

ALEC. Why, you cold-blooded little kitty. It's lucky for some that the Lord gave you a pug nose.

(*Enter* MRS. CONNAGE.)

MRS. CONNAGE. Where on earth is Rosalind?

ALEC. (*Brilliantly*) Of course you've come to the best people to find out. She'd naturally be with us.

MRS. CONNAGE. Her father has marshalled eight bachelor millionaires to meet her.

ALEC. You might form a squad and march through the halls.

MRS. CONNAGE. I'm perfectly serious—for all I know she may be at the Cocoanut Grove* with some football player on the night of her début. You look left and I'll——

ALEC. (*Flippantly*) Hadn't you better send the butler through the cellar?

MRS. CONNAGE. (*Perfectly serious*) Oh, you don't think she'd be there?

CECELIA. He's only joking, mother.

ALEC. Mother had a picture of her tapping a keg of beer with some high hurdler.

MRS. CONNAGE. Let's look right away.

(*They go out.* ROSALIND *comes in with* GILLESPIE.)

GILLESPIE. Rosalind—   Once more I ask you. Don't you care a blessed thing about me?

(AMORY *walks in briskly.*)

AMORY. My dance.

ROSALIND. Mr. Gillespie, this is Mr. Blaine.

GILLESPIE. I've met Mr. Blaine. From Lake Geneva, aren't you?

AMORY. Yes.

GILLESPIE. (*Desperately*) I've been there. It's in the—the Middle West, isn't it?

AMORY. (*Spicily*) Approximately. But I always felt that I'd rather be provincial hot-tamale than soup without seasoning.

GILLESPIE. What!

AMORY. Oh, no offense.

(GILLESPIE *bows and leaves.*)

ROSALIND. He's too much *people*.

AMORY. I was in love with a *people* once.

ROSALIND. So?

AMORY. Oh, yes—her name was Isabelle—nothing at all to her except what I read into her.

ROSALIND. What happened?

AMORY. Finally I convinced her that she was smarter than I was—then she threw me over. Said I was critical and impractical, you know.

ROSALIND. What do you mean impractical?

AMORY. Oh—drive a car, but can't change a tire.

ROSALIND. What are you going to do?

AMORY. Can't say—run for President, write——

ROSALIND. Greenwich Village?

AMORY. Good heavens, no—I said write—not drink.

ROSALIND. I like business men. Clever men are usually so homely.

AMORY. I feel as if I'd known you for ages.

ROSALIND. Oh, are you going to commence the "pyramid" story?

AMORY. No—I was going to make it French. I was Louis XIV and you were one of my—my— (*Changing his tone.*) Suppose—we fell in love.

ROSALIND. I've suggested pretending.

AMORY. If we did it would be very big.

ROSALIND. Why?

AMORY. Because selfish people are in a way terribly capable of great loves.

ROSALIND. (*Turning her lips up*) Pretend.

  (*Very deliberately they kiss.*)

AMORY. I can't say sweet things. But you *are* beautiful.

ROSALIND. Not that.

AMORY. What then?

ROSALIND. (*Sadly*) Oh, nothing—only I want sentiment, real sentiment—and I never find it.

AMORY. I never find anything else in the world—and I loathe it.

ROSALIND. It's so hard to find a male to gratify one's artistic taste.

  (*Some one has opened a door and the music of a waltz surges into the room.* ROSALIND *rises.*)

ROSALIND. Listen! they're playing "Kiss Me Again."*

  (*He looks at her.*)

AMORY. Well?

ROSALIND. Well?

AMORY. (*Softly —the battle lost*) I love you.

ROSALIND. I love you—now.

  (*They kiss.*)

AMORY. Oh, God, what have I done?

ROSALIND. Nothing. Oh, don't talk. Kiss me again.

AMORY. I don't know why or how, but I love you—from the moment I saw you.

ROSALIND. Me too—I—I—oh, to-night's to-night.

(*Her brother strolls in, starts and then in a loud voice says:* "Oh, excuse me," *and goes.*)

ROSALIND. (*Her lips scarcely stirring*) Don't let me go—I don't care who knows what I do.

AMORY. Say it!

ROSALIND. I love you—now. (*They part.*) Oh—I am very youthful, thank God—and rather beautiful, thank God—and happy, thank God, thank God—(*She pauses and then, in an odd burst of prophecy, adds*) Poor Amory!

(*He kisses her again.*)

Kismet

Within two weeks Amory and Rosalind were deeply and passionately in love. The critical qualities which had spoiled for each of them a dozen romances were dulled by the great wave of emotion that washed over them.

"It may be an insane love-affair," she told her anxious mother, "but it's not inane."

The wave swept Amory into an advertising agency early in March, where he alternated between astonishing bursts of rather exceptional work and wild dreams of becoming suddenly rich and touring Italy with Rosalind.

They were together constantly, for lunch, for dinner, and nearly every evening—always in a sort of breathless hush, as if they feared that any minute the spell would break and drop them out of this paradise of rose and flame. But the spell became a trance, seemed to increase from day to day; they began to talk of marrying in July—in June. All life was transmitted into terms of their love, all experience, all desires, all ambitions, were nullified—their senses of humor crawled into corners to sleep; their former love-affairs seemed faintly laughable and scarcely regretted juvenilia.

For the second time in his life Amory had had a complete bouleversement and was hurrying into line with his generation.

A Little Interlude

Amory wandered slowly up the avenue and thought of the night as inevitably his—the pageantry and carnival of rich dusk and dim streets . . . it seemed that he had closed the book of fading harmonies at last and stepped into the sensuous vibrant walks of life. Everywhere these countless lights, this promise of a night of streets and singing—he moved in a half-dream through the crowd as if expecting to meet Rosalind hurrying toward him with eager feet from every corner. . . . How the unforgetable faces of dusk would blend to her, the myriad footsteps, a thousand overtures, would blend to her footsteps; and there would be more drunkenness than wine in the softness of her eyes on his. Even his dreams now were faint violins drifting like summer sounds upon the summer air.

The room was in darkness except for the faint glow of Tom's cigarette where he lounged by the open window. As the door shut behind him, Amory stood a moment with his back against it.

"Hello, Benvenuto Blaine.* How went the advertising business to-day?"

Amory sprawled on a couch.

"I loathed it as usual!" The momentary vision of the bustling agency was displaced quickly by another picture.

"My God! She's wonderful!"

Tom sighed.

"I can't tell you," repeated Amory, "just how wonderful she is. I don't want you to know. I don't want any one to know."

Another sigh came from the window—quite a resigned sigh.

"She's life and hope and happiness, my whole world now."

He felt the quiver of a tear on his eyelid.

"Oh, *Golly*, Tom!"

Bitter Sweet

"Sit like we do," she whispered.

He sat in the big chair and held out his arms so that she could nestle inside them.

"I knew you'd come to-night," she said softly, "like summer, just when I needed you most . . . darling . . . darling . . ."

His lips moved lazily over her face.

"You *taste* so good," he sighed.

"How do you mean, lover?"

"Oh, just sweet, just sweet . . ." he held her closer.

"Amory," she whispered, "when you're ready for me I'll marry you."

"We won't have much at first."

"Don't!" she cried. "It hurts when you reproach yourself for what you can't give me. I've got your precious self—and that's enough for me."

"Tell me . . ."

"You know, don't you? Oh, you know."

"Yes, but I want to hear you say it."

"I love you, Amory, with all my heart."

"Always, will you?"

"All my life—　Oh, Amory——"

"What?"

"I want to belong to you. I want your people to be my people. I want to have your babies."

"But I haven't any people."

"Don't laugh at me, Amory. Just kiss me."

"I'll do what you want," he said.

"No, I'll do what *you* want. We're *you*—not me. Oh, you're so much a part, so much all of me . . ."

He closed his eyes.

"I'm so happy that I'm frightened. Wouldn't it be awful if this was—was the high point? . . ."

She looked at him dreamily.

"Beauty and love pass, I know. . . . Oh, there's sadness, too. I suppose all great happiness is a little sad. Beauty means the scent of roses and then the death of roses——"

"Beauty means the agony of sacrifice and the end of agony. . . ."

"And, Amory, we're beautiful, I know. I'm sure God loves us——"

"He loves you. You're his most precious possession."

"I'm not his, I'm yours. Amory, I belong to you. For the first time I regret all the other kisses; now I know how much a kiss can mean."

Then they would smoke and he would tell her about his day at the office—and where they might live. Sometimes, when he was particularly loquacious, she went to sleep in his arms, but he loved that Rosalind—all Rosalinds as he had never in the world loved any one else. Intangibly fleeting, unrememberable hours.

Aquatic Incident

One day Amory and Howard Gillespie meeting by accident downtown took lunch together, and Amory heard a story that delighted him.

Gillespie after several cocktails was in a talkative mood; he began by telling Amory that he was sure Rosalind was slightly eccentric.

He had gone with her on a swimming party up in Westchester County, and some one mentioned that Annette Kellerman* had been there one day on a visit and had dived from the top of a rickety, thirty-foot summer-house. Immediately Rosalind insisted that Howard should climb up with her to see what it looked like.

A minute later, as he sat and dangled his feet on the edge, a form shot by him; Rosalind, her arms spread in a beautiful swan dive, had sailed through the air into the clear water.

"Of course *I* had to go, after that—and I nearly killed myself. I thought I was pretty good to even try it. Nobody else in the party tried it. Well, afterward Rosalind had the nerve to ask me why I stooped over when I dove. 'It didn't make it any easier,' she said, 'it just took all the courage out of it.' I ask you, what can a man do with a girl like that? Unnecessary, I call it."

Gillespie failed to understand why Amory was smiling delightedly all through lunch. He thought perhaps he was one of these hollow optimists.

Five Weeks Later

Again the library of the Connage house. ROSALIND *is alone, sitting on the lounge staring very moodily and unhappily at nothing. She has changed perceptibly—she is a trifle thinner for one thing; the light in her eyes is not so bright; she looks easily a year older.*

Her mother comes in, muffled in an opera-cloak. She takes in ROSALIND *with a nervous glance.*

MRS. CONNAGE. Who is coming to-night?

(ROSALIND *fails to hear her, at least takes no notice.*)

MRS. CONNAGE. Alec is coming up to take me to this Barrie play, "Et tu, Brutus."* (*She perceives that she is talking to herself.*) Rosalind! I asked you who is coming to-night?

ROSALIND. (*Starting*) Oh—what—oh—Amory——

MRS. CONNAGE. (*Sarcastically*) You have so *many* admirers lately that I couldn't imagine *which* one. (ROSALIND *doesn't answer.*) Dawson Ryder is more patient than I thought he'd be. You haven't given him an evening this week.

ROSALIND. (*With a very weary expression that is quite new to her face.*) Mother—please——

MRS. CONNAGE. Oh, *I* won't interfere. You've already wasted over two months on a theoretical genius who hasn't a penny to his name, but *go* ahead, waste your life on him. I won't interfere.

ROSALIND. (*As if repeating a tiresome lesson*) You know he has a little income—and you know he's earning thirty-five dollars a week in advertising——

MRS. CONNAGE. And it wouldn't buy your clothes. (*She pauses but* ROSALIND *makes no reply*.) I have your best interests at heart when I tell you not to take a step you'll spend your days regretting. It's not as if your father could help you. Things have been hard for him lately and he's an old man. You'd be dependent absolutely on a dreamer, a nice, well-born boy, but a dreamer—merely clever. (*She implies that this quality in itself is rather vicious*.)

ROSALIND. For heaven's sake, mother——

(*A maid appears, announces Mr. Blaine who follows immediately.* AMORY'S *friends have been telling him for ten days that he "looks like the wrath of God," and he does. As a matter of fact he has not been able to eat a mouthful in the last thirty-six hours*.)

AMORY. Good evening, MRS. CONNAGE.

MRS. CONNAGE. (*Not unkindly*) Good evening, Amory. (AMORY *and* ROSALIND *exchange glances—and* ALEC *comes in.* ALEC'S *attitude throughout has been neutral. He believes in his heart that the marriage would make* AMORY *mediocre and* ROSALIND *miserable, but he feels a great sympathy for both of them*.)

ALEC. Hi, Amory!

AMORY. Hi, Alec! Tom said he'd meet you at the theatre.

ALEC. Yeah, just saw him. How's the advertising to-day? Write some brilliant copy?

AMORY. Oh, it's about the same. I got a raise—(*Every one looks at him rather eagerly*)—of two dollars a week. (*General collapse*.)

MRS. CONNAGE. Come, Alec, I hear the car.

(*A good night, rather chilly in sections. After* MRS. CONNAGE *and* ALEC *go out there is a pause.* ROSALIND *still stares moodily at the fireplace.* AMORY *goes to her and puts his arm around her*.)

AMORY. Darling girl.

(*They kiss. Another pause and then she seizes his hand, covers it with kisses and holds it to her breast*.)

ROSALIND. (*Sadly*) I love your hands, more than anything. I see them often when you're away from me—so tired; I know every line of them. Dear hands!

(*Their eyes meet for a second and then she begins to cry—a tearless sobbing.*)

AMORY. Rosalind!

ROSALIND. Oh, we're so darned pitiful!

AMORY. Rosalind!

ROSALIND. Oh, I want to die!

AMORY. Rosalind, another night of this and I'll go to pieces. You've been this way four days now. You've got to be more encouraging or I can't work or eat or sleep. (*He looks around helplessly as if searching for new words to clothe an old, shop-worn phrase.*) We'll have to make a start. I *like* having to make a start together. (*His forced hopefulness fades as he sees her unresponsive.*) What's the matter? (*He gets up suddenly and starts to pace the floor.*) It's Dawson Ryder, that's what it is. He's been working on your nerves. You've been with him every afternoon for a week. People come and tell me they've seen you together, and I have to smile and nod and pretend it hasn't the slightest significance for me. And you won't tell me anything as it develops.

ROSALIND. Amory, if you don't sit down I'll scream.

AMORY. (*Sitting down suddenly beside her*) Oh, Lord.

ROSALIND. (*Taking his hand gently*) You know I love you, don't you?

AMORY. Yes.

ROSALIND. You know I'll always love you——

AMORY. Don't talk that way; you frighten me. It sounds as if we weren't going to have each other. (*She cries a little and rising from the couch goes to the armchair.*) I've felt all afternoon that things were worse. I nearly went wild down at the office—couldn't write a line. Tell me everything.

ROSALIND. There's nothing to tell, I say. I'm just nervous.

AMORY. Rosalind, you're playing with the idea of marrying Dawson Ryder.

ROSALIND. (*After a pause*) He's been asking me to all day.

AMORY. Well, he's got his nerve!

ROSALIND. (*After another pause*) I like him.

AMORY. Don't say that. It hurts me.

ROSALIND. Don't be a silly idiot. You know you're the only man I've ever loved, ever will love.

AMORY. (*Quickly*) Rosalind, let's get married—next week.

ROSALIND. We can't.

AMORY. Why not?

ROSALIND. Oh, we can't. I'd be your squaw—in some horrible place.

AMORY. We'll have two hundred and seventy-five dollars a month all told.

ROSALIND. Darling, I don't even do my own hair, usually.

AMORY. I'll do it for you.

ROSALIND. (*Between a laugh and a sob*) Thanks.

AMORY. Rosalind, you *can't* be thinking of marrying some one else. Tell me! You leave me in the dark. I can help you fight it out if you'll only tell me.

ROSALIND. It's just—us. We're pitiful, that's all. The very qualities I love you for are the ones that will always make you a failure.

AMORY. (*Grimly*) Go on.

ROSALIND. Oh—it *is* Dawson Ryder. He's so reliable, I almost feel that he'd be a—a background.

AMORY. You don't love him.

ROSALIND. I know, but I respect him, and he's a good man and a strong one.

AMORY. (*Grudgingly*) Yes—he's that.

ROSALIND. Well—here's one little thing. There was a little poor boy we met in Rye Tuesday afternoon—and, oh, Dawson took him on his lap and talked to him and promised him an Indian suit—and next day he remembered and bought it—and, oh, it was so sweet and I couldn't help thinking he'd be so nice to—to our children—take care of them—and I wouldn't have to worry.

AMORY. (*In despair*) Rosalind! Rosalind!

ROSALIND. (*With a faint roguishness*) Don't look so consciously suffering.

AMORY. What power we have of hurting each other!

ROSALIND. (*Commencing to sob again*) It's been so perfect—you and I. So like a dream that I'd longed for and never thought I'd find. The first real unselfishness I've ever felt in my life. And I can't see it fade out in a colorless atmosphere!

AMORY. It won't—it won't!

ROSALIND. I'd rather keep it as a beautiful memory—tucked away in my heart.

AMORY. Yes, women can do that—but not men. I'd remember always, not the beauty of it while it lasted, but just the bitterness, the long bitterness.

ROSALIND. Don't!

AMORY. All the years never to see you, never to kiss you, just a gate shut and barred—you don't dare be my wife.

ROSALIND. No—no—I'm taking the hardest course, the strongest course. Marrying you would be a failure and I never fail—if you don't stop walking up and down I'll scream!

(*Again he sinks despairingly onto the lounge.*)

AMORY. Come over here and kiss me.

ROSALIND. No.

AMORY. Don't you *want* to kiss me?

ROSALIND. To-night I want you to love me calmly and coolly.

AMORY. The beginning of the end.

ROSALIND. (*With a burst of insight*) Amory, you're young. I'm young. People excuse us now for our poses and vanities, for treating people like Sancho* and yet getting away with it. They excuse us now. But you've got a lot of knocks coming to you——

AMORY. And you're afraid to take them with me.

ROSALIND. No, not that. There was a poem I read somewhere—you'll say Ella Wheeler Wilcox* and laugh—but listen:

> "For this is wisdom—to love and live,
>   To take what fate or the gods may give,
>   To ask no question, to make no prayer,
>   To kiss the lips and caress the hair,
>   Speed passion's ebb as we greet its flow,
>   To have and to hold, and, in time—let go."*

AMORY. But we haven't had.

ROSALIND. Amory, I'm yours—you know it. There have been times in the last month I'd have been completely yours if you'd said so. But I can't marry you and ruin both our lives.

AMORY. We've got to take our chance for happiness.

ROSALIND. Dawson says I'd learn to love him.

(AMORY *with his head sunk in his hands does not move. The life seems suddenly gone out of him.*)

ROSALIND. Lover! Lover! I can't do with you, and I can't imagine life without you.

AMORY. Rosalind, we're on each other's nerves. It's just that we're both high-strung, and this week——

(*His voice is curiously old. She crosses to him and taking his face in her hands, kisses him.*)

ROSALIND. I can't, Amory. I can't be shut away from the trees and flowers, cooped up in a little flat, waiting for you. You'd hate me in a narrow atmosphere. I'd make you hate me.

(*Again she is blinded by sudden uncontrolled tears.*)

AMORY. Rosalind——

ROSALIND. Oh, darling, go— Don't make it harder! I can't stand it——

AMORY. (*His face drawn, his voice strained*) Do you know what you're saying? Do you mean forever?

(*There is a difference somehow in the quality of their suffering.*)

ROSALIND. Can't you see——

AMORY. I'm afraid I can't if you love me. You're afraid of taking two years' knocks with me.

ROSALIND. I wouldn't be the Rosalind you love.

AMORY. (*A little hysterically*) I can't give you up! I can't, that's all! I've got to have you!

ROSALIND. (*A hard note in her voice*) You're being a baby now.

AMORY. (*Wildly*) I don't care! You're spoiling our lives!

ROSALIND. I'm doing the wise thing, the only thing.

AMORY. Are you going to marry Dawson Ryder?

ROSALIND. Oh, don't ask me. You know I'm old in some ways—in others—well, I'm just a little girl. I like sunshine and pretty things and cheerfulness—and I dread responsibility. I don't want to think about pots and kitchens and brooms. I want to worry whether my legs will get slick and brown when I swim in the summer.

AMORY. And you love me.

ROSALIND. That's just why it has to end. Drifting hurts too much. We can't have any more scenes like this.

(*She draws his ring from her finger and hands it to him. Their eyes blind again with tears.*)

AMORY. (*His lips against her wet cheek*) Don't! Keep it, please—oh, don't break my heart!

(*She presses the ring softly into his hand.*)

ROSALIND. (*Brokenly*) You'd better go.

AMORY. Good-bye——

(*She looks at him once more, with infinite longing, infinite sadness.*)

ROSALIND. Don't ever forget me, Amory——

AMORY. Good-bye——

(*He goes to the door, fumbles for the knob, finds it—she sees him throw back his head—and he is gone. Gone—she half starts from the lounge and then sinks forward on her face into the pillows.*)

ROSALIND. Oh, God, I want to die! (*After a moment she rises and with her eyes closed feels her way to the door. Then she turns and looks once more at the room. Here they had sat and dreamed: that tray she had so often filled with matches for him; that shade that they had discreetly lowered one long Sunday afternoon. Misty-eyed she stands and remembers; she speaks aloud.*) Oh, Amory, what have I done to you?

(*And deep under the aching sadness that will pass in time, Rosalind feels that she has lost something, she knows not what, she knows not why.*)

CHAPTER II

EXPERIMENTS IN CONVALESCENCE

THE Knickerbocker Bar, beamed upon by Maxfield Parrish's jovial, colorful "Old King Cole," was well crowded. Amory stopped in the entrance and looked at his wrist-watch; he wanted particularly to know the time, for something in his mind that catalogued and classified liked to chip things off cleanly. Later it would satisfy him in a vague way to be able to think "that thing ended at exactly twenty minutes after eight on Thursday, June 10, 1919." This was allowing for the walk from her house—a walk concerning which he had afterward not the faintest recollection.

He was in rather grotesque condition: two days of worry and nervousness, of sleepless nights, of untouched meals, culminating in the emotional crisis and Rosalind's abrupt decision—the strain of it had drugged the foreground of his mind into a merciful coma. As he fumbled clumsily with the olives at the free-lunch table, a man approached and spoke to him, and the olives dropped from his nervous hands.

"Well, Amory . . ."

It was some one he had known at Princeton; he had no idea of the name.

"Hello, old boy—" he heard himself saying.

"Name's Jim Wilson—you've forgotten."

"Sure, you bet, Jim. I remember."

"Going to reunion?"

"You know!" Simultaneously he realized that he was not going to reunion.

"Get overseas?"

Amory nodded, his eyes staring oddly. Stepping back to let some one pass, he knocked the dish of olives to a crash on the floor.

"Too bad," he muttered. "Have a drink?"

Wilson, ponderously diplomatic, reached over and slapped him on the back.

"You've had plenty, old boy."

Amory eyed him dumbly until Wilson grew embarrassed under the scrutiny.

"Plenty, hell!" said Amory finally. "I haven't had a drink to-day."

Wilson looked incredulous.

"Have a drink or not?" cried Amory rudely.

Together they sought the bar.

"Rye high."

"I'll just take a Bronx."*

Wilson had another; Amory had several more. They decided to sit down. At ten o'clock Wilson was displaced by Carling, class of '15. Amory, his head spinning gorgeously, layer upon layer of soft satisfaction setting over the bruised spots of his spirit, was discoursing volubly on the war.

"'S a mental was'e," he insisted with owl-like wisdom. "Two years my life spent inalleshual vacuity. Los' idealism, got be physcal anmal," he shook his fist expressively at Old King Cole, "got be Prussian 'bout ev'thing, women 'specially. Use' be straight 'bout women college. Now don'givadam." He expressed his lack of principle by sweeping a seltzer bottle with a broad gesture to noisy extinction on the floor, but this did not interrupt his speech. "Seek pleasure where find it for to-morrow die. 'At's philos'phy for me now on."

Carling yawned, but Amory, waxing brilliant, continued:

"Use' wonder 'bout things—people satisfied compromise, fif'y-fif'y att'tude on life. Now don' wonder, don' wonder—" He became so emphatic in impressing on Carling the fact that he didn't wonder that he lost the thread of his discourse and concluded by announcing to the bar at large that he was a "physcal anmal."

"What are you celebrating, Amory?"

Amory leaned forward confidentially.

"Cel'brating blowmylife. Great moment blow my life. Can't tell you 'bout it——"

He heard Carling addressing a remark to the bartender:

"Give him a bromo-seltzer."

Amory shook his head indignantly.

"None that stuff!"

"But listen, Amory, you're making yourself sick. You're white as a ghost."

Amory considered the question. He tried to look at himself in the mirror but even by squinting up one eye could only see as far as the row of bottles behind the bar.

"Like som'n solid. We go get some—some salad."

He settled his coat with an attempt at nonchalance, but letting go of the bar was too much for him, and he slumped against a chair.

"We'll go over to Shanley's," suggested Carling, offering an elbow.

With this assistance Amory managed to get his legs in motion enough to propel him across Forty-second Street.

Shanley's was very dim. He was conscious that he was talking in a loud voice, very succinctly and convincingly, he thought, about a desire to crush people under his heel. He consumed three club sandwiches, devouring each as though it were no larger than a chocolate-drop. Then Rosalind began popping into his mind again, and he found his lips forming her name over and over. Next he was sleepy, and he had a hazy, listless sense of people in dress suits, probably waiters, gathering around the table. . . .

. . . He was in a room and Carling was saying something about a knot in his shoe-lace.

"Nemmine," he managed to articulate drowsily. "Sleep in 'em. . . ."

Still Alcoholic

He awoke laughing and his eyes lazily roamed his surroundings, evidently a bedroom and bath in a good hotel. His head was whirring and picture after picture was forming and blurring and melting before his eyes, but beyond the desire to laugh he had no entirely conscious reaction. He reached for the 'phone beside his bed.

"Hello—what hotel is this—?

"'Knickerbocker? All right, send up two rye highballs——"

He lay for a moment and wondered idly whether they'd send up a bottle or just two of those little glass containers. Then, with an effort, he struggled out of bed and ambled into the bathroom.

When he emerged, rubbing himself lazily with a towel, he found the bar boy with the drinks and had a sudden desire to kid him. On reflection he decided that this would be undignified, so he waved him away.

As the new alcohol tumbled into his stomach and warmed him, the isolated pictures began slowly to form a cinema reel of the day before. Again he saw Rosalind curled weeping among the pillows, again he felt her tears against his cheek. Her words began ringing in his ears: "Don't ever forget me, Amory—don't ever forget me——"

"Hell!" he faltered aloud, and then he choked and collapsed on the bed in a shaken spasm of grief. After a minute he opened his eyes and regarded the ceiling.

"Damned fool!" he exclaimed in disgust, and with a voluminous sigh rose and approached the bottle. After another glass he gave way loosely to the luxury of tears. Purposely he called up into his mind little incidents of the vanished spring, phrased to himself emotions that would make him react even more strongly to sorrow.

"We were so happy," he intoned dramatically, "so very happy." Then he gave way again and knelt beside the bed, his head half-buried in the pillow.

"My own girl—my own— Oh——"

He clenched his teeth so that the tears streamed in a flood from his eyes.

"Oh . . . my baby girl, all I had, all I wanted! . . . Oh, my girl, come back, come back! I need you . . . need you . . . we're so pitiful . . . just misery we brought each other. . . . She'll be shut away from me. . . . I can't see her; I can't be her friend. It's got to be that way—it's got to be——"

And then again:

"We've been so happy, so very happy. . . ."

He rose to his feet and threw himself on the bed in an ecstasy of sentiment, and then lay exhausted while he realized slowly that he had been very drunk the night before, and that his head was spinning again wildly. He laughed, rose, and crossed again to Lethe. . . .

At noon he ran into a crowd in the Biltmore bar, and the riot began again. He had a vague recollection afterward of discussing French poetry with a British officer who was introduced to him as "Captain Corn, of his Majesty's Foot," and he remembered attempting to recite "Clair de Lune"* at luncheon; then he slept in a big, soft chair until almost five o'clock when another crowd found and woke him; there followed an alcoholic dressing of several temperaments for the ordeal of dinner. They selected theatre tickets at Tyson's for a play that had a four-drink programme—a play with two monotonous voices, with turbid, gloomy scenes, and lighting effects that were hard to follow when his eyes behaved so amazingly. He imagined afterward that it must have been "The Jest."* . . .

. . . Then the Cocoanut Grove, where Amory slept again on a little balcony outside. Out in Shanley's, Yonkers, he became almost logical, and by a careful control of the number of high-balls he drank, grew quite lucid and garrulous. He found that the party consisted of five men, two of whom he knew slightly; he became righteous about paying his share of the expense and insisted in a loud voice on arranging everything then and there to the amusement of the tables around him. . . .

Some one mentioned that a famous cabaret star was at the next table, so Amory rose and, approaching gallantly, introduced himself . . . this involved him in an argument, first with her escort and then with the head-waiter—Amory's attitude being a lofty and exaggerated courtesy . . . he consented, after being confronted with irrefutable logic, to being led back to his own table.

"Decided to commit suicide," he announced suddenly.

"When? Next year?"

"Now. To-morrow morning. Going to take a room at the Commodore, get into a hot bath and open a vein."

"He's getting morbid!"

"You need another rye, old boy!"

"We'll all talk it over to-morrow."

But Amory was not to be dissuaded, from argument at least.

"Did you ever get that way?" he demanded confidentially fortaccio.

"Sure!"

"Often?"

"My chronic state."

This provoked discussion. One man said that he got so depressed sometimes that he seriously considered it. Another agreed that there was nothing to live for. "Captain Corn," who had somehow rejoined the party, said that in his opinion it was when one's health was bad that one felt that way most. Amory's suggestion was that they should each order a Bronx, mix broken glass in it, and drink it off. To his relief no one applauded the idea, so having finished his high-ball, he balanced his chin in his hand and his elbow on the table—a most delicate, scarcely noticeable sleeping position, he assured himself—and went into a deep stupor. . . .

He was awakened by a woman clinging to him, a pretty woman, with brown, disarranged hair and dark blue eyes.

"Take me home!" she cried.

"Hello!" said Amory, blinking.

"I like you," she announced tenderly.

"I like you too."

He noticed that there was a noisy man in the background and that one of his party was arguing with him.

"Fella I was with's a damn fool," confided the blue-eyed woman. "I hate him. I want to go home with you."

"You drunk?" queried Amory with intense wisdom.

She nodded coyly.

"Go home with him," he advised gravely. "He brought you."

At this point the noisy man in the background broke away from his detainers and approached.

"Say!" he said fiercely. "I brought this girl out here and you're butting in!"

Amory regarded him coldly, while the girl clung to him closer.

"You let go that girl!" cried the noisy man.

Amory tried to make his eyes threatening.

"You go to hell!" he directed finally, and turned his attention to the girl.

"Love first sight," he suggested.

"I love you," she breathed and nestled close to him. She *did* have beautiful eyes.

Some one leaned over and spoke in Amory's ear.

"That's just Margaret Diamond. She's drunk and this fellow here brought her. Better let her go."

"Let him take care of her, then!" shouted Amory furiously. "I'm no W. Y. C. A. worker, am I?—am I?"

"Let her go!"

"It's *her* hanging on, damn it! Let her hang!"

The crowd around the table thickened. For an instant a brawl threatened, but a sleek waiter bent back Margaret Diamond's fingers until she released her hold on Amory, whereupon she slapped the waiter furiously in the face and flung her arms about her raging original escort.

"Oh, Lord!" cried Amory.

"Let's go!"

"Come on, the taxis are getting scarce!"

"Check, waiter."

"C'mon, Amory. Your romance is over."

Amory laughed.

"You don't know how true you spoke. No idea. 'At's the whole trouble."

Amory on the Labor Question

Two mornings later he knocked at the president's door at Bascome and Barlow's advertising agency.

"Come in!"

Amory entered unsteadily.

"'Morning, Mr. Barlow."

Mr. Barlow brought his glasses to the inspection and set his mouth slightly ajar that he might better listen.

"Well, Mr. Blaine. We haven't seen you for several days."

"No," said Amory. "I'm quitting."

"Well—well—this is——"

"I don't like it here."

"I'm sorry. I thought our relations had been quite—ah—pleasant. You seemed to be a hard worker—a little inclined perhaps to write fancy copy——"

"I just got tired of it," interrupted Amory rudely. "It didn't matter a damn to me whether Harebell's flour was any better than any one else's. In fact, I never ate any of it. So I got tired of telling people about it—oh, I know I've been drinking——"

Mr. Barlow's face steeled by several ingots of expression.

"You asked for a position——"

Amory waved him to silence.

"And I think I was rottenly underpaid. Thirty-five dollars a week—less than a good carpenter."

"You had just started. You'd never worked before," said Mr. Barlow coolly.

"But it took about ten thousand dollars to educate me where I could write your darned stuff for you. Anyway, as far as length of service goes, you've got stenographers here you've paid fifteen a week for five years."

"I'm not going to argue with you, sir," said Mr. Barlow rising.

"Neither am I. I just wanted to tell you I'm quitting."

They stood for a moment looking at each other impassively and then Amory turned and left the office.

A Little Lull

Four days after that he returned at last to the apartment. Tom was engaged on a book review for *The New Democracy* on the staff of which he was employed. They regarded each other for a moment in silence.

"Well?"

"Well?"

"Good Lord, Amory, where'd you get the black eye—and the jaw?"

Amory laughed.

"That's a mere nothing."

He peeled off his coat and bared his shoulders.

"Look here!"

Tom emitted a low whistle.

"What hit you?"

Amory laughed again.

"Oh, a lot of people. I got beaten up. Fact." He slowly replaced his shirt. "It was bound to come sooner or later and I wouldn't have missed it for anything!"

"Who was it?"

"Well, there were some waiters and a couple of sailors and a few stray pedestrians, I guess. It's the strangest feeling. You ought to get beaten up just for the experience of it. You fall down after a while and everybody sort of slashes in at you before you hit the ground—then they kick you."

Tom lighted a cigarette.

"I spent a day chasing you all over town, Amory. But you always kept a little ahead of me. I'd say you've been on some party."

Amory tumbled into a chair and asked for a cigarette.

"You sober now?" asked Tom quizzically.

"Pretty sober. Why?"

"Well, Alec has left. His family had been after him to go home and live, so he——"

A spasm of pain shook Amory.

"Too bad."

"Yes, it is too bad. We'll have to get some one else if we're going to stay here. The rent's going up."

"Sure. Get anybody. I'll leave it to you, Tom."

Amory walked into his bedroom. The first thing that met his glance was a photograph of Rosalind that he had intended to have framed, propped up against a mirror on his dresser. He looked at it unmoved. After the vivid mental pictures of her that were his portion at present, the portrait was curiously unreal. He went back into the study.

"Got a cardboard box?"

"No," answered Tom, puzzled. "Why should I have? Oh, yes—there may be one in Alec's room."

Eventually Amory found what he was looking for and, returning to his dresser, opened a drawer full of letters, notes, part of a chain, two little handkerchiefs, and some snap-shots. As he transferred them carefully to the box his mind wandered to some place in a book where the hero, after preserving for a year a cake of his lost love's soap, finally washed his hands with it. He laughed and began to hum "After you've gone"* . . . ceased abruptly. . .

The string broke twice, and then he managed to secure it, dropped the package into the bottom of his trunk, and having slammed the lid returned to the study.

"Going out?" Tom's voice held an undertone of anxiety.

"Uh-huh."

"Where?"

"Couldn't say, old keed."

"Let's have dinner together."

"Sorry. I told Sukey Brett I'd eat with him."

"Oh."

"Bye-bye."

Amory crossed the street and had a high-ball; then he walked to Washington Square and found a top seat on a bus. He disembarked at Forty-third Street and strolled to the Biltmore bar.

"Hi, Amory!"

"What'll you have?"

"Yoho! Waiter!"

Temperature Normal

The advent of prohibition with the "thirsty-first" put a sudden stop to the submerging of Amory's sorrows, and when he awoke one morning to find that the old bar-to-bar days were over, he had neither remorse for the past three weeks nor regret that their repetition was impossible. He had taken the most violent, if the weakest, method to shield himself from the stabs of memory, and while it was not a course he would have prescribed for others, he found in the end that it had done its business: he was over the first flush of pain.

Don't misunderstand! Amory had loved Rosalind as he would never love another living person. She had taken the first flush of his youth and brought from his unplumbed depths tenderness that had surprised him, gentleness and unselfishness that he had never given to another creature. He had later love-affairs, but of a different sort: in those he went back to that, perhaps, more typical frame of mind, in which the girl became the mirror of a mood in him. Rosalind had drawn out what was more than passionate admiration; he had a deep, undying affection for Rosalind.

But there had been, near the end, so much dramatic tragedy, culminating in the arabesque nightmare of his three weeks' spree, that he was emotionally worn out. The people and surroundings that he remembered as being cool or delicately artificial, seemed to promise him a refuge. He wrote a cynical story which featured his father's funeral and despatched it to a magazine, receiving in return a check for sixty dollars and a request for more of the same tone. This tickled his vanity, but inspired him to no further effort.

He read enormously. He was puzzled and depressed by "A Portrait of the Artist as a Young Man"; intensely interested by "Joan and Peter" and "The Undying Fire,"* and rather surprised by his discovery through a critic named Mencken of several excellent American novels: "Vandover and the Brute," "The Damnation of Theron Ware," and "Jennie Gerhardt."* Mackenzie, Chesterton, Galsworthy, Bennett,* had sunk in his appreciation from sagacious, life-saturated geniuses to merely diverting contemporaries. Shaw's aloof clarity and brilliant consistency and the gloriously intoxicated efforts of H. G. Wells to fit the key of romantic symmetry into the elusive lock of truth, alone won his rapt attention.

He wanted to see Monsignor Darcy, to whom he had written when he landed, but he had not heard from him; besides he knew that a visit to Monsignor would entail the story of Rosalind, and the thought of repeating it turned him cold with horror.

In his search for cool people he remembered Mrs. Lawrence, a very intelligent, very dignified lady, a convert to the church, and a great devotee of Monsignor's.

He called her on the 'phone one day. Yes, she remembered him perfectly; no, Monsignor wasn't in town, was in Boston she thought; he'd promised to come to dinner when he returned. Couldn't Amory take luncheon with her?

"I thought I'd better catch up, Mrs. Lawrence," he said rather ambiguously when he arrived.

"Monsignor was here just last week," said Mrs. Lawrence regretfully. "He was very anxious to see you, but he'd left your address at home."

"Did he think I'd plunged into Bolshevism?" asked Amory, interested.

"Oh, he's having a frightful time."

"Why?"

"About the Irish Republic. He thinks it lacks dignity."

"So?"

"He went to Boston when the Irish President* arrived and he was greatly distressed because the receiving committee, when they rode in an automobile, *would* put their arms around the President."

"I don't blame him."

"Well, what impressed you more than anything while you were in the army? You look a great deal older."

"That's from another, more disastrous battle," he answered, smiling in spite of himself. "But the army—let me see—well, I discovered that physical courage depends to a great extent on the physical shape a man is in. I found that I was as brave as the next man—it used to worry me before."

"What else?"

"Well, the idea that men can stand anything if they get used to it, and the fact that I got a high mark in the psychological examination."

Mrs. Lawrence laughed. Amory was finding it a great relief to be in this cool house on Riverside Drive, away from more condensed New York and the sense of people expelling great quantities of breath into a little space. Mrs. Lawrence reminded him vaguely of Beatrice, not in temperament, but in her perfect grace and dignity. The house, its furnishings, the manner in which dinner was served, were in immense contrast to what he had met in the great places on Long Island, where the servants were so obtrusive that they had positively to be bumped out of the way, or even in the houses of more conservative "Union Club" families. He wondered if this air of symmetrical restraint, this grace, which he felt was continental, was distilled through Mrs. Lawrence's New England ancestry or acquired in long residence in Italy and Spain.

Two glasses of sauterne at luncheon loosened his tongue, and he talked, with what he felt was something of his old charm, of religion and literature and the menacing phenomena of the social order. Mrs. Lawrence was ostensibly pleased with him, and her interest was especially in his mind; he wanted people to like his mind again—after a while it might be such a nice place in which to live.

"Monsignor Darcy still thinks that you're his reincarnation, that your faith will eventually clarify."

"Perhaps," he assented. "I'm rather pagan at present. It's just that religion doesn't seem to have the slightest bearing on life at my age."

When he left her house he walked down Riverside Drive with a feeling of satisfaction. It was amusing to discuss again such subjects as this young poet, Stephen Vincent Benét, or the Irish Republic. Between the rancid accusations of Edward Carson and Justice Cohalan* he had completely tired of the Irish question; yet there had been a time when his own Celtic traits were pillars of his personal philosophy.

There seemed suddenly to be much left in life, if only this revival of old interests did not mean that he was backing away from it again—backing away from life itself.

Restlessness

"I'm tres old and tres bored, Tom," said Amory one day, stretching himself at ease in the comfortable window-seat. He always felt most natural in a recumbent position.

"You used to be entertaining before you started to write," he continued. "Now you save any idea that you think would do to print."

Existence had settled back to an ambitionless normality. They had decided that with economy they could still afford the apartment, which Tom, with the domesticity of an elderly cat, had grown fond of. The old English hunting prints on the wall were Tom's, and the large tapestry by courtesy, a relic of decadent days in college, and the great profusion of orphaned candlesticks and the carved Louis XIV chair in which no one could sit more than a minute without acute spinal disorders—Tom claimed that this was because one was sitting in the lap of Montespan's wraith*—at any rate, it was Tom's furniture that decided them to stay.

They went out very little: to an occasional play, or to dinner at the Ritz or the Princeton Club. With prohibition the great rendezvouz had received their death wounds; no longer could one wander to the Biltmore bar at twelve or five and find congenial spirits, and both Tom and Amory had outgrown the passion for dancing with mid-Western or New Jersey debbies at the Club-de-Vingt (surnamed the "Club de Gink") or the Plaza. Rose Room—besides even that required several cocktails "to come down to the intellectual level of the women present," as Amory had once put it to a horrified matron.

Amory had lately received several alarming letters from Mr. Barton—the Lake Geneva house was too large to be easily rented; the best rent obtainable at present would serve this year to little more than pay for the taxes and necessary improvements; in fact, the lawyer suggested that the whole property was simply a white elephant on Amory's hands. Nevertheless, even though it might not yield a cent for the next three years, Amory decided with a vague sentimentality that for the present, at any rate, he would not sell the house.

This particular day on which he announced his ennui to Tom had been quite typical. He had risen at noon, lunched with Mrs. Lawrence, and then ridden abstractedly homeward atop one of his beloved buses.

"Why shouldn't you be bored," yawned Tom. "Isn't that the conventional frame of mind for the young man of your age and condition?"

"Yes," said Amory speculatively, "but I'm more than bored; I am restless."

"Love and war did for you."

"Well," Amory considered, "I'm not sure that the war itself had any great effect on either you or me—but it certainly ruined the old backgrounds, sort of killed individualism out of our generation."

Tom looked up in surprise.

"Yes it did," insisted Amory. "I'm not sure it didn't kill it out of the whole world. Oh, Lord, what a pleasure it used to be to dream I might be a really great dictator or writer or religious or political leader—and now even a Leonardo da Vinci or Lorenzo de Medici couldn't be a real old-fashioned bolt in the world. Life is too huge and complex. The world is so overgrown that it can't lift its own fingers, and I was planning to be such an important finger——"

"I don't agree with you," Tom interrupted. "There never were men placed in such egotistic positions since—oh, since the French Revolution."

Amory disagreed violently.

"You're mistaking this period when every nut is an individualist for a period of individualism. Wilson has only been powerful when he has represented; he's had to compromise over and over again. Just as soon as Trotsky and Lenin take a definite, consistent stand they'll become merely two-minute figures like Kerensky. Even Foch* hasn't half the significance of Stonewall Jackson. War used to be the most individualistic pursuit of man, and yet the popular heroes of the war had neither authority nor responsibility: Guynemer and Sergeant York. How could a schoolboy make a hero of Pershing?* A big man has no time really to do anything but just sit and be big."

"Then you don't think there will be any more permanent world heroes?"

"Yes—in history—not in life. Carlyle would have difficulty getting material for a new chapter on 'The Hero as a Big Man.'"*

"Go on. I'm a good listener to-day."

"People try so hard to believe in leaders now, pitifully hard. But we no sooner get a popular reformer or politician or soldier or writer or philosopher—a Roosevelt, a Tolstoi, a Wood,* a Shaw, a Nietzsche, than the cross-currents of criticism wash him away. My Lord, no man can stand prominence these days. It's the surest path to obscurity. People get sick of hearing the same name over and over."

"Then you blame it on the press?"

"Absolutely. Look at you; you're on *The New Democracy*, considered the most brilliant weekly in the country, read by the men who do things and all that. What's your business? Why, to be as clever, as interesting, and as brilliantly cynical as possible about every man, doctrine, book, or policy that is assigned you to deal with. The more strong lights, the more spiritual scandal you can throw on the matter, the more money they pay you, the more the people buy the issue. You, Tom d'Invilliers, a blighted Shelley, changing, shifting, clever, unscrupulous, represent the critical consciousness of the race—   Oh, don't protest, I know the stuff. I used to write book reviews in college; I considered it rare sport to refer to the latest honest, conscientious effort to propound a theory or a remedy as a 'welcome addition to our light summer reading.' Come on now, admit it."

Tom laughed, and Amory continued triumphantly.

"We *want* to believe. Young students try to believe in older authors, constituents try to believe in their Congressmen, countries try to believe in their statesmen, but they *can't*. Too many voices, too much scattered, illogical, ill-considered criticism. It's worse in the case of newspapers. Any rich, unprogressive old party with that particularly grasping, acquisitive form of mentality known as financial genius can own a paper that is the intellectual meat and drink of thousands of tired, hurried men, men too involved in the business of modern living to swallow anything but predigested food. For two cents the voter buys his politics, prejudices, and philosophy. A year later there is a new political ring or a change in the paper's ownership, consequence: more confusion, more contradiction, a sudden inrush of new ideas, their tempering, their distillation, the reaction against them——"

He paused only to get his breath.

"And that is why I have sworn not to put pen to paper until my ideas either clarify or depart entirely; I have quite enough sins on my soul without putting dangerous, shallow epigrams into people's heads; I might cause a poor, inoffensive capitalist to have a vulgar liaison with a bomb, or get some innocent little Bolshevik tangled up with a machine-gun bullet——"

Tom was growing restless under this lampooning of his connection with *The New Democracy*.

"What's all this got to do with your being bored?"

Amory considered that it had much to do with it.

"How'll I fit in?" he demanded. "What am I for? To propagate the race? According to the American novels we are led to believe that the 'healthy American boy' from nineteen to twenty-five is an entirely sexless animal. As a matter of fact, the healthier he is the less that's true. The only alternative to letting it get you is some violent interest. Well, the war is over; I believe too much in the responsibilities of authorship to write just now; and business, well, business speaks for itself. It has no connection with anything in the world that I've ever been interested in, except a slim, utilitarian connection with economics.

What I'd see of it, lost in a clerkship, for the next and best ten years of my life would have the intellectual content of an industrial movie."

"Try fiction," suggested Tom.

"Trouble is I get distracted when I start to write stories—get afraid I'm doing it instead of living—get thinking maybe life is waiting for me in the Japanese gardens at the Ritz or at Atlantic City or on the lower East Side.

"Anyway," he continued, "I haven't the vital urge. I wanted to be a regular human being but the girl couldn't see it that way."

"You'll find another."

"God! Banish the thought. Why don't you tell me that 'if the girl had been worth having she'd have waited for you'? No, sir, the girl really worth having won't wait for anybody. If I thought there'd be another I'd lose my remaining faith in human nature. Maybe I'll play—but Rosalind was the only girl in the wide world that could have held me."

"Well," yawned Tom, "I've played confidant a good hour by the clock. Still, I'm glad to see you're beginning to have violent views again on something."

"I am," agreed Amory reluctantly. "Yet when I see a happy family it makes me sick at my stomach——"

"Happy families try to make people feel that way," said Tom cynically.

Tom the Censor

There were days when Amory listened. These were when Tom, wreathed in smoke, indulged in the slaughter of American literature. Words failed him.

"Fifty thousand dollars a year," he would cry. "My God! Look at them, look at them—Edna Ferber, Gouverneur Morris,* Fannie Hurst,* Mary Roberts Rinehart—not producing among 'em one story or novel that will last ten years. This man Cobb*—I don't think he's either clever or amusing—and what's more, I don't think very many people do, except the editors. He's just groggy with advertising. And—oh Harold Bell Wright* oh Zane Grey——"

"They try."

"No, they don't even try. Some of them *can* write, but they won't sit down and do one honest novel. Most of them *can't* write, I'll admit. I believe Rupert Hughes* tries to give a real, comprehensive picture of American life, but his style and perspective are barbarous. Ernest Poole and Dorothy Canfield* try but they're hindered by their absolute lack of any sense of humor; but at least they crowd their work instead of spreading it thin. Every author ought to write every book as if he were going to be beheaded the day he finished it."

"Is that double entente?"

"Don't slow me up! Now there's a few of 'em that seem to have some cultural background, some intelligence and a good deal of literary felicity but they just simply won't write honestly; they'd all claim there was no public for good stuff. Then why the devil is it that Wells, Conrad, Galsworthy, Shaw, Bennett, and the rest depend on America for over half their sales?"

"How does little Tommy like the poets?"

Tom was overcome. He dropped his arms until they swung loosely beside the chair and emitted faint grunts.

"I'm writing a satire on 'em now, calling it 'Boston Bards and Hearst Reviewers.'"*

"Let's hear it," said Amory eagerly.

"I've only got the last few lines done."

"That's very modern. Let's hear 'em, if they're funny."

Tom produced a folded paper from his pocket and read aloud, pausing at intervals so that Amory could see that it was free verse:

> "So
> Walter Arensberg,
> Alfred Kreymborg,
> Carl Sandburg,
> Louis Untermeyer,
> Eunice Tietjens,
> Clara Shanafelt,
> James Oppenheim,
> Maxwell Bodenheim,
> Richard Glaenzer,
> Scharmel Iris,
> Conrad Aiken,
> I place your names here
> So that you may live
> If only as names,
> Sinuous, mauve-colored names,
> In the Juvenilia
> Of my collected editions."

Amory roared.

"You win the iron pansy. I'll buy you a meal on the arrogance of the last two lines."

Amory did not entirely agree with Tom's sweeping damnation of American novelists and poets. He enjoyed both Vachel Lindsay and Booth Tarkington, and admired the conscientious, if slender, artistry of Edgar Lee Masters.

"What I hate is this idiotic drivel about 'I am God—I am man—I ride the winds—I look through the smoke—I am the life sense.'"

"It's ghastly!"

"And I wish American novelists would give up trying to make business romantically interesting. Nobody wants to read about it, unless it's crooked business. If it was an entertaining subject they'd buy the life of James J. Hill* and not one of these long office tragedies that harp along on the significance of smoke——"

"And gloom," said Tom. "That's another favorite, though I'll admit the Russians have the monopoly. Our specialty is stories about little girls who break their spines and get adopted by grouchy old men because they smile so much. You'd think we were a race of cheerful cripples and that the common end of the Russian peasant was suicide——"

"Six o'clock," said Amory, glancing at his wrist-watch. "I'll buy you a grea' big dinner on the strength of the Juvenilia of your collected editions."

Looking Backward

July sweltered out with a last hot week, and Amory in another surge of unrest realized that it was just five months since he and Rosalind had met. Yet it was already hard for him to visualize the heart-whole boy who had stepped off the transport, passionately desiring the adventure of life. One night while the heat, overpowering and enervating, poured into the windows of his room he struggled for several hours in a vague effort to immortalize the poignancy of that time.

The February streets, wind-washed by night, blow full of strange half-intermittent damps, bearing on wasted walks in shining sight wet snow plashed into gleams under the lamps, like golden oil from some divine machine, in an hour of thaw and stars.

Strange damps—full of the eyes of many men, crowded with life borne in upon a lull. . . . Oh, I was young, for I could turn again to you,

most finite and most beautiful, and taste the stuff of half-remembered
dreams, sweet and new on your mouth.

. . . There was a tanging in the midnight air—silence was dead and
sound not yet awoken—Life cracked like ice!—one brilliant note and
there, radiant and pale, you stood . . . and spring had broken. (The icicles
were short upon the roofs and the changeling city swooned.)

Our thoughts were frosty mist along the eaves; our two ghosts kissed,
high on the long, mazed wires—eerie half-laughter echoes here and leaves
only a fatuous sigh for young desires; regret has followed after things she
loved, leaving the great husk.

Another Ending

In mid-August came a letter from Monsignor Darcy, who had
evidently just stumbled on his address:

My dear Boy: —

Your last letter was quite enough to make me worry about you. It was
not a bit like yourself. Reading between the lines I should imagine that
your engagement to this girl is making you rather unhappy, and I see
you have lost all the feeling of romance that you had before the war. You
make a great mistake if you think you can be romantic without religion.
Sometimes I think that with both of us the secret of success, when we
find it, is the mystical element in us: something flows into us that enlarges
our personalities, and when it ebbs out our personalities shrink; I should
call your last two letters rather shrivelled. Beware of losing yourself in the
personality of another being, man or woman.

His Eminence Cardinal O'Neill and the Bishop of Boston are staying
with me at present, so it is hard for me to get a moment to write, but I wish
you would come up here later if only for a week-end. I go to Washington
this week.

What I shall do in the future is hanging in the balance. Absolutely
between ourselves I should not be surprised to see the red hat of a cardinal
descend upon my unworthy head within the next eight months. In any
event, I should like to have a house in New York or Washington where you
could drop in for week-ends.

Amory, I'm very glad we're both alive; this war could easily have been
the end of a brilliant family. But in regard to matrimony, you are now at the
most dangerous period of your life. You might marry in haste and repent at
leisure, but I think you won't. From what you write me about the present
calamitous state of your finances, what you want is naturally impossible.
However, if I judge you by the means I usually choose, I should say that
there will be something of an emotional crisis within the next year.

Do write me. I feel annoyingly out of date on you.
With greatest affection,

THAYER DARCY.

Within a week after the receipt of this letter their little household fell precipitously to pieces. The immediate cause was the serious and probably chronic illness of Tom's mother. So they stored the furniture, gave instructions to sublet and shook hands gloomily in the Pennsylvania Station. Amory and Tom seemed always to be saying good-bye.

Feeling very much alone, Amory yielded to an impulse and set off southward, intending to join Monsignor in Washington. They missed connections by two hours, and, deciding to spend a few days with an ancient, remembered uncle, Amory journeyed up through the luxuriant fields of Maryland into Ramilly County. But instead of two days his stay lasted from mid-August nearly through September, for in Maryland he met Eleanor.

CHAPTER III

YOUNG IRONY

FOR years afterward when Amory thought of Eleanor he seemed still to hear the wind sobbing around him and sending little chills into the places beside his heart. The night when they rode up the slope and watched the cold moon float through the clouds, he lost a further part of him that nothing could restore; and when he lost it he lost also the power of regretting it. Eleanor was, say, the last time that evil crept close to Amory under the mask of beauty, the last weird mystery that held him with wild fascination and pounded his soul to flakes.

With her his imagination ran riot and that is why they rode to the highest hill and watched an evil moon ride high, for they knew then that they could see the devil in each other. But Eleanor—did Amory dream her? Afterward their ghosts played, yet both of them hoped from their souls never to meet. Was it the infinite sadness of her eyes that drew him or the mirror of himself that he found in the gorgeous clarity of her mind? She will have no other adventure like Amory, and if she reads this she will say:

"And Amory will have no other adventure like me."

Nor will she sigh, any more than he would sigh.

Eleanor tried to put it on paper once:

> "The fading things we only know
>   We'll have forgotten . . .
>   Put away . . .
> Desires that melted with the snow,
>   And dreams begotten
>   This to-day:
> The sudden dawns we laughed to greet,
>   That all could see, that none could share,
> Will be but dawns . . . and if we meet
>   We shall not care.
>
> Dear . . . not one tear will rise for this . . .
>   A little while hence
>   No regret
> Will stir for a remembered kiss—

> Not even silence,
> When we've met,
> Will give old ghosts a waste to roam,
> Or stir the surface of the sea . . .
> If gray shapes drift beneath the foam
> We shall not see."

They quarrelled dangerously because Amory maintained that *sea* and *see* couldn't possibly be used as a rhyme. And then Eleanor had part of another verse that she couldn't find a beginning for:

> ". . . But wisdom passes . . . still the years
> Will feed us wisdom. . . . Age will go
> Back to the old— For all our tears
> We shall not know."

Eleanor hated Maryland passionately. She belonged to the oldest of the old families of Ramilly County and lived in a big, gloomy house with her grandfather. She had been born and brought up in France. . . . I see I am starting wrong. Let me begin again.

Amory was bored, as he usually was in the country. He used to go for far walks by himself—and wander along reciting "Ulalume" to the corn-fields, and congratulating Poe for drinking himself to death in that atmosphere of smiling complacency. One afternoon he had strolled for several miles along a road that was new to him, and then through a wood on bad advice from a colored woman . . . losing himself entirely. A passing storm decided to break out, and to his great impatience the sky grew black as pitch and the rain began to splatter down through the trees, become suddenly furtive and ghostly. Thunder rolled with menacing crashes up the valley and scattered through the woods in intermittent batteries. He stumbled blindly on, hunting for a way out, and finally, through webs of twisted branches, caught sight of a rift in the trees where the unbroken lightning showed open country. He rushed to the edge of the woods and then hesitated whether or not to cross the fields and try to reach the shelter of the little house marked by a light far down the valley. It was only half past five, but he could see scarcely ten steps before him, except when the lightning made everything vivid and grotesque for great sweeps around.

Suddenly a strange sound fell on his ears. It was a song, in a low, husky voice, a girl's voice, and whoever was singing was very close to him. A year before he might have laughed, or trembled; but in his restless mood he only stood and listened while the words sank into his consciousness:

> *"Les sanglots longs*
> *Des violons*
> *De l'automne*
> *Blessent mon cœur*
> *D'une langueur*
> *Monotone."*

The lightning split the sky, but the song went on without a quaver. The girl was evidently in the field and the voice seemed to come vaguely from a haystack about twenty feet in front of him.

Then it ceased; ceased and began again in a weird chant that soared and hung and fell and blended with the rain:

> *"Tout suffocant*
> *Et blême quand*
> *Sonne l'heure*
> *Je me souviens*
> *Des jours anciens*
> *Et je pleure. . . ."**

"Who the devil is there in Ramilly County," muttered Amory aloud, "who would deliver Verlaine in an extemporaneous tune to a soaking haystack?"

"Somebody's there!" cried the voice unalarmed. "Who are you?—Manfred,* St. Christopher, or Queen Victoria?"

"I'm Don Juan!" Amory shouted on impulse, raising his voice above the noise of the rain and the wind.

A delighted shriek came from the haystack.

"I know who you are—you're the blond boy that likes 'Ulalume'—I recognize your voice."

"How do I get up?" he cried from the foot of the haystack, whither he had arrived, dripping wet. A head appeared over the edge—it was so dark that Amory could just make out a patch of damp hair and two eyes that gleamed like a cat's.

"Run back!" came the voice, "and jump and I'll catch your hand—no, not there—on the other side."

He followed directions and as he sprawled up the side, knee-deep in hay, a small, white hand reached out, gripped his, and helped him onto the top.

"Here you are, Juan," cried she of the damp hair. "Do you mind if I drop the Don?"

"You've got a thumb like mine!" he exclaimed.

"And you're holding my hand, which is dangerous without seeing my face." He dropped it quickly.

As if in answer to his prayers came a flash of lightning and he looked eagerly at her who stood beside him on the soggy haystack, ten feet above the ground. But she had covered her face and he saw nothing but a slender figure, dark, damp, bobbed hair, and the small white hands with the thumbs that bent back like his.

"Sit down," she suggested politely, as the dark closed in on them. "If you'll sit opposite me in this hollow you can have half of the raincoat, which I was using as a water-proof tent until you so rudely interrupted me."

"I was asked," Amory said joyfully; "you asked me—you know you did."

"Don Juan always manages that," she said, laughing, "but I shan't call you that any more, because you've got reddish hair. Instead you can recite 'Ulalume' and I'll be Psyche, your soul."

Amory flushed, happily invisible under the curtain of wind and rain. They were sitting opposite each other in a slight hollow in the hay with the raincoat spread over most of them, and the rain doing for the rest. Amory was trying desperately to see Psyche, but the lightning refused to flash again, and he waited impatiently. Good Lord! supposing she wasn't beautiful—supposing she was forty and pedantic—heavens! Suppose, only suppose, she was mad. But he knew the last was unworthy. Here had Providence sent a girl to amuse him just as it sent Benvenuto Cellini men to murder, and he was wondering if she was mad, just because she exactly filled his mood.

"I'm not," she said.

"Not what?"

"Not mad. I didn't think you were mad when I first saw you, so it isn't fair that you should think so of me."

"How on earth—"

As long as they knew each other Eleanor and Amory could be "on a subject" and stop talking with the definite thought of it in their heads, yet ten minutes later speak aloud and find that their minds had followed the same channels and led them each to a parallel idea, an idea that others would have found absolutely unconnected with the first.

"Tell me," he demanded, leaning forward eagerly, "how do you know about 'Ulalume'—how did you know the color of my hair? What's your name? What were you doing here? Tell me all at once!"

Suddenly the lightning flashed in with a leap of overreaching light and he saw Eleanor, and looked for the first time into those eyes of hers. Oh, she was magnificent—pale skin, the color of marble in starlight, slender brows, and eyes that glittered green as emeralds in the blinding glare. She was a witch, of perhaps nineteen, he judged, alert and dreamy and with the tell-tale white line over her upper lip that was a weakness and a delight. He sank back with a gasp against the wall of hay.

"Now you've seen me," she said calmly, "and I suppose you're about to say that my green eyes are burning into your brain."

"What color is your hair?" he asked intently. "It's bobbed,* isn't it?"

"Yes, it's bobbed. I don't know what color it is," she answered, musing, "so many men have asked me. It's medium, I suppose— No one ever looks long at my hair. I've got beautiful eyes, though, haven't I? I don't care what you say, I have beautiful eyes."

"Answer my question, Madeline."*

"Don't remember them all—besides my name isn't Madeline, it's Eleanor."

"I might have guessed it. You *look* like Eleanor—you have that Eleanor look. You know what I mean."

There was a silence as they listened to the rain.

"It's going down my neck, fellow lunatic," she offered finally.

"Answer my questions."

"Well—name of Savage, Eleanor; live in big old house mile down road; nearest living relation to be notified, grandfather—Ramilly Savage; height, five feet four inches; number on watch-case, 3077 W; nose, delicate aquiline; temperament, uncanny——"

"And me," Amory interrupted, "where did you see me?"

"Oh, you're one of *those* men," she answered haughtily, "must lug old self into conversation. Well, my boy, I was behind a hedge sunning myself one day last week, and along comes a man saying in a pleasant, conceited way of talking:

> "'And now when the night was senescent'
> (says he)

'And the star dials pointed to morn
At the end of the path a liquescent'
                                            (says he)
'And nebulous lustre was born.'*

So I poked my eyes up over the hedge, but you had started to run, for some unknown reason, and so I saw but the back of your beautiful head. 'Oh!' says I, 'there's a man for whom many of us might sigh,' and I continued in my best Irish——"

"All right," Amory interrupted. "Now go back to yourself."

"Well, I will. I'm one of those people who go through the world giving other people thrills, but getting few myself except those I read into men on such nights as these. I have the social courage to go on the stage, but not the energy; I haven't the patience to write books; and I never met a man I'd marry. However, I'm only eighteen."

The storm was dying down softly and only the wind kept up its ghostly surge and made the stack lean and gravely settle from side to side. Amory was in a trance. He felt that every moment was precious. He had never met a girl like this before—she would never seem quite the same again. He didn't at all feel like a character in a play, the appropriate feeling in an unconventional situation—instead, he had a sense of coming home.

"I have just made a great decision," said Eleanor after another pause, "and that is why I'm here, to answer another of your questions. I have just decided that I don't believe in immortality."

"Really! how banal!"

"Frightfully so," she answered, "but depressing with a stale, sickly depression, nevertheless. I came out here to get wet—like a wet hen; wet hens always have great clarity of mind," she concluded.

"Go on," Amory said politely.

"Well—I'm not afraid of the dark, so I put on my slicker and rubber boots and came out. You see I was always afraid, before, to say I didn't believe in God—because the lightning might strike me—but here I am and it hasn't, of course, but the main point is that this time I wasn't any more afraid of it than I had been when I was a Christian Scientist, like I was last year. So now I know I'm a materialist and I was fraternizing with the hay when you came out and stood by the woods scared to death."

"Why, you little wretch—" cried Amory indignantly. "Scared of what?"

"*Yourself!*" she shouted, and he jumped. She clapped her hands and laughed. "See—see! Conscience—kill it like me! Eleanor Savage, materiologist—no jumping, no starting, come early——"

"But I *have* to have a soul," he objected. "I can't be rational—and I won't be molecular."

She leaned toward him, her burning eyes never leaving his own and whispered with a sort of romantic finality:

"I thought so, Juan, I feared so—you're sentimental. You're not like me. I'm a romantic little materialist."

"I'm not sentimental—I'm as romantic as you are. The idea, you know, is that the sentimental person thinks things will last—the romantic person has a desperate confidence that they won't." (This was an ancient distinction of Amory's.)

"Epigrams. I'm going home," she said sadly. "Let's get off the haystack and walk to the cross-roads."

They slowly descended from their perch. She would not let him help her down and motioning him away arrived in a graceful lump in the soft mud where she sat for an instant, laughing at herself. Then she jumped to her feet and slipped her hand into his, and they tiptoed across the fields, jumping and swinging from dry spot to dry spot. A transcendent delight seemed to sparkle in every pool of water, for the moon had risen and the storm had scurried away into western Maryland. When Eleanor's arm touched his he felt his hands grow cold with deadly fear lest he should lose the shadow brush with which his imagination was painting wonders of her. He watched her from the corners of his eyes as ever he did when he walked with her—she was a feast and a folly and he wished it had been his destiny to sit forever on a haystack and see life through her green eyes. His paganism soared that night and when she faded out like a gray ghost down the road, a deep singing came out of the fields and filled his way homeward. All night the summer moths flitted in and out of Amory's window; all night large looming sounds swayed in mystic revery through the silver grain—and he lay awake in the clear darkness.

September

Amory selected a blade of grass and nibbled at it scientifically.

"I never fall in love in August or September," he proffered.

"When then?"

"Christmas or Easter. I'm a liturgist."

"Easter!" She turned up her nose. "Huh! Spring in corsets!"

"Easter *would* bore spring, wouldn't she? Easter has her hair braided, wears a tailored suit."

> "Bind on thy sandals, oh, thou most fleet.
> Over the splendor and speed of thy feet——"*

quoted Eleanor softly, and then added: "I suppose Hallowe'en is a better day for autumn than Thanksgiving."

"Much better—and Christmas eve does very well for winter, but summer . . ."

"Summer has no day," she said. "We can't possibly have a summer love. So many people have tried that the name's become proverbial. Summer is only the unfulfilled promise of spring, a charlatan in place of the warm balmy nights I dream of in April. It's a sad season of life without growth. . . . It has no day."

"Fourth of July," Amory suggested facetiously.

"Don't be funny!" she said, raking him with her eyes.

"Well, what could fulfil the promise of spring?"

She thought a moment.

"Oh, I suppose heaven would, if there was one," she said finally, "a sort of pagan heaven—you ought to be a materialist," she continued irrelevantly.

"Why?"

"Because you look a good deal like the pictures of Rupert Brooke."

To some extent Amory tried to play Rupert Brooke as long as he knew Eleanor. What he said, his attitude toward life, toward her, toward himself, were all reflexes of the dead Englishman's literary moods. Often she sat in the grass, a lazy wind playing with her short hair, her voice husky as she ran up and down the scale from Grantchester to Waikiki.* There was something most passionate in Eleanor's reading aloud. They seemed nearer, not only mentally, but physically, when they read, than when she was in his arms, and this was often, for they fell half into love almost from the first. Yet was Amory capable of love now? He could, as always, run through the emotions in a half hour, but even while they revelled in their imaginations, he knew that neither of them could care as he had cared once before—I suppose that was why they turned to Brooke, and Swinburne, and Shelley. Their chance was to make everything fine and finished and rich and imaginative; they must bend tiny golden tentacles from his imagination to hers, that would take the place of the great, deep love that was never so near, yet never so much of a dream.

One poem they read over and over; Swinburne's "Triumph of Time," and four lines of it rang in his memory afterward on warm nights when he saw the fireflies among dusky tree trunks and heard the low drone of many frogs. Then Eleanor seemed to come out of the night and stand by him, and he heard her throaty voice, with its tone of a fleecy-headed drum, repeating:

> *"Is it worth a tear, is it worth an hour,*
> *To think of things that are well outworn;*
> *Of fruitless husk and fugitive flower,*
> *The dream foregone and the deed foreborne?"**

They were formally introduced two days later, and his aunt told him her history. The Ramillys were two: old Mr. Ramilly and his granddaughter, Eleanor. She had lived in France with a restless mother whom Amory imagined to have been very like his own, on whose death she had come to America, to live in Maryland. She had gone to Baltimore first to stay with a bachelor uncle, and there she insisted on being a débutante at the age of seventeen. She had a wild winter and arrived in the country in March, having quarrelled frantically with all her Baltimore relatives, and shocked them into fiery protest. A rather fast crowd had come out, who drank cocktails in limousines and were promiscuously condescending and patronizing toward older people, and Eleanor with an esprit that hinted strongly of the boulevards, led many innocents still redolent of St. Timothy's and Farmington, into paths of Bohemian naughtiness. When the story came to her uncle, a forgetful cavalier of a more hypocritical era, there was a scene, from which Eleanor emerged, subdued but rebellious and indignant, to seek haven with her grandfather who hovered in the country on the near side of senility. That's as far as her story went; she told him the rest herself, but that was later.

Often they swam and as Amory floated lazily in the water he shut his mind to all thoughts except those of hazy soap-bubble lands where the sun splattered through wind-drunk trees. How could any one possibly think or worry, or do anything except splash and dive and loll there on the edge of time while the flower months failed.

Let the days move over—sadness and memory and pain recurred outside, and here, once more, before he went on to meet them he wanted to drift and be young.

There were days when Amory resented that life had changed from an even progress along a road stretching ever in sight, with the scenery merging and blending, into a succession of quick, unrelated scenes—two years of sweat and blood, that sudden absurd instinct for paternity that Rosalind had stirred; the half-sensual, half-neurotic quality of this autumn with Eleanor. He felt that it would take all time, more than he could ever spare, to glue these strange cumbersome pictures into the scrap-book of his life. It was all like a banquet where he sat for this half-hour of his youth and tried to enjoy brilliant epicurean courses.

Dimly he promised himself a time where all should be welded together. For months it seemed that he had alternated between being borne along a stream of love or fascination, or left in an eddy, and in the eddies he had not desired to think, rather to be picked up on a wave's top and swept along again.

"The despairing, dying autumn and our love—how well they harmonize!" said Eleanor sadly one day as they lay dripping by the water.

"The Indian summer of our hearts—" he ceased.

"Tell me," she said finally, "was she light or dark?"

"Light."

"Was she more beautiful than I am?"

"I don't know," said Amory shortly.

One night they walked while the moon rose and poured a great burden of glory over the garden until it seemed fairy-land with Amory and Eleanor, dim phantasmal shapes, expressing eternal beauty in curious elfin love moods. Then they turned out of the moonlight into the trellised darkness of a vine-hung pagoda, where there were scents so plaintive as to be nearly musical.

"Light a match," she whispered. "I want to see you."

Scratch! Flare!

The night and the scarred trees were like scenery in a play, and to be there with Eleanor, shadowy and unreal, seemed somehow oddly familiar. Amory thought how it was only the past that ever seemed strange and unbelievable. The match went out.

"It's black as pitch."

"We're just voices now," murmured Eleanor, "little lonesome voices. Light another."

"That was my last match."

Suddenly he caught her in his arms.

"You *are* mine—you know you're mine!" he cried wildly . . . the moonlight twisted in through the vines and listened . . . the fireflies hung upon their whispers as if to win his glance from the glory of her eyes.

The End of Summer

"No wind is stirring in the grass; not one wind stirs . . . the water in the hidden pools, as glass, fronts the full moon and so inters the golden token in its icy mass," chanted Eleanor to the trees that skeletoned the body of the night. "Isn't it ghostly here? If you can hold your horse's feet up, let's cut through the woods and find the hidden pools."

"It's after one, and you'll get the devil," he objected, "and I don't know enough about horses to put one away in the pitch dark."

"Shut up, you old fool," she whispered irrelevantly, and, leaning over, she patted him lazily with her riding-crop. "You can leave your old plug in our stable and I'll send him over to-morrow."

"But my uncle has got to drive me to the station with this old plug at seven o'clock."

"Don't be a spoil-sport—remember, you have a tendency toward wavering that prevents you from being the entire light of my life."

Amory drew his horse up close beside, and, leaning toward her, grasped her hand.

"Say I am—*quick*, or I'll pull you over and make you ride behind me."

She looked up and smiled and shook her head excitedly.

"Oh, do!—or rather, don't! Why are all the exciting things so uncomfortable, like fighting and exploring and ski-ing in Canada? By the way, we're going to ride up Harper's Hill. I think that comes in our programme about five o'clock."

"You little devil," Amory growled. "You're going to make me stay up all night and sleep in the train like an immigrant all day to-morrow, going back to New York."

"Hush! some one's coming along the road—let's go! *Whoo-ee-oop!*" And with a shout that probably gave the belated traveller a series of shivers, she turned her horse into the woods and Amory followed slowly, as he had followed her all day for three weeks.

The summer was over, but he had spent the days in watching Eleanor, a graceful, facile Manfred, build herself intellectual and imaginative pyramids while she revelled in the artificialities of the temperamental teens and they wrote poetry at the dinner-table.

When Vanity kissed Vanity, a hundred happy Junes ago, he pondered o'er her breathlessly, and, that all men might ever know, he rhymed her eyes with life and death:

"Thru Time I'll save my love!" he said . . . yet Beauty vanished with his breath, and, with her lovers, she was dead . . .

—Ever his wit and not her eyes, ever his art and not her hair:

"Who'd learn a trick in rhyme, be wise and pause before his sonnet there" . . . So all my words, however true, might sing you to a thousandth June, and no one ever *know* that you were Beauty for an afternoon.

So he wrote one day, when he pondered how coldly we thought of the "Dark Lady of the Sonnets," and how little we remembered her as the great man wanted her remembered. For what Shakespeare *must* have desired, to have been able to write with such divine despair, was that the lady should live . . . and now we have no real interest in her. . . . The irony of it is that if he had cared *more* for the poem than for the lady the sonnet would be only obvious, imitative rhetoric and no one would ever have read it after twenty years. . . .

This was the last night Amory ever saw Eleanor. He was leaving in the morning and they had agreed to take a long farewell trot by the cold moonlight. She wanted to talk, she said—perhaps the last time in her life that she could be rational (she meant pose with comfort). So they had turned into the woods and rode for half an hour with scarcely a word, except when she whispered "Damn!" at a bothersome branch—whispered it as no other girl was ever able to whisper it. Then they started up Harper's Hill, walking their tired horses.

"Good Lord! It's quiet here!" whispered Eleanor; "much more lonesome than the woods."

"I hate woods," Amory said, shuddering. "Any kind of foliage or underbrush at night. Out here it's so broad and easy on the spirit."

"The long slope of a long hill."

"And the cold moon rolling moonlight down it."

"And thee and me, last and most important."

It was quiet that night—the straight road they followed up to the edge of the cliff knew few footsteps at any time. Only an occasional negro cabin, silver-gray in the rock-ribbed moonlight, broke the long line of bare ground; behind lay the black edge of the woods like a dark frosting on white cake, and ahead the sharp, high horizon. It was much colder—so cold that it settled on them and drove all the warm nights from their minds.

"The end of summer," said Eleanor softly. "Listen to the beat of our horses' hoofs—'tump-tump-tump-a-tump.' Have you ever been feverish and had all noises divide into 'tump-tump-tump' until you could swear eternity was divisible into so many tumps? That's the way I feel—old horses go tump-tump. . . . I guess that's the only thing that separates horses and clocks from us. Human beings can't go 'tump-tump-tump' without going crazy."

The breeze freshened and Eleanor pulled her cape around her and shivered.

"Are you very cold?" asked Amory.

"No, I'm thinking about myself—my black old inside self, the real one, with the fundamental honesty that keeps me from being absolutely wicked by making me realize my own sins."

They were riding up close by the cliff and Amory gazed over. Where the fall met the ground a hundred feet below, a black stream made a sharp line, broken by tiny glints in the swift water.

"Rotten, rotten old world," broke out Eleanor suddenly, "and the wretchedest thing of all is me—oh, *why* am I a girl? Why am I not a stupid—? Look at you; you're stupider than I am, not much, but some, and you can lope about and get bored and then lope somewhere else, and you can play around with girls without being involved in meshes of sentiment, and you can do anything and be justified—and here am I with the brains to do everything, yet tied to the sinking ship of future matrimony. If I were born a hundred years from now, well and good, but now what's in store for me—I have to marry, that goes without saying. Who? I'm too bright for most men, and yet I have to descend to their level and let them patronize my intellect in order to get their attention. Every year that I don't marry I've got less chance for a first-class man. At the best I can have my choice from one or two cities and, of course, I have to marry into a dinner-coat.

"Listen," she leaned close again, "I like clever men and good-looking men, and, of course, no one cares more for personality than I do. Oh, just one person in fifty has any glimmer of what sex is. I'm hipped on Freud and all that, but it's rotten that every bit of *real* love in the world is ninety-nine per cent passion and one little soupçon of jealousy." She finished as suddenly as she began.

"Of course, you're right," Amory agreed. "It's a rather unpleasant overpowering force that's part of the machinery under everything. It's like an actor that lets you see his mechanics! Wait a minute till I think this out. . . ."

He paused and tried to get a metaphor. They had turned the cliff and were riding along the road about fifty feet to the left.

"You see every one's got to have some cloak to throw around it. The mediocre intellects, Plato's second class, use the remnants of romantic chivalry diluted with Victorian sentiment—and we who consider ourselves the intellectuals cover it up by pretending that it's another side of us, has nothing to do with our shining brains; we pretend that the fact that we realize it is really absolving us from being a prey to it. But the truth is that sex is right in the middle of our purest abstractions, so close that it obscures vision. . . . I can kiss you now and will. . . ." He leaned toward her in his saddle, but she drew away.

"I can't—I can't kiss you now—I'm more sensitive."

"You're more stupid then," he declared rather impatiently. "Intellect is no protection from sex any more than convention is . . ."

"What is?" she fired up. "The Catholic Church or the maxims of Confucius?"

Amory looked up, rather taken aback.

"That's your panacea, isn't it?" she cried. "Oh, you're just an old hypocrite, too. Thousands of scowling priests keeping the degenerate Italians and illiterate Irish repentant with gabble-gabble about the sixth and ninth commandments.* It's just all cloaks, sentiment and spiritual rouge and panaceas. I'll tell you there *is* no God, not even a definite abstract goodness; so it's all got to be worked out for the individual by the individual here in high white foreheads like mine, and you're too much the prig to admit it." She let go her reins and shook her little fists at the stars.

"If there's a God let him strike me—strike me!"

"Talking about God again after the manner of atheists," Amory said sharply. His materialism, always a thin cloak, was torn to shreds by Eleanor's blasphemy. . . . She knew it and it angered him that she knew it.

"And like most intellectuals who don't find faith convenient," he continued coldly, "like Napoleon and Oscar Wilde and the rest of your type, you'll yell loudly for a priest on your death-bed."

Eleanor drew her horse up sharply and he reined in beside her.

"Will I?" she said in a queer voice that scared him. "Will I? Watch! *I'm going over the cliff!*" And before he could interfere she had turned and was riding breakneck for the end of the plateau.

He wheeled and started after her, his body like ice, his nerves in a vast clangor. There was no chance of stopping her. The moon was under a cloud and her horse would step blindly over. Then some ten feet from the edge of the cliff she gave a sudden shriek and flung herself sideways—plunged from her horse and, rolling over twice, landed in a pile of brush five feet from the edge. The horse went over with a frantic whinny. In a minute he was by Eleanor's side and saw that her eyes were open.

"Eleanor!" he cried.

She did not answer, but her lips moved and her eyes filled with sudden tears.

"Eleanor, are you hurt?"

"No; I don't think so," she said faintly, and then began weeping.

"My horse dead?"

"Good God— Yes!"

"Oh!" she wailed. "I thought I was going over. I didn't know——"

He helped her gently to her feet and boosted her onto his saddle. So they started homeward; Amory walking and she bent forward on the pommel, sobbing bitterly.

"I've got a crazy streak," she faltered, "twice before I've done things like that. When I was eleven mother went—went mad—stark raving crazy. We were in Vienna——"

All the way back she talked haltingly about herself, and Amory's love waned slowly with the moon. At her door they started from habit to kiss good night, but she could not run into his arms, nor were they stretched to meet her as in the week before. For a minute they stood there, hating each other with a bitter sadness. But as Amory had loved himself in Eleanor, so now what he hated was only a mirror. Their poses were strewn about the pale dawn like broken glass. The stars were long gone and there were left only the little sighing gusts of wind and the silences between . . . but naked souls are poor things ever, and soon he turned homeward and let new lights come in with the sun.

A Poem that Eleanor Sent Amory Several Years Later

"Here, Earth-born, over the lilt of the water,
    Lisping its music and bearing a burden of light,
Bosoming day as a laughing and radiant daughter . . .
    Here we may whisper unheard, unafraid of the night.
Walking alone . . . was it splendor, or what, we were bound with,
    Deep in the time when summer lets down her hair?
Shadows we loved and the patterns they covered the ground with
    Tapestries, mystical, faint in the breathless air.

That was the day . . . and the night for another story,
    Pale as a dream and shadowed with pencilled trees—
Ghosts of the stars came by who had sought for glory,
    Whispered to us of peace in the plaintive breeze,
Whispered of old dead faiths that the day had shattered,
    Youth the penny that bought delight of the moon;
That was the urge that we knew and the language that mattered
    That was the debt that we paid to the usurer June.

Here, deepest of dreams, by the waters that bring not
    Anything back of the past that we need not know,
What if the light is but sun and the little streams sing not,
    We are together, it seems . . . I have loved you so . . .
What did the last night hold, with the summer over,
    Drawing us back to the home in the changing glade?
What leered out of the dark in the ghostly clover?
    God! . . . till you stirred in your sleep . . . and were wild afraid . . .

Well . . . we have passed . . . we are chronicle now to the eerie.
    Curious metal from meteors that failed in the sky;
Earth-born the tireless is stretched by the water, quite weary,
    Close to this ununderstandable changeling that's I . . .
Fear is an echo we traced to Security's daughter;
    Now we are faces and voices . . . and less, too soon,
Whispering half-love over the lilt of the water . . .
    Youth the penny that bought delight of the moon."

A Poem Amory Sent to Eleanor and Which He Called "Summer Storm"

"Faint winds, and a song fading and leaves falling,
Faint winds, and far away a fading laughter . . .
And the rain and over the fields a voice calling . . .

Our gray blown cloud scurries and lifts above,
Slides on the sun and flutters there to waft her
Sisters on. The shadow of a dove
Falls on the cote, the trees are filled with wings;
And down the valley through the crying trees
The body of the darker storm flies; brings
With its new air the breath of sunken seas
And slender tenuous thunder . . .
                                        But I wait . . .
Wait for the mists and for the blacker rain—
Heavier winds that stir the veil of fate,
Happier winds that pile her hair;
                                        Again
They tear me, teach me, strew the heavy air
Upon me, winds that I know, and storm.

There was a summer every rain was rare;
There was a season every wind was warm. . . .
And now *you* pass me in the mist . . . your hair
Rain-blown about you, damp lips curved once more
In that wild irony, that gay despair
That made you old when we have met before;
Wraith-like you drift on out before the rain,
Across the fields, blown with the stemless flowers,
With your old hopes, dead leaves and loves again—
Dim as a dream and wan with all old hours
(Whispers will creep into the growing dark . . .
Tumult will die over the trees)
                                        Now night
Tears from her wetted breast the splattered blouse
Of day, glides down the dreaming hills, tear-bright,
To cover with her hair the eerie green . . .
Love for the dusk . . . Love for the glistening after;
Quiet the trees to their last tops . . . serene . . .

Faint winds, and far away a fading laughter . . ."

CHAPTER IV

THE SUPERCILIOUS SACRIFICE

ATLANTIC CITY. Amory paced the board walk at day's end, lulled by the everlasting surge of changing waves, smelling the half-mournful odor of the salt breeze. The sea, he thought, had treasured its memories deeper than the faithless land. It seemed still to whisper of Norse galleys ploughing the water world under raven-figured flags, of the British dreadnoughts, gray bulwarks of civilization steaming up through the fog of one dark July into the North Sea.

"Well—Amory Blaine!"

Amory looked down into the street below. A low racing car had drawn to a stop and a familiar cheerful face protruded from the driver's seat.

"Come on down, goopher!" cried Alec.

Amory called a greeting and descending a flight of wooden steps approached the car. He and Alec had been meeting intermittently, but the barrier of Rosalind lay always between them. He was sorry for this; he hated to lose Alec.

"Mr. Blaine, this is Miss Waterson, Miss Wayne, and Mr. Tully."

"How d'y do?"

"Amory," said Alec exuberantly, "if you'll jump in we'll take you to some secluded nook and give you a wee jolt of Bourbon."

Amory considered.

"That's an idea."

"Step in—move over, Jill, and Amory will smile very handsomely at you."

Amory squeezed into the back seat beside a gaudy, vermilion-lipped blonde.

"Hello, Doug Fairbanks," she said flippantly. "Walking for exercise or hunting for company?"

"I was counting the waves," replied Amory gravely. "I'm going in for statistics."

"Don't kid me, Doug."

When they reached an unfrequented side street Alec stopped the car among deep shadows.

"What you doing down here these cold days, Amory?" he demanded, as he produced a quart of Bourbon from under the fur rug.

Amory avoided the question. Indeed, he had had no definite reason for coming to the coast.

"Do you remember that party of ours, sophomore year?" he asked instead.

"Do I? When we slept in the pavilions up in Asbury Park——"

"Lord, Alec! It's hard to think that Jesse and Dick and Kerry are all three dead."

Alec shivered.

"Don't talk about it. These dreary fall days depress me enough."

Jill seemed to agree.

"Doug here is sorta gloomy anyways," she commented. "Tell him to drink deep—it's good and scarce these days."

"What I really want to ask you, Amory, is where you are——"

"Why, New York, I suppose——"

"I mean to-night, because if you haven't got a room yet you'd better help me out."

"Glad to."

"You see, Tully and I have two rooms with bath between at the Ranier, and he's got to go back to New York. I don't want to have to move. Question is, will you occupy one of the rooms?"

Amory was willing, if he could get in right away.

"You'll find the key in the office; the rooms are in my name."

Declining further locomotion or further stimulation, Amory left the car and sauntered back along the board walk to the hotel.

He was in an eddy again, a deep, lethargic gulf, without desire to work or write, love or dissipate. For the first time in his life he rather longed for death to roll over his generation, obliterating their petty fevers and struggles and exultations. His youth seemed never so vanished as now in the contrast between the utter loneliness of this visit and that riotous, joyful party of four years before. Things that had been the merest commonplaces of his life then, deep sleep, the sense of beauty around him, all desire, had flown away and the gaps they left were filled only with the great listlessness of his disillusion.

"To hold a man a woman has to appeal to the worst in him." This sentence was the thesis of most of his bad nights, of which he felt this was to be one. His mind had already started to play variations on the subject. Tireless passion, fierce jealousy, longing to possess and crush—these alone were left of all his love for Rosalind; these remained to him as payment for the loss of his youth—bitter calomel under the thin sugar of love's exaltation.

In his room he undressed and wrapping himself in blankets to keep out the chill October air drowsed in an armchair by the open window.

He remembered a poem he had read months before:

> "Oh staunch old heart who toiled so long for me,
> I waste my years sailing along the sea——"

Yet he had no sense of waste, no sense of the present hope that waste implied. He felt that life had rejected him.

"Rosalind! Rosalind!" He poured the words softly into the half-darkness until she seemed to permeate the room; the wet salt breeze filled his hair with moisture, the rim of a moon seared the sky and made the curtains dim and ghostly. He fell asleep.

When he awoke it was very late and quiet. The blanket had slipped partly off his shoulders and he touched his skin to find it damp and cold.

Then he became aware of a tense whispering not ten feet away.

He became rigid.

"Don't make a sound!" It was Alec's voice. *"Jill—do you hear me?"*

"Yes—" breathed very low, very frightened. They were in the bathroom.

Then his ears caught a louder sound from somewhere along the corridor outside. It was a mumbling of men's voices and a repeated muffled rapping. Amory threw off the blankets and moved close to the bathroom door.

"My God!" came the girl's voice again. "You'll have to let them in."

"Sh!"

Suddenly a steady, insistent knocking began at Amory's hall door and simultaneously out of the bathroom came Alec, followed by the vermilion-lipped girl. They were both clad in pajamas.

"Amory!" an anxious whisper.

"What's the trouble?"

"It's house detectives. My God, Amory—they're just looking for a test-case——"

"Well, better let them in."

"You don't understand. They can get me under the Mann Act."*

The girl followed him slowly, a rather miserable, pathetic figure in the darkness.

Amory tried to plan quickly.

"You make a racket and let them in your room," he suggested anxiously, "and I'll get her out by this door."

"They're here too, though. They'll watch this door."

"Can't you give a wrong name?"

"No chance. I registered under my own name; besides, they'd trail the auto license number."

"Say you're married."

"Jill says one of the house detectives knows her."

The girl had stolen to the bed and tumbled upon it; lay there listening wretchedly to the knocking which had grown gradually to a pounding. Then came a man's voice, angry and imperative:

"Open up or we'll break the door in!"

In the silence when this voice ceased Amory realized that there were other things in the room besides people . . . over and around the figure crouched on the bed there hung an aura, gossamer as a moonbeam, tainted as stale, weak wine, yet a horror, diffusively brooding already over the three of them . . . and over by the window among the stirring curtains stood something else, featureless and indistinguishable, yet strangely familiar. . . . Simultaneously two great cases presented themselves side by side to Amory; all that took place in his mind, then, occupied in actual time less than ten seconds.

The first fact that flashed radiantly on his comprehension was the great impersonality of sacrifice—he perceived that what we call love and hate, reward and punishment, had no more to do with it than the date of the month. He quickly recapitulated the story of a sacrifice he had heard of in college: a man had cheated in an examination; his roommate in a gust of sentiment had taken the entire blame—due to the shame of it the innocent one's entire future seemed shrouded in regret and failure, capped by the ingratitude of the real culprit. He had finally taken his own life—years afterward the facts had come out. At the time the story had both puzzled and worried Amory. Now he realized the truth; that sacrifice was no purchase of freedom. It was like a great elective office, it was like an inheritance of power—to certain people at certain times an essential luxury, carrying with it not a guarantee but a responsibility, not a security but an infinite risk. Its very momentum might drag him down to ruin—the passing of the emotional wave that made it possible might leave the one who made it high and dry forever on an island of despair.

. . . Amory knew that afterward Alec would secretly hate him for having done so much for him. . . .

. . . All this was flung before Amory like an opened scroll, while ulterior to him and speculating upon him were those two breathless, listening forces: the gossamer aura that hung over and about the girl and that familiar thing by the window.

Sacrifice by its very nature was arrogant and impersonal; sacrifice should be eternally supercilious.

*Weep not for me but for thy children.**

That—thought Amory—would be somehow the way God would talk to me.

Amory felt a sudden surge of joy and then like a face in a motion-picture the aura over the bed faded out; the dynamic shadow by the window, that was as near as he could name it, remained for the fraction of a moment and then the breeze seemed to lift it swiftly out of the room. He clenched his hands in quick ecstatic excitement . . . the ten seconds were up. . . .

"Do what I say, Alec—do what I say. Do you understand?"

Alec looked at him dumbly—his face a tableau of anguish.

"You have a family," continued Amory slowly. "You have a family and it's important that you should get out of this. Do you hear me?" He repeated clearly what he had said. "Do you hear me?"

"I hear you." The voice was curiously strained, the eyes never for a second left Amory's.

"Alec, you're going to lie down here. If any one comes in you act drunk. You do what I say—if you don't I'll probably kill you."

There was another moment while they stared at each other. Then Amory went briskly to the bureau and, taking his pocket-book, beckoned peremptorily to the girl. He heard one word from Alec that sounded like "penitentiary," then he and Jill were in the bathroom with the door bolted behind them.

"You're here with me," he said sternly. "You've been with me all evening."

She nodded, gave a little half cry.

In a second he had the door of the other room open and three men entered. There was an immediate flood of electric light and he stood there blinking.

"You've been playing a little too dangerous a game, young man!" Amory laughed.

"Well?"

The leader of the trio nodded authoritatively at a burly man in a check suit.

"Ah right, Olson."

"I got you, Mr. O'May," said Olson, nodding. The other two took a curious glance at their quarry and then withdrew, closing the door angrily behind them.

The burly man regarded Amory contemptuously.

"Didn't you ever hear of the Mann Act? Coming down here with her," he indicated the girl with his thumb, "with a New York license on your car—to a hotel like *this*." He shook his head implying that he had struggled over Amory but now gave him up.

"Well," said Amory rather impatiently, "what do you want us to do?"

"Get dressed, quick—and tell your friend not to make such a racket." Jill was sobbing noisily on the bed, but at these words she subsided sulkily and, gathering up her clothes, retired to the bathroom. As Amory slipped into Alec's B. V. D.'s he found that his attitude toward the situation was agreeably humorous. The aggrieved virtue of the burly man made him want to laugh.

"Anybody else here?" demanded Olson, trying to look keen and ferret-like.

"Fellow who had the rooms," said Amory carelessly. "He's drunk as an owl, though. Been in there asleep since six o'clock."

"I'll take a look at him presently."

"How did you find out?" asked Amory curiously.

"Night clerk saw you go up-stairs with this woman."

Amory nodded; Jill reappeared from the bathroom, completely if rather untidily arrayed.

"Now then," began Olson, producing a note-book, "I want your real names—no damn John Smith or Mary Brown."

"Wait a minute," said Amory quietly. "Just drop that big-bully stuff. We merely got caught, that's all."

Olson glared at him.

"Name?" he snapped.

Amory gave his name and New York address.

"And the lady?"

"Miss Jill——"

"Say," cried Olson indignantly, "just ease up on the nursery rhymes. What's your name? Sarah Murphy? Minnie Jackson?"

"Oh, my God!" cried the girl cupping her tear-stained face in her hands. "I don't want my mother to know. I don't want my mother to know."

"Come on now!"

"Shut up!" cried Amory at Olson.

An instant's pause.

"Stella Robbins," she faltered finally. "General Delivery, Rugway, New Hampshire."

Olson snapped his note-book shut and looked at them very ponderously.

"By rights the hotel could turn the evidence over to the police and you'd go to penitentiary, you would, for bringin' a girl from one state to 'nother f'r immoral purp'ses"—he paused to let the majesty of his words sink in. "But—the hotel is going to let you off."

"It doesn't want to get in the papers," cried Jill fiercely. "Let us off! Huh!"

A great lightness surrounded Amory. He realized that he was safe and only then did he appreciate the full enormity of what he might have incurred.

"However," continued Olson, "there's a protective association among the hotels. There's been too much of this stuff, and we got a 'rangement with the newspapers so that you get a little free publicity. Not the name of the hotel, but just a line sayin' that you had a little trouble in 'lantic City. See?"

"I see."

"You're gettin' off light—damn light—but——"

"Come on," said Amory briskly. "Let's get out of here. We don't need a valedictory."

Olson walked through the bathroom and took a cursory glance at Alec's still form. Then he extinguished the lights and motioned them to follow him. As they walked into the elevator Amory considered a piece of bravado—yielded finally. He reached out and tapped Olson on the arm.

"Would you mind taking off your hat? There's a lady in the elevator."

Olson's hat came off slowly. There was a rather embarrassing two minutes under the lights of the lobby while the night clerk and a few belated guests stared at them curiously; the loudly dressed girl with bent head, the handsome young man with his chin several points aloft; the inference was quite obvious. Then the chill outdoors—where the salt air was fresher and keener still with the first hints of morning.

"You can get one of those taxis and beat it," said Olson, pointing to the blurred outline of two machines whose drivers were presumably asleep inside.

"Good-bye," said Olson. He reached in his pocket suggestively,* but Amory snorted, and, taking the girl's arm, turned away.

"Where did you tell the driver to go?" she asked as they whirled along the dim street.

"The station."

"If that guy writes my mother——"

"He won't. Nobody'll ever know about this—except our friends and enemies."

Dawn was breaking over the sea.

"It's getting blue," she said.

"It does very well," agreed Amory critically, and then as an after-thought: "It's almost breakfast-time—do you want something to eat?"

"Food—" she said with a cheerful laugh. "Food is what queered the party. We ordered a big supper to be sent up to the room about two o'clock. Alec didn't give the waiter a tip, so I guess the little bastard snitched."

Jill's low spirits seemed to have gone faster than the scattering night. "Let me tell you," she said emphatically, "when you want to stage that sorta party stay away from liquor, and when you want to get tight stay away from bedrooms."

"I'll remember."

He tapped suddenly at the glass and they drew up at the door of an all-night restaurant.

"Is Alec a great friend of yours?" asked Jill as they perched themselves on high stools inside, and set their elbows on the dingy counter.

"He used to be. He probably won't want to be any more—and never understand why."

"It was sorta crazy you takin' all that blame. Is he pretty important? Kinda more important than you are?"

Amory laughed.

"That remains to be seen," he answered. "That's the question."

The Collapse of Several Pillars

Two days later back in New York Amory found in a newspaper what
he had been searching for—a dozen lines which announced to whom
it might concern that Mr. Amory Blaine, who "gave his address" as,
etc., had been requested to leave his hotel in Atlantic City because of
entertaining in his room a lady *not* his wife.

Then he started, and his fingers trembled, for directly above was
a longer paragraph of which the first words were:

"Mr. and Mrs. Leland R. Connage are announcing the engagement
of their daughter, Rosalind, to Mr. J. Dawson Ryder, of Hartford,
Connecticut——"

He dropped the paper and lay down on his bed with a frightened,
sinking sensation in the pit of his stomach. She was gone, definitely,
finally gone. Until now he had half unconsciously cherished the hope
deep in his heart that some day she would need him and send for
him, cry that it had been a mistake, that her heart ached only for the
pain she had caused him. Never again could he find even the sombre
luxury of wanting her—not this Rosalind, harder, older—nor any
beaten, broken woman that his imagination brought to the door of
his forties—Amory had wanted her youth, the fresh radiance of her
mind and body, the stuff that she was selling now once and for all.
So far as he was concerned, young Rosalind was dead.

A day later came a crisp, terse letter from Mr. Barton in Chicago,
which informed him that as three more street-car companies had
gone into the hands of receivers he could expect for the present no
further remittances. Last of all, on a dazed Sunday night, a telegram
told him of Monsignor Darcy's sudden death in Philadelphia five
days before.

He knew then what it was that he had perceived among the
curtains of the room in Atlantic City.

CHAPTER V

THE EGOTIST BECOMES A PERSONAGE

"A fathom deep in sleep I lie
With old desires, restrained before,
To clamor lifeward with a cry,
As dark flies out the greying door;
And so in quest of creeds to share
I seek assertive day again . . .
But old monotony is there:
Endless avenues of rain.

Oh, might I rise again! Might I
Throw off the heat of that old wine,
See the new morning mass the sky
With fairy towers, line on line;
Find each mirage in the high air
A symbol, not a dream again . . .
But old monotony is there:
Endless avenues of rain."

UNDER the glass porte cochère* of a theatre Amory stood, watching the first great drops of rain splatter down and flatten to dark stains on the sidewalk. The air became gray and opalescent; a solitary light suddenly outlined a window over the way; then another light; then a hundred more danced and glimmered into vision. Under his feet a thick, iron-studded skylight turned yellow; in the street the lamps of the taxi-cabs sent out glistening sheens along the already black pavement. The unwelcome November rain had perversely stolen the day's last hour and pawned it with that ancient fence, the night.

The silence of the theatre behind him ended with a curious snapping sound, followed by the heavy roaring of a rising crowd and the interlaced clatter of many voices. The matinée was over.

He stood aside, edged a little into the rain to let the throng pass. A small boy rushed out, sniffed in the damp, fresh air and turned up the collar of his coat; came three or four couples in a great hurry; came a further scattering of people whose eyes as they emerged glanced invariably, first at the wet street, then at the rain-filled air, finally at the dismal sky; last a dense, strolling mass that depressed him with its heavy odor compounded of the tobacco smell of the men and the fetid sensuousness of stale powder on women. After the thick crowd came another scattering; a stray half-dozen; a man on crutches; finally the rattling bang of folding seats inside announced that the ushers were at work.

New York seemed not so much awakening as turning over in its bed. Pallid men rushed by, pinching together their coat-collars; a great swarm of tired, magpie girls from a department-store crowded along with shrieks of strident laughter, three to an umbrella; a squad of marching policemen passed, already miraculously protected by oilskin capes.

The rain gave Amory a feeling of detachment, and the numerous unpleasant aspects of city life without money occurred to him in threatening procession. There was the ghastly, stinking crush of the subway—the car cards* thrusting themselves at one, leering out like dull bores who grab your arm with another story; the querulous worry as to whether some one isn't leaning on you; a man deciding not to give his seat to a woman, hating her for it; the woman hating him for not doing it; at worst a squalid phantasmagoria of breath, and old cloth on human bodies and the smells of the food men ate—at best just people—too hot or too cold, tired, worried.

He pictured the rooms where these people lived—where the patterns of the blistered wall-papers were heavy reiterated sunflowers on green and yellow backgrounds, where there were tin bathtubs and gloomy hallways and verdureless, unnamable spaces in back of the buildings; where even love dressed as seduction—a sordid murder around the corner, illicit motherhood in the flat above. And always there was the economical stuffiness of indoor winter, and the long summers, nightmares of perspiration between sticky enveloping walls . . . dirty restaurants where careless, tired people helped themselves to sugar with their own used coffee-spoons, leaving hard brown deposits in the bowl.

It was not so bad where there were only men or else only women; it was when they were vilely herded that it all seemed so rotten. It was some shame that women gave off at having men see them tired and poor—it was some disgust that men had for women who were tired and poor. It was dirtier than any battle-field he had seen, harder to contemplate than any actual hardship moulded of mire and sweat and danger, it was an atmosphere wherein birth and marriage and death were loathsome, secret things.

He remembered one day in the subway when a delivery boy had brought in a great funeral wreath of fresh flowers, how the smell of it had suddenly cleared the air and given every one in the car a momentary glow.

"I detest poor people," thought Amory suddenly. "I hate them for being poor. Poverty may have been beautiful once, but it's rotten now. It's the ugliest thing in the world. It's essentially cleaner to be corrupt and rich than it is to be innocent and poor." He seemed to see again a figure whose significance had once impressed him—a well-dressed young man gazing from a club window on Fifth Avenue and saying something to his companion with a look of utter disgust. Probably, thought Amory, what he said was: "My God! Aren't people horrible!"

Never before in his life had Amory considered poor people. He thought cynically how completely he was lacking in all human sympathy. O. Henry had found in these people romance, pathos, love, hate—Amory saw only coarseness, physical filth, and stupidity. He made no self-accusations: never any more did he reproach himself for feelings that were natural and sincere. He accepted all his reactions as a part of him, unchangeable, unmoral. This problem of poverty transformed, magnified, attached to some grander, more dignified attitude might some day even be his problem; at present it roused only his profound distaste.

He walked over to Fifth Avenue, dodging the blind, black menace of umbrellas, and standing in front of Delmonico's hailed an autobus. Buttoning his coat closely around him he climbed to the roof, where he rode in solitary state through the thin, persistent rain, stung into alertness by the cool moisture perpetually reborn on his cheek. Somewhere in his mind a conversation began, rather resumed its place in his attention. It was composed not of two voices, but of one, which acted alike as questioner and answerer:

Question.—Well—what's the situation?

Answer.—That I have about twenty-four dollars to my name.

Q.—You have the Lake Geneva estate.

A.—But I intend to keep it.

Q.—Can you live?

A.—I can't imagine not being able to. People make money in books and I've found that I can always do the things that people do in books. Really they are the only things I can do.

Q.—Be definite.

A.—I don't know what I'll do—nor have I much curiosity. To-morrow I'm going to leave New York for good. It's a bad town unless you're on top of it.

Q.—Do you want a lot of money?

A.—No. I am merely afraid of being poor.

Q.—Very afraid?

A.—Just passively afraid.

Q.—Where are you drifting?

A.—Don't ask *me!*

Q.—Don't you care?

A.—Rather. I don't want to commit moral suicide.

Q.—Have you no interests left?

A.—None. I've no more virtue to lose. Just as a cooling pot gives off heat, so all through youth and adolescence we give off calories of virtue. That's what's called ingenuousness.

Q.—An interesting idea.

A.—That's why a "good man going wrong" attracts people. They stand around and literally *warm themselves* at the calories of virtue he gives off. Sarah makes an unsophisticated remark and the faces simper in delight—"How *innocent* the poor child is!" They're warming themselves at her virtue. But Sarah sees the simper and never makes that remark again. Only she feels a little colder after that.

Q.—All your calories gone?

A.—All of them. I'm beginning to warm myself at other people's virtue.

Q.—Are you corrupt?

A.—I think so. I'm not sure. I'm not sure about good and evil at all any more.

Q.—Is that a bad sign in itself?

A.—Not necessarily.

Q.—What would be the test of corruption?

A.—Becoming really insincere—calling myself "not such a bad fellow," thinking I regretted my lost youth when I only envy the delights of losing it. Youth is like having a big plate of candy. Sentimentalists think they want to be in the pure, simple state they were in before they ate the candy. They don't. They just want the fun of eating it all over again. The matron doesn't want to repeat her girlhood—she wants to repeat her honeymoon. I don't want to repeat my innocence. I want the pleasure of losing it again.

Q.—Where are you drifting?

This dialogue merged grotesquely into his mind's most familiar state—a grotesque blending of desires, worries, exterior impressions and physical reactions.

One Hundred and Twenty-seventh Street—or One Hundred and Thirty-seventh Street. . . . Two and three look alike—no, not much. Seat damp . . . are clothes absorbing wetness from seat, or seat absorbing dryness from clothes? . . . Sitting on wet substance gave appendicitis, so Froggy Parker's mother said. Well, he'd had it—I'll sue the steamboat company, Beatrice said, and my uncle has a quarter interest—did Beatrice go to heaven? . . . probably not— He represented Beatrice's immortality, also love-affairs of numerous dead men who surely had never thought of him . . . if it wasn't appendicitis, influenza maybe. What? One Hundred and Twentieth Street? That must have been One Hundred and Twelfth back there. One One Two instead of One Two Seven. Rosalind not like Beatrice, Eleanor like Beatrice, only wilder and brainier. Apartments along here expensive—probably hundred and fifty a month—maybe two hundred. Uncle had only paid hundred a month for whole great big house in Minneapolis. Question—were the stairs on the left or right as you came in? Anyway, in 12 Univee they were straight back and to the left. What a dirty river—want to go down there and see if it's dirty—French rivers all brown or black, so were Southern rivers. Twenty-four dollars meant four hundred and eighty doughnuts. He could live on it three months and sleep in the park. Wonder where Jill was—Jill Bayne, Fayne, Sayne—what the devil—neck hurts, darned uncomfortable seat. No desire to sleep with Jill, what could Alec see in her? Alec had a coarse taste in women. Own taste the best; Isabelle, Clara, Rosalind, Eleanor, were all-American. Eleanor would pitch, probably southpaw. Rosalind was outfield, wonderful hitter, Clara first base, maybe. Wonder what Humbird's body looked like now. If he himself hadn't been bayonet instructor he'd have gone up to line three months sooner, probably been killed. Where's the darned bell——

The street numbers of Riverside Drive were obscured by the mist and dripping trees from anything but the swiftest scrutiny, but Amory had finally caught sight of one—One Hundred and

Twenty-seventh Street. He got off and with no distinct destination followed a winding, descending sidewalk and came out facing the river, in particular a long pier and a partitioned litter of shipyards for miniature craft: small launches, canoes, rowboats, and catboats. He turned northward and followed the shore, jumped a small wire fence and found himself in a great disorderly yard adjoining a dock. The hulls of many boats in various stages of repair were around him; he smelled sawdust and paint and the scarcely distinguishable flat odor of the Hudson. A man approached through the heavy gloom.

"Hello," said Amory.

"Got a pass?"

"No. Is this private?"

"This is the Hudson River Sporting and Yacht Club."

"Oh! I didn't know. I'm just resting."

"Well—" began the man dubiously.

"I'll go if you want me to."

The man made non-committal noises in his throat and passed on. Amory seated himself on an overturned boat and leaned forward thoughtfully until his chin rested in his hand.

"Misfortune is liable to make me a damn bad man," he said slowly.

In the Drooping Hours

While the rain drizzled on Amory looked futilely back at the stream of his life, all its glitterings and dirty shallows. To begin with, he was still afraid—not physically afraid any more, but afraid of people and prejudice and misery and monotony. Yet, deep in his bitter heart, he wondered if he was after all worse than this man or the next. He knew that he could sophisticate himself finally into saying that his own weakness was just the result of circumstances and environment; that often when he raged at himself as an egotist something would whisper ingratiatingly: "No. Genius!" That was one manifestation of fear, that voice which whispered that he could not be both great and good, that genius was the exact combination of those inexplicable grooves and twists in his mind, that any discipline would curb it to mediocrity. Probably more than any concrete vice or failing Amory despised his own personality—he loathed knowing that to-morrow and the thousand days after he would swell pompously at a compliment and sulk at an ill word like a third-rate musician or a first-class actor.

He was ashamed of the fact that very simple and honest people usually distrusted him; that he had been cruel, often, to those who had sunk their personalities in him—several girls, and a man here and there through college, that he had been an evil influence on; people who had followed him here and there into mental adventures from which he alone rebounded unscathed.

Usually, on nights like this, for there had been many lately, he could escape from this consuming introspection by thinking of children and the infinite possibilities of children—he leaned and listened and he heard a startled baby awake in a house across the street and lend a tiny whimper to the still night. Quick as a flash he turned away, wondering with a touch of panic whether something in the brooding despair of his mood had made a darkness in its tiny soul. He shivered. What if some day the balance was overturned, and he became a thing that frightened children and crept into rooms in the dark, approached dim communion with those phantoms who whispered shadowy secrets to the mad of that dark continent upon the moon. . . .

Amory smiled a bit.

"You're too much wrapped up in yourself," he heard some one say. And again——

"Get out and do some real work——"

"Stop worrying——"

He fancied a possible future comment of his own.

"Yes—I was perhaps an egotist in youth, but I soon found it made me morbid to think too much about myself."

Suddenly he felt an overwhelming desire to let himself go to the devil—not to go violently as a gentleman should, but to sink safely and sensuously out of sight. He pictured himself in an adobe house in Mexico, half-reclining on a rug-covered couch, his slender, artistic fingers closed on a cigarette while he listened to guitars strumming melancholy undertones to an age-old dirge of Castile and an olive-skinned, carmine-lipped girl caressed his hair. Here he might live a strange litany, delivered from right and wrong and from the hound of heaven and from every God (except the exotic Mexican one who was pretty slack himself and rather addicted to Oriental scents)—delivered from success and hope and poverty into that long chute of indulgence which led, after all, only to the artificial lake of death.

There were so many places where one might deteriorate pleasantly: Port Said, Shanghai, parts of Turkestan, Constantinople, the South Seas—all lands of sad, haunting music and many odors, where lust could be a mode and expression of life, where the shades of night skies and sunsets would seem to reflect only moods of passion: the colors of lips and poppies.

Still Weeding

Once he had been miraculously able to scent evil as a horse detects a broken bridge at night, but the man with the queer feet in Phœbe's room had diminished to the aura over Jill. His instinct perceived the fetidness of poverty, but no longer ferreted out the deeper evils in pride and sensuality.

There were no more wise men; there were no more heroes; Burne Holiday was sunk from sight as though he had never lived; Monsignor was dead. Amory had grown up to a thousand books, a thousand lies; he had listened eagerly to people who pretended to know, who knew nothing. The mystical reveries of saints that had once filled him with awe in the still hours of night, now vaguely repelled him. The Byrons and Brookes who had defied life from mountain tops were in the end but flaneurs and poseurs, at best mistaking the shadow of courage for the substance of wisdom. The pageantry of his disillusion took shape in a world-old procession of Prophets, Athenians, Martyrs, Saints, Scientists, Don Juans, Jesuits, Puritans, Fausts, Poets, Pacifists; like costumed alumni at a college reunion they streamed before him as their dreams, personalities, and creeds had in turn thrown colored lights on his soul; each had tried to express the glory of life and the tremendous significance of man; each had boasted of synchronizing what had gone before into his own rickety generalities; each had depended after all on the set stage and the convention of the theatre, which is that man in his hunger for faith will feed his mind with the nearest and most convenient food.

Women—of whom he had expected so much; whose beauty he had hoped to transmute into modes of art; whose unfathomable instincts, marvellously incoherent and inarticulate, he had thought to perpetuate in terms of experience—had become merely consecrations to their own posterity. Isabelle, Clara, Rosalind, Eleanor, were all removed by their very beauty, around which men had swarmed, from the possibility of contributing anything but a sick heart and a page of puzzled words to write.

Amory based his loss of faith in help from others on several sweeping syllogisms. Granted that his generation, however bruised and decimated from this Victorian war, were the heirs of progress. Waving aside petty differences of conclusions which, although they might occasionally cause the deaths of several millions of young men, might be explained away—supposing that after all Bernard Shaw and Bernhardi, Bonar Law and Bethmann-Hollweg* were mutual heirs of progress if only in agreeing against the ducking of witches—waiving the antitheses and approaching individually these men who seemed to be the leaders, he was repelled by the discrepancies and contradictions in the men themselves.

There was, for example, Thornton Hancock, respected by half the intellectual world as an authority on life, a man who had verified and believed the code he lived by, an educator of educators, an adviser to Presidents—yet Amory knew that this man had, in his heart, leaned on the priest of another religion.

And Monsignor, upon whom a cardinal rested, had moments of strange and horrible insecurity—inexplicable in a religion that explained even disbelief in terms of its own faith: if you doubted the devil it was the devil that made you doubt him. Amory had seen Monsignor go to the houses of stolid philistines, read popular novels furiously, saturate himself in routine, to escape from that horror.

And this priest, a little wiser, somewhat purer, had been, Amory knew, not essentially older than he.

Amory was alone—he had escaped from a small enclosure into a great labyrinth. He was where Goethe was when he began "Faust"; he was where Conrad was when he wrote "Almayer's Folly."

Amory said to himself that there were essentially two sorts of people who through natural clarity or disillusion left the enclosure and sought the labyrinth. There were men like Wells and Plato, who had, half unconsciously, a strange, hidden orthodoxy, who would accept for themselves only what could be accepted for all men— incurable romanticists who never, for all their efforts, could enter the labyrinth as stark souls; there were on the other hand sword-like pioneering personalities, Samuel Butler, Renan,* Voltaire, who progressed much slower, yet eventually much further, not in the direct pessimistic line of speculative philosophy but concerned in the eternal attempt to attach a positive value to life. . . .

Amory stopped. He began for the first time in his life to have a strong distrust of all generalities and epigrams. They were too easy, too dangerous to the public mind. Yet all thought usually reached the public after thirty years in some such form: Benson and Chesterton had popularized Huysmans and Newman; Shaw had sugar-coated Nietzsche and Ibsen and Schopenhauer. The man in the street heard the conclusions of dead genius through some one else's clever paradoxes and didactic epigrams.

Life was a damned muddle . . . a football game with every one off-side and the referee gotten rid of—every one claiming the referee would have been on his side. . . .

Progress was a labyrinth . . . people plunging blindly in and then rushing wildly back, shouting that they had found it . . . the invisible king—the élan vital—the principle of evolution . . . writing a book, starting a war, founding a school. . . .

Amory, even had he not been a selfish man, would have started all inquiries with himself. He was his own best example—sitting in the rain, a human creature of sex and pride, foiled by chance and his own temperament of the balm of love and children, preserved to help in building up the living consciousness of the race.

In self-reproach and loneliness and disillusion he came to the entrance of the labyrinth.

Another dawn flung itself across the river; a belated taxi hurried along the street, its lamps still shining like burning eyes in a face white from a night's carouse. A melancholy siren sounded far down the river.

Monsignor

Amory kept thinking how Monsignor would have enjoyed his own funeral. It was magnificently Catholic and liturgical. Bishop O'Neill sang solemn high mass and the cardinal gave the final absolutions. Thornton Hancock, Mrs. Lawrence, the British and Italian ambassadors, the papal delegate, and a host of friends and priests were there—yet the inexorable shears had cut through all these threads that Monsignor had gathered into his hands. To Amory it was a haunting grief to see him lying in his coffin, with closed hands upon his purple vestments. His face had not changed, and, as he never knew he was dying, it showed no pain or fear. It was Amory's dear old friend, his and the others'—for the church was full of people with daft, staring faces, the most exalted seeming the most stricken.

The cardinal, like an archangel in cope and mitre, sprinkled the holy water; the organ broke into sound; the choir began to sing the *Requiem Eternam.**

All these people grieved because they had to some extent depended upon Monsignor. Their grief was more than sentiment for the "crack in his voice or a certain break in his walk," as Wells put it. These people had leaned on Monsignor's faith, his way of finding cheer, of making religion a thing of lights and shadows, making all light and shadow merely aspects of God. People felt safe when he was near.

Of Amory's attempted sacrifice had been born merely the full realization of his disillusion, but of Monsignor's funeral was born the romantic elf who was to enter the labyrinth with him. He found something that he wanted, had always wanted and always would want—not to be admired, as he had feared; not to be loved, as he had made himself believe; but to be necessary to people, to be indispensable; he remembered the sense of security he had found in Burne.

Life opened up in one of its amazing bursts of radiance and Amory suddenly and permanently rejected an old epigram that had been playing listlessly in his mind: "Very few things matter and nothing matters very much."

On the contrary, Amory felt an immense desire to give people a sense of security.

The Big Man with Goggles

On the day that Amory started on his walk to Princeton the sky was a colorless vault, cool, high and barren of the threat of rain. It was a gray day, that least fleshly of all weathers; a day of dreams and far hopes and clear visions. It was a day easily associated with those abstract truths and purities that dissolve in the sunshine or fade out in mocking laughter by the light of the moon. The trees and clouds were carved in classical severity; the sounds of the countryside had harmonized to a monotone, metallic as a trumpet, breathless as the Grecian urn.

The day had put Amory in such a contemplative mood that he caused much annoyance to several motorists who were forced to slow up

considerably or else run him down. So engrossed in his thoughts was he
that he was scarcely surprised at that strange phenomenon—cordiality
manifested within fifty miles of Manhattan—when a passing car
slowed down beside him and a voice hailed him. He looked up and saw
a magnificent Locomobile* in which sat two middle-aged men, one of
them small and anxious looking, apparently an artificial growth on the
other who was large and begoggled and imposing.

"Do you want a lift?" asked the apparently artificial growth, glancing from the corner of his eye at the imposing man as if for some
habitual, silent corroboration.

"You bet I do. Thanks."

The chauffeur swung open the door, and, climbing in, Amory
settled himself in the middle of the back seat. He took in his com-
panions curiously. The chief characteristic of the big man seemed to
be a great confidence in himself set off against a tremendous boredom
with everything around him. That part of his face which protruded
under the goggles was what is generally termed "strong"; rolls of
not undignified fat had collected near his chin; somewhere above
was a wide thin mouth and the rough model for a Roman nose, and,
below, his shoulders collapsed without a struggle into the powerful
bulk of his chest and belly. He was excellently and quietly dressed.
Amory noticed that he was inclined to stare straight at the back of
the chauffeur's head as if speculating steadily but hopelessly some
baffling hirsute problem.

The smaller man was remarkable only for his complete submersion
in the personality of the other. He was of that lower secretarial type
who at forty have engraved upon their business cards: "Assistant to
the President," and without a sigh consecrate the rest of their lives
to second-hand mannerisms.

"Going far?" asked the smaller man in a pleasant disinterested
way.

"Quite a stretch."

"Hiking for exercise?"

"No," responded Amory succinctly, "I'm walking because I can't
afford to ride."

"Oh."

Then again:

"Are you looking for work? Because there's lots of work," he
continued rather testily. "All this talk of lack of work. The West is

especially short of labor." He expressed the West with a sweeping, lateral gesture. Amory nodded politely.

"Have you a trade?"

No—Amory had no trade.

"Clerk, eh?"

No—Amory was not a clerk.

"Whatever your line is," said the little man, seeming to agree wisely with something Amory had said, "now is the time of opportunity and business openings." He glanced again toward the big man, as a lawyer grilling a witness glances involuntarily at the jury.

Amory decided that he must say something and for the life of him could think of only one thing to say.

"Of course I want a great lot of money——"

The little man laughed mirthlessly but conscientiously.

"That's what every one wants nowadays, but they don't want to work for it."

"A very natural, healthy desire. Almost all normal people want to be rich without great effort—except the financiers in problem plays, who want to 'crash their way through.' Don't you want easy money?"

"Of course not," said the secretary indignantly.

"But," continued Amory disregarding him, "being very poor at present I am contemplating socialism as possibly my forte."

Both men glanced at him curiously.

"These bomb throwers—" The little man ceased as words lurched ponderously from the big man's chest.

"If I thought you were a bomb thrower I'd run you over to the Newark jail. That's what I think of Socialists."

Amory laughed.

"What are you," asked the big man, "one of these parlor Bolsheviks, one of these idealists? I must say I fail to see the difference. The idealists loaf around and write the stuff that stirs up the poor immigrants."

"Well," said Amory, "if being an idealist is both safe and lucrative, I might try it."

"What's your difficulty? Lost your job?"

"Not exactly, but—well, call it that."

"What was it?"

"Writing copy for an advertising agency."

"Lots of money in advertising."

Amory smiled discreetly.

"Oh, I'll admit there's money in it eventually. Talent doesn't starve any more. Even art gets enough to eat these days. Artists draw your magazine covers, write your advertisements, hash out rag-time for your theatres. By the great commercializing of printing you've found a harmless, polite occupation for every genius who might have carved his own niche. But beware the artist who's an intellectual also. The artist who doesn't fit—the Rousseau, the Tolstoi, the Samuel Butler, the Amory Blaine——"

"Who's he?" demanded the little man suspiciously.

"Well," said Amory, "he's a—he's an intellectual personage not very well known at present."

The little man laughed his conscientious laugh, and stopped rather suddenly as Amory's burning eyes turned on him.

"What are you laughing at?"

"These *intellectual* people——"

"Do you know what it means?"

The little man's eyes twitched nervously.

"Why, it *usually* means——"

"It *always* means brainy and well-educated," interrupted Amory. "It means having an active knowledge of the race's experience." Amory decided to be very rude. He turned to the big man. "The young man," he indicated the secretary with his thumb, and said young man as one says bell-boy, with no implication of youth, "has the usual muddled connotation of all popular words."

"You object to the fact that capital controls printing?" said the big man, fixing him with his goggles.

"Yes—and I object to doing their mental work for them. It seemed to me that the root of all the business I saw around me consisted in overworking and underpaying a bunch of dubs who submitted to it."

"Here now," said the big man, "you'll have to admit that the laboring man is certainly highly paid—five and six hour days—it's ridiculous. You can't buy an honest day's work from a man in the trades-unions."

"You've brought it on yourselves," insisted Amory. "You people never make concessions until they're wrung out of you."

"What people?"

"Your class; the class I belonged to until recently; those who by inheritance or industry or brains or dishonesty have become the moneyed class."

"Do you imagine that if that road-mender over there had the money he'd be any more willing to give it up?"

"No, but what's that got to do with it?"

The older man considered.

"No, I'll admit it hasn't. It rather sounds as if it had though."

"In fact," continued Amory, "he'd be worse. The lower classes are narrower, less pleasant and personally more selfish—certainly more stupid. But all that has nothing to do with the question."

"Just exactly what is the question?"

Here Amory had to pause to consider exactly what the question was.

Amory Coins a Phrase

"When life gets hold of a brainy man of fair education," began Amory slowly, "that is, when he marries he becomes, nine times out of ten, a conservative as far as existing social conditions are concerned. He may be unselfish, kind-hearted, even just in his own way, but his first job is to provide and to hold fast. His wife shoos him on, from ten thousand a year to twenty thousand a year, on and on, in an enclosed treadmill that hasn't any windows. He's done! Life's got him! He's no help! He's a spiritually married man."

Amory paused and decided that it wasn't such a bad phrase.

"Some men," he continued, "escape the grip. Maybe their wives have no social ambitions; maybe they've hit a sentence or two in a 'dangerous book' that pleased them; maybe they started on the treadmill as I did and were knocked off. Anyway, they're the congressmen you can't bribe, the Presidents who aren't politicians, the writers, speakers, scientists, statesmen who aren't just popular grab-bags for a half-dozen women and children."

"He's the natural radical?"

"Yes," said Amory. "He may vary from the disillusioned critic like old Thornton Hancock, all the way to Trotsky. Now this spiritually unmarried man hasn't direct power, for unfortunately the spiritually married man, as a by-product of his money chase, has garnered in the great newspaper, the popular magazine, the influential weekly—so that Mrs. Newspaper, Mrs. Magazine, Mrs. Weekly can have a better limousine than those oil people across the street or those cement people 'round the corner."

"Why not?"

"It makes wealthy men the keepers of the world's intellectual conscience and, of course, a man who has money under one set of social institutions quite naturally can't risk his family's happiness by letting the clamor for another appear in his newspaper."

"But it appears," said the big man.

"Where?—in the discredited mediums. Rotten cheap-papered weeklies."

"All right—go on."

"Well, my first point is that through a mixture of conditions of which the family is the first, there are these two sorts of brains. One sort takes human nature as it finds it, uses its timidity, its weakness, and its strength for its own ends. Opposed is the man who, being spiritually unmarried, continually seeks for new systems that will control or counteract human nature. His problem is harder. It is not life that's complicated, it's the struggle to guide and control life. That is his struggle. He is a part of progress—the spiritually married man is not."

The big man produced three big cigars, and proffered them on his huge palm. The little man took one, Amory shook his head and reached for a cigarette.

"Go on talking," said the big man. "I've been wanting to hear one of you fellows."

Going Faster

"Modern life," began Amory again, "changes no longer century by century, but year by year, ten times faster than it ever has before—populations doubling, civilizations unified more closely with other civilizations, economic interdependence, racial questions, and—we're *dawdling* along. My idea is that we've got to go very much faster." He slightly emphasized the last words and the chauffeur unconsciously increased the speed of the car. Amory and the big man laughed; the little man laughed, too, after a pause.

"Every child," said Amory, "should have an equal start. If his father can endow him with a good physique and his mother with some common sense in his early education, that should be his heritage. If the father can't give him a good physique, if the mother has spent in chasing men the years in which she should have been preparing herself to educate her children, so much the worse for the child. He shouldn't be artificially bolstered up with money, sent to these horrible tutoring schools, dragged through college . . . Every boy ought to have an equal start."

"All right," said the big man, his goggles indicating neither approval nor objection.

"Next I'd have a fair trial of government ownership of all industries."

"That's been proven a failure."

"No—it merely failed. If we had government ownership we'd have the best analytical business minds in the government working for something besides themselves. We'd have Mackays instead of Burlesons;* we'd have Morgans in the Treasury Department; we'd have Hills running interstate commerce. We'd have the best lawyers in the Senate."

"They wouldn't give their best efforts for nothing. McAdoo*——"

"No," said Amory, shaking his head. "Money isn't the only stimulus that brings out the best that's in a man, even in America."

"You said a while ago that it was."

"It is, right now. But if it were made illegal to have more than a certain amount the best men would all flock for the one other reward which attracts humanity—honor."

The big man made a sound that was very like *boo*.

"That's the silliest thing you've said yet."

"No, it isn't silly. It's quite plausible. If you'd gone to college you'd have been struck by the fact that the men there would work twice as hard for any one of a hundred petty honors as those other men did who were earning their way through."

"Kids—child's play!" scoffed his antagonist.

"Not by a darned sight—unless we're all children. Did you ever see a grown man when he's trying for a secret society—or a rising family whose name is up at some club? They'll jump when they hear the sound of the word. The idea that to make a man work you've got to hold gold in front of his eyes is a growth, not an axiom. We've done that for so long that we've forgotten there's any other way. We've made a world where that's necessary. Let me tell you"—Amory became emphatic—"if there were ten men insured against either wealth or starvation, and offered a green ribbon for five hours' work a day and a blue ribbon for ten hours' work a day, nine out of ten of them would be trying for the blue ribbon. That competitive instinct only wants a badge. If the size of their house is the badge they'll sweat their heads off for that. If it's only a blue ribbon, I damn near believe they'll work just as hard. They have in other ages."

"I don't agree with you."

"I know it," said Amory nodding sadly. "It doesn't matter any more though. I think these people are going to come and take what they want pretty soon."

A fierce hiss came from the little man.

"Machine-guns!"

"Ah, but you've taught them their use."

The big man shook his head.

"In this country there are enough property owners not to permit that sort of thing."

Amory wished he knew the statistics of property owners and non-property owners; he decided to change the subject.

But the big man was aroused.

"When you talk of 'taking things away,' you're on dangerous ground."

"How can they get it without taking it? For years people have been stalled off with promises. Socialism may not be progress, but the threat of the red flag is certainly the inspiring force of all reform. You've got to be sensational to get attention."

"Russia is your example of a beneficent violence, I suppose?"

"Quite possibly," admitted Amory. "Of course, it's overflowing just as the French Revolution did, but I've no doubt that it's really a great experiment and well worth while."

"Don't you believe in moderation?"

"You won't listen to the moderates, and it's almost too late. The truth is that the public has done one of those startling and amazing things that they do about once in a hundred years. They've seized an idea."

"What is it?"

"That however the brains and abilities of men may differ, their stomachs are essentially the same."

The Little Man Gets His

"If you took all the money in the world," said the little man with much profundity, "and divided it up in equ——"

"Oh, shut up!" said Amory briskly and, paying no attention to the little man's enraged stare, he went on with his argument.

"The human stomach—" he began; but the big man interrupted rather impatiently.

"I'm letting you talk, you know," he said, "but please avoid stomachs. I've been feeling mine all day. Anyway, I don't agree with one-half you've said. Government ownership is the basis of your whole argument, and it's invariably a beehive of corruption. Men won't work for blue ribbons, that's all rot."

When he ceased the little man spoke up with a determined nod, as if resolved this time to have his say out.

"There are certain things which are human nature," he asserted with an owl-like look, "which always have been and always will be, which can't be changed."

Amory looked from the small man to the big man helplessly.

"Listen to that! *That's* what makes me discouraged with progress. *Listen* to that! I can name offhand over one hundred natural phenomena that have been changed by the will of man—a hundred instincts in man that have been wiped out or are now held in check by civilization. What this man here just said has been for thousands of years the last refuge of the associated mutton-heads of the world. It negates the efforts of every scientist, statesman, moralist, reformer, doctor, and philosopher that ever gave his life to humanity's service. It's a flat impeachment of all that's worth while in human nature. Every person over twenty-five years old who makes that statement in cold blood ought to be deprived of the franchise."

The little man leaned back against the seat, his face purple with rage. Amory continued, addressing his remarks to the big man.

"These quarter-educated, stale-minded men such as your friend here, who *think* they think; every question that comes up, you'll find his type in the usual ghastly muddle. One minute it's 'the brutality and inhumanity of these Prussians'—the next it's 'we ought to exterminate the whole German people.' They always believe that 'things are in a bad way now,' but they 'haven't any faith in these idealists.' One minute they call Wilson 'just a dreamer, not practical'—a year later they rail at him for making his dreams realities. They haven't clear logical ideas on one single subject except a sturdy, stolid opposition to all change. They don't think uneducated people should be highly paid, but they won't see that if they don't pay the uneducated people their children are going to be uneducated too, and we're going round and round in a circle. That—is the great middle class!"

The big man with a broad grin on his face leaned over and smiled at the little man.

"You're catching it pretty heavy, Garvin; how do you feel?"

The little man made an attempt to smile and act as if the whole matter were so ridiculous as to be beneath notice. But Amory was not through.

"The theory that people are fit to govern themselves rests on this man. If he can be educated to think clearly, concisely, and logically, freed of his habit of taking refuge in platitudes and prejudices and sentimentalisms, then I'm a militant Socialist. If he can't, then I don't think it matters much what happens to man or his systems, now or hereafter."

"I am both interested and amused," said the big man. "You are very young."

"Which may only mean that I have neither been corrupted nor made timid by contemporary experience. I possess the most valuable experience, the experience of the race, for in spite of going to college I've managed to pick up a good education."

"You talk glibly."

"It's not all rubbish," cried Amory passionately. "This is the first time in my life I've argued Socialism. It's the only panacea I know. I'm restless. My whole generation is restless. I'm sick of a system where the richest man gets the most beautiful girl if he wants her, where the artist without an income has to sell his talents to a button manufacturer. Even if I had no talents I'd not be content to work ten years, condemned either to celibacy or a furtive indulgence, to give some man's son an automobile."

"But, if you're not sure——"

"That doesn't matter," exclaimed Amory. "My position couldn't be worse. A social revolution might land me on top. Of course I'm selfish. It seems to me I've been a fish out of water in too many outworn systems. I was probably one of the two dozen men in my class at college who got a decent education; still they'd let any well-tutored flathead play football and *I* was ineligible, because some silly old men thought we should *all* profit by conic sections. I loathed the army. I loathed business. I'm in love with change and I've killed my conscience——"

"So you'll go along crying that we must go faster."

"That, at least, is true," Amory insisted. "Reform won't catch up to the needs of civilization unless it's made to. A laissez-faire policy is like spoiling a child by saying he'll turn out all right in the end. He will—if he's made to."

"But you don't believe all this Socialist patter you talk."

"I don't know. Until I talked to you I hadn't thought seriously about it. I wasn't sure of half of what I said."

"You puzzle me," said the big man, "but you're all alike. They say Bernard Shaw, in spite of his doctrines, is the most exacting of all dramatists about his royalties. To the last farthing."

"Well," said Amory, "I simply state that I'm a product of a versatile mind in a restless generation—with every reason to throw my mind and pen in with the radicals. Even if, deep in my heart, I thought we were all blind atoms in a world as limited as a stroke of a pendulum, I and my sort would struggle against tradition; try, at least, to displace old cants with new ones. I've thought I was right about life at various times, but faith is difficult. One thing I know. If living isn't a seeking for the grail it may be a damned amusing game."

For a minute neither spoke and then the big man asked:

"What was your university?"

"Princeton."

The big man became suddenly interested; the expression of his goggles altered slightly.

"I sent my son to Princeton."

"Did you?"

"Perhaps you knew him. His name was Jesse Ferrenby. He was killed last year in France."

"I knew him very well. In fact, he was one of my particular friends."

"He was—a—quite a fine boy. We were very close."

Amory began to perceive a resemblance between the father and the dead son and he told himself that there had been all along a sense of familiarity. Jesse Ferrenby, the man who in college had borne off the crown that he had aspired to. It was all so far away. What little boys they had been, working for blue ribbons——

The car slowed up at the entrance to a great estate, ringed around by a huge hedge and a tall iron fence.

"Won't you come in for lunch?"

Amory shook his head.

"Thank you, Mr. Ferrenby, but I've got to get on."

The big man held out his hand. Amory saw that the fact that he had known Jesse more than outweighed any disfavor he had created by his opinions. What ghosts were people with which to work! Even the little man insisted on shaking hands.

"Good-bye!" shouted Mr. Ferrenby, as the car turned the corner and started up the drive. "Good luck to you and bad luck to your theories."

"Same to you, sir," cried Amory, smiling and waving his hand.

*"Out of the Fire, Out of the Little Room"**

Eight hours from Princeton Amory sat down by the Jersey roadside and looked at the frost-bitten country. Nature as a rather coarse phenomenon composed largely of flowers that, when closely inspected, appeared moth-eaten, and of ants that endlessly traversed blades of grass, was always disillusioning; nature represented by skies and waters and far horizons was more likable. Frost and the promise of winter thrilled him now, made him think of a wild battle between St. Regis and Groton, ages ago, seven years ago—and of an autumn day in France twelve months before when he had lain in tall grass, his platoon flattened down close around him, waiting to tap the shoulders of a Lewis gunner.* He saw the two pictures together with somewhat the same primitive exaltation—two games he had played, differing in quality of acerbity, linked in a way that differed them from Rosalind or the subject of labyrinths which were, after all, the business of life.

"I am selfish," he thought.

"This is not a quality that will change when I 'see human suffering' or 'lose my parents' or 'help others.'

"This selfishness is not only part of me. It is the most living part.

"It is by somehow transcending rather than by avoiding that selfishness that I can bring poise and balance into my life.

"There is no virtue of unselfishness that I cannot use. I can make sacrifices, be charitable, give to a friend, endure for a friend, lay down my life for a friend—all because these things may be the best possible expression of myself; yet I have not one drop of the milk of human kindness."

The problem of evil had solidified for Amory into the problem of sex. He was beginning to identify evil with the strong phallic worship in Brooke and the early Wells. Inseparably linked with evil was beauty—beauty, still a constant rising tumult; soft in Eleanor's voice, in an old song at night, rioting deliriously through life like superimposed waterfalls, half rhythm, half darkness. Amory knew that every time he had reached toward it longingly it had leered out at him with the grotesque face of evil. Beauty of great art, beauty of all joy, most of all the beauty of women.

After all, it had too many associations with license and indulgence. Weak things were often beautiful, weak things were never good. And in this new loneness of his that had been selected for what greatness he might achieve, beauty must be relative or, itself a harmony, it would make only a discord.

In a sense this gradual renunciation of beauty was the second step after his disillusion had been made complete. He felt that he was leaving behind him his chance of being a certain type of artist. It seemed so much more important to be a certain sort of man.

His mind turned a corner suddenly and he found himself thinking of the Catholic Church. The idea was strong in him that there was a certain intrinsic lack in those to whom orthodox religion was necessary, and religion to Amory meant the Church of Rome. Quite conceivably it was an empty ritual but it was seemingly the only assimilative, traditionary bulwark against the decay of morals. Until the great mobs could be educated into a moral sense some one must cry: "Thou shalt not!" Yet any acceptance was, for the present, impossible. He wanted time and the absence of ulterior pressure. He wanted to keep the tree without ornaments, realize fully the direction and momentum of this new start.

The afternoon waned from the purging good of three o'clock to the golden beauty of four. Afterward he walked through the dull ache of a setting sun when even the clouds seemed bleeding and at twilight he came to a graveyard. There was a dusky, dreamy smell of flowers and the ghost of a new moon in the sky and shadows everywhere. On an impulse he considered trying to open the door of a rusty iron vault built into the side of a hill; a vault washed clean and covered with late-blooming, weepy watery-blue flowers that might have grown from dead eyes, sticky to the touch with a sickening odor.

Amory wanted to *feel* "William Dayfield, 1864."

He wondered that graves ever made people consider life in vain. Somehow he could find nothing hopeless in having lived. All the broken columns and clasped hands and doves and angels meant romances. He fancied that in a hundred years he would like having young people speculate as to whether his eyes were brown or blue, and he hoped quite passionately that his grave would have about it an air of many, many years ago. It seemed strange that out of a row of Union soldiers two or three made him think of dead loves and dead lovers, when they were exactly like the rest, even to the yellowish moss.

Long after midnight the towers and spires of Princeton were visible, with here and there a late-burning light—and suddenly out of the clear darkness the sound of bells. As an endless dream it went on; the spirit of the past brooding over a new generation, the chosen youth from the muddled, unchastened world, still fed romantically on the mistakes and half-forgotten dreams of dead statesmen and poets. Here was a new generation, shouting the old cries, learning the old creeds, through a revery of long days and nights; destined finally to go out into that dirty gray turmoil to follow love and pride; a new generation dedicated more than the last to the fear of poverty and the worship of success; grown up to find all Gods dead, all wars fought, all faiths in man shaken. . . .

Amory, sorry for them, was still not sorry for himself—art, politics, religion, whatever his medium should be, he knew he was safe now, free from all hysteria—he could accept what was acceptable, roam, grow, rebel, sleep deep through many nights. . . .

There was no God in his heart, he knew; his ideas were still in riot; there was ever the pain of memory; the regret for his lost youth—yet the waters of disillusion had left a deposit on his soul, responsibility and a love of life, the faint stirring of old ambitions and unrealized dreams. But—oh, Rosalind! Rosalind! . . .

"It's all a poor substitute at best," he said sadly.

And he could not tell why the struggle was worth while, why he had determined to use to the utmost himself and his heritage from the personalities he had passed. . . .

He stretched out his arms to the crystalline, radiant sky.

"I know myself," he cried, "but that is all."

EXPLANATORY NOTES

1 *Well . . . Brooke*: from the final lines of Brooke's poem 'Tiare Tahiti' (1915).

Experience . . . Wilde: from Act III of *Lady Windermere's Fan* (1893).

3 *Sigourney Fay*: Father Cyril Sigourney Webster Fay (1875–1919), a prominent Catholic priest whom Fitzgerald met in 1912 and who became a father figure for him; he served as the model for Monsignor Darcy in *This Side of Paradise*.

9 *Bar Harbor*: a resort on the coast of Maine frequented at this time by the wealthy and well connected.

Queen Margherita: Margherita di Savoia (1851–1926), who was queen of Italy from 1878 to 1900 and queen dowager from 1900 to 1926.

10 *Coronado*: a resort in southern California, catering to the wealthy.

Newport: a resort in Rhode Island, the site of many mansions of the wealthy.

"Do and Dare" . . . "Frank on the Lower Mississippi": *Do or Dare* (1884), a novel by Horatio Alger Jr. (1834–99); *Frank on the Lower Mississippi* (1867), a novel by Harry Castlemon, a pseudonym for Charles Austin Fosdick.

Waldorf: a fashionable New York hotel, then located at Fifth Avenue and 33rd Street.

Bernhardt's: Sarah Bernhardt, the famous French-born actress (1844–1923), who toured extensively in the US and Europe.

"Fêtes Galantes": a poetry collection (1869) by Paul Verlaine (1844–96).

Hot Springs: a fashionable resort in Arkansas.

11 *Pasadena to Cape Cod*: Pasadena was a fashionable resort in California for the wealthy; Cape Cod, on the Massachusetts coast, was a similar summer destination.

12 *Asheville*: a resort community in the western mountains of North Carolina.

16 *"trade-lasts"*: the understanding that when one gives a compliment, they will receive one in return.

Arrow-collar: detachable shirt collar worn by fashionable men of the day.

19 *graphophone*: a machine, invented by Alexander Graham Bell, which played music on wax-covered discs through a large horn.

20 *"Arsène Lupin"*: a play by Francis de Croisset and Maurice Leblanc, first performed in the US in 1909, and featuring Leblanc in the role of the title character, a gentleman criminal.

20 *McGovern of Minnesota*: John Francis McGovern was, in 1909, the first University of Minnesota football player named to the first-string All-American team.

Three-fingered Brown . . . Christy Mathewson: Mordecai 'Three-finger' (because he was missing half of the index finger on his right hand) Brown (1876–1948) pitched for the Chicago Cubs and St Louis Cardinals in the first decade of the twentieth century; Mathewson (1880–1925) was a pitcher for the New York Giants during the same period. Both are in baseball's Hall of Fame.

"For the Honor . . ." . . . "Gunga Din": R. H. Barbour's boys' book *For the Honor of the School* (1900); Louisa May Alcott's novel *Little Women* (1869); Robert Chambers's novel *The Common Law* (1911) presents alternatives to marriage; Alphonse Daudet's novel *Sappho* (1884) deals with crime and prostitution in Paris; Robert Service's poem 'The Shooting of Dan McGrew' (1907); Jeffery Farnol's adventure novel *The Broad Highway* (1910); Edgar Allan Poe's macabre short story 'The Fall of the House of Usher' (1839); Elinor Glyn's romantic novel *Three Weeks* (1907); Annie Fellows Johnston's novel *Mary Ware* (1908); Rudyard Kipling's poem 'Gunga Din' (1892).

The Police Gazette . . . Jim-Jam Jems: *The Police Gazette* was a periodical that featured sensational crime; *Jim-Jam Gems* was a similarly focused pocket-sized mass-circulation magazine.

Henty biases . . . Rinehart: G. A. Henty (1832–1902) wrote a series of boys' adventure novels based on events in military history including *Under Drake's Flag* (1883), *With Clive in India* (1884), and *With Roberts to Pretoria* (1902); Mary Roberts Rinehart (1876–1956) was an American writer of mystery novels, among them *The Circular Staircase* (1908) and *The Man in Lower Ten* (1909).

23 *Brooks*: Brooks Brothers, a fashionable New York clothing store.

"Bull": 'Bull' Durham Smoking Tobacco, used in rolling one's own cigarettes.

26 *a Turner sunset*: the English painter J. M. W. Turner (1775–1851) was especially famous for landscapes. Fitzgerald compares Turner's vivid colours, especially in his sunsets, to Darcy's attire when in his robes.

27 *Bonnie Prince Charlie . . . Hannibal—*: two heroes of lost causes: Charles Edward Stuart (1720–88) was the last of his family to claim, unsuccessfully, the British throne and became a national hero in Scotland as 'Bonnie Prince Charlie'; and Hannibal (247–182? BC) was a Carthaginian general who fought unsuccessfully against Rome in the Second Punic War (218–201 BC).

28 *Parnell and Gladstone and Bismarck*: three late nineteenth-century European political leaders: Charles Stewart Parnell (1846–91) was the leader of the Irish nationalist movement; William Ewart Gladstone (1809–98) was

four times English prime minister between 1868 and 1894; and Otto von Bismarck (1815–98) was chancellor of Prussia from 1862 to 1890.

Biltmore Teas and Hot Springs golf-links: tea-dances at New York's Biltmore Hotel and golf games at The Homestead, a resort in the mountains of Virginia.

"The Beloved Vagabond" and "Sir Nigel": *The Beloved Vagabond* (1900) and *Sir Nigel* (1906) are romantic novels by W. J. Locke and Arthur Conan Doyle respectively.

30 *nabiscos . . . "The White Company"*: cookies made by the National Biscuit Company; and a romantic historical novel (1891) by Arthur Conan Doyle.

31 *the chariot-race sign on Broadway*: the climactic scene of Lew Wallace's novel *Ben-Hur* (1880) was depicted, with simulated movement, on a large, electric advertising sign.

"The Little Millionaire": a musical play (1911), written and directed by and starring George M. Cohan.

32 *Roland and Horatius, Sir Nigel and Ted Coy*: Roland was the legendary knight of Charlemagne immortalized in the medieval French epic *La Chanson de Roland*; Horatius was the legendary sixth-century BC Roman hero who held a bridge against invading Etruscans; Sir Nigel is the titular hero of Arthur Conan Doyle's novel of 1906, set in the Middle Ages; and Edward H. 'Ted' Coy was a football star at Yale from 1906 to 1909.

33 *"The Gentleman . . . Thursday"*: Booth Tarkington's novel *The Gentleman from Indiana* (1899); Robert Louis Stevenson's short-story collection *New Arabian Nights* (1882); W. J. Locke's novel *The Morals of Marcus Ordeyne* (1905); G. K. Chesterton's novel *The Man Who Was Thursday* (1908).

"Stover at Yale": O. M. Johnson's boys' novel (1912), which depicts 'Dink' Stover's college adventures.

Robert Chambers . . . Oppenheim: Robert W. Chambers (1865–1933) was the best-selling American novelist who wrote *The King in Yellow* (1895) and *Ashes of Empire* (1897); David Graham Phillips (1867–1911) was an American novelist and muckraking journalist; E. Phillips Oppenheim (1866–1946) was a British novelist whose mysteries and espionage fictions included *The Mysterious Mr. Sabin* (1901) and *The Double Traitor* (1920).

34 *Harstrum's*: the Harstrum School in Norwalk, Connecticut, a remedial school that prepared students for admission to Yale.

Sheff: Yale's Sheffield Scientific School, a three-year course of study, admission to which was considered easier than to Yale's regular four-year undergraduate programme.

locomotor ataxia: a syphilis of the spinal cord resulting in the loss of motor control and paralysis.

36 *"tapped for Skull and Bones"*: the most coveted and secret of the senior societies at Yale.

37 *Gibson Girls*: popular pen-and-ink drawings of fashionable young women by artist Charles Dana Gibson.

38 *the freshman cap*: first-year students at many American colleges and universities of the day were required to wear skullcaps for the first term.

tiger pictures: Princeton's athletic teams are nicknamed The Tigers.

40 *"By the Sea"*: Harold R. Atteridge and Harry Carroll's 1914 song 'By the Beautiful Sea.'

41 *the heavy blue and crimson lines*: the most important games of Princeton's football season were and are against Yale and Harvard, whose school colours are, respectively, blue and crimson.

44 *Fatimas*: Fatima Turkish Blend Cigarettes.

45 *Golden Treasury*: an anthology of English poetry edited by Francis Turner Palgrave entitled *Golden Treasury of the Best Songs and Lyrical Poems of the English Language*, first published in 1861 and reissued multiple times.

46 *Farmington . . . Dana Hall*: fashionable girls' private schools of the day: Miss Porter's School in Farmington, Connecticut; the Misses Masters School in Dobbs Ferry, New York; Westover near Middlebury, Connecticut; and Dana Hall in Wellesley, Massachusetts.

the Twin Cities: St Paul and Minneapolis, Minnesota.

47 *St. Timothy*: St Timothy's School for Girls in Catonsville, Maryland, another fashionable private school.

"Mrs. Warren's Profession": George Bernard Shaw's controversial play about prostitution, first published in 1893 but not produced until 1905 in the US and 1925 in England.

Stephen Phillips: an English poet (1868–1915), who was known for his verse dramas.

"Come into the Garden, Maude": the first words of poem XII in Alfred Lord Tennyson's *Maud, and Other Poems* (1855), frequently recited by students. Fitzgerald misspells Maud.

48 *'Patience'*: an operetta (1881) by W. S. Gilbert and Arthur Sullivan that included a character who was a satirical portrayal of Oscar Wilde.

'The Picture of Dorian Gray': Oscar Wilde's 1891 novel, referred to several times by Amory, who compares its young hero's dissolute lifestyle to his own.

49 *"Mystic . . . Merci"*: 'Mystic and Somber Dolores' is an allusion to line 7 of Algernon Charles Swinburne's poem 'Dolores' (1866); 'La Belle Dame Sans Merci' is a poem by John Keats (1819).

"Fingal O'Flahertie": Wilde's full name was Oscar Fingal O'Flahertie Wills Wilde.

Sudermann, Robert Hugh Benson: Hermann Sudermann (1857–1928) was a German Naturalist playwright; Robert Hugh Benson (1871–1914) was an English priest and novelist who wrote *The Light Invisible* (1903) and *The Lord of the World* (1907).

the Savoy Operas: because they premiered at London's Savoy Theatre, Gilbert and Sullivan's operettas were known as the Savoy Operas.

Lord Dunsany's poems: Edward John Moreton Drax Plunkett (Lord Dunsany) was an Irish poet and playwright (1878–1957).

50 *'Hearts and Flowers'*: Mary D. Brine and Theodore Moses Tobani's sentimental song (1899).

"Asleep or waking . . . for a fleck . . . ": the first stanza of Swinburne's 'Laus Veneris', published in his *Poems and Ballads* (1866).

53 *Elis*: nickname given to Yale students; Elihu Yale (1649–1721) was an early benefactor for whom the school is named.

55 *Midnight Frolic*: the roof garden located above New York's New Amsterdam Theatre; impresario Florenz Ziegfeld owned and operated it.

Williams: Williams College in Williamstown, Massachusetts.

56 *"Thaïs"* . . . *"Carmen"*: *Thaïs* is an opera (1894) by Jules Massenet, based on Anatole France's novel of 1890. *Carmen* is an opera (1875) by Georges Bizet, based on Prosper Mérimée's novel of 1852. Fitzgerald thus invites a comparison between Isabelle's free lifestyle and that of the two titular heroines.

62 *Stutzes*: the Stutz bearcat was a fashionable two-seat sports car of the 1910s and 1920s.

63 *"Babes in the Woods"*: a popular song written by Jerome Kern and Schuyler Greene for their Broadway musical *Very Good Eddie* (1915).

65 *black balls*: in order to be asked to join a Princeton eating club, one had to be elected by the members, who dropped white or black balls into a box; one black ball would eliminate a candidate.

67 *Deal Beach . . . Asbury Park*: Deal Beach was a fashionable resort on the New Jersey coast; Asbury Park is a town in the same area.

68 *"Oh, winter's rains . . . flower of——"*: from a speech by the Chorus in stanza 4 of Swinburne's *Atalanta in Calydon* (1865); Fitzgerald misquotes the lines slightly.

69 *Ganymede*: cupbearer to the god Zeus in Greek mythology.

71 *"Beaches . . . came"*: from the second stanza of Rudyard Kipling's poem 'Lukannon' in his *The Jungle Book* (1894).

72 *Corneille and Racine*: the pre-eminent French playwrights of the seventeenth century, Pierre Corneille (1606–84) and Jean Racine (1639–99).

74 *"Love Moon"* . . . *"Good-bye, Boys, I'm Through"*: 'Love Moon' was a song by Anne Caldwell and Ivan Caryll from the Broadway musical *Chin-Chin* (1914); 'Good-bye Boys' was a 1913 song by Andrew B. Sterling, William Dillon, and Harry von Tilzer; but Fitzgerald is more likely referring to 'Good-bye Girls, I'm Through', a song by Ivan Caryll and John Golden, also from *Chin-Chin*.

75 *Franks*: a fashionable New York shoe store.

76 *'silver-snarling trumpets'*: from line 31 of Keats's 'The Eve of St Agnes' (1820).

81 *"All the perfumes . . . little hand"*: from Act V, scene 1, of *Macbeth*; Fitzgerald misquotes slightly.

82 *Greenwich Country Club*: in Greenwich, Connecticut, on Long Island Sound in south-western Connecticut.

84 *"Each life . . . been happy"*: stanza 16 of Robert Browning's 'Youth and Art', from his *Dramatis Personae* (1864); Fitzgerald misquotes slightly.

conditioned men: Princeton students in academic trouble.

91 *Lafayette Escadrille*: a French fighter squadron that included American volunteers; it began flying missions in May 1916, two months before the US entered the First World War, and became the 103rd Pursuit Squadron of the US Army Air Corps in 1919.

94 *John Fox, Jr.*: an American journalist and fiction writer (1863–1919), author of the romantic novels *The Little Shepherd of Kingdom Come* (1903) and *The Trail of the Lonesome Pine* (1908).

"What Every Middle-Aged Woman . . . of the Yukon": J. M. Barrie's play *What Every Woman Knows* (1918); and Robert W. Service's poetry collection *The Spell of the Yukon* (1915).

96 *General Booth*: William Booth (1829–1912), the founder of the Salvation Army in 1878.

97 *jitney waiter*: a waiter who accepts small tips, derived from the term for a bus or train that charged a small fare.

104 *"The New Machiavelli"*: a novel (1911) by H. G. Wells.

105 *"None Other . . . Research Magnificent"*: Robert Hugh Benson's novel *None Other Gods* (1911); Compton Mackenzie's novel *Sinister Street* (1913); H. G. Wells's novel *The Research Magnificent* (1915).

106 *Woodrow*: Woodrow Wilson (1856–1924), who was president of Princeton during the First World War, tried unsuccessfully to abolish the college's eating clubs.

107 *the Masses*: a radical monthly magazine that focused on the troubles of the American worker.

108 *'Varieties of Religious Experience'*: William James's treatise on natural religion, delivered originally as lectures in 1901–2 and published in 1902.

Edward Carpenter: a British author and social reformer (1844–1929).

'Kreutzer Sonata': a novel (1890) by Tolstoy.

109 *Huysmans and Bourget*: Joris Karl Huysmans (1848–1907) was a French decadent novelist; Paul Bourget (1852–1935) was a French critic and psychological novelist.

Ralph Adams Cram: an American architect (1863–1942) who served as supervising architect at Princeton.

115 *Philadelphian Society*: a collegiate religious organization whose members were often planning to enter the ministry.

116 *Savonarola*: the Dominican friar Girolamo Savonarola ruled Florence after the fall of the Medici and was known as a moralistic foe of immorality and of corruption in the clergy.

'*He who is not with me is against me*': from Matthew 12: 30.

118 *Sir Oliver Lodge*: a British scientist (1851–1940) interested in reconciling science and religion, who believed in survival after death.

119 *preceptors*: instructors at Princeton who taught small discussion groups and were generally regarded as among the best teachers on campus.

120 *Amelia-like*: Amelia Osborne, the modest widow in Thackeray's novel *Vanity Fair* (1848).

128 *Stephen*: Acts 5–6.

129 *Peter the Hermit*: the French priest and military officer (1050–1115) who proposed the First Crusade to Pope Urban II.

130 *Germany in 1870*: supporters of Germany in the Franco-Prussian War.

131 "*Poor Butterfly*": a song by John L. Golden and Raymond Hubbell from the Broadway musical *The Big Show* (1916).

132 *Von Hindenburg*: Paul von Hindenburg (1847–1934), the leader of the German military in the First World War.

Burr and Light-Horse Harry Lee: probably Aaron Burr Sr. (1716–57), who was president of Princeton and the father of the vice-president of the US, who was a Princeton graduate; Henry 'Light-Horse Harry' Lee (1756–1818), another Princeton graduate who became a Revolutionary War hero for his daring missions.

133 *Messalina*: Valeria Messalina, the third wife of Roman emperor Claudius, known for her lascivious ways.

Heraclitus: the fifth-century BC Greek philosopher who believed that 'all things change'.

141 *Donald Hankey*: a British soldier killed in action in October 1916 whose essays were collected in *A Student in Arms* (1917) and *A Student in Arms, Second Series* (1917).

145 "*Cherry Ripe*," . . . *Maxfield Parrish*: *Cherry Ripe* was a popular painting of a young girl by Sir John Everett Millais; Sir Edwin Henry Landseer (1802–73) was a British artist, known for his paintings of dogs; Maxfield Parrish (1870–1966) was an American artist and illustrator.

150 *you don't mind — do you?*: social custom of the day dictated that young people call each other by their family names upon first acquaintance.

152 *Spence*: the Spence School for Girls, an exclusive private school in New York.

155 *Coronas*: cigarettes aimed at an upscale market; girls of Cecelia's age were not supposed to smoke in public.

157 *since the French officers went back*: during the First World War, French officers in colourful uniforms frequently attended social events in New York.

158 *Cocoanut Grove*: a fashionable rooftop nightclub above the Century Theatre in New York.

159 *"Kiss Me Again"*: a song (1905) by Henry Blossom and Victor Herbert which had a popular revival in 1915.

161 *Benvenuto Blaine*: the allusion is to Benvenuto Cellini (1500–71), the sixteenth-century Italian sculptor, author, and goldsmith known for his outspoken and boastful autobiography, begun in 1558 but not published until 1730.

163 *Annette Kellerman*: an Australian swimmer (1887–1975) who became a stage and screen actress and was known as the 'Million Dollar Mermaid'.

"Et tu, Brutus": the reference is to J. M. Barrie's fantasy play *Dear Brutus* (1917).

167 *Sancho*: Don Quixote frequently chides his squire, Sancho Panza, for being a peasant.

Ella Wheeler Wilcox: an American newspaperwoman and popular poet who published more than twenty volumes of verse.

"For this is wisdom . . . let go": from Lawrence Hope's (pseud. for Adela Florence [Cory] Nicolson) 'The Teak Forest' in her *India's Love Lyrics* (1902); Fitzgerald misquotes slightly.

171 *"Rye high . . . a Bronx"*: a rye highball mixes rye whiskey with either soda water or ginger ale; a Bronx mixes gin, vermouth, and orange juice.

173 *"Clair de Lune"*: a poem by the French poet Paul Verlaine collected in *Fêtes galantes* (1869).

Tyson's . . . "The Jest": Tyson's was a Broadway ticket agency that had counters in most major New York hotels; a play with 'a four-drink programme' was one with five acts and four intervals; 'The Jest' was a play (1919) with a medieval setting by the Italian dramatist Sam Binelli.

178 *"After you've gone"*: a song (1918) by Henry Creamer and Turner Layton.

179 *"Joan . . . Fire"*: two novels by H. G. Wells, published in 1918 and 1919, respectively.

"Vandover . . . Gerhardt": novels by Frank Norris, Harold Frederic, and Theodore Dreiser, published in 1914, 1896, and 1911 respectively.

Bennett: the British novelist Arnold Bennett (1867–1931), best known for his *The Old Wives' Tale* (1908).

180 *the Irish President*: Eamon de Valera, president of Ireland's Sinn Fein party, came to the US in 1919 seeking financial assistance and political recognition for the Irish Republic.

181 *Edward Carson and Justice Cohalan*: Edward Carson (1854–1935) was an Irish Protestant politician who led opposition to Irish Home Rule; Daniel Florence Cohalan was a New York Supreme Court judge, who, in support of the Irish revolution, advocated German air raids on England.

182 *Montespan's wraith*: Louis XIV's mistress, Madame de Montespan, tried to poison her court rivals and was accused of participating in the Black Mass.

183 *Foch*: Ferdinand Foch (1851–1929), known as Marshal Foch, commanded the Allied Forces in the First World War.

Guynemer . . . Sergeant York . . . Pershing: during the First World War Georges Marie Guynemer (1894–1917) was a famous and highly successful French fighter pilot; Alvin Cullum York (1887–1964), popularly known as Sergeant York, was an American hero; John J. Pershing (1860–1948), 'Black Jack', commanded American troops.

'The Hero as a Big Man': refers to the English prose writer Thomas Carlyle's *On Heroes, Hero-worship, and the Heroic in History* (1841).

Wood: the American politician and military man Leonard Wood (1860–1927) was Chief of Staff of the US Army from 1910 to 1914 and was under consideration as the Republican presidential nominee in 1920.

185 *Gouverneur Morris*: an American novelist (1876–1953), author of *Ellen and Mr. Man* (1904) and *The Penalty* (1913).

Fannie Hurst: an American writer of popular fiction, including *Every Soul Hath Its Song* (1916) and *Humoresque: A Laugh on Life With a Tear Behind It* (1920).

Cobb: the American humorist, short-story writer, and dramatist Irvin S. Cobb (1876–1944), author of *Old Judge Priest* (1915) and *The Life of the Party* (1919).

Harold Bell Wright: an American local-colour novelist whose works included *Shepherd of the Hills* (1907) and *The Winning of Barbara Worth* (1911).

Rupert Hughes: an American journalist, novelist, and dramatist, author of *Music Lovers' Cyclopedia* (1914), the novel *What Will People Say?* (1914), and the play *Excuse Me* (1911).

186 *Ernest Poole and Dorothy Canfield*: American novelists of the period: Poole (1880–1950) was the author of *The Harbor* (1915) and *His Family* (1917), which won the Pulitzer Prize; Canfield, later Dorothy Canfield Fisher (1879–1958), was the author of *The Squirrel Cage* (1912) and *The Day of Glory* (1918).

'Boston Bards and Hearst Reviewers': this refers to Byron's satirical *English Bards and Scotch Reviewers* (1809).

"So . . . collected editions": besides Sandburg, Untermeyer, and Aiken, these poets, all of whose work appeared in *The New Poetry* (1917), an anthology edited by Harriet Monroe, editor of *Poetry* magazine, and who

were popular at that time, are now no longer highly regarded. Walter Arensberg (1878–1954) was the author of *Poems* (1914) and *Idols* (1916); Alfred Kreymborg (1883–1966) was the author of *Mushrooms* (1916); Eunice Tietjens (1884–1944) was an editor of *Poetry* whose books included *Profiles from China* (1917); Clara Shanafelt (1861–1957) contributed to *Poetry*; James Oppenheim (1882–1932) was the editor of *Seven Arts* magazine and author of *Monday Morning* (1909) and *Songs for the New Age* (1914); Maxwell Bodenheim (1893–1954) was a poet and novelist whose books of verse included *Minna and Myself* (1918) and *Introducing Irony* (1922); Richard Glaenzer (1876–1937) was the author of *Beggar and King* (1917) and *Literary Snapshots* (1920); Scharmel Iris (1889–1964) was the author of *Lyric of a Lad* (1914).

187 *James J. Hill*: an American railroad tycoon (1838–1916) and resident of St Paul.

192 *"Les sanglots . . . Monotone" . . . "Tout suffocant . . . je pleure . . ."*: from the French poet Paul Verlaine's 'Chanson d'automne' in his *Poèmes saturniens* (1866).

Manfred: the titular hero of Byron's dramatic poem (1817).

194 *bobbed*: for a woman of Eleanor's age to wear her hair bobbed was an indication of her nonconformity.

Madeline: this refers to Lady Madeline Usher, who returns from being dead in Poe's story 'The Fall of the House of Usher' (1839).

195 *'And now . . . was born'*: from Poe's 'Ulalume: A Ballad' (1847); Fitzgerald misquotes slightly.

197 *"Bind on thy sandals . . . thy feet———"*: from a speech by the Chorus in Swinburne's *Atalanta in Calydon* (1865).

Grantchester to Waikiki: this refers to poems by Rupert Brooke, 'Waikiki' (1913) and 'The Old Vicarage, Grantchester' (1912).

198 *"Is it worth . . . deed foreborne?"*: from Swinburne's 'The Triumph of Time' in his *Poems and Ballads* (1866); Fitzgerald misquotes slightly.

203 *the sixth and ninth commandments*: the Sixth Commandment is 'Thou shalt not kill'; the Ninth Commandment is 'Thou shalt not bear false witness against thy neighbour' (Exodus 20).

209 *the Mann Act*: passed by Congress in 1910, the Mann Act made it illegal—and punishable by time in jail—for an individual to assist or participate in the transportation of a woman across state lines 'for immoral purposes'.

211 *Weep not for me but for thy children*: from Luke 23: 28–9; Fitzgerald condenses the original.

214 *He reached in his pocket suggestively*: he is indicating that Amory might want to give him some money for not arresting him.

216 *porte-cochère*: the roof over the entrance to a theatre; in the first edition, the word here is 'portcullis', which is the heavy gate to a medieval castle.

217 *car cards*: advertisements on cards that appeared above the windows in subway cars.

224 *Bernhardi, Bonar Law and Bethmann-Hollweg*: Friedrich von Bernhardi (1849–1930) was a Prussian general and author of the novel *Germany and the Next War* (1911) in which he asserted Germany's right to wage war; Bonar Law (1858–1923) was a British statesman who formed a coalition government with Lloyd George during the First World War; Theobald von Bethmann-Hollweg (1856–1921) was chancellor of Germany and encouraged his country's participation in the First World War as a distraction from its internal problems.

Renan: the French critic, writer, and scholar Joseph Ernest Renan (1823–92), whose *La Vie de Jésus* (*The Life of Jesus*) (1863) contended that Jesus was not the Son of God but rather a human being divinely inspired.

226 *the Requiem Eternam*: the Mass for the dead of the Roman Catholic faith.

227 *Locomobile*: an expensive automobile of the day, owned primarily by the very wealthy; it was open to the air, which is why those riding in it are wearing goggles.

232 *Mackays instead of Burlesons*: Clarence Hungerford Mackay (1874–1938) was a prominent and philanthropically inclined Catholic businessman of the day whose first wife, Katherine Mackay, was a leading suffragette; Albert Sidney Burleson (1863–1937) was an American politician who served as Postmaster General during the First World War and sought to ban from the mail any material critical of government policy.

McAdoo: William G. McAdoo (1863–1941) was Secretary of the Treasury from 1913 to 1918 and director general of railways from 1917 to 1919.

237 *"Out of the Fire, Out of the Little Room"*: from Rupert Brooke's 'The Night Journey' in his *1914 and Other Poems* (1915).

Lewis gunner: a light machine gun used by the American and British forces in the First World War.

American Literature

British and Irish Literature

Children's Literature

Classics and Ancient Literature

Colonial Literature

Eastern Literature

European Literature

Gothic Literature

History

Medieval Literature

Oxford English Drama

Poetry

Philosophy

Politics

Religion

The Oxford Shakespeare

A complete list of Oxford World's Classics, including Authors in Context, Oxford English Drama, and the Oxford Shakespeare, is available in the UK from the Marketing Services Department, Oxford University Press, Great Clarendon Street, Oxford OX2 6DP, or visit the website at www.oup.com/uk/worldsclassics.

In the USA, visit www.oup.com/us/owc for a complete title list.

Oxford World's Classics are available from all good bookshops. In case of difficulty, customers in the UK should contact Oxford University Press Bookshop, 116 High Street, Oxford OX1 4BR.

HENRY ADAMS	The Education of Henry Adams
LOUISA MAY ALCOTT	Little Women
SHERWOOD ANDERSON	Winesburg, Ohio
CHARLES BROCKDEN BROWN	Wieland; or The Transformation and Memoirs of Carwin, The Biloquist
WILLA CATHER	My Ántonia O Pioneers!
KATE CHOPIN	The Awakening and Other Stories
JAMES FENIMORE COOPER	The Deerslayer The Last of the Mohicans The Pathfinder The Pioneers The Prairie
STEPHEN CRANE	The Red Badge of Courage
J. HECTOR ST. JEAN DE CRÈVECŒUR	Letters from an American Farmer
FREDERICK DOUGLASS	Narrative of the Life of Frederick Douglass, an American Slave
THEODORE DREISER	Sister Carrie
F. SCOTT FITZGERALD	The Great Gatsby The Beautiful and Damned
BENJAMIN FRANKLIN	Autobiography and Other Writings
CHARLOTTE PERKINS GILMAN	The Yellow Wall-Paper and Other Stories
ZANE GREY	Riders of the Purple Sage
NATHANIEL HAWTHORNE	The Blithedale Romance The House of the Seven Gables The Marble Faun The Scarlet Letter Young Goodman Brown and Other Tales

WASHINGTON IRVING	The Sketch-Book of Geoffrey Crayon, Gent.
HENRY JAMES	The Ambassadors
	The American
	The Aspern Papers and Other Stories
	The Awkward Age
	The Bostonians
	Daisy Miller and Other Stories
	The Europeans
	The Golden Bowl
	The Portrait of a Lady
	The Spoils of Poynton
	The Turn of the Screw and Other Stories
	Washington Square
	What Maisie Knew
	The Wings of the Dove
JACK LONDON	The Call of the Wild, White Fang and Other Stories
	John Barleycorn
	The Sea-Wolf
	The Son of the Wolf
HERMAN MELVILLE	Billy Budd, Sailor and Selected Tales
	The Confidence-Man
	Moby-Dick
FRANK NORRIS	McTeague
FRANCIS PARKMAN	The Oregon Trail
EDGAR ALLAN POE	The Narrative of Arthur Gordon Pym of Nantucket and Related Tales
	Selected Tales
HARRIET BEECHER STOWE	Uncle Tom's Cabin
HENRY DAVID THOREAU	Walden

	Late Victorian Gothic Tales
JANE AUSTEN	Emma
	Mansfield Park
	Persuasion
	Pride and Prejudice
	Selected Letters
	Sense and Sensibility
MRS BEETON	Book of Household Management
MARY ELIZABETH BRADDON	Lady Audley's Secret
ANNE BRONTË	The Tenant of Wildfell Hall
CHARLOTTE BRONTË	Jane Eyre
	Shirley
	Villette
EMILY BRONTË	Wuthering Heights
ROBERT BROWNING	The Major Works
JOHN CLARE	The Major Works
SAMUEL TAYLOR COLERIDGE	The Major Works
WILKIE COLLINS	The Moonstone
	No Name
	The Woman in White
CHARLES DARWIN	The Origin of Species
THOMAS DE QUINCEY	The Confessions of an English Opium-Eater
	On Murder
CHARLES DICKENS	The Adventures of Oliver Twist
	Barnaby Rudge
	Bleak House
	David Copperfield
	Great Expectations
	Nicholas Nickleby
	The Old Curiosity Shop
	Our Mutual Friend
	The Pickwick Papers

GUY DE MAUPASSANT	**A Day in the Country and Other Stories** **A Life** **Bel-Ami** **Mademoiselle Fifi and Other Stories** **Pierre et Jean**
PROSPER MÉRIMÉE	**Carmen and Other Stories**
MOLIÈRE	**Don Juan and Other Plays** **The Misanthrope, Tartuffe, and Other Plays**
BLAISE PASCAL	**Pensées and Other Writings**
ABBÉ PRÉVOST	**Manon Lescaut**
JEAN RACINE	**Britannicus, Phaedra, and Athaliah**
ARTHUR RIMBAUD	**Collected Poems**
EDMOND ROSTAND	**Cyrano de Bergerac**
MARQUIS DE SADE	**The Crimes of Love** **The Misfortunes of Virtue and Other Early Tales**
GEORGE SAND	**Indiana**
MME DE STAËL	**Corinne**
STENDHAL	**The Red and the Black** **The Charterhouse of Parma**
PAUL VERLAINE	**Selected Poems**
JULES VERNE	**Around the World in Eighty Days** **Captain Hatteras** **Journey to the Centre of the Earth** **Twenty Thousand Leagues under the Seas**
VOLTAIRE	**Candide and Other Stories** **Letters concerning the English Nation**

ANTON CHEKHOV

About Love and Other Stories
Early Stories
Five Plays
The Princess and Other Stories
The Russian Master and Other Stories
The Steppe and Other Stories
Twelve Plays
Ward Number Six and Other Stories

FYODOR DOSTOEVSKY

Crime and Punishment
Devils
A Gentle Creature and Other Stories
The Idiot
The Karamazov Brothers
Memoirs from the House of the Dead
Notes from the Underground and
      The Gambler

NIKOLAI GOGOL

Dead Souls
Plays and Petersburg Tales

ALEXANDER PUSHKIN

Eugene Onegin
The Queen of Spades and Other Stories

LEO TOLSTOY

Anna Karenina
The Kreutzer Sonata and Other Stories
The Raid and Other Stories
Resurrection
War and Peace

IVAN TURGENEV

Fathers and Sons
First Love and Other Stories
A Month in the Country